# A DEATH at
# The Potawatomi Club

STEPHEN TIMBERS

DORRANCE
PUBLISHING CO
EST 1920
Pittsburgh, Pennsylvania 15222

Dorrance Publishing Co
585 Alpha Drive
Pittsburgh, PA 15238
Visit our website at *www.dorrancebookstore.com*

ISBN: 978-1-6853-7223-1
eISBN: 978-1-6853-7732-8

*For Elaine*
*you made it all possible*

_____

# CONTENTS

## CHAPTER ONE

"Brendan, I'm running late. Traffic," Charlie Bailey alerted the golf course starter from his car phone.

"Don't worry, Mr. B. We had a big party here last night. Everyone seems to be arriving late today."

"Good. Please tell Mr. Stanhope that I'm coming and will meet him on the first tee."

"Will do, but he's not here yet either."

They both laughed and Charlie hung up.

Ten minutes later Charlie raced his big engine BMW convertible down the driveway of the ancient, esteemed Potawatomi Club. He felt upbeat, anxious to play his match. Besides, what could be better than a tranquil Sunday morning in June?

The only signs of life he noticed in these deftly landscaped environs were two senior caddies sipping coffee, waiting for the first members to arrive.

They nodded recognition to Charlie. One scurried into the bag room to retrieve his clubs, and the other walked over to where Charlie was parking.

"Can I help you with anything?" Seamus asked.

"No, thanks." Charlie answered as he maneuvered his lean, six-foot, two-inch frame out of his car. "Living in Chicago I forget sometimes how quiet Lake Forest is. I should know; I grew up here. It's too early for church, so it's just the birds and us. Right, Seamus? Remind me, when do the padres ring the bells?"

"I'm told the town don't allow the church bells 'til nine o'clock, Mr. Bailey. Where I come from in Ireland, the fathers rang the bells at seven to wake up all the Saturday night drunks and get 'em to mass by eight. Of course, everyone's too proper here to drink like us reprobates. No need to prompt the laity."

"Oh, the people drink, all right. They just want their sleep, too."

"Will you be hittin' balls first, Mr. Bailey? And are you meetin' up with anyone today?"

"Bring out Mr. Stanhope's clubs if you will. We should be teeing off by seven." Charlie turned and walked towards the men's locker room. He loved to banter with the caddies—especially Seamus, who had worked at the club for many years. Charlie himself had been playing at the club since he was a boy— after his parents moved from the city into the large, classic estate less than a mile from the club. He smiled to himself as he opened the clubhouse door.

He was amused and pleased that the men's locker room had undergone an extensive renovation a year before. Little changed at Potawatomi over the years. The members preferred its stately, well-appointed comfort—"old shoe" many said. But something had to be done with this room with its dated, metal lockers and well-worn carpet. A bold board of directors had approved the creation of a showplace of polished dark brown wood lockers and benches, softened by the subtle green plaid of the carpet and draperies. Still, the décor retained an overall impression of power and masculinity.

The older members continued to grumble that the club spent too much money on such sumptuousness, although Charlie suspected that they secretly relished the luxurious furnishings. Most controversial was the sunken ten by fifteen foot, heated soaking pool off the shower room—referred to as the "roman bath". Considering the often chilly days of April and October, the men past their prime should have welcomed it as a vehicle to soothe their aching muscles.

At this hour the locker room was empty—as Charlie had hoped. That guaranteed no one would be playing ahead of him and his partner, Jack Stanhope, slowing their speedy play. For them, the perfect round lasted three hours at most. Combine that pace with the sun slowly warming the morning air and the fragrance of freshly mown grass, Charlie could not imagine a better way to spend the morning.

As Charlie walked toward a sink in the washroom, something caught his eye in the new pool beyond the showers - a floating dark mass. He nearly walked by, but the image of that object pulled him back. As he approached Charlie realized it was a man fully dressed, floating face-down.

Heart pounding, Charlie jumped into the pool and lifted the man enough to get his face out of the water. One look told him he was dead. Charlie pushed the bloated, ashen body to the side of the pool and struggled to roll him onto the tile floor. Succeeding, Charlie climbed out and straddled the man. He started to administer CPR, hoping against hope. Gradually the horror of the situation became clear. Nothing would bring this man back. After five frustrating minutes Charlie stopped his futile attempts. As a marine in Vietnam he had witnessed death multiple times, but this was different. This wasn't war. This was the Potawatomi Club. No one died here. The world had just turned upside down. Revulsion crept thorough him. He felt powerless.

Needing to do something—anything—productive, Charlie stood and ran into the main locker room towards the attendant's room.

"Javier, Javier."

A second later he saw Javier between locker bays and waved to him to follow. As they neared the corpse, Javier gasped. "Mr. Bradshaw!"

"Scottie Bradshaw?" Charlie asked. Javier, nodding, looked as if he might cry.

Then Charlie peered down and barely recognized his old fiend—the ghastly face, white and distorted. He noticed also a black and blue bruise on the right forehead. This can't be, he thought.

He knew Scottie well. The Bradshaws had lived in Lake Forest for decades. They were close friends. Charlie had played golf with him just five weeks before. He was even a client of the firm.

How could this have happened? The club hosted parties for

its members almost every weekend. Maybe Scottie had been there last night, had too much to drink, came up to the locker room to relieve himself, stumbled in the pool, hit his head on the edge, and been unable to climb out. A pure guess. Scottie did drink a lot. Whatever had happened, Charlie needed to notify the club manager and the police.

Charlie looked at Javier, who was clearly shocked, and said, "Go find Mr. Scobie or whoever is in charge at this hour. Tell him what has happened and ask him to call the police right away."

Javier nodded and ran in the direction of the club manager's office. Charlie did not know what to do next. He felt confused, disoriented. "Is this really happening?" he asked himself. He did not want to stay with the corpse. He decided to go outside and instructed the golf staff to keep the members and other staff out of the locker room.

As he stepped into the fresh air, he almost collided with Jack. Charlie moved to block the door.

"Jack, hold on. Don't go in. Scottie Bradshaw drowned in the soaking pool."

"What?" Jack said incredulously. "Scottie's dead? Here?"

"Could you stay here until the police come to keep everyone out?"

"Fine," Jack said, and shook his head. "Scottie Bradshaw. Unreal. Unreal."

"I'll alert the caddie master and the pro shop," Charlie said turning away.

After talking to the head pro, Charlie was still bewildered

as to what to do. For a minute he considered leaving and driving over to Henry Bradshaw's house. The family needed to know and they would be devastated. But he also understood that the police would have questions for him.

As a rule he felt confident in any situation, but now he was shaken. He had to regain control of himself, or he would be useless to help. He wandered towards the parking lot. What was his duty: to inform friends and family of this tragedy first—out of respect—or to wait for the police? Confused, he did neither. He drove to his mother's house.

## CHAPTER TWO

"Mother, I was so disoriented I didn't recognize Scottie," Charlie said, sitting in his mother's kitchen and recounting what had happened at the Club. "Only when our locker room attendant said so, I could see the pale, bloated face was his."

"I understand," Claire Bailey said slumping in a chair across the table from her son looking stone-faced. "What a terrifying discovery. Dottie and Henry will be shattered. After you call Henry, I'll telephone Dottie. She's such a special friend. It's best they hear from us before the police contact them. The police won't be compassionate.'

"Call now," Claire said. "Then go upstairs and shower. You're dripping wet and you stink. You have plenty of clean clothes in your old bedroom."

She paused, staring out the window. Charlie sat across from her trying to control his breathing. Finally he went upstairs.

Fifteen minutes later Charlie came downstairs and found his mother sitting in the library sobbing.

"I told Henry," Charlie reported. "Clearly he was upset and shocked. But he didn't want to talk about it. He said he would call the police immediately. He thanked me for notifying him right away."

"That's Henry. Always polite—even when his son is dead. I know him. He hides the pain. Dottie was crushed when I called. Scottie was her little boy. This accident is so sad.'

'Dottie said to me sobbing, "He was only in his early thirties. Mothers aren't supposed to bury their children."

"I know," Charlie agreed sorrowfully. "Don't think poorly of me if I don't stay now. I'll be back, but I expect that the police will want to ask me some questions."

"Of course, Charlie. Drive over. Come back for lunch."

He found his car parked in the four-car garage. James, the butler, must have moved it from where he had left it in a hurry in front of the house. Driving the short, less than a mile return to the club, Charlie thought about how close his family has been with the Bradshaws. Starting with his parents decades ago in Chicago, Lake Forest, and Palm Beach, Florida. One of his best friends growing up was Jamie, Scottie's older brother. In addition to the personal bonds Charlie also had business connections overseeing money for them through his investment management firm.

Pulling into the club parking lot Charlie noticed three police cars and a couple of officers near the locker room door. The first person he saw as he left his car was Jack Stanhope.

"There you are," Jack said. "The police are looking for you. The sergeant seemed angry that you weren't around. They questioned me, but I only knew what you told me. You better talk to them now. There's the sergeant by the main entrance with Scobie."

Charlie strode over to the imposing figure with the nametag "Sergeant Rumson". Charlie introduced himself catching a glimpse of the officer's communications device and firearm.

"Where the hell have you been?" Rumson barked, taking out a pen and pad. "You left an investigation scene."

"Sorry. I had to change my soaked clothes and let the Bradshaws know what happened."

"Hold on. What happened to your clothes?"

"I gave them to my mother's housekeeper to wash and iron."

"I don't believe it," Rumson shook his head obviously upset. "Your clothes are part of the crime scene."

"What crime scene?" Charlie asked.

"That's what it is until we find otherwise. I need those clothes!"

"I'll get them for you later."

"Damn!" Rumson said irritated.

Then the officer asked, "Tell me what happened this morning."

Charlie then described how and when he found Scottie's body, what he did, and whom he had talked to. The sergeant wrote rapidly on his pad frowning all the time.

"So you moved the body?"

"Of course. I would have been disrespectful to leave him in the pool. Besides I wasn't certain Scottie was dead at first."

"Why did you perform CPR?"

"I thought I might revive him, but stopped when I had no response."

"Did you use mouth-to-mouth resuscitation?"

"No."

"But you sat on the body?"

"Astride. For a minute or two."

"Then you fled the scene."

"No. I went to my mother's—a mile away, got dry clothes, and came back to see you."

"Mister Bailey, don't be so cocky," Rumson said sharply. "You touched the deceased, disturbed important evidence, and disappeared. You need a better explanation of what you did."

"This was an accident. I stumbled upon it. That's all there is to it."

"We'll be the judge of that. How do you know it was an accident? Did you see the deceased fall? Are you telling me everything?"

"I didn't see the accident. What else could it be?"

"How well did you know the deceased?"

"Quite well. The Bradshaws have been good friends of my family for many years. Also Scottie was a client of mine."

At that point another police officer came up to Sergeant Rumson and whispered something. Rumson gave Charlie a hard look, told him that he had other questions and left with his patrolman.

Charlie wandered into the clubhouse and found a comfortable chair in the library to wait for Sergeant Rumson. He used the time to collect his thoughts. He was surprised that Rumson had been so combative and skeptical when questioning him. Of course, Scottie's death was an accident. He had seen him across the living room at the club the night before. Charlie had met some friends for drinks before heading downtown to Chicago for dinner with Kate Milano, his girlfriend. He knew there was a dinner dance that night and assumed Scottie was there for that event. Scottie was a big drinker and could have gone up to the locker room to relieve himself. Possibly he could have stumbled and slipped into the roman bath. Pure speculation—but possible.

The bruise on his head could have happened if he hit a side of the pool when he fell. The accident must have occurred very late or another partygoer coming to pee would have noticed the body floating in the next room—and might have saved him. Scottie had been unlucky. Life can be so fragile. Coming from a wealthy, prestigious family guaranteed nothing.

Sergeant Rumson peaked into the library from the doorway and frowned upon seeing Charlie.

"You keep on disappearing, Mr. Bailey. Stop that. This is a very serious matter."

"Believe me, I understand the gravity," Charlie responded. "Scottie's death is a dreadful tragedy. I wish it could be undone."

"Well, it can't," Rumson said approaching and taking out his pad. "Where do you live?"

"In Chicago. 1500 Lake Shore Drive."

"You're here awfully early. Lake Forest is a long way from the city. Did you stay overnight?

"No. I drove up this morning."

"An early bird. Do you come here that early every weekend?"

"When I can. I like early golf."

Rumson looked skeptical as he wrote something down. Charlie then mentioned his friend and business relationship with Scottie and his having seen him the night before.

"So you see Mr. Bradshaw, drive to the city and come back first thing. Can anyone confirm your movements?"

"Wait a minute," Charlie said angrily. "I don't like the tone of your questions."

"Get used to it. So you are refusing to answer a question. Expect to hear from the Lake County Major Crimes Task Force in a day or two. Meantime, be available and stay out of the locker room."

"Major Crimes? For an accident? I never refused to answer."

"We will determine that," Rumson said then put his pad away and left.

Charlie stared at the door, stunned by the accusatory attitude of the police officer. He thought that Rumson had been watching too many police dramas on television. He was suspicious of everything. Crazy.

Charlie stood up and walked out of the club. He looked for Jack briefly, but, not seeing him, assumed he had left. Then Charlie returned to his car. He wanted to see how his mother was dealing with the news and also to tell her of Rumson's behavior.

James met Charlie at the front door and directed him to the sunroom. "Your mother is quite upset. She is reading a book to calm herself."

Charlie walked through the foyer and the living room to the

pleasant little room with large windows facing southwest. Claire was sitting in a large white wicker chair holding a small book.

"What are you reading, Mother?"

Claire Bailey seemed startled at first but then she smiled on seeing Charlie. "Come sit by me. I am reading a wonderful book written by a priest about coping with the loss of a child. I want to understand what Dottie and Henry are experiencing."

Charlie sat on the ottoman near her. She went on, "This terrible event shows that no matter how rich and successful you are bad things happen. Henry's law firm must be the most prominent in Chicago. He built it up from scratch. And the Bradshaws are so admired and respected socially here and in the city. Who would have expected that a tragedy would befall them?"

"You're right, Mother."

"Did you finish with the police at the club?"

"Rather they finished with me. The sergeant in charge took his job quite seriously — in fact he was outrageous. He was skeptical of everything I told him. He suggested that I was dodging him and asked if someone could verify my coming and going."

"The nerve," Claire snapped. "Who does he think he is?"

"Beyond disbelieving what I told him, he insinuated that Scottie's death was not an accident."

"What? Does he think Scottie was murdered? At the club? In Lake Forest?"

"He didn't rule it out."

"What a scandal that would be," Claire stated considering the idea. "Just last week at bridge Sally Kirkland was discussing crime here in Lake County. She quoted some source who wrote that while murders averaged one a month in the county murders are so rare in Lake Forest that only one has occurred here during the past decade—a crime of passion that the local police solved instantaneously. Of course, not by a club member."

"I seem to remember that."

"Of course you do. Our gossip-starved neighbors talked of little else for two months. I shudder to think what people and the press would do if Scottie has been killed. The notoriety, the embarrassment, the added hurt to Dottie and Henry. Also the fear that a murderer is present in our midst."

"Stop, Mother," Charlie demanded. "You are going overboard with this unlikely notion. Scottie's death was a tragic accident. The sergeant was just being dramatic."

As he spoke, for the first time Charlie wondered if Sergeant Rumson might have a point.

## CHAPTER THREE

Reluctantly Charlie agreed to stay for lunch. He usually spent the time with his mother after Saturday morning golf before returning to the city in the afternoon. But after the events of the last hour he wanted to drive home to trigger the duties his firm was required to perform when a client died. However, his mother needed him now. He sensed she wanted to talk—to voice the consequences of Scottie's death.

At noon, James called Charlie from the library where he had been reading the papers to lunch with his mother in the sunroom. As soon as the mulligatawny soup was served, Mrs. Bailey started as if their previous conversation had briefly been interrupted.

"I do hope they have the service here in Lake Forest rather than downtown. In Chicago there will be all those business types who barely know the Bradshaws. And the minister at All Saints would be very upset that he could not have it in his church."

"Mother, everything will be handled beautifully."

"Well, Charlie, it's important that these things be done right. Everyone will expect that with Dottie everything is *comme il faut*."

"Certainly."

"And then there is the money."

"Yes?"

"Don't you have all the Bradshaw money, darling?"

"Not really. We manage the accounts for Henry and Dottie and some generation-skipping trusts for the children, including Scottie. They were all set up by Edward Bradshaw. The Old Fiduciary Bank and Trust is the trustee and we just manage the investments."

"Well, I'm sure you have done a good job. You are clever with bonds and stocks, just like your father was."

"The bank and the lawyers will take care of Scottie's affairs. I don't' know who the executor is but we'll freeze Scottie's trusts until we get instructions."

"Is there much money there?"

"The family has a great deal — not Scottie, but the family."

They paused as James came in and swapped the soup setting for a shrimp salad plate. When he left, Claire said suddenly, "I know it was an accident, but you have to wonder when someone dies unnaturally and the family has a lot of money."

"Don't go there, Mother. Let's change the subject."

"Yes, the funeral. Maybe I can offer to arrange for a soprano from the Lyric Opera. Knowing the Bradshaws, the service will be quite grand.'

"Poor Dottie," Claire continued. "Things have been going so well for them. Jamie's success at Goodman, Bates and Phillipa's marriage to Lawleigh Sims.'

'Dottie does concede that Scottie has his issues. She said that at parties he often drank too much and paid unwanted attention to younger women—even dates of other men. And he was accused of misbehaving. She worried that he would never grow up. Then on several occasions friends of hers complained that Scottie's investment ideas had lost them money. That sort of gripe embarrassed her. She and Henry also felt that he lived way beyond his means. He was so unlike his brother."

Claire shook her head and looked at her uneaten salad. Apparently lost in thought, she then looked up and said, "You may not know but Henry's father, Edward, helped your grandfather get into the club here—and the other clubs in Palm Beach, too. Back in those days, Catholics weren't always accepted in clubs. But Edward Bradshaw would brook no religious prejudice. He knew that grandfather Terrence Bailey was a man of character and substance and would be a valuable member in any club he joined. So Edward talked to all the right people and they asked your grandfather to join. We owe Edward Bradshaw a large debt of gratitude. Of course, Henry has never brought up the subject. He has too much class.

"I know that the Bradshaws have been special friends," Charlie concurred.

Claire continued her reflections. "Are you certain it was an accident? As I said, Dottie admitted that Scottie wasn't a saint."

"I hope it was an accident."

"Lord knows. The press will have a field day. It'll be the same in Palm Beach. You remember problems, even if it wasn't a murder. If this is murder, everyone will want to have their say. The fuss!"

"Well, let's not get ahead of ourselves. We need to focus on comforting the Bradshaw family."

Charlie thought that the past ten minutes had been vintage Claire Bailey. She felt sincere sorrow for her friends' loss. But she saw everything through the prism of historical relationships and social status. Her mind jumped around from topic to topic. She tended to be blunt, so some misconstrued that as insensitivity.

In her late sixties, she was bright, trim, and attractive. Her principal capitulation to age was that she had let her hair go white. She had lost Robbie, Charlie's father, ten years before, and, as she told Charlie several times, the memory of her husband and their activities over the years caused her pain when she stopped to reflect.

Charlie noticed increasingly over the past few years that she had difficulty dealing with change. She felt reassured by a schedule and constancy in her relationships. Death and surprises upset her enormously. She marveled at her friends who accepted change with equanimity. She worried that their calmness came with age. After all, she and her friends had seen a lot. She just reacted differently from them.

Claire stared out the sunroom windows, then sighed, "I'm not hungry. You must be eager to drive back downtown. Thank you for listening to a tired, old woman."

"Mother, I love you. But you're right I should be on my way.

I have dinner with Kate."

"Don't tell me. You know what I think of Miss Milano. You can do better. She grew up on a farm, for heaven's sake. How do you expect her to fulfill the social responsibilities that will arise as your wife?"

Charlie listened reluctantly. His mother was tired, out of sorts. She had criticized Kate Milano many times. Charlie knew he should keep silent, but this time he responded out of pique.

"Look, she's intelligent, spirited, engaging, and beautiful. A hundred men are waiting to date her. Besides, her father's farm is over eight hundred acres."

"Probably corn and soybeans," Claire retorted trying to belittle Charlie's comment. "Twice as many lovely women are dying to have you ask them out—girls who come from fine families that we've known for years."

"I disagree. She's remarkable—not a fortune hunter, a catch. And don't look down on farmers when our glorious Irish ancestors were potato farmers before they immigrated."

Claire looked glum and exhausted. She seemed to have lost interest in arguing. Charlie came over and kissed her cheek and left.

Charlie tried calling Sam Dixon, the portfolio manager for the Bradshaw accounts, from the car before he left the driveway. Getting no response, he left a message on Sam's answering machine, "Call me at home. Scottie Bradshaw was found dead this morning. We need to review his trusts to follow the instructions."

As Charlie started to drive, a police car pulled in blocking him. Sergeant Rumson got out and walked directly to Charlie in his car.

"Going somewhere Mr. Bailey? I came to get your clothes. I hope you haven't thrown them out."

"No. James will have them—all freshly laundered," Charlie sneered.

"That's another mistake you made," Rumson snapped. "Make sure you don't take any trips until we finish interviewing you. Understand?"

"Yes," Charlie answered, "Now would you move your car?"

Steaming Charlie pulled out and drove down a leafy street where the trees formed a canopy. The effect of this *allée* made him feel that he was driving through a green tunnel illuminated by the sun. The result was restful, as if he was surrounded by a protective cocoon that could keep life nourished and private forever. Just what he needed. In Lake Forest, it could be no other way. The beauty of the trees and landscaped grounds, the magnificent set-back mansions, the graceful allure of the parks and lakes, and the carefully maintained serenity came at a price of enduring a steady stream of sightseers driving by, and pointing fingers,—probably wondering who lived there. Charlie knew also that since the nature of the town's residents eschewed ostentation and conceit, the tourists would never have their questions answered.

His review ended abruptly as he turned onto Route 41 and encountered heavy traffic heading south to Chicago. Auto dealerships, gas stations, fast-food restaurants, and shopping centers lined the road giving bold contrast to the tranquil hamlet he had just left. Despite the attention this drive demanded Charlie mulled over Sergeants Rumson's accusatory demeanor. Charlie had done nothing but been the first to find Scottie and pull his body out of the roman bath. Rumson was out of line.

Then his mother had criticized Kate once again. She was too caught up in social class definition of people. She is a product of the wealthy family she was born to. Funny, when she agreed to marry Dad, she had to defend his modest upbringing to her parents. In a way history is repeating.

Kate is the most exciting woman he had met since his wife, Solange, had died in a car accident five years ago. Kate is someone I might marry.

But most troubling was the death of Scottie. He grew up with Scottie's older brother and sister. Jamie had been Charlie's constant companion until college. They had been tennis doubles partners at the club and had gone to the same parties. They had attended two different prep schools but always hung out together each summer. In their twenties they had been groomsmen in each other's weddings. Although during the past decade they had been busy with business and family and saw each other less as a result, they had remained good friends.

Scottie was the little bratty brother they had tried to leave behind. Still Jamie and Scottie were bonded in a special way. Jamie would be shattered when he heard the news. Charlie vowed to call him the next day after Jamie talked with his parents and sister.

# CHAPTER FOUR

Fifteen minutes later Charlie was able to reach Sam Dixon from his car phone. They agreed to meet at the Bailey, Richardson, and O'Neill offices where they could talk interrupted.

Two hours later Dixon walked into Charlie's office dressed in golf attire.

"I'm glad you didn't change," Charlie said. "We need to have answers by the first thing tomorrow. We both know the drill. The trust documents will tell us what we can do."

"Terrible tragedy," Sam said, and sat back down in front of Charlie's desk. He placed three thick files across from his boss. He acted businesslike in spite of wearing a polo shirt and short pants. He waited while Charlie flipped through the Bradshaw documents.

"Good," Charlie remarked. "You're already ahead of me."

"I have access to all of my clients' privileged documents though the security file on my computer - both here and at home. I had time to glance at Scottie's trust and investment portfolio. Nothing unusual. No trades are open pending close. We're free to act to protect the assets. His brother is co-trustee with their bank. I'll talk to Jamie and the bank tomorrow."

"Is there a lot of money in the investment account?" Charlie asked.

"It is substantial, although the trust was not funded with much initially.

"His father didn't want Scottie to have enough money to squander. He said that I should watch closely that his son did not go behind his back to invade his trusts."

"I hope we wrote the trusts tight enough so that couldn't happen," Charlie commented.

"They are tight- as Henry requested," Sam assured his boss. "As you know, Scottie was divorced and had no children. The trust was set up for him to receive the inheritance when his parents passed away."

"And who are the beneficiaries of Scottie's estate?" Charlie asked.

"We don't have his will in our files. So I suspect that the money in the trust goes to his bother and sister. I'll check with the bank tomorrow."

The phone rang, and Charlie answered it without thinking. A reporter from the *Chicago Tribune* identified herself as Sue Grossman and said she had questions about Scottie Bradshaw's death.

"Why are you calling me?" Charlie asked. He rolled his eyes and raised his eyebrows looking at Sam. Sam pointed at himself and then at the door. Charlie gestured Sam to stay.

"An employee of the Potawatomi Club said you found the

body in the men's locker room."

"I have no comment. The Lake Forest police are handling the matter. Talk to them."

Charlie hung up quickly.

"Sam,that was the *Trib*. I'm astonished they found me so quickly."

"I'm sure that that won't be the last call," Sam remarked.

"I shouldn't have answered the phone."

Charlie turned back and reached for a file, but added, "See what's going on. The Bradshaws are prominent—newsworthy. Even an accidental death is good for a story. Where were we?"

Just then the phone rang again. Charlie glanced at the call reader and recognized Kate's cell number. He laughed at his last statement and picked up. He held up a finger to tell Sam to wait a minute. He told her about Scottie's death and invited her to come over to his apartment for dinner and a full explanation.

When Charlie hung up and Sam resumed their discussion covering several details and contingencies.

"I'll be ready tomorrow," Sam promised. "You don't think it was a suicide? That might change lots of things - like insurance, probate, *et cetera.*"

Charlie shrugs his shoulders as to say "Who knows now?"

\* \* \*

Charlie arrived at his apartment emotionally drained. On the elevator he closed his eyes and breathed deeply. When the elevator door opened Kate was standing at the apartment door with a glass of pinot noir. He smiled wanly at her welcoming face.

"You look like you could use this. Ken Wright Vineyards, Oregon."

"Thanks. I need a kiss also."

"Of course."

Charlie stepped forward and made sure he kissed her lips.

With his wine in one hand and his arm around Kate, they walked into the living room and sat down on the couch. He told her everything, including the details of his police interview and the reporter's call.

"Wait until you see your answering machine. It says you have nine calls. That's a lot more than your usual. I told you to delist your number."

"I know, I know," Charlie responded, feeling embarrassed. "And I will. Then only you will be able to call me."

"I'd like that, handsome. But you can add your mom—and some friends. Seriously, though, what do you think happened?" She leaned into him and stroked his arm.

"The more I think of it, I doubt Scottie's death was an accident. I've noticed him drinking a lot at parties, but I've never seen him fall down drunk. Plus, the locker room urinals are in a separate room from the roman bath. So I don't know why he was there, much less how he could drown.

"Who would want to kill Scottie Bradshaw?" Kate asked. She stood up and circled the couch while Charlie thought.

"Can I refill your glass?"

Then the doorbell rang.

"That would be the Chinese I ordered. I'll get it."

Charlie watched Kate take her purse and give the building's bellman money to pay the delivery boy downstairs.

"Can I help?" Charlie asked.

"No. I'll have everything ready in a minute. Charlie stood by as Kate set the table with plates, napkins and chopsticks and put the containers between their places."

"I hope you don't mind that I didn't get out the silver," she said, pouring wine.

He smiled at her sense of humor and appreciated her taking charge. He looked at this lovely, caring woman he had known intimately for a couple of years. Kate was accomplishing something he never thought would happen. She was slowly filling the gap in his heart after Solange's death. She had respected his distance but occasionally seemed impatient that he hadn't proposed to her. He just needed more time. He hoped that his emotional struggle wouldn't chase her away.

Kate was different from his elegant, worldly, aristocratic French Solange. Kate was artistic, bright, athletic, young, affectionate, and attentive. If he made a wine analogy, Solange was a premier grand cru Bordeaux and Kate was an exciting Napa cult cab. Both were made from similar grapes and equally rare and wonderful.

"You asked me before the food arrived who might kill Scottie," Charlie said. "I don't know, but he had lots of enemies. As charming as he could be, I have heard that he had been involved in a handful of investment schemes that went bad. Sam Dixon, who knows the family as well as anyone, didn't trust him and had been asked by Scottie to dip into his future inheritance."

"So, did he?"

"Sam refused, and according to Sam Scottie resented our firm because we didn't help him. Of course, no matter what he asked, we wouldn't violate the language of the trusts. Scottie's grandfather and father set up these trusts for a purpose. And the bank and our firm have a fiduciary duty to follow the original instructions."

"Being a stockbroker himself, Scottie must have known what you could and could not do," Kate offered.

"I'm sure he knew, but from what Sam said, he may have been desperate."

"Well, the police will delve into his situation, especially if they suspect foul play."

"I know," Charlie continued. "But I don't have anything more to tell the police than what I have. I hope they just leave us alone. Unfortunately, in the course of the investigation I see our firm being mentioned. That could be unsettling to some of our clients. I hope they refrain from calling and asking questions I will not answer. That would put me in an awkward position."

"Do you think the Bradshaw trusts you manage have any bearing on the death?"

"I have no idea."

"If there anything I can do, please let me help." "Thanks for the offer."

"There's the phone again."

They looked at each other. Charlie frowned, "Let it ring. I'm not in the mood to talk with anyone tonight."

| § |

# CHAPTER FIVE

At eight o'clock every Monday morning, Charlie gathered his key partners and staff in the large conference room to discuss the usual topics: the markets, economic events, client matters, and prospective clients. Most of the staff had been in the office since seven a.m. preparing trade tickets, talking to research analysts on the East Coast, and planning the week. Charlie's audience seemed especially alert and he assumed that was so because they expected him to talk about Scottie Bradshaw.

The conference room was full - all twenty-five seats. Charlie sat in his customary chair at the table - middle right.

He leaned forward and made eye contact with a couple of his senior portfolio managers.

"Let's begin with the news. As the media have reported, our client Scottie Bradshaw died this weekend. I shall be the firm's only spokesman. Refer any media inquiries to me. If a client asks you for information, tell him you know only what's in the papers. We must be sensitive to the Bradshaw family's privacy. Don't speculate."

"What if the police contact us?" Dieter Keller, a senior analyst, asked.

"Be polite, and direct them to me. If I'm not in, have them call our general counsel, Bob Underwood."

"Sam said you found the body. Is that true?"

Charlie was annoyed to hear that Sam had revealed that and glared his way. He would have to take him aside later and emphasize that his directions applied to everyone.

"True. Pure chance. But that is the type of detail we shouldn't comment on. We will conduct business as usual and I'll keep you informed."

Charlie looked around the group and sensed that they understood how serious he was. Then he asked Dieter to open the discussion of securities markets and business topics.

A half-hour later Charlie adjourned the meeting. In the hallway Kathy, his secretary, looking nervous, stopped him and whispered that two policemen were in the reception area waiting to see him.

Charlie nodded and turned immediately in the other

direction to greet them. They stood when he approached, he noted their plain clothes, signally that they were detectives.

"Good morning. I am Charlie Bailey, the General Partner of Bailey, Richardson, and O'Neill. How can I help you?"

"I am Detective John Riordan of the Chicago PD, and this is Investigator Paul Victor of the Lake Forest Police Department, assigned to the Lake County Sherriff Office's Major Crimes Task Force."

"We're here to ask you a few questions about yesterday," the other office said.

"Fine, follow me."

Charlie led the two to a small adjacent conference room, where he offered them coffee or water.

"No thanks," Detective Riordan declined.

The police officers sat across the table from Charlie. Riordan was rather short and pudgy, with a ruddy face. He was dressed in a rumpled sport coat and plain tan tie. He looked to be in his fifties. Victor wore a sport coat with a Lake Forest Police Department badge on the breast pocket. This man was tall and muscular and looked several years younger than the other officer. Charlie noted a handgun on his belt under the open blazer.

Charlie began, "I'm happy to help but I already told the Lake Forest police all I know. I am curious though: Why are you here from a Major Crimes Task Force? What major crime?"

"We are investigating all possibilities," Victor explained. "My unit draws its members from the police departments of the local communities and investigates all active and cold cases involving potential major crime. Now let me ask you a few questions. How did you know the deceased?"

Charlie repeated what he had told Sergeant Rumson the day before. While he was talking, he wondered if the police had already determined the death to be foul play. He guessed that the importance of the Bradshaw political influence had prompted the police to assign the top investigative unit.

"Where were you Saturday night?" Victor continued, taking notes.

"I had a drink in the grill at the club after an afternoon round of golf with an assistant pro, Brian Jensen. Then I drove home to Chicago where I remained until I returned to the club early morning Sunday."

"Did you see the deceased on Saturday?"

"Briefly, as I was leaving. I saw him getting out of his car across the parking lot."

"Did you talk to him?"

"No."

"Did you attend the party at the Potawatomi Club?" "No."

"Did you see anyone going to the party?"

"I noticed a handful of couples heading in the direction of the club patio where the party was supposed to be."

"Can anyone verify your whereabouts Saturday night?"

"Of course, Kate, Kate Milano, was with me at home." "Who is Kate Milano?"

"She is my girlfriend."

"Was she with you all night?"

"That's none of your business."

"It might be. When did Miss Milano arrive and leave?"

Charlie glowered at the officer.

"She met me at seven o'clock at a restaurant—Tru. We ate and came back to my apartment around nine. She left early the next morning, when I drove to Lake Forest to play golf."

"Thank you, Mr. Bailey, but our job is to learn by asking questions. You said that you found the body in the roman bath, but when club's security guard switched off the locker room lights after the party, he didn't notice a body. In addition, the attendant, Javier, arrived at six-fifteen and didn't see a body before he went to the kitchen for coffee."

Investigator Victor paused, looked at his note pads and then glanced up at Charlie. "Yet you, a personal and business acquaintance of the deceased, found his body a few minutes later in the locker room. How do you explain that?"

Charlie looked at the investigator with disbelief. What is this all about? *Is he accusing me with murder? Is he accusing me of murder??*

"I can't explain why Javier and the security guard didn't notice the body. They would have to go through the bathroom and shower area to reach the roman bath. Maybe they didn't check in there."

"But you did. Why?"

"I happened to notice the body out of the corner of my eye. I had finished applying sunscreen at the middle sink, then turned to go back to the main locker area. That's when I saw a dark shape. If I had used a different sink, I would not have been able to see along the shower stalls to the bath. Go there. You'll understand."

Charlie frowned. He was not happy with his answers. He thought he sounded flustered and vulnerable. His body temperature rose.

"You touched the body?" Victor said.

"Of course, I had to get it out of the water."

"Why? You could have left it there. Did you touch the body beforehand?"

"What? Of course not! What are you implying?"

"Calm down, Mr. Bailey. Let's move on. You said that the

deceased was a client of your firm. Wasn't Mr. Bradshaw a broker or financial advisor?"

"Yes."

"Why would a financial advisor hire another financial company to manage his money?"

"He wouldn't need us, if it were his money outright. Scottie was an income beneficiary of some trusts and a remainderman in others."

"A remainderman? What's that?" Detective Riordan asked suddenly interested.

"That's a legal term, it means he would receive the corpus or principal of the trust after certain events transpired—often the death of the income beneficiary."

"Huh? Speak English, please," Riordan demanded.

"There can be one or several trusts. In a simple case Scottie received income from the interest earned from our investing but could not touch the principal—except for specific needs. If the trust did not have an expiration date, a remainderman—could be a relative, school, foundation, or other entity—would receive the original principal plus gains when Scottie died.

"What are those needs?"

"Whatever the trust allows—medical expenses, a new house, schooling. The named trustee would have to agree to permit such a distribution."

"So the deceased could have drawn on these trusts if he could convince the trustee."

"Yes, but only for those specific needs."

"So these remaindermen benefit from Mr. Bradshaw's death."

"Technically. I doubt those beneficiaries would have wanted Scottie to die."

"Could a Bradshaw be a remainderman of these trusts?"

"Yes, but the trust would spell that out."

Detective Riordan whistled out loud and smiled. He went silent then and Victor picked up the questioning. "So with a trust who hires you?

"In some cases, the trustee bank. In other trusts we are specifically named as the manager. For instance, Scottie's father, Henry Bradshaw, set up some trusts with us named. In no cases would Scottie have hired us. I take that back. He did hire us two years ago for part of his personal portfolio—not a trust. He said that he was happy with the performance of the trusts and thought we might help him."

"Who would have benefited financially from Scottie Bradshaw's death?"

"I do not know. I haven't seen his will. I suggest that you talk to the trustee bank and the law firm that wrote his will and the trusts. The law firm is probably Bradshaw, Evans. The bank is Old Fiduciary Bank and Trust. At any rate, they may not even be permitted to give you the information you want. You may need a court order."

"Would your firm benefit from Mr. Bradshaw's death?"

Charlie was trying hard to control himself. He prided himself on his integrity and the firm's stellar fiduciary reputation. This cop was crossing the line of honest inquiry with his innuendos. His suggestions were defamatory to a firm which Charlie had built ethical brick upon ethical brick.

"No," Charlie bristled. "Losing a client like Scottie Bradshaw hurts us — personally and professionally. We mourn his passing. But I can assure you that that is not the type of thing we think about — *ever*."

"Still, did you have any reason to dislike Mr. Bradshaw personally?" Riordan asked as he stared at the charcoal drawings on the wall.

"Scottie Bradshaw was a client, and I treated him with respect but did not encourage a close friendship."

"Well, that's all the questions we have for you right now," the investigator ended abruptly. "Is there someone at this firm who would be more intimate with the details of the Bradshaw Trusts than you are?"

"Why don't you leave cards, and I'll have someone contact you with the employees and service providers on these accounts. I'll have that information by this afternoon." He paused, then looked at the detective. "Detective Riordan, you did not ask many questions. Should I deal only with Investigator Victor?"

He replied, "This is a Lake County case. Investigator Victor is in charge. I'd lead if Cook County were the jurisdiction."

As Charlie stood up to let them out, Riordan again stared at the drawings, then pointed and asked, "Are those real? I mean the bull and bear pictures. They say Picasso."

"We're an investment firm. They speak to our struggle with

the markets. I borrowed them from my mother."

"Nice touch. Offices in the Rookery building with Picassos on the wall."

"Detectives, Kathy will show you out."

Charlie did not like the tone of John Riordan's last comment but at least the officer recognized the historical importance of the architecturally significant Rookery building on LaSalle Street, the center of Chicago's financial district.

After the detectives had left, Charlie returned to his office feeling angry and depressed. Why the interest in me?" Why the concern about my whereabouts and the firm's duties regarding the trusts? They would not have asked such questions, if they thought this tragedy was an accident.

Unable to concentrate on his inbox or office memos, Charlie looked out his window until he regained his composure. So the police did not believe that the death was an accident. Neither did he. As irritating as their visit was, he felt confident that they would turn their attention away from him once they had real clues.

Kathy stuck her head around the door. "Your phone has been ringing off the hook."

"Make a list of all clients who call. I'll call them back later today. Screen my personal calls. You'll know who to put through. Tell any broker who calls to talk to the analysts or traders. You know how to handle them."

"Don't forget, you are on the dais for the Economic Club's luncheon. Federal Reserve Chairman Powell is talking."

He sighed remembering his commitment: "Okay. I'll walk

over at noon. This has already been a busy day."

"One last thing, Mr. Bailey. This article was in today's *Trib*."

Charlie scanned it for his name.

"Following the death of Scott Bradshaw at the Potawatomi Club in Lake Forest, the Lake County Coroner's Office issued the following statement:

"The decedent, Scott Bradshaw, was found in a pool of water with wet clothes. The autopsy revealed water in the lungs; accordingly the probable cause of death and the manner of death are undetermined. An Inquest will take place next month to record an official cause of death.'

Mr. Bradshaw was a broker at the firm of Collins, Lang in Chicago and son of prominent attorney Henry Bradshaw. His body was discovered early Sunday morning in a locker room pool. Police will not confirm whether the death was an accident or homicide."

Charlie was relieved that he was not mentioned. In addition the coroner's statement did not state that the death was an accident. That meant the police would continue to pursue the case and might want to question him again.

He shook his head and asked himself why it hadn't rained yesterday so he wouldn't have gone to play golf. But he had. Now he should call Henry Bradshaw again to express his condolences and see if he could help the family in any way. Then he would call his close friend, Jamie, to check on how he was coping.

# CHAPTER SIX

After the police interview Charlie had just started to think about business when Chris Stewart, a portfolio manager, walked into his office and announced, "Rumors are flying around the Street that Chairman Powell is going to surprise us all and suggest at lunch today that the Fed is going to tighten monetary policy immediately. The markets are going crazy and have already built in between a twenty-five to fifty basis point increase in the Fed Funds rate. If true, such a policy reversal indicates the chairman means business in fighting inflation and isn't afraid of pre-empting the market."

"You are right. If he announces such a policy change, all hell is going to break loose. The market has not been expecting such a move so soon. Everyone will have to adjust their portfolios. Call a meeting immediately. Chris, have Kathy get all the portfolio managers in the big conference room in ten minutes."

As Chris Stewart left, Steve Zimmerman appeared at Charlie's door looking sheepish. Steve was a freshman at Northwestern University and son of a client. Charlie liked to bring in college students each summer and expose them to the investment business. Two of his current research analysts had begun as interns.

"Excuse me, Mr. Bailey. I heard three of the analysts talking about a possible Federal Reserve policy change. They seemed shocked by that prospect. I know I sound stupid, but what does it mean? Why is it important?"

"Steve, you are stupid only if you don't ask. As you know, the Fed is in charge of the nation's monetary policy. It operates independently of the federal government and tries to supply our financial system with the right amount of money to support economic growth with modest inflation. Until now the Fed has been pumping money into the economy to encourage growth. Investors are speculating that the Fed will start to withdraw money from the banking system which action could lead to increased short term rates. That will slow the economy because every borrower will have to pay more for loans."

Steve nodded but still looked puzzled. He asked, "Why would the Fed want to do that?"

"It's a balancing act, but the Fed probably feels that economic activity and inflation are building up too fast. They may think it is prudent to slow things down."

"Does that mean that the Fed wants a recession?"

"No, not at all. If the economy were a car, the Fed is tapping on the brakes, not slamming them on. Still, a change in policy means we'll have to adjust our portfolios as some investments do better in different types of monetary actions than others."

"What kind of investments do better?"

"Great question. We are going to have a meeting now to discuss how we need to reposition our portfolios if the policy change takes place. Sit in the back and listen. Don't expect to comprehend everything this time. Understand that this change - if it occurs—is significant and may make investing in common stocks and bonds more difficult in the near term. Come with me."

Charlie felt relieved that he had conducted himself professionally, in this conversation with Steve. He disliked the young man. Steve had an annoying tone in his voice and dressed more like a rock band drummer than a businessman. His long ponytail hair was kept in place with a rubber band. He had a diamond earring in one ear. A tattoo on his neck peaked out over the collar of his shirt. Plus, Kathy had reported that Steve had propositioned one of the young file clerks.

Charlie had taken him aside a week ago to explain the need for standards in a firm like this, in both dress and conduct. He had described the firm's culture as "buttoned-down." Steve responded that he understood that this firm was fussy. He would try to do what was expected but he had to be "himself".

Charlie had bit his tongue at that remark. He had instead put a call into Steve's father, a client for ten years. Unfortunately he was traveling in China for two weeks. So Charlie decided to put up with Steve for the time being, but his days were numbered.

The portfolio managers and analysts had already assembled in the large conference room when Charlie entered. He understood that the firm's portfolios were not structured to deal with a new period of rising interest rates, his managers would have to review each portfolio and make adjustments.

As usual, Charlie took charge of the meeting. Although the firm had many highly intelligent, experienced investment professionals, Charlie's keen analytical mind and years of excellent market calls made him the natural leader. And the firm's success was built on his reputation as a savvy investor for his clients. Part of his mental process was that he encouraged constructive challenges to his ideas before deciding what to do. Often he altered his preconception when he heard a compelling contrasting argument. He enjoyed a give and take. Today, though, speed of action was more important than nuanced analysis. That might come later. Now they had a short time frame to act.

Charlie began, "We have had three years of Fed ease of the money supply. And I still see only a few signs of excess or pressures on inflation. However, it appears that Powell doesn't want to wait for such evidence and wants to be ahead of the curve. So, right policy or not, we need to act. Granted, we are hearing only rumors, but he is talking at lunch today - I'll be there - and the markets are already assuming an inevitable tightening of policy. We need to get started. Let's get ready to act quickly. We all know it will take us time to make all the necessary changes."

Most of the managers nodded in agreement and waited for instructions.

"We'll do the simple things first. In the bond portfolios, shorten durations and upgrade quality. Treasuries should be the first choice because they are the most liquid. We might even use Treasuries temporarily in municipal-bond portfolios until we can find sufficient high-grade, shorter-maturity tax-exempts.

"In stock portfolios, move out of major cyclicals and be selective on banks and financials. In general, raise cash."

Sam Dixon raised his hand and asked, "How sensitive should we be to creating tax liabilities in personal accounts through selling?"

"It's better to pay a tax than lose money," Charlie responded. "Remember my dad's favorite line: 'More money has been lost trying to avoid taxes than being at the end of a gun.' In those cases where income is very important and the clients are long-term investors, go easy on these moves."

"Currencies? Short positions?" Sam asked.

"The dollar should appreciate; so take off any dollar hedges. Also, look at using derivatives to protect the value of the portfolio—short positions, paired trades, or credit default swaps, if permitted. Share any of these ideas with the other managers who are not here. Most importantly, get on the phone to clients, trustees, and co-trustees. Explain what we are intending to do and why it makes sense. This advice applies to both advisory and discretionary accounts."

"Charlie, I can see that these changes will keep us busy for three or four weeks," Kyle Wagner, a portfolio manager, estimated.

"Whatever it takes. If you have a vacation planned, see if you can delay it. If not, have adequate backup. I'll be in every day. Thank you all."

"You can count on us," Chris Stewart said while getting up.

Charlie felt good about this group. They had been through these major transitions before, and his team always rose to the occasion. One of the reasons the firm had been successful for so many years was because the staff communicated well with clients. They were realistic in setting expectations, had never talked down to clients, and were responsive to every concern. The proof of this approach was that clients rarely left the firm to go to a competitor.

Charlie signaled to Steve Zimmerman and the two other interns who were in the room to join him in his office. He sat them down on the couch and a chair opposite him and said,

"You can learn from that meeting. You may not have understood all the investment jargon we used. Eventually you will. But what is most important is that we recognized a significant change in the investment environment and are moving to act consistently for all our clients. We'll speak with one voice to everyone. No portfolio manager will go off on his own. Our clients expect us to treat them equally and to our best thinking. We have built this business on those principles."

"Here, here," Steve chimed.

The other interns looked at Steve as if he were strange. Charlie merely rolled his eyes skyward and dismissed the group.

After the interns left Charlie could feel his adrenaline surging as it always did when a major inflection point in the financial market occurred. He loved the challenge. A major event like a Fed policy change happened only every couple of years, so this was an important day. The firm would earn its fees today and over the next few weeks.

---

This salutary feeling did not last. His mind shifted to the earlier meeting with the police. His stomach seized for an instance. This investigation could not have come at a worse time. He hoped this police matter would fade away, but he had a foreboding that it would only become bigger and bigger.

****

On Tuesday, Federal Reserve policy-makers raised short-term interest rates a full half percent—just as Chairman Powell had hinted at lunch the day before. Charlie and his investment team were pleased that they had had the time to talk to their clients—even if it was only a day early. In reaction to the chairman's comments and the Fed's announcement, the stock and bond market fell sharply. Investors were expecting that further rate increases would follow over the next twelve months.

Charlie used this event as a teaching moment and called the three interns in to his office again. "You might wonder why investment professionals can be calm when the value of their clients' portfolios decline, as they have the past two days. After all, the point of investing is to grow the value of assets. But we have a broad perspective. We recognize that when certain events occur, market prices will decline. That's part of life. The challenge in such times is to protect the value of assets at least somewhat—if not in whole. In this instance, this firm lessened the full impact of the falling markets on its clients' portfolios. In other words, the effect could have been worse. The firm saved our clients some money in a difficult situation. This is not reason for a celebration, but we feel vindicated. Had we done nothing our clients would be worse off."

Steve spoke up, "Dad will be happy to hear that."

Kathy appeared at the door and said, "I'm sorry to interrupt but Paul Victor is on the phone for you."

The interns left and Charlie took the call.

"Mr. Bailey, regarding the Scott Bradshaw case," Paul began without pleasantries. "I notice that your firm paid substantial sums to Mr. Scott Bradshaw's bank account throughout the year. What did he do to deserve those payments from you?"

The investigator's aggressive tone reminded Charlie that he was not free to focus entirely on work.

"I think, Officer Victor—is that what I should call you? Investigator, detective, officer?"

"I am called 'investigator' as a member of the Task Force. That is the same as a 'detective'. My rank in the Lake Forest Police Department is 'patrol officer'. You can call me whatever you want. I'll know what you mean."

"Okay, Investigator Victor. Let me clarify about the funds paid out to Mr. Bradshaw," Charlie responded. "That money is not the firm's. It belongs to several Bradshaw trusts, which are invested primarily in stocks and bonds. These securities pay dividends and interest periodically, and according to the terms of the trust we instruct the custodial bank to pay the amounts collected to the income beneficiary—in this case, Scottie Bradshaw. We serve as investment manager, but the assets we manage do not belong to us. And in fact the actual payments come from the trustee bank—not Bailey Richardson."

"Old Fiduciary told us that your firm determines how much money comes from these trusts, but I'll accept your explanation. But you did not answer my question. Did Mr. Bradshaw deserve these payments?"

Charlie frowned. The police officer was asking for a value judgment.

"Deserve? That was not for me to decide. The original grantor of the trust, Scottie's grandfather, made that judgment. We try to balance the various needs of the beneficiaries: income, capital preservation, and growth. But we don't second-guess the intentions of the client who established the terms of the trust."

"Thank you for educating me, Mr. Bailey," Victor said sounding insincere, "But if Mr. Bradshaw wanted more money, wouldn't he have come to you and asked for it?"

"Mr. Bradshaw may have had several sources of income, but it is possible that he would come here to us to let us know if he needed more. We are also bound by the terms of the trust to try to meet the needs and desires of all the income beneficiaries and the remainderman."

"Did Scott Bradshaw ask you for more money?" Paul persisted.

"From time to time Mr. Bradshaw requested that he receive higher income and special distributions from the corpus of the trust. The trust did provide for distributions from principal for heavy medical expenses, but that was never the case with Scottie Bradshaw."

"Did you accommodate his requests?" Paul bore in further.

"We did all we could to satisfy his demands within the language of the trusts," Charlie answered carefully.

"Usually his requests did not supersede the trusts' terms."

"And when they did, you turned him down?"

"Yes."

"Did he threaten you or anyone?"

Charlie paused, exasperated. This line of questioning was combative and distasteful. Charlie tried to deflect it.

"Investigator Victor, I did not deal with Scottie Bradshaw directly, and I did not hear of any threats. I would not expect to hear of threats made by anyone of Scottie Bradshaw's character."

"Did you consider Mr. Bradshaw a nuisance?"

"No. It is not unusual to want more income from a trust."

At that point, the investigator changed his line of inquiry and asked a series of purely informational questions about Bailey Richardson and O'Neill and requested some biographical background about Sam Dixon. He concluded by asking, "By the way, did you like Mr. Bradshaw?"

"You asked me that yesterday. My answer is the same: I have had limited contact with Mr. Bradshaw over the years.

He was a bit younger then I; so I knew him as a client and saw him infrequently otherwise. But he came from a wonderful family and seemed to have intelligence, energy, and charm. I know his parents and older brother, Jamie, better. His sister, Phillipa, I have only met once."

"So you don't want to answer my question?"

"I answered your question. Twice now."

Paul Victor paused and said, "That's all for now. I may call you again."

After that unpleasant interview, Charlie wandered out to his company's trading floor thirty feet from his office to see how the markets were doing. It was an open room where six traders sat around a central desk, each with a computer and monitor built into the desk consoles. Above on the wall several television monitors displayed real time securities and currency markets and streaming current news.

On one of the wall-mounted screens a local news program showed Scottie's picture. Charlie focused on the closed captioning scrolling across the bottom of the display. "Investigators are pursuing all angles, including investigation of the deceased's relationship with the prestigious investment firm of Bailey, Richardson, which caters to the wealthy and socially connected. That firm's head, Charles Bailey, discovered the deceased on Sunday morning."

Charlie suddenly felt as if he had fallen down a tunnel. Both his reputation and that of the firm were being called into question. A wave of nausea came over him and he headed toward the men's room. Alone he stood at the sink scooping water onto his face and swallowed some.

He looked into the mirror and took several deep breaths until his heart rate slowed. He knew he needed to contact his lawyer. He had thought about calling Bob Underwood earlier but the matter had seemed more nettlesome than serious. He reasoned that with time it would fade away. Now, after this broadcast, he feared that his reputation and the firm's would suffer a nightmare of public innuendo. And worse—they might accuse him of murder.

"Kathy, get Bob Underwood on the phone. Better yet, ask him to meet me in the downstairs lobby as soon as he has a chance."

Thirty minutes later they met and walked to the coffee shop on the ground floor of the Chicago Board of Trade. They sat at a secluded table and ordered coffee.

"I cleared my schedule when Kathy called," Bob said. "I wasn't surprised to hear from you. I've seen the news reports."

Bob looked his usual conservative self: short haircut, pin-striped navy suit tailored to his lean six foot frame, white but-toned-down shirt, and blue polka-dot tie.

"So Bob, what do you think I should do?"

"My first reaction is that you are being a bit paranoid. Of course you did not commit a crime."

Charlie laughed in spite of himself. Bob, who used to play tennis with Charlie's father, had known him since he was born and served as outside general counsel for Bailey, Richardson since its inception. Few other men could have been so forthright without a risk of Charlie bristling.

"Why do you think you are being implicated?" Bob continued. "Did the police say something?"

"Not directly, but they asked where I had been the night before, and they knew that Scottie came to us several times to ask for more money than the trusts we manage threw off."

"They assumed conflicts between Scottie and your firm?"

"Which never existed."

"Of course there weren't," Bob agreed adjusting his wire-rim glasses. "The big thing, Charlie, is to answer the authorities' questions truthfully but don't offer anything beyond their questions. Be helpful but don't set forth any opinions or theories. Seemingly innocent comments can lead to unintended consequences. The best thing that could happen is that the police solve the crime they think occurred. Then life will return to normal."

"Should I try to help them speed along the process, if I can? Their line of questioning and the media reports I witnessed today on TV really bothered me. I feel I need to do something."

"Stay out of it. I know you want to put this all behind you, but I am not sure how you could accomplish that. By solving the crime - if there is one? I would not recommend that. You have no experience in criminal investigations, and too much involvement may lead the police to think you have something to hide. As far as the press, direct them to me, and I shall try to disabuse them of any notions of your involvement.'

"Remember me to your mom. She still is the most elegant and beautiful woman of her set."

"I'll do that. I'm sure she'd say you have too much of the blarney in you. Sweet-tongued lawyer."

Charlie walked with Bob out to the sidewalk and thanked him again. Then he went back up to his office and private bathroom. He had recognized that he was perspiring and had been embarrassed that his palm was sweaty when he shook Bob's hand.

He rinsed his face again with cool water. The stress of the morning had hit him. He felt events were getting out of hand. *I'm losing it*, he thought. *I was defensive with Paul Victor. I shouldn't have been. I must do something. It's unlike me to be only reactive. How do I get control of this runaway train?*

He sat at his desk, ignoring his message slips, tapping his pen on his blotter, and considering his options. I can't be passive. Maybe I could be more helpful to the police about Scottie Bradshaw's business problems and his talent for angering people. I could ask some of my industry and social contacts about who might have held a grudge. I might learn something that would be value added to the police.

*Still, Bob warned me against any involvement. My efforts could backfire. The police might conclude that I am too interested in this death to be blameless.*

Mindlessly he brought up his emails on his computer. The last five were from friends offering condolences that the news was running stories tying him to Scotties' death.

*Damn it. I can't merely stand by. I have to be involved now until I am exonerated in all minds.*

# CHAPTER SEVEN

"Of course the police interview and the media reporting have been painful," Kate commiserated. "But you have no experience in investigation. You're a money manager. A lovable one."

Kate reached across the table to touch Charlie's hand. He squeezed back but didn't smile.

"I don't trust the police to get to the bottom of Scottie's death quickly," Charlie declared. "If this drags on for weeks and we are still mentioned in connection with the investigation, we'll be damaged. Clients and prospects will lose confidence that we are the right firm for them. Some of the staff might start to interview elsewhere."

Kate had listened patiently as Charlie had vented as soon as they had sat down for dinner at one of their favorite Italian restaurants, Spiaggia. She knew from experience that after he had expressed his annoyance for a few minutes he would usually calm down. This time was different. The stakes were higher.

The waiter helped the process by interrupting him asking for their drink order.

"What?" Charlie said confused for a moment.

Kate tried to help. "Two pinot grigios, please. Santa Margharita."

The waiter nodded and went off.

"After meeting with Bob I found a reporter parked out at our receptionist's desk. He rushed up and started at me with a question. I was so angry that I exploded. I shouted, "Get out. Leave." Then he pulled out his iPhone and began taking a video of me. I tried to knock his camera out of his hand but missed. I turned to our receptionist and ordered her to call security. I looked one last time at the reporter and fled down the corridor. I know I reacted wrong. We'll probably see the tape on a TV report."

"What else could you do?" Kate said, "He provoked you."

Charlie took two deep breaths and a drink of water.

"Sorry, Kate. I need to focus on dinner."

They sat quietly for a few minutes. She wondered how far she should go in opposing his idea about an investigation.

The waiter brought the glasses of wine, mentioned the specials, and left. Charlie continued his monologue,

"I know a lot of people who knew Scottie; I am in the same financial industry. If the resolution of what happened requires knowledge of financial instruments of schemes, I am in a better position than the police."

Kate remained unconvinced and took a sip of wine to slow Charlie down while she considered a stronger reply. Then she countered "All true. But with due respect, that may not be enough. If this were fraud or a white-collar crime, I might agree with you. But if this is murder, you are not an expert. And if it is murder, the killer won't want you sniffing around. I am worried that what you are considering could be unsafe."

"I think I can help the police without anyone knowing what I am doing."

Kate realized that the personal safety argument would probably not register with him. She knew him as fearless—an invincible alpha male. She was arguing uphill.

"You know, you are a stubborn guy. It's hard for you to stand back and wait for things to play out. You can be analytical, thoughtful, and strategic but then a switch clicks and you have to act- boldly, fully committed. Two sides of the same man."

"It's the curse of a money manager. Events occurring all the time can affect my view of the markets and individual holdings in a portfolio. I have to remain composed and weigh the changes taking place. But once I have decided that I need to act I must not procrastinate, or my clients may lose money. Get conviction and place your bets—knowing that I won't be right all the time."

Kate saw the belief in his eyes and heard the steel in his voice. She tried her last argument, "Have you considered what the Bradshaws might think if they heard you were conducting your personal investigation? How would they react to your meddling?"

Charlie frowned and thought for a minute. He responded slowly and with conviction. "As it stands, they may share the suspicion about me. I must clear any doubts. I can't trust the police to do that. In addition, they must be interested in a quick resolution of who's responsible. They won't have closure until they know. If I speed the process, they'll be happy I helped."

Kate didn't agree with is argument but felt resigned to the inevitable.

"I admire you. I am far less analytical and more driven by emotion. If I were you, I would not get involved. I'd be afraid. Catching a murderer isn't like buying stocks. But I know you won't rest until you solve this thing. I may have a few sleepless nights worrying about you, but I'll be supportive."

Charlie smiled wanly, not seeming to be taking in what she said. Then he answered, "I am going to start with Jamie Bradshaw. I have know him for ages, and he should know who had it in for his brother."

Kate hid her annoyance that he did not seem to appreciate the negative impact on her peace of mind of his decision. She remained silent hoping that time and events would change his resolve.

Charlie arranged to have lunch at noon the next day with Jamie Bradshaw. Ostensively, they were to talk about the trusts and how Scottie's death might influence the way Sam Dixon invested the money. They agreed to meet in a private room at the Fort Dearborn Club where Jamie was a member. It was a short walk from Charlie's office in the Loop, Chicago's downtown business district.

Charlie greeted Scottie Bradshaw's older brother in a private dining room on the third floor with a sincere embrace. Jamie was dressed in a grey flannel suit with a white shirt and blue tie, appropriate to his position as a principal in Goodman, Bates, a large, prestigious private equity firm. He had tears in his eyes as he sat down.

"Jamie," Charlie began, "I am terribly sorry about your brother. I hope you and your parents are able to deal with the grief. It's tough. Believe me that I am disconcerted to have been the one who found him. If I could have done anything to save him, I would have."

"That's all right, Charlie. Don't feel guilty. You couldn't have done anything. My family is consoled that it wasn't a stranger who found him." Jamie paused and asked rhetorically, "Do you think he would still be alive if you had arrived earlier?"

"No. The police seem to think Scottie died Saturday night. So even if I arrived an hour earlier to play golf, I would have been too late. In a way I wish someone else had found Scottie. If someone had been there that night, he might have been able to revive him. Ironically the police seem to be suspicious of me because I found Scottie and had a business relationship with him."

"I'm sure this questioning is normal procedure," Jamie offered.

"Still, the implication bothers me," Charlie admitted.

"Don't worry, Charlie. Nothing will come of the police's interest. My parents and I appreciate your making yourself available to them."

"Of course, I will do that. Maybe I can help with some of Scottie's personal and business history. I am sure that you and your family would like to know what happened."

"Yes, of course. But don't trouble yourself. My dad and I believe it was an accident. We hope that the police will put this to rest soon."

Charlie felt an urge to tell Jamie that he would go beyond the police inquiry and do more personally. But because of Kate's admonition last night he decided to wait. There would be another time to tell Jamie.

"My parents tell me that Claire has been very helpful. Thank her for me."

"I will. When will the viewing and the service take place?"

"We decided to have everything in the city. It should be more convenient for a majority of people. So viewing on Thursday evening and the religious service on Friday morning at St. James's. The casket will be closed. We want everyone to remember Scottie as handsome and vital."

"My mother and I will be there, and I am certain Kate will want to pay her respects."

"We know you and your mother will always be there for us. We appreciate it."

As Jamie examined the menu, Charlie reflected on the Fort Dearborn Club and how important it was in the business and social fabric of the city.

Lunch at clubs had been a long tradition in Chicago. In fact, several of the clubs dated back to right after the Great Chicago Fire of 1871, which destroyed half the city. In the late nineteenth century, successful business men and financiers in Chicago conducted most of their business in the morning and then moved on to their clubs to enjoy lunch, meet friends, make deals, play cards, smoke cigars, and drink a cognac or whiskey. At three p.m. they would stroll back to the office to check on business or have their driver take them home. A few had private railroad cars to share with friends on the trips up to their mansions in the suburbs. In more recent times, club members felt bound to their offices and returned promptly after lunch at one-thirty or two.

As the way people conducted business and communicated with each other changed—business had grown more impersonal and global - critics thought these clubs had become anachronistic and predicted their demise. Several had closed over the years, but those that accommodated change and attracted a top-notch membership of people with like interests continued to thrive.

Historically, most of these clubs were organized around a single purpose, such as support of the arts, public affairs, commerce or athletics. Some clubs offered only meals, while the more elaborate like this one had paneled libraries, huge reading rooms, squash courts, indoor swimming pools, and guest rooms.

The Fort Dearborn Club was one of the oldest, most respected, and diverse. Its membership was a Who's Who of Chicago industry, law, finance, architecture, accounting, government, health care, and the media. Originally a bastion of white males, as times changed, these clubs invited women, blacks, and Latinos to join. As always, the common currency for membership was success and influence. Although Charlie belonged to the Chicago Club, a similar club, whenever he ate here, he recognized more acquaintances in the hallways and the large, main dining room.

For his meeting with Jamie Bradshaw, Charlie welcomed Jamie's invitation because the Club was extremely discreet. The staff was trained that anything that was said stayed within the walls. Indeed, almost as a metaphor, the club was built with thick, stone walls. It was a stand-alone building, dominating the street with the massive façade executed in the Romanesque architectural style of H.H. Richardson

In appreciation of this tradition Charlie felt comfortable discussing financial matters. After they ordered lunch, Charlie became businesslike.

"I'm glad we could get together because I wanted to talk to you about the trusts we manage. Since Scottie had no children and was divorced, you and your heirs and Phillipa and her heirs will receive his interest in the trusts. As you know, you have shared with him and some trusts already. Your grandfather and father set up other trusts only for Scottie, with your sister and you as beneficiaries. Sam Dixon will call you with the details. We'll need to know if this change in circumstances requires us to manage the money differently."

Jamie paused, then said, "Let me think about everything for a week or so, and then I'll get back to Sam. Phillipa will probably ask me what I think. I'll also talk to my parents. At any rate, as you know, my needs are different from Scottie's. He was always out of money."

"Why was that?" Charlie asked as delicately as he could.

"Scottie was always chasing some fantastic scheme. He would get an enthusiastic and then try to entice his friends and clients to join him. Inevitably, things went badly, and he made all sorts of excuses."

Jamie shook his head in disgust and added, "Remember that fraudulent Canadian Mining Company with the vanishing gold finds in Indonesia a few years back? Put his clients in it. He also loved every technology stock with a concept but no assets during the Internet bubble and derivatives security—everything from instruments that captured the volatility of bonds, to electricity supply, to weather forecasts, to whatever." Jamie threw his hands in the air and looked around the small room in a conspiratorial way. "He didn't have a clue how they worked, but that didn't stop him. Lost a ton of money for his friends and clients. Dad and I talked to him from time to time, but being an orthodox broker/money manager was too tame for him. I am sure Collins, Lang would have fired him long ago if he hadn't been the son of Henry Bradshaw."

"I had no idea Scottie created all these problems," Charlie observed but was not surprised.

"Yes, he did. He tried to get me to arrange a job for him at Goodman, Bates. Of course that is the last thing I wanted. He did enough damage to clients at Collins, Lang."

Jamie paused. He had raised his voice, becoming increasingly irritated as he described his inept and goof-off brother.

Then Jamie calmed down. "But, I shouldn't speak ill of the dead. He was still my brother, and we'll all miss him."

"Yes, we'll miss him," Charlie agreed.

Charlie didn't blame Jamie for being upset. He would have been as well if he had had a brother like Scottie. It was okay to vent at this time—with a friend.

"Sorry to change the subject, but if I need to get some information regarding Scottie's employee benefits for our files, whom can I contact?"

"His boss at Collins, Lang was Steve Keller. I don't know his number."

"Don't worry. I can find it."

The waiter sat down their lunches. Charlie was amused that they both ordered turkey and cheese sandwiches with a small salad. Considering the three-page menu and the prominence of the club, a meal that could be bought at the local deli for under ten dollars seemed impolite. Yet, simple fare is what most members ordered. Times had changed since the good old days of indulgence.

After a conversation about the Chicago Cubs and the political impasse in Springfield on the state budget, Charlie asked, "And how are you, Jamie? I was sorry to hear of your divorce; I thought to call you but I know it's difficult to talk about such things. How are your children? Do you see them frequently?"

"Young Jamie and Hillary are fine. They live only a few blocks away, and I see them most weekends. They seem to like the Latin School and have many friends. Unfortunately, I travel a great deal with my work and I'm probably not as good of a father as I should be."

Then Jamie pushed back abruptly from the table. "Now I

have to run. I have another appointment. Mom mentioned that Claire might be able to get a soprano from the Lyric Opera to sing at Scottie's service. We appreciate your mother's help - Friday, remember."

They both stood and shook hands. Jamie said, "I'll see you at the viewing tomorrow," and left.

As Charlie watched him leave, he worried that Jamie seemed upset. He hoped he had not been rude mentioning his divorce.

Reviewing their conversation, he was surprised how forthcoming Jamie had been about Scottie's failures. His friend's grief was genuine as was his animosity toward his brother. Scottie had sullied the Bradshaw name and squandered some of its wealth. It was a natural for Jamie to express mixed emotions.

Based on just this first meeting, Charlie wondered what else he might learn about Scottie as he talked to others who dealt with him. From Jamie's comments there must be many people who had a motive to see Scottie gone. Would anyone go so far as to kill him? He was sure that he would hear lots of complaints. For the sake of the Bradshaws he'd like to find who could have murdered Scottie. He was eager to talk to Steve Keller next.

# CHAPTER EIGHT

"Good evening, Mr. Bailey," Jose, the doorman at Charlie's building said with a slight Spanish accent. "Two police detectives came by this afternoon."

"What did they want, Jose?"

"To know if you were here last Saturday night. I told them it wasn't my shift. Was that okay?"

"Fine. Did they leave then?"

"No, they asked to speak with the super."

Charlie tried to control his anger that the police felt they needed to verify his alibi. He wondered if his situation was a topic of interest among his neighbors in the building.

"Jose, I have been meaning to ask you these last couple of days, have any residents asked you about me? You might have seen me mentioned in the news."

Jose looked down and seemed suddenly awkward. "I'm not supposed to talk about any of the residents' business. If anyone asks, I say 'I don't know'."

"But did anyone mention that I had been on the news?"

"Maybe three or four, but I said 'I don't know anything'."

Nosey neighbors, Charlie thought. Typical of rich people without enough to do.

Jose changed the subject to something more comfortable. "It was a pleasure to meet your mother this morning."

"Thanks for keeping her company until I arrived. I was only about five minutes late."

"My pleasure. Her chauffeur parked her car in the back garage."

"I'm glad it all worked out. We went to a funeral together and parking here and taking a cab made more sense than trying to have her search for a lot near the church. She came down from Lake Forest. Has Miss Milano arrived yet?"

"No."

"When she arrives, just send her up."

Charlie entered the lobby on his way to the elevator, intent on talking to the super. He noticed the building's president, Alberto Botin, talking to a middle-aged couple by the sitting area and hoped that he could go upstairs uninterrupted.

"Charlie, wait a second," Alberto called out. "I want you to meet Jack and Sandra Scott. They are applying to buy the Beyhoffer apartment. I just interviewed them. It would be good for them to meet another resident."

Charlie was not in a mood to stop but how could he refuse without being rude? Of course he knew what Alberto probably wanted. The process of buying an apartment in a cooperative owned building entails approval by the board of directors and several owner-residents. He had gone through it himself ten years before. Since every resident was responsible for his pro-rata share of the building's expenses, Charlie had an interest in ensuring that the Scotts were acceptable socially and capable of paying maintenance and assessments. If the Scotts had come for an interview, that meant that they had already submitted an audited financial statement and six letters of recommendations attesting to their good character and suitability.

Alberto wanted to add a letter from Charlie, whose opinion carried a lot of weight with the board. The process was undemocratic, but it was legal and the way that the vintage, desirable buildings in Chicago worked.

Jack Scott approached and extended his hand. "Charlie, you may not remember me, but we met at an Economics Club luncheon last year. Bill Clinton was the speaker. I sat next to you."

"I thought you looked familiar," Charlie lied.

Meanwhile Sandy Scott had joined them and said, "I grew up in Lake Forest. My parents know your mother. They used to play golf at the Potawatomi Club."

Charlie still drew a blank on the Scotts but conceded that he was likely at fault in not remembering them. "Of course. I'll have to tell her I saw you today." Feeling embarrassed, he felt obliged to make positive comments about the building, its staff, and its residents. He said that, if they were accepted, the neighbors would welcome them warmly, and they should enjoy the privacy and comfort of this wonderful building. After a few more minutes of pleasant conversation Charlie felt he could leave politely. The

Scotts seemed to him likely to be accepted by the board, and his mind was consumed by other matters.

Once in his apartment Charlie called down to the super. "I heard that two detectives were here looking for me today. What did they want?"

"They asked about last Saturday night and Sunday morning. Had I seen you? That sort of thing. I told them I was off on Saturday but saw you leave for the golf course Sunday. Remember, we talked as Will Heinen brought up your car? He had parked it late Saturday."

"Of course. Did Heinen say about midnight?"

"Yes."

Charlie had forgotten their chat, but now he felt relieved that someone could vouch for him late Saturday.

Fifteen minutes later Kate arrived at his tenth floor, three-bedroom apartment with a precooked dinner in a paper bag. Since she did not have her briefcase, Charlie assumed that she had stopped after work at her apartment three blocks away to check her mail and change clothes.

"You look different from how you looked at the funeral," Charlie said, greeting her at the door with a kiss.

"A black dress and stockings didn't seem right for a casual dinner at my boyfriend's place."

"I like you in anything—and nothing," Charlie nuzzled her neck.

"Dream on, Don Juan."

"That's no dream."

"Right you are," she laughed.

Kate took the dinner into the kitchen to reheat the food while Charlie opened a bottle of white wine from his private collection brought up from the basement of the co-op and housed in a small refrigerator under the countertop.

"Let me pour you a glass of this excellent five year old Chardonnay," Charlie said cheerfully. "It'll make warming up dinner more agreeable."

They sat down at the table in the center of the kitchen and clinked glasses.

Charlie enjoyed looking at Kate's clothes. Most of the women his age dressed in a conservative, vintage style that their mothers had at their age: skirts to the knees, tailored blouses, cardigan sweaters, pearls, gold bracelets and watches, flats or low heels—comfortable, expensive clothes. They avoided bold patterns, wild colors, and low décolleté. They looked refined, classic, and often beautiful. At night out on the town they brought out the designer clothes and shoes and expensive jewelry.

Kate was different. She was younger—and an artist. She told Charlie that in high school she took every art course offered. Her grades and boards were splendid in all subjects but her heart was in the creative courses. Against the wishes of her farming family she started college at Parsons in New York with the goal of becoming a fashion designer. After a few months while she loved her teachers and fellow students, she missed painting and sculpting and three-dimensional design. Fashion had not excited her enough. So in her second year she had enrolled in the art department at Northwestern. Her living closer to home and going to a school they had heard of pleased her parents.

Still this period in her life had a significant influence on how she dressed. Her sense of color and fabric were strong. She embraced new designs and shopped at the big retailers but also the smaller trendy shops and boutiques found on the side streets. Charlie liked the energy and creativity of her selections and looked forward to seeing each new ensemble she put together. The downside was that his mother and some of his friends were uncomfortable with her outfits, disliking an alternative look. Tonight she wore purple capri pants and a ruffled long-sleeved light yellow blouse, ballet slippers, and the yellow and white hairband. Charlie smiled at his free-spirited girlfriend.

"This wine is delicious." Kate said.

"I'm glad you liked it. It's Talbott Chardonnay—Cuvee Cynthia. It's excellent year after year."

They sat waiting for their dinner to heat up.

Don't you agree that the funeral service today was exceptional?" Charlie asked. "The church was decked out impeccably, the flowers spectacular, the music superb—especially the soprano from the Lyric Opera—and the eulogies spot on. Too often at funerals, I feel that the speakers barely know the deceased as a person and only recite the highlights of his or her accomplishments. Things you could read in the newspaper's obituary. But this time even the clergyman seem to know Scottie."

Kate nodded her head in agreement and added, "In my opinion, the best eulogy was Jamie's. He was magnificent—especially with the amusing anecdotes from their childhood. He captured Scottie's energy and charm."

"And he had a sense of profound loss," Charlie said sincerely.

"Of course, we were only hearing part of the story, but that was the part of the story the audience wanted to hear. I think most people were moved."

Charlie reached over to pour her more wine.

"I admit I was impressed by the church service—and touched," Kate agreed. "But we shouldn't be surprised. Anything Dorothy Bradshaw organizes would be first-class and dramatic. Everyone knows that. It was her way of saying goodbye to her son and she spared nothing. Besides the family and friends, I recognized the mayor and many other politicians, lawyers, and powerbrokers. The gathering of the socialites was *toute Chicago*. The Bradshaws are held in high esteem by everyone, it seems."

"Mother pointed out to me that there were lots of people who drove in from when Winnetka, Kenilworth, Lake Forest, Hinsdale, and the Barrington. And it was classy of Lauren Bradshaw to come. Most divorcees would skip the funeral of her ex."

Charlie saw Kate looks serious, "As flawless as the occasion was, I sensed an awkwardness from things left unsaid -that Scottie was probably murdered, and no one knows who is responsible. I couldn't help but notice that several people stared at you and then quickly averted their eyes when you've looked their way."

"I saw that too. I guess I am toxic at this point to some people. More reason to solve the mystery of Scottie's death."

"Did anyone talk to you about it?"

"Not a church, but last night at Donellan's Corey Webster said he hoped the police would find the person responsible soon. One or two others also suggested that the death wasn't an accident. Corey wanted to know if I knew anything. I told him no. I did notice that Jamie in his eulogy described Scottie's death as 'untimely' — not 'untoward'."

"I am sorry if my leaving right after the funeral was 'unto-ward'," Kate apologized. "I wanted to stay and talk to your mother, but I had a deadline to turn in my artwork for a prospective account. I hope your mother was not offended."

"Nope. She understands that women of your generation work at jobs."

"I fear that your mother means 'women of your class'."

"I didn't say that and neither did she," Charlie corrected her.

"I know I am being defensive."

"All of our families emigrated to America at some point. Forget it. Nonsense."

"I'll try. I do like her. I am happy that your mother looks so healthy today."

"Thanks. She's healthy — at least for now," Charlie agreed. "But you never know. As long as she takes her pills and not gets too excited, her heart should be all right. She hasn't had an episode in five months. But you know that. I worry that the Scottie tragedy, might be putting too much stress on her."

"I worry about the affects of her health and Scottie's death have on you."

"Thank you for your concern, and I'm okay even if I don't look or act as such. Ex-Marine, money manager, former football player. I can take anything."

"Do you mind if I laugh? The Charlie I know it's sweet and cuddly."

"I am a master of disguise. Let's eat."

When Kate was cleaning up after dinner, Charlie went to his library. He thought back at his conversation with Kate about her sensitivity to class disparity.

He had had this give and take with Kate several times before. She came from a wonderful upper middle-class family, graduated from Northwestern, was an award-winning artist, and worked at a top advertising agency. Plus she was a tall, athletic brunette with model looks. He found her extremely smart, engaging, and sexy. She was different from the women he grew up with — better. She seemed enthusiastic and committed to him. Still friends had told him on occasion that they had seen her out with other men — at restaurants, a basketball game, at a picnic in Lincoln Park. Maybe she was hiding her reservations about him.

Charlie couldn't blame her. His first wife, the brilliant, bubbly, exotically French Solange, had died in an automobile accident three years before. He had buried her physically but not emotionally — yet. Kate would have to wait. But he knew he had to let Solange go — sooner than later — or lose Kate.

\* \* \*

Kate left Charlie's apartment shortly after dinner. She said that she had work to do. Her mood had turned sour and he attributed it to her comments about his mother's view of her. She might have stayed with Charlie. He welcomed their intimate moments. But Charlie didn't question her excuse for leaving.

When she was gone, Charlie went back into his library and looked out at Lake Shore Drive and Lake Michigan. The sky was turning dark, and the light from passing cars and apartment buildings gave a magical feeling to this cityscape.

He poured a port from a decanter and pulled out a pen and legal pad to write down what he remembered from his meeting that afternoon with Steve Keller, Scottie's boss. Charlie had called to arrange a meeting.

"Come right over, Mr. Bailey. I know your firm. It's a slow Friday afternoon and I have a little to do until the market closes."

Charlie walked over to the Collins, Lang offices in the Willis Tower. He expected security to be tight but Keller had left his name with the guards; so he attached his nametag and took the middle bank elevators to the sixty-fifth floor.

Charlie saw from the elevator roster that Collins, Lang occupied four floors—meaning that it was a medium- sized brokerage house. Charlie's firm had done some trading with it in past years, but he didn't know it well.

"I'm sorry I missed the funeral," Steve Keller said on greeting Charlie by the receptionist desk. "We were frantic this morning. The markets are still reeling from the rate increase. After lunch everything slowed down. I guess the traders got a head start on the weekend."

Charlie followed him into his small glass office. He was surprised that Steve had not attended the funeral of his former associate. His absence raised a red flag.

"Scottie was a good producer for us for his five years with the firm. I can't remember who he worked for before—some small outfit."

"Was he on commission or paid by fees?" Charlie asked in a casual fashion.

"Mainly commission. Most of his accounts were advisory—not discretionary. Collins, Lang acted as agent. He also had a few clients as part of our firm's wrap account programs."

Charlie understood that wrap accounts bundle research, trading costs, and advice under one fee—higher than a purely commission arrangement or a straight portfolio management fee. A broker like Scottie might prefer wrap arrangement because his fees resulted in a more consistent payout than commissions. Commissions were only paid if there was activity in an account.

"Did Scottie see himself as a portfolio manager?"

"No. More of an asset allocator and idea generator."

"Did he use other packaged products—like mutual funds or ETF's to diversify his clients' assets?"

"To some extent. What he did the most was come up with big investment ideas and convince clients to buy the relevant stocks or bonds."

As they talked, Charlie knew that he had met Steve before. He strained to remember the context. Suddenly he recalled interviewing Steve for a job at Bailey, Richardson two or three years before. Charlie had passed on him because Sam thought that Steve had been careless in his description of what his responsibilities were at Collins, Lang. Sam felt that he might be indiscreet at times with their conservative clients.

If Sam was correct, Charlie hoped that Steve would be imprudent in his assessment of Scottie's activities. He studied Steve and thought he was awkward and nervous. Steve kept shifting in his chair and played with a pen in his hand. Charlie sensed that Steve knew he had probably already shared too much information. Charlie preferred that Steve feel relaxed.

Steve suddenly straightened up, leaned forward and asked, "Why are you interested in his business? You said on the phone that Scottie had some trusts with you where he was a beneficiary. Since he is dead, what do you care about how he did business?"

"In case a challenge to the estate comes forth because of actions Scottie may have taken. I heard he was involved in some risky investments."

Charlie had expected Keller's question and made this explanation to elicit comments about Scottie's investment history. There was only a remote possibility that his firm could be brought into a challenge to the estate from a creditor or a client of Scottie's. He smiled to himself when Keller accepted his shaky explanation and opened up about Scottie's activities.

"There are many things you should know," Steve said seemingly relieved to have been asked.

"Scottie was neither smart nor a hard worker. He was charming and entertained clients elaborately, but his advantage was the Bradshaw name. Clients assumed he was kind of an insider, privy to things. Everything he said was legal and he did not misrepresent anything. But people will believe what they want to think."

"Did he make money for his clients? Were there any complaints?"

Steve looked out the window, away from Charlie, and blurted out, "There have been complaints from clients of his previous employers. They alleged that Scottie had precipitated some losses in their accounts. As a consequence, before Collins, Lang hired him, we researched the complaints and decided he was okay."

*Keep talking*, thought Charlie.

"I remember one in particular. A Canadian mining company recorded discovering substantial gold deposits in Indonesia. Since these deposits were in a secret, remote location, they could not be independently verified. The CEO and corporate VP in charge of exploration were so convincing, the stock rocketed. The corporate executives sold their stock holdings, and everyone was happy—for about a year. When the gold finds never ended up in the company's revenues, investors became suspicious and asked questions. Eventually, the exploration VP cracked and admitted the mine had been 'salted'. The house of cards collapsed; the CEO fled the country to the Cayman Islands. Investors lost millions. Scottie had been a big believer in the company and had put most of his clients in the investment."

"But could Scottie have known about the fraud?"

"We didn't think so when we hired him. He did make a lot of commissions, so I had my doubts. At least he didn't promote Rite Aid, Enron, or WorldCom."

"Small solace, I guess," Charlie offered. "Anything similar here—under you?"

"Well, the mutual fund timing service."

That comment peaked Charlie's interest. A couple of years before, the SEC had uncovered an after-close scandal involving mutual funds. The abuses were widespread, and several fund groups were censured.

"Timing services are legitimate. Did Scottie get involved and late trading?"

"He was never charged, although the SEC targeted us. Whatever the facts, the firm shut down his service upon my recommendation. The SEC never penalized the firm."

How could a little guy like Scottie have been involved in this type of illegal activity? All Charlie could think of was that Scottie may have led his hedge fund clients to the fund groups that permitted after close trading. That meant aiding and abetting wrongdoing.

Charlie sensed that Steve was trying hard to maintain that he was a vigilant supervisor. Maybe he was hoping that Charlie would reconsider his decision not to hire him before?

"It sounds as if supervising Scottie was a hair-raising experience for you."

"That's an understatement."

"Any other questionable activities?" Charlie encouraged the loquacious Steve.

"We were always worried about his derivatives trading. He had some big losses there. But to give him credit, recently he recommended a series of merger and acquisition ideas that worked out well. In fact, this success attracted many hedge fund investors who started trading more frequently with us. Management liked that."

Considering the problems Scottie created for his firm, Steve had sufficient motive to seeing Scottie gone—especially since he probably couldn't fire a person like a Bradshaw without the blessing of his firm's senior executives. Maybe enough motive to see him dead—particularly if Steve had been involved in Scottie's schemes.

More essential, even if Steve had only been an ineffective boss he would know which clients have lost money through Scottie and may have been mad enough to get even. This conversation had not only educated Charlie regarding Scottie's dubious business practices but also might have unearthed multiple suspects to the death.

"The police have been here this week?" Charlie asked in an offhanded way.

"Yes. They interviewed me and copied his trading records. We could have asked for a court order, but I felt there was no harm, seeing as Scottie's death was an accident."

"Of course. They're just doing their job."

"Must have been a shock, finding the body."

Charlie winced. Everyone seemed to know about the connection.

"Sure was."

"What did he look like?"

That was a weird question. It was time to leave this man who
said more than he should.

Charlie stood up and said, "The police told me not to talk
about anything. I don't want to be rude, but I have to get back to
the office."

On the way out Charlie thanked Steve for his help and said
he would need to get more information later.

"For the estate," Steve added.

Charlie thought he saw Steve wink. If so, Steve was telling
Charlie that the "estate" reason was unlikely, but that he would
be willing to help in any way he could. Time will tell.

In his library that night Charlie wrote down the ways Steve
Keller might be helpful. First, Steve was a suspect. Second, Steve
would have access to the names of other suspects. Third, Steve
was a willing resource to bring forth information on Scottie's
shady dealings. Charlie had someone close to Scottie who he
could use.

# CHAPTER NINE

The caller ID on Kate's phone made her a happy lady.

"I like calling you at work. This way I know you aren't out with a secret admirer," Charlie kidded Kate.

"Maybe I should have more mystery in my life. Keep you on your toes."

"You are too smart and beautiful for me to take you for granted. And I was impressed with you when you told me this morning that you had to go to work on a Saturday. I didn't know whether or not to believe you. Now I'm a believer."

Kate swiveled right and left in her office chair amused by the conversation. Her artwork for the client presentation by the new business department was laid out on her desk and on a cork-board on the wall. She had told Charlie that Brett McDougal, a leading account executive of Hunter Freeman, had asked for her specifically to help win business of the major consumer products company. If his presentation on Monday were successful, her art work would appear in in countless advertisements in maga-zines, newspapers, newspapers, and TV slots for the next six months.

"You should talk, Charlie dear. How many times have you had to cancel our weekend plans to go to your office because of some crisis?"

"Touché. From your enthusiastic description of this project over dinner a few nights ago, I know it is very important to you. You'll be running that advertising firm before too long."

"You know, I am more artist then businesswomen. If I could have made a living as a sculptress, I would have."

"I know you tried—with your studies and the tie-in with Suzie Walsh's gallery. I'm proud of you that you did that for those two and a half years."

"Thanks. You're did help by buying those bronzes and those pieces of jewelry."

Kate knew he gave them to his mother, who never wears them. I wish I could do something right in her opinion.

"They're terrific."

"Anyway, I now get a paycheck every two weeks and I do like the freedom I have in the Creative Department."

"You've been promoted twice and do a wonderful job. I get a kick every time I see an ad with your work."

Kate moved her chair closer to her desk and searched for a note she had made earlier. "You are probably calling me to see if I got in touch with my friend, Maureen Turner, and with Joe Urbanski at the *Trib*. Both owe me a call back."

"I have total confidence in you, honey."

That morning Charlie had surprised her by asking her to call Maureen, who organized big functions at the Potawatomi club.

Kate knew Maureen from grade school in DeKalb. Kate had put her onto the job when Charlie mentioned it to her. She and Maureen always chatted a few minutes whenever Charlie brought Kate to the club. Charlie wanted to see a list of guests at the club party last Saturday night.

Kate was uneasy about asking. Charlie was putting her and Maureen in an awkward position as club rosters were private. Kate wanted to help him but feared the request might be over the line.

She remembered pointing that out, "Charlie, she may feel compromised. I don't want her to risk her job."

"Try. That list is important. If she is uncomfortable, she can say so."

Kate had agreed reluctantly. Next time she would put up more of the fight.

The call to Joe was easier. Through her job she knew lots of people at the *Chicago Tribune*. Her artwork for various ad campaigns appeared there almost daily. He will tell her which reporters were investigating the Bradshaw story. Anyway their bylines appeared with each article.

"Charlie, I have to go," Kate said, trying to hide her irritation with him checking on her when she was busy.

The pressure of putting her presentation in final form was getting to her. Plus Charlie's requests. She needed to return to her work. What was that word Charlie likes to use to show off his vocabulary? *Persiflage.* Yes, frivolous banter.

Ten minutes later, her cell phone rang.

"Kate, what can I do for you?" Maureen asked.

Kate explained what Charlie wanted and added that she was embarrassed to ask.

"What does he want it for? We don't usually do that?"

Charlie had suggested that if Maureen wanted a reason, Kate should say that he had seen someone arrive at the party and could not remember his name. The list would jog his memory. Kate knew that this was a lie and a lame excuse.

So instead, Kate answered, "The police have been asking him a lot of questions and he would feel better if he could have a couple of the attendees confirm he was not there. But if you are uncomfortable, he said that he would ask the club president for the list."

"No need to do that, but I am nervous. You understand?" Maureen said softly. "But you are a friend and Charlie is a member. Promise me that you won't use the names commercially or tell anybody."

"I promise," Kate vowed.

Kate hung up feeling very bad. She hated to be part of this request. The only redeeming aspect of the situation was that Kate also wanted Charlie's name exonerated.

And attachment to an email arrived a few minutes later. Kate fowarded it to Charlie without opening it. She wanted nothing to do with it.

As she was becoming engrossed again in her project, Joe from the *Trib* Advertising Department called.

"I got your message. The local news desk considers that the

Bradshaw death and ongoing story will be assigned now to George Kenney. Since George is our society reporter, they must see that angle as the most relevant. I hope that is what you need."

Kate thanked him and hung up surprised that the *Trib* assumed that Scottie's death was an accident or suicide. Otherwise it would have assigned a criminal investigative reporter.

She had met George several times. Charlie knew him from grade school. His nickname was "Peaches" because of his pale pink complexion and rounded body. He covered society news, as Claire Bailey described, "irreverently." Charlie mentioned on several occasions that despite the journalist's upper class pedigree, his drool and judgmental comments had made him many enemies. If past was a prediction, Peaches would make sure to embarrass the classy Potawatomi Club because of a member's death at a party on its grounds. Moreover, if the coroner deemed the death homicide—not an accident—Peaches would have a field day.

She left a message for Charlie about Peaches and then returned to her work. Distracted by the interruptions brought on by Charlie's requests, she sat back and considered their relationship. He was the man she had always wanted—despite the ten year age difference. She admired his success, work ethic, high standards, and intelligence. He was also witty, handsome, and religious. He would make a great father. He appreciated her background and career and encouraged her to continue to succeed in her work. She was ambitious and needed self-esteem.

But he hadn't committed yet. They did almost everything together including sharing secrets and sexual intimacy, acting like equals, and being a couple in public. Yet after a year of a close, romantic relationship, he had not proposed. She wanted marriage, had brought up the subject, and felt frustrated. Moreover her parents and friends pressured her. Her mother said she should move on if Charlie couldn't get its priorities straight.

Other men continued to ask her out and several times this past year she had accepted. None of them had appealed to her compared to Charlie and she felt guilty about these occasions - guilty towards Charlie and guilty to her dates if she were misleading them. While she did not mention these men to Charlie, she was convinced that one of his friends would tell him what they saw. Her objective was obvious: make Charlie jealous enough to propose.

He was always so decisive in his business. Why not in this relationship? Even though Claire Bailey had always been pleasant to her, she was certain that the woman didn't approve of her— her background, her job, her personality. Maybe she was the type of mother that no woman was good enough for her son. Still Charlie had married Solange; perhaps Solange was more like Claire.

At moments like this, Kate wanted to confront Charlie. Maybe it was time for her to make the decision to end things. She couldn't bear to lose him, but she wasn't going to wait forever. He could make her furious and she was beginning to feel like a fool.

As chance would have it, that afternoon Marc d'Amboise a recent transfer from Hunter, Freeman's Paris office, came by and asked "Kate, I am new to Chicago and would love to know more about its restaurants, cultural institutions, and politics. Frankly, I would also like to know more about you. Would you take compassion on an expat Frenchman and have dinner with me?"

This cheesy approach amused Kate. Marc sounded like a teenager, but, after her thoughts about dating earlier, his timing was opportune. Also he was quite handsome and a few women in the office had referred to him as intelligent, suave, and knowledgeable about art.

She hesitated but then thought, *"What the heck"* and said, "I would be delighted to introduce you to Chicago. Some time next week works for me — after I turn in this project."

As he left smiling, Kate wondered *"Have I done the right thing?"*

She did not want to be unfaithful to Charlie, but maybe a little competition might light a fire under him. And Marc might be an entertaining dinner partner. So next time she would say yes.

\* \* \*

When Charlie returned from the fitness center, he listened to Kate's message.

He was ambivalent about Peaches whom he saw regularly at various benefits, social functions, and the Bailey, Richardson offices. Sam managed most of the Peaches money — inherited from his socially connected mother. His regular job was to write short pieces for the Society column, citing the social powerhouses at an event, celebrating the individual (inevitably a woman) who organized the affair, estimating how much money was raised (if it was a benefit), highlighting the fashionable dress, and cajoling select attendees to have their pictures taken. Although his Society columns infuriated most people at one time or another, Charlie thought Peaches was excellent at writing light feature stories. But the fluff of social events in no way prepared Peaches to cover a serious story like this. In Charlie's mind, Peaches would be way over his head.

What bothered Charlie the most in this case was that Peaches would probably weave a social connection role through the story. He would likely play up Charlie's involvement. Nothing good will come of that.

On the other hand, Charlie might have an opportunity to use their familiar relationship to his advantage, to learn where the police were going with the case. Peaches liked to talk—especially after a few glasses of champagne—and Charlie sensed that his biggest problem might be separating substance from gossip. So Charlie made a mental note to call him for lunch as soon as possible.

In the meantime, Charlie needed to look at the party list. The party had been of moderate size—137 attendees. Charlie had been to countless club parties of this ilk. He could imagine how it was structured. The club would serve cocktails outside on the lawn overlooking the attractively designed old golf course with its abundance of trees, lakes, and streams. Then they would serve dinner on the large terrace dotted with linen-clothed tables for four to eight guests. Candles and floral centerpieces would adorn each table. The band would have played upbeat tempos during cocktails, ballads during the buffet dinner, and dance music as the desserts were presented as the sun set.

After dessert the older members of the club would oblige their spouses with a single dance and then offer polite excuses to the younger set and leave for home. The remaining crowd would be the actual young and the middle-aged who thought they were young. During the next four or five hours this group would drink, talk, and dance to the point of exhaustion and inebriation. This pattern of behavior seldom varied. Young and old liked it that way and enjoyed themselves.

Now he scanned the names for some anomaly or for someone he knew well who might talk about what happened night—especially anything unusual.

Unfortunately, nobody fit his criteria. He knew or recognized attendees, - club members, their sons and daughters or close relatives, and local guests. No surprises. He didn't notice anyone with a reputation for loose lips.

Then a better idea struck Charlie—the staff. The old-timers knew the members well enough to detect something out of the ordinary. Of course, the club's code of conduct prohibited discussion with the staff about members, but Charlie believed some of them trusted him to be discreet.

An instance supporting Charlie's belief was the matter of a certain young lady, the daughter of a prominent member, who a few years before had sexually harassed a summer intern on the staff and threatened him when he demurred. The intern had in turn explained his precarious situation to a senior member of the dining staff, Peter Sawyer. Peter, in turn, asked Charlie for his help.

Satisfied this story was accurate, Charlie quietly handled the matter with tactful but direct questions with the club manager, club president, and the unfortunate girl's father. As a consequence, the amorous young lady in question was sent quietly to spend the rest of the summer with her grandparents in Maine.

Charlie reasoned that if he were lucky, Peter might remember something significant at the party. He picked up the phone and after a few minutes tracked down Peter.

"Peter. I have a delicate question for you. I wonder if you can be circumspect. If, however, you feel awkward answering, just say no."

"Mr. Bailey, I would be honored to help if I can. You have been so supportive of all of us, whenever we needed it."

Charlie started cautiously, "Were you on duty at the party before Mr. Bradshaw's unfortunate accident?"

"Yes, from setup to cleanup. I was mainly serving drinks and cleaning up spills during the course of the party."

"Did you notice anything unusual? Were there any accidents or altercations out of the ordinary?"

"In fact, yes. The party went well until the end. The members seemed to like the meal and the band. The young people stayed until a little after twelve. But they left *en masse* after a fight between two members dampened spirits.

"Let me get back to that incident, but first did you see Mr.

Scottie Bradshaw there?"

"Oh, yes. He was there with some of his friends—Mr. Spencer, Mr. Arnold and his wife, and Mr. and Mrs. Kind."

Charlie checked their names on the list and pulled out a club book from a drawer for future reference.

"Did Mr. Bradshaw drink much or seem agitated?"

"Mr. Bailey, I really shouldn't answer that," Peter replied slowly.

"I understand. But we need to know all we can about what led to the accident. To give the Bradshaws peace of mind."

"As I told the investigators, the young Mr. Bradshaw arrived alone but met with his friends immediately. He drank and joked and ate with his group. When the crowd started to dance, Mr. Bradshaw asked two or three of the college girls who had come without escorts to dance—members' daughters and their friends. Is this what you want?"

"Yes, please go on."

"Later on, I noticed that Mr. Bradshaw was primarily dancing and talking with Miss Tansey."

Charlie remembered seeing a svelte teenager in tennis whites eating lunch with her parents on the bluestone patio two or three years before. She would be about twenty now.

"Do you mean the Tansey daughter who is quite a bit younger than Mr. Bradshaw? Taylor Tansey?"

"Oh, yes, Mr. Bailey."

Charlie wrote her name down. "Go on. Did Mr. Bradshaw behave?"

"Mr. Bradshaw stumbled a couple of times while they were dancing and one time he fell. I rushed to pick him up. He had hit his head on a table leg but wasn't bleeding. He sat for a while. After five minutes he staggered over to where Miss Tansey was sitting, grabbed her hand, and led her out in the darkness onto the lawn. I couldn't see them well but a few minutes later Miss Tansey came back, grabbed her purse and strode to the clubhouse. Clearly seemed upset. I saw her stop on her way out and talk to her brother, William. I thought she was crying."

"Did Will do anything?"

"Mr. Tansey approached Mr. Bradshaw and shouted at him."

"What did he say?"

"Mr. Tansey was incensed and screamed some foul language I'd like not to repeat. He accused Mr. Bradshaw of assaulting his sister."

"I get the picture. What did Scottie do?"

"He lunged at Mr. Tansey, hit him in the face and Mr. Tansey fell."

"Mr. Tansey called him an asshole and tried to get up. Mr. Bradshaw kicked him in the ribs and legs. A few members rushed over and restrained Mr. Bradshaw by his arms. One of the members said, 'Cut this shit out'. Mr. Bradshaw was screaming obscenities. Mr. Jamie Bradshaw joined the group and shouted at his brother to shut up. Someone yelled at Mr. Jamie, 'What's wrong with you? Can't you control your brother?'

"Mr. Scottie pulled away from Mr. Jamie and glared at everyone. He then stalked off towards the men's locker room. Mr.

Tansey was bleeding from his mouth but refused my help. He then called out for his sister, found her, and left with her through the main clubhouse."

"Wow! What a story," Charlie said. "Does this sort of thing happen at the club?"

"Never in my time here," Peter added.

"I imagine the party broke up then."

"Yes. The band started to play but everyone was gone in five minutes."

"Including Jamie Bradshaw?"

"I suppose. People left in different directions. I can't say who went with who."

"Peter, do you remember Scottie Bradshaw talking with anyone other than his friends?"

"Just the band manager."

"Has the club used that band before?"

"No."

"How did you know that the man was the manager?"

"I asked him who he was. He arrived late—just when it was getting dark. I didn't recognize him, so I went up to him and asked what he wanted. He said he was the band's manager and had been with another of his bands earlier in the evening. He just said his job was to make sure the band did a good job for us."

"What did he look like?"

"Tall and stocky. He wore a business suit. He had a New York accent. Like on TV. He stood on the side behind the band where it was dark."

Charlie made a note. Here was someone who was not usually at the party. "Did he talk to any of the members?"

"No one that I saw. Now that I think, I don't remember him even talking to the band."

"Would you recognize him if you saw him again?"

"I'm not sure, Mr. Bailey. Our conservation was over quickly, and he stood in the dark."

"Did you see him leave?"

"No."

"Did the Bradshaws spend any time together?"

"They were at different tables."

"Thanks for your help. What happened with Scottie Bradshaw is a mystery to me. By the way, did the police question anyone from the club about the party and Mr. Bradshaw?"

"Oh, yes indeed. A group of them talked to both the Sunday and Monday shifts. They were very thorough."

"Thanks, Peter. You have been very helpful."

Charlie tried to imagine the ugly scene at the party. Strange that Jamie had not mentioned what occurred. Maybe he was too embarrassed by Scottie's conduct. Charlie was certain that Scottie had humiliated the family many times.

Scottie's behavior with young Taylor Tansey had enraged Will. Feeding that anger, Scottie had bloodied Will in the fight. Was that enough to result in Will murdering Scottie later that evening? Hard to tell. But from what Steve Keller had said, there were many others who had plenty of reasons to kill Scottie. *I should make a list.*

## | § |

## CHAPTER TEN

"Thank you, Charlie, for inviting me to brunch," Claire Bailey said warmly. "I haven't been to the Racquet Club in years. The clubhouse is looking marvelous. And it's always wonderful to be in the city—despite the weather."

Charlie was walking his mother to the second floor dining room where a sumptuous buffet table was visible from the hall. The rich aroma kindled his appetite. The maître d' let them to a table for three near the window. Rain was pelting down.

"I don't usually have the pleasure of my mother's company twice a week."

"I had to come into the city to return a cardigan your uncle gave me for my birthday. You know purple isn't my color. I could have returned it on Friday after Scottie's funeral, but I wanted to be free in case Dottie needed me."

Claire looked around, "Where is Kate? I thought she was joining us."

"She is. After mass this morning she went to her office for a little while. She is nervous about a presentation she is making tomorrow."

"Of course, but she's late. It's not the first time. She's devoted to her job, I guess. As you've said, she's made quite a success for herself. Naturally she'll have to give that up if she marries you. Are you going to propose? She practically lives with you. Her mother can't be happy about that. I wouldn't be—with a daughter."

"All in good time. She's a big girl. She doesn't need her mother's approval."

"Charles Bailey, I'm not talking about her; I'm talking about you. You need a wife. If you think she is the one, go ahead. If you have reservations, move on. Lord knows there a hundred suitable women who would want you. You are quite a catch.

'I know that losing Solange was cruel and painful. But you can't turn back the clock. The right wife will make you happy."

Charlie looked around the room at a loss for words. He never admitted it to his mother, but he missed Solange every day. They were a great couple. She challenged him and made their interactions fun and memorable.

Considering his mother's comments about Kate, he was relieved to see Kate walk into the room. "Here she is."

Charlie stood and watched Kate kiss his mother on the cheek and then turn to kiss him. The trio made small talk as they examined the menu and eyed the buffet table. Kate told Claire about her presentation and Claire bemoaned the days of rain that had prevented her from gardening.

"Dear, are you still doing the drawing and sculpting you did when you were on your own?" Claire asked.

"Some. I wish I had more time. Fortunately my work at the agency pushes me to be creative."

"When you have a chance, you should consider joining some non-for-profit boards. They need creative minds. If you like I'll introduce you to the right people. All my friends' daughters volunteer in this way."

"Thank you, Mrs. Bailey. I'll take you up on your generous offer when I have more free time at work."

Charlie did not like the direction this interchange was taking, so he offered, "Shall we visit the buffet?"

Back at the table, Claire brought up Scottie's death. "Have the police confirmed that Scottie had an accident? I'm told he often drank too much."

"I haven't heard anything new," Charlie said. "I'm touchy when the media mentions Bailey, Richardson or my name."

"There's nothing to worry about, is there?" Claire asked.

"I don't know. I talked to Sam Dixon an hour ago and he reported that a handful of our conservative clients don't like publicity associated with a death. Tomorrow we'll go over our client list to identify anyone at risk of leaving us. Unfortunately I know of a few."

"Then on my way out the door to come here Alberto Botin saw me in the lobby and asked that I not mention our apartment building in connection with this affair. He added that a couple of my neighbors had groused about the notoriety my involvement could bring to 1500 Lake Shore Drive."

"The people in your building are as bad as the members of

the Potawatomi Club," Claire huffed. "They seem to ignore the fact that you merely found the body and tried to revive him. At times I surmise that they think you murdered poor Scottie."

"Charlie, have you told your mother what you're doing?" Kate asked.

"Not yet," Charlie admitted. "Now is not a good time. These reactions and inquiries infuriate me. I need to do two related things: control the reputational damage taking place and encourage the police to solve the mystery of Scottie's death. If the death were an accidental fall and drowning, announce that and the attention will fade away. If there was foul play, identify the murderer and the public focus will be on him."

"I was afraid that you might mention the possibility of a murder," Claire said. "Do you think that possible?"

"Yes. A lot of people didn't like Scottie. He lost money for several of his clients. He treated women badly. He embarrassed his family and friends regularly. As recently as Saturday night at the party, he got into a fight with Billy Tansey."

"Billy? He's such a nice young man," Claire declared.

"Apparently Scottie made an unwanted pass at Billy's sister."

"Taylor? She's only a child," Claire said angrily. "The club is no place for fights."

"Scottie was no gentleman. If the death was no accident, the police will have several individuals to look at."

"Oh, the fuss if he was killed! Dottie would be shocked. She's already nearly inconsolable. Kate, did you know him?"

"I did—a little bit. A friend of mine invited me to come to

her school's dance when I was fifteen. I was a sophomore at Sacred Heart then. It was a girls' school and boys were asked to join the event. Scottie asked me to dance. I was more naïve than I am today. I could smell alcohol on his breath while we were on the floor. He touched me where he shouldn't have. I broke away and ran to the ladies room. I cried not knowing if I had done the wrong thing or he had been rude. I called my dad and he drove into the city and picked me up. My girlfriends teased me later but I didn't ever want to see Scottie again."

"You were quite right," said Claire matter-of-factly.

"I'm sure you did nothing to encourage him. If Dottie had known, she would have disciplined him in a way he would have never forgotten. The gall!"

"After that I tried to avoid Scottie. I had to go to his wedding to Lauren McKay because my parents knew her mother—from college. Otherwise I saw Scottie only when I was with Charlie."

"Kate told me the story," Charlie added. "I made sure Kate did not have to talk to him, although knowing Scottie I suspect he didn't remember the incident anyway."

"Kate dear. Why were you at Sacred Heart?"

"After grade school, my parents thought that the high schools near the farm were poor. So my dad rented an apartment in Chicago and enrolled me in Sacred Heart. Mom lived with me during the week and we went out to the farm on weekends. When I started at Northwestern my parents dropped the apartment."

"Smart parents," Claire said.

The trio were finishing their meal when Charlie saw Claire

look up as if she had just remembered something.

"You said that you would engage in damage control. What do you mean by that?"

"Two things. We'll call those clients who voiced any concerns over the publicity. Sam Dixon will help me. The other imitative will be to tip the influence of the *Trib's* coverage away from us. Kate was able to learn today that Peaches Kenney is the reporter on the story. I'm going to talk to him and convince him that we should not be part of any article. Our relationship should mean something."

"George Kenney. I know his parents," Claire recalled. "They were important socially thirty years ago. Lived on the Gold Coast a few buildings south of you. Entertained often and were fixtures on the benefit circuits. The fact that George turned out gay didn't seem to faze them. I haven't seen much of them since your father died and I cut back on the Chicago social merry-go-round. Are they in good health?"

"They are both frail, but their minds are still there," Charlie answered. "I enjoy our client luncheons twice a year."

"You know, she got George his job at the *Trib*. He had bounced around aimlessly—fashion, interior decoration, art gallery work. Dottie told me that his mother knew Sally Goodyear the society editor, and talked her into taking George under her wing. She retired and now George is the man—or boy or whatever. Anyway, he knows everyone because he went to all the parties for years. Some of his articles are fun."

"Now he gets to go to the big galas for free," Charlie said.

"Don't be malicious," Kate warned.

"Excuse me. Bad manners. His father took me aside several years ago and said that a fool and his money are soon parted. He said, "Take care of George's trust funds. He needs you.""

"Now you need him," Kate added. "To write the Scottie story without you."

"Don't take him too lightly," Claire advised. "George may be Peaches to you but he is his father's son to me."

## CHAPTER ELEVEN

Charlie did not sleep that night. Kate had gone to her apartment to work on her presentation and couldn't see him for a couple of days. He was annoyed with himself. Normally he made decisions easily: running a company, making investments, playing sports, judging people. He despised wishy-washy people. Yet, here he was hesitant, indecisive about Kate—beautiful, loving Kate. She had been amazingly patient. Maybe she had been too easy with him? She had not given him a deadline or ultimatum on their relationship.

For a time the memory of Solange had weighed on him. But Kate was not replacing Solange. Kate was herself: unique, special in her own way. She balanced his faults. She was funnier, less stubborn, more stylish, more passionate and patient than he. Charlie liked that she was different. Some differences were inevitable. Her background and experience defined her: liberal family, farm life, modest travel outside the States, little exposure to the trappings and practices of the rich. Still, they shared many likes: classical art, country music, pinot noir, young children, Paris, E.M. Forster, chocolate chip ice cream, tulips, cellos, BMWs, and the Chicago Bears.

Charlie stopped this analysis, sat up in bed, and checked the clock. Enough. He was getting nowhere. He had to decide to propose or end the relationship. I'm not being fair to her. I'll give myself a deadline—two weeks. Propose or move on.

He felt happy, relived, excited, and impatient to talk to her. So he got up, showered, shaved and went outside for a walk enjoying the sunrise. He felt as giddy as a seventeen year old. His life was about to change—one way or the other.

"Charlie, I must advise you to deal posthaste with this unfortunate publicity," Sam Dixon said on Monday morning. "It's bad enough that the markets are down after the Fed raised interest rates, but some of our clients don't like that their money manager is mentioned in the same breath as a possible murder. Two major clients have even asked if it is difficult to move their investment portfolios to Goldman, Sachs."

Charlie was comfortable with Sam. He valued his advice. Sam was fifteen years older, but their social and educational backgrounds were similar: old family, Chicago, ivy-league, conservative politically, committed to doing what's best for the client. Sitting across from Charlie in a blue, pin-striped suit smartly pressed, trade-mark blue bowtie, and shined black wing-tipped shoes, Sam cast an avuncular air. His bushy eyebrows barely touched the tops of his horned-rimmed glasses. Charlie understood that this was a man who commanded a strong sense of self.

Charlie answered, "Make me a list and I'll call personally anyone with qualms and try to calm them down. Moreover I am going to do everything I can to get the Bradshaw death off the front page."

Charlie considered telling Sam that he had taken the initiative to do some sleuthing but decided not to at this time.

"Not all is dire," Sam said changing the subject. "You should be pleased that our communication efforts regarding the market correction and our portfolio changes have been well-received."

"That is good news. Keep the information flowing. Emphasize that when markets go down, our actions try to minimize inevitable declines in portfolio values. We can't perform miracles, but the actions we took have reduced the damage."

"The concept of a 'lesser loss' is a difficult strategy to convey."

"Agreed, but silence is worse. Clients want to hear from us."

Sam started to get up to leave, but Charlie stopped him, "Anything new on Scottie Bradshaw?"

"The bank called and wants us to continue managing the money until it can approve a distribution. I'll keep you informed."

\* \* \*

"Over here," Charlie said loudly and gestured to Peaches as he entered the Oak Tree restaurant. "I have a table by the window."

Charlie had chosen one of the very public, mid-priced restaurants serving downtown shoppers. Oak Tree was located on the ground floor of one of those popular, multi-use structures finding its way into most large cities, combining an upscale indoor mall, a hotel, and condominiums. At 900 North Michigan Avenue it added to Chicago's skyline and attracted shoppers, tourists, and residents to the downtown area.

Rather than inviting Peaches to lunch at one of the prestigious social clubs like The Casino or Racquet Club, where they would have been recognized, Charlie opted to blend in with the hurried shoppers. Moreover, the *Tribune* prohibited reporters from receiving gifts in any form—including lunch. At the Oak Tree they could split the check.

"Peaches, you look good. Always punctual," Charlie joked.

"My reputation for being late is overblown. Mother taught me to be on time. Anyway, I have a new strategy. I set my watch twenty minutes ahead."

"And what a watch that is. You must have a trust fund to own a Breguet like that."

"Oh, a mere trifle. We reporters file hefty 1040s."

They both laughed. Charlie had known Peaches since childhood. He considered him a friend—and understood his sense of humor. He enjoyed and anticipated this banter.

"Actually, it was my father's. I merely updated the

band. My boyfriend is envious. By the way, you, of all people, know what is in my trust funds."

"*Touché*. But I know nothing of your love life."

As Peaches chatted, Charlie studied him. His tan suit was conservative, but his tie boldly patterned orange shouted, "Notice me!" His glasses were round and dark blue. Missing was the diamond stud he usually wore in his right earlobe. Charlie smiled inwardly that without the diamond this outfit was Peaches attempt to being serious. After all, the *Trib* had given him a somber assignment—the Bradshaw death.

"It's just as well," Peaches responded. "I have such awful taste in men. Speaking of romance—and doing my job- when am I going to hear about you and that delicious Kate Milano? Marriage perhaps?"

The server arrived, to Charlie's relief.

"Shall we order?" replied Charlie.

Both selected Greek salads with grilled chicken. Peaches ordered a white wine while Charlie asked for iced tea.

"Come on, Charlie. You can't avoid my question so easily. I am head over heels about Kate. An artist. You know many people think I have a creative side—fashion design. Kate would be good for you—complement your intensely rational personality. Your wedding would be the event of the year."

"You flatter me. But if we elope, Peaches, you will be the first to know—after my mother, of course."

"Oh, yes, the formidable Claire Bailey, of Curtis lineage. One of the dowager queens of Lake Forest."

"Watch it," Charlie warned.

"Mea culpa," Peaches giggled, holding up his hand in surrender. "We never see her anymore. She's well, I trust?"

"She could be better. Her heart is giving her troubles. Add to that, her close friend, Dottie Bradshaw's grief. She's feeling the stress."

"I'm sorry to hear that. Your mother seems much too young to be having heart issues. But to change the subject. I hope you are kidding about eloping. You would deprive me of a big wedding story—the lifeblood of my column. It is so hard to write Society in Chicago. It's not like New York. Chicago people are so hardworking and goal oriented. And we go to bed early. It's so boring. Please don't add to my depression by eloping."

"My heart bleeds for you."

"At the risk of being obvious, I suppose you were shaken to find young Bradshaw at the Potawatomi."

Charlie switched to a serious tone, "True. Tragic occurrence."

"The death must be causing quite a stir in Lake Forest. I can imagine that the senior protectors of the Lake Forest image of propriety are aghast about all the fuss. You know, it can't happen here. And it didn't help that poor Scottie was such a black sheep."

"Now, Peaches, calm down," Charlie said feeling obliged to defend his friends. "The Bradshaws are very well respected and liked. No one in the community wished ill on Scottie or his family. This unfortunate accident could have happened any-where."

"Accident? That's not what the police thought at first, when they saw the bruises on his head and neck. You didn't know that?" asked Peaches.

"I had that impression when the police talked to me during the first couple of days after the incident. By their tone I thought they suspected me of something. Unnerving. Annoying. But I guess that's their job."

"Well, you're safe. The police think now that he must have gone into the men's locker room to relieve himself. He probably stepped too close to the roman bath, slipped, hit his head, and drowned. The police used the word *trauma*. At any rate, they now think it was an accident. Case closed. So there will be no article under my byline. *Quel domage.* I don't usually get a chance to cover a murder—sex, scandal, divorce, yes. But murder? No."

"I am sorry you are disappointed, but I am relieved that the Bradshaws will have closure and Scottie can rest in peace."

Charlie was genuinely pleased to hear that Peaches would not be writing anything more. But he was incredulous that the police could dismiss the possibility of murder. Maybe Peaches had misunderstood or the police wanted to be secretive.

"You know, Charlie. I was at that party for an hour or two. Purely personal, not on the *Trib's* dime. I had dinner with my cousin and then watched the college boys dance for awhile. I saw Scottie Bradshaw looking drunk as usual, and was pawing some young girl. I missed the scandalous fight people are talking about. Not loudly mind you. After all, Scottie was a Bradshaw. He was a despicable person. A year or two ago he called on my mother. He asked to be her broker. She said she gave him a chance, and he lost her some sizable amount of money. She's still angry."

"I didn't know that."

"A side of me says 'good riddance'. I can be mean, you know."

"We all have failings," Charlie said, trying not to smile.

They split the bill, and Charlie walked with Peaches out to the street, "I'm glad the police have closed the door on Scottie's death. However, if you hear they are reconsidering the case, I would like to know. Henry and Jamie are good friends. They need to know the truth."

"Of course," Peaches agreed. "But you might hold off. Maybe I just want it to be a murder. Deep down I believe it was no accident."

Charlie caught a cab back to the office and reviewed the conversation. He had known Peaches for so long that he was no longer shocked by anything he said. On balance, Charlie found him amusing, although one had to be careful what one said, since a thoughtless remark might end up on the society page. He had not noticed Peaches' name on the party list, but he was probably listed as George or just guest.

Charlie was surprised that the police had told the press that the death was an accident. But if the police and the press were dropping the case, the public notoriety of last week would fade and his business would return to normal. They would stop pestering him. Sam Dixon would be happy and so would Charlie.

One wildcard that he had to consider was the political influence of Henry Bradshaw. His contacts may have pressured the police to say publically that the death was an accident while they were still pursing the case. He would want the end of the focus on Scottie's bad deeds and the notoriety of a murder in Lake Forest. Besides, according to mother, Dottie Bradshaw was an emotional wreck. The police could always open the case in the future after time had defused the current attention. Whatever the truth, Charlie was not ready to stop his investigation.

# CHAPTER TWELVE

"Don't be stubborn," Kate insisted. "Peaches told you that the police think Scottie's death was an accident. It's time to drop it and get on with life."

"But I don't believe the accident explanation, Peaches doesn't either—and I doubt the police do as well. Whatever their reasons they want the press to back off."

Charlie and Kate sat at a table in a niche away from the door and the long, brass bar in an anteroom of a restaurant near her office. He had called her to meet after he arrived home from a quick trip to Italy and Abu Dhabi to calm the anxieties of a handful of his clients about the recent stock market gyrations. He said he missed her and wanted to celebrate her successful presentation at work.

Kate had missed him, but more than that wanted to get him to agree to drop his personal investigation into the death. If it had been an accident, he and his company were in the clear and any further work was a waste of time. If Scottie had been murdered, she felt he was in over his head. The killer might learn what he was doing and he would be at risk. What Charlie was doing affected himself—and herself as well.

So far their discussion had not gone well. The more they talked, the angrier she became.

"Haven't you heard a word I've said? You have no business investigating a murder. It's dangerous. While you're out playing detective, I'm worrying. I don't want to worry. What do you gain?"

"For me, if there is renewed talk of murder, the spotlight comes back at me. More importantly, the Bradshaws are my friends- especially Jamie. They need to know who did it. What if the police believe it was an accident, and it wasn't? Who would be looking?"

"Not you, I would hope."

Kate was seething inside. Why had she chosen such a headstrong, inflexible man? She pushed her drink aside and slid along the banquette. She stood up, "I've had enough. You're pigheaded—won't listen to reason. I'm going home."

Charlie looked dumbfounded.

"Why are you so angry? I'm trying to explain."

"I need to calm down," Kate answered. "At home, alone."

"I know you are flying to New York tomorrow," Charlie said as she started to leave. "Do you still want me to drive you to the airport?"

"No. I'll ask Marc to do it. He's going too."

Charlie remained seated, and watched her leave.

She hailed a cab outside the restaurant and reached her building ten minutes later.

Hiding her anger, she greeted her doorman outside her North State Parkway apartment house.

"Robert, you're looking dapper today. I like the summer uniforms. Were there any deliveries today?"

"Yes, some roses came a half hour ago. I put them on the table outside your door."

What poor timing she thought as she took the elevator to her eighth floor landing. The card identified Charlie. "*Fleurs* for my *fleur*. See you tonight. Love, C."

Kate's mood changed to regret and exasperation. This evening she and Charlie might have dressed up and had a special dinner. Instead Charlie wanted to play detective.

*What am I doing? I love him more than any other man I have ever know. But he can upset me like no one else. I'll never change him. His confidence and strong will are part of his attractiveness. Sometimes when Marc comes on to me at work, I think why don't I encourage him. He would be much easier than Charlie—not as complex. I know he likes me. I guess I prefer the Charlie challenge. The higher you reach, the greater the reward.*

As she changed her clothes to something comfortable- a white, cotton top and blue jeans—she glanced wistfully at the black Armani dress she had almost worn that evening. And the Christian Louboutin shoes. Another night perhaps.

Then Kate sat down to do some work and then remembered that she had left her iPad in her car. She would need it for her trip. She took the elevator down to the parking garage floor. With

its storage lockers and mechanical systems, it took up most of
the first three above-ground floors. She disliked this structure because the back area was open to the elements. Every cold wind
and snowstorm would in onto the cars. A chain link fence
stretched across the concrete supports for security purposes, but
Kate was never satisfied with the arrangement.

She unlocked her tan Lexus, slid into the driver's seat, and
set her purse next to her. As Kate was checking her iPad, she
thought she heard a high-pitched hissing sound to her right. Looking down she saw a fat, dark coil on the floor. The object moved
again, and Kate recognized what it was.

Her heart stopped for a moment, and then she leapt out the
door, chest pounding, and ran about twenty yards away from the
car. Unmistakably a black snake was in her car. "Manuel!" she
shrieked for the attendant. She stumbled towards the ramp near his
office. "Manuel!" She turned to see him racing toward her. Kate
could not speak but pointed him toward her car, its door open. The
snake's head and a foot of its body slithered out. Manuel dashed
forward and slammed the door. The head and half of the body shot
up across the garage floor. It spasmed and died on the concrete.

Kate screamed in horror. The snake seemed everywhere and
the thought of the severed half, smashed and bleeding in her car,
made her sick. She leaned against a concrete post,
hyperventilating, and threw up.

"I'll be right back," Manuel said. "Do you want help to your
apartment?"

Kate shook her head, trying to stand still and collect herself.

After a minute or two Manuel returned with an armful of rags and a plastic bucket of sloshing water. She watched from a distance not wanting to see what he was doing but unable to look away. He glanced over his shoulder and approached her.

"Miss Milano, the snake is dead. I'll clean up the blood stains out of your car, but it'll take time. Please go up to your apartment, and I'll call you when I'm finished. Here's your purse from the car."

"Are there any others?" Kate asked, quivering.

"Not in your car. I'll look around the garage. I don't know where it could have come from. Maybe another car or the open fence in the back. Very strange. Never happened before. Your car was locked?"

"I'm sure it was," she said faintly.

Maybe it wasn't, though yesterday she had been excited to see Charlie on his return today, and she may have forgotten. That explanation was more palatable than someone breaking into her car and putting the snake there. Why would anyone do that?"

"I'll call the building's manager and report the incident," Manuel promised.

In a daze Kate nodded and walked to the elevator. Once in her apartment she poured a glass of water with shaking hands and called Charlie.

"Charlie," she sobbed into the phone.

"What's wrong?"

"Please come over. My place. Something terrible happened. I need you."

"I'll be right over."

Kate composed herself as best she could in the ten minutes it took Charlie to arrive. The moment he came in the door she burst into tears. He held her and stroked her back as she sobbed. Finally she stopped and let him lead her to the couch to sit down.

"Tell me," he said, holding her hands.

When she finished, Charlie kissed her and offered to get her a drink. She said she felt calmer and safe with him there.

The phone rang. "Shall I answer?" Charlie asked.

"No. I'm sure it's Manuel. I'll take it."

Instead she heard a man's muffled voice. "Tell your boyfriend to stay out of matters that don't concern him, or things will get worse for you."

"Who is this?" Kate demanded.

The phone disconnected.

"Is your car ready?" Charlie asked, handing her a glass of wine.

Frightened Kate told Charlie what the man said.

"So Scottie was murdered," Charlie declared. "Has to be. Whoever is behind this doesn't know that the police planned to close the case. If he hadn't done this crazy snake thing, he could have gotten away with murder. But why did he target you?"

After a pause, Kate said, "See. This thing is dangerous. You have to stop and let the police do their job."

"I agree we must call the police. I know you are angry, but let's think about it first. Look, you are still shaking."

Charlie sat back on the couch and hugged Kate, who started

to sob again.

"Let's pack you up and go to my place," Charlie suggested.

Kate needed no encouragement and headed back to her bedroom to find her things. She stayed in her top and jeans but wiped off the tears. She kept toiletries, nightgown and other necessities at Charlie's, so she only packed a work outfit for her trip tomorrow—including the iPad that Manuel had retrieved for her.

When she came back to her living room, Charlie said he would take her down to the lobby and leave her for a few minutes so that he could look at her car. He wanted to see the area and ask Manuel if anyone had been around the garage before Kate arrived.

Afterwards he drove her in his car the few blocks to his building. There they ate frozen dinners he kept in his refrigerator. Kate had no appetite and tried to talk of other things, but the incident with the snake and the threat on the phone were all she could think about. Eventually they retired to bed, where Charlie held Kate close until she fell asleep exhausted.

Charlie could not sleep. He stared at the ceiling hearing Kate's steady breathing next to him. He was very angry at himself for having put Kate at risk. Maybe he had been too headstrong to insist on pursuing Scottie's murderer. He had wanted to clear his name, but if he had left well enough alone, the police would have dropped their interest in him anyway. They had concluded the incident was an accident.

*If I hadn't been nosing around, the murderer would never have thought of threatening Kate. It is too late now to change that.*

Now he felt an even greater urgency to uncover the murderer- to protect Kate and Claire. It was foolish to think that if he stopped pursuing the matter, as the mysterious man on the phone demanded, the threat would disappear.

He had to tell the police and let them know what happened to Kate and about the threatening phone call. They would have to reopen the case as a homicide. He would insist they provide some protection for Kate. But calling Investigator Victor was a complex issue. Victor might be angry that they had come to the wrong conclusion regarding the death. He would also be upset to learn that Charlie also had been investigating the incident— in his amateurish way. They already thought him suspicious. Finally, might they believe him about the attack and phone call? They might think that he was fabricating a story to cast suspicion away from himself. Thank goodness for Manuel. Still as much as Paul Victor might distrust and dislike him, Charlie knew that protecting Kate was paramount and that everyone would be safer if Scottie's killer could be found. He had to notify the police.

The next morning Kate appeared in the kitchen dressed for her trip and searching for coffee.

"Why don't you stay home today? Go to a movie or shopping. Anything to distract you."

"No. This trip is crucial. It'll take my mind off that terrible snake."

"I hope so," Charlie said. "But call me immediately if you get any more calls."

"Of course. Right now my biggest fear is opening my car. I may have to buy a new car."

"When you're ready to get into your car, let me know. I'll want to be there."

"Before I leave, let's settle something. You're going to call the police? And you're going to stop meddling in the investigation?"

Charlie could sense her anger beneath the surface. Fair enough. She had been the target of the murderer. He didn't want to start a new argument so he said, "I'll call Paul Victor within the hour. I'll have to admit I had been snooping around. He'll jump all over me for ignoring his admonitions. I'll have to agree to behave. Besides the last thing I was is for you to be put in danger."

Kate did not smile but she seemed to be satisfied.

After Kate left, Charlie called Paul Victor and described what happened to Kate.

He ended his account by urging the detective to trace the call and to check to see if Kate's garage had security cameras.

"What have you been doing to prompt the attack?" Paul asked. "Who did you talk to about what?"

"I just talked to a few people about who disliked Scottie. Since you recently told the media that the death was an accident, I thought that I could go back to my normal life."

"What? We never announced a finding. Where did you hear that? This case is active. Stop getting involved. You don't know what you are doing, and you could harm the investigation."

"I thought I could be of help," Charlie said defensively. "But after yesterday we know someone has been watching our activities. It's imperative that you provide protection for Kate Milano."

"We don't' have that kind of manpower, even if your story is true. We can't assign personnel every time some one sees a snake or gets a prank phone call."

"I assure you, Investigator Victor, that this is a very serious matter."

"We take Mr. Bradshaw's death very seriously and are analyzing any and all evidence we find. But you need to keep your nose out of this. Understand?"

Paul Victor emphasized this last demand by raising his voice, slowing down, and speaking directly.

*But so what? Charlie thought. He had Kate to protect. The good news was that the police were continuing to investigate. The bad news was that he and Kate were on their own.*

*I'll hire someone to provide security. Then I'll convince Kate to take a vacation with me to put this behind her. I need to patch things up.*

Those actions would be defensive. Charlie vowed also to go on the offense. He would have to review every conversation he had had during the past two weeks. There must be a clue as to who wanted him to back off. *That way I can redeem myself in*

*Kate's eyes by nabbing the man who terrorized her. The hell with the police. If they won't protect her, I sure will.*

# CHAPTER THIRTEEN

"Snake?" Claire Bailey reacted on the phone to Charlie's account of the events of the day before. "Certainly. That might frighten someone. They scare the bejesus out of me. I am surprised though that your girl, Kate, was shaken. She's a farm girl after all. She must have lived with snakes growing up."

'Your story reminds me of the prank you and your Dad played on me. Remember, you buried a dead garter snake in my vegetable garden just before I went to plant tomato seeds? I think my heart stopped for ten seconds. You two had a good laugh."

"That reminds me, mother. You are taking your heart medication?"

"I'm okay. Following doctor's orders."

"Good. About Kate, the attempt to scare her worked. She was already in a state having argued with me earlier and then the surprise in her garage."

"What did you argue about?"

"My efforts to find Scottie's murderer. Peaches had said that the police had decided it was an accident; so Kate concluded I should stop. I told her that Peaches had to be wrong—that Scottie had been killed. If so, Kate reasoned, that was more reason to stop. A murderer would be dangerous the closer I come to him."

"On this point I agree with Kate. You could get hurt—or put Kate at risk. That fact has just been proven. A snake now. What's next?"

Charlie frowned at the kitchen phone. He didn't want to argue with his mother. But he had to make one last point. "If the murderer is not found, the Bradshaws will never have closure. They'll always wonder. Our friends. Moreover, I still have to clear my name."

"Admittedly. Dottie and Henry are beside themselves with sadness. Murder or accident, they would like to see the public aspect go away. They are very private people."

"After what happened to Kate, I am going to try to convince her to take a few days with me away from here. She needs a break. I thought Palm Beach. In the summer not many people are there and the place is beautiful. We can stay at the Colony instead of opening up your house. What do you think?"

"You know what I think of her, but if you must go, Palm Beach will be quiet and far away from gossip about Scottie Bradshaw. By coincidence I suggested to Dottie yesterday to escape to there for her peace of mind. Who know, you may run into them there."

* * * *

"You know I wouldn't be coming if you hadn't offered a private plane," Kate joked as she buckled her belt on the leather seat facing Charlie.

"Nothing but the best for my lady," Charlie said.

He had had a difficult time convincing Kate to take a short vacation. She was committed to a big project at work and unwilling to admit that the scare bothered her. She told Charlie that after a good night's sleep, she had almost forgotten about the snake incident. Charlie knew her well enough to dismiss her brave front. Her eyes told him otherwise.

He had suggested that they fly on Wednesday and stay the weekend. He would use his firm's small office there to stay on top of the turmoil in the markets, and she could rest and read by the pool at The Colony Hotel.

Charlie's plane was an eight-passenger Citation he used on demand through a fractional ownership program, which entitled him to substantial airtime each year. While he had to pay a monthly maintenance charge, a plane was available at most airports given two hours' notice.

The two-man crew at the General Aviation Jetport at the Palwaukee airport had taken their bags and invited them aboard. One of the pilots reviewed the aircraft's safety features and amenities and served cocktails and snacks. Then he climbed up into the cockpit, and they took off.

"Why aren't we staying at your Mother's house?" Kate asked.

"The hurricane shutters are attached around the windows, and I didn't want to bother the caretaker with taking them down for just a few days. We'll be safe and comfortable at the Colony."

"You prefer it to the Breakers?" Kate asked, sipping her mimosa.

"I want to see the Colony since they poured a lot of money into modernizing it. The next time, if you wish, I'll take you to the Breakers. Of course, when it is convenient, I'd ask to stay at Mother's. It's beautiful and convenient to the town."

"Either place is fine with me."

"You'll enjoy the shops on Worth Avenue. Some are the best in the world. Shop all you like and we can eat at Renato's, Taboo, or Café Boulud. It's off-season, so I would be surprised if we see anyone we know."

"You spoil me. Keep it up."

Kate located her book and started to read. Charlie read some memos and looked up occasionally to check on her. She seemed relaxed. Then her brow furrowed and she glanced over at him.

"I shouldn't think about the snake again, but I am curious what you saw when you left me in the lobby for a few minutes after we left my apartment?"

"I went up to where your car was parked. Manuel was still there, scrubbing the interior. I asked where the snake was. He pointed to the garbage bin."

"Did you look at it?"

"Yes. It looked at least three feet long."

She shuddered. "Was someone trying to kill me? Was it poisonous, do you think?"

"No. It was a black rat snake—harmless but scary. I'm sorry for putting you in this situation."

She sighed and shook her head in disgust. "I know you never expected this. I forgive you."

"I was determined to find out how the snake got there," Charlie continued. "Behind the building are four stand-alone townhouses, each with a backyard abutting your apartment house. The yards have brick or flagstone patios with wrought-iron chairs and tables and gardens along the perimeters with a four-foot concrete wall in the back next to your garage."

"So a man with a snake in a cloth bag could easily sneak into these yards and climb over the fence," Kate suggested.

"Right. Was your car locked?"

"I thought so, since the alarm didn't sound. I trust the other residents, and an attendant is always on duty. I'll remember to lock it from now on."

"I'm sure you will." He smiled and reached to squeeze her hand.

"How did the intruder know when to call you after the incident? I looked down the ramp and I could see the sidewalk in front of the building. He could have stood there watching. The sidewalk was busy at that time of day. He could have heard you scream and seen Manuel running up the ramp to the second level. He could have waited ten minutes and then used a pay phone to make the threatening call."

"That's logical." Kate agreed. "Maybe you do have a talent as an investigator."

"If so, I wish I didn't have to use it," Charlie confessed.

Charlie did not intend to put off restarting his investigation just because they were in Palm Beach. Now time was more critical than ever. Ideas grow cold if not pursued quickly. When Charlie had called Paul Victor, he had seemed to think that Charlie had invented the snake and phone call and without a doubt did not want Charlie's help. So Charlie thought that the next thing to do was to follow up with some of the partygoers - particularly the Tansey girl. In addition, now he had a new avenue of inquiry: remembering whom he had talked to about his investigation and trying to tie them back directly to the party scene.

After they landed, the plane taxied to the General Aviation terminal, where the hotel's limousine met them.

As they drove away from the airport the driver asked, "First time in Palm Beach? I'm happy to be a travel guide."

Charlie smiled but Kate said, "My first time. What do I need to know?"

"Palm Beach is a special place," the driver began changing his voice to try to sound like a newscaster. "It's a barrier island sixteen miles long, separated from the mainland and the city of West Palm Beach by the Intracoastal Waterway, which runs up most of the eastern coast of the United States. That separation—between the island and the mainland—is more than physical, however. It is money, mindset, and glamour."

Charlie felt the urge to laugh but quelled it. This driver clearly had done this narrative before. Charlie looked at him and noticed he had a golf visor on.

"Palm Beach is like no others," the driver went on. "It has wealth beyond imagination. The residents do not have the normal worries of the average Americans: family budget, job security, the cost of health care and gasoline, and the quality of public schools. Palm Beachers think about social prominence, philanthropy, cultural and artistic events, clothes, cars, planes, polo and yachts. Most of their houses are exquisitely furnished and magnificently landscaped."

"Are you a member of the Chamber of Commerce," Kate joked. "You obviously practice this presentation. It is quite polished."

"I conduct a historical walking tour three mornings a week—a good break from driving. I dress up with a blue blazer, white pants, bowtie, and a straw hat."

"I'd like to see that," Kate said, sounding enthusiastic.

"No visor then," Charlie whispered to Kate.

"I'll give you my card a the Colony. My name is Stan Slutsky." He then continued his narrative, "Despite their opulence, these mansions are second or third homes or 'beach houses' to a majority of the residents. These people have larger homes and estates up north or in Europe. While many of the residents passionately protect their privacy and anonymity and avoid glitz, others just as passionately compete with one another over the glamour associated with clothes, boats, and parties. Some of the newer owners hire publicists to ensure that their names and pictures appear in the right publications. This type of activity tends to evoke both amusement and jealousy from rich non-Palm Beachers and hatred or aspiration from the rest of the world."

Charlie could not keep quiet any longer. "Hold on. I doubt

most of the world cares anything about Palm Beach. My family has been coming here for over eighty years, and we are happy to live under the radar. The people you refer to are recent arrivals with high-profile careers. They carry on the same way in their New York, LA, Dallas, or London homes. Is this description part of your walking tour?"

"Yes, I've been doing this for five years," Stan said, sounding defensive. "The tips are bigger if I entertain my clients. I rarely run into someone like you. Eighty years. You are almost a founding family. Your father must have been here when this sandbar was wild, speculative real estate. Who would have thought these properties would become the most expensive in the country? I bet you belong to all the elite clubs like the Everglades, Bath and Tennis, Four Arts and such. What is your name?"

The last thing Charlie was going to do was to give this chatty guy his name. His family made it a practice to maintain a low profile and let others dominate the society pages. The Baileys had nothing to prove in this playground of the rich.

Charlie deflected the question by saying to Kate, "Look, we are about to cross the Intracoastal on the middle bridge, called the Royal Palm Bridge. Across the bridge is Palm Beach."

He never tired of driving on Royal Palm Way. This boulevard, lined with sixty-foot royal palms, boasting a superb collection of private banks and money management firms on one side and a school, the rec center, a park, and the Society of the Four Arts on the other. He pointed to the right to show Kate the small but elegant office of Bailey, Richardson, where Charlie intended to spend the afternoon. The limo turned right on South County road, past several upscale galleries, boutiques, and restaurants, past Worth Avenue, and then left onto Hammon Avenue to The Colony Club—a British Colonial gem in the heart of the island.

Despite being early, they found that their suite was ready, and they went up to it immediately. They unpacked quickly. Kate urged Charlie to go off to his office which he had said on the plane that he wanted to visit.

"Go, Charlie. I'll fend for myself. I'll have a salad by the pool, and then make my way down Worth Avenue. I don't need your help to shop."

Charlie kissed Kate goodbye and took a taxi to his office. He spent the first thirty minutes catching up with his office manager and two portfolio managers who handled local clients. Fortunately, the financial markets were stable—apparently finished with the volatility of the past week.

Sequestering himself in his office, Charlie considered his strategy. He wanted to talk to Taylor Tansey but had no idea how to reach her. His options were to call her parents or try Maureen Turner at the club. He decided that the Tanseys might not want their daughter questioned about the party.

He reached for the phone and called Maureen. "Thank you for sending me that list of party attendees," he began. "It helped me remember a couple of the guests. I must be getting old."

"If you are old, I hate to think what I am."

"You don't look a day over thirty to me. But that list made me remember that I promised Taylor Tansey to answer some career-related questions for one of her classes. I can't find her phone number and would rather not call her dad for it. Might you have a listing for her? I'd be grateful."

Maureen indicated that they might have something in the member's database and retrieved a number and address in less than a minute. "Here it is." Then there was an awkward silence. "I'm not sure the information is correct," she said at last. "It says she graduated from Indiana a year ago and is a marketing trainee at a local company."

"Yes," Charlie said quickly. "She's thinking of graduate school."

After another pause, she gave Charlie the work number.

"You're a godsend. I'll call immediately. She sounds well situated, but I may be helpful anyway."

Charlie felt guilty lying to Maureen, but he would have gotten Taylor's number one way or another. He had merely taken a shortcut. To try to make amends for his ruse, he would offer Taylor some career advice and send Maureen some thank you flowers.

That offer was how he began his conversation with Taylor when he reached her. He said that her father had sung her praises to him and he wanted to help promising young people get ahead.

"I did have another reason to call you," Charlie admitted eventually. "If you don't mind talking about Scottie Bradshaw. You know I found him the morning after the dinner dance. I think he approached you the night of the accident."

"I didn't know him well, Mr. Bailey, but, if I can help, I'll try. It's like really wired to like talk to someone one day, and he's dead the next. This experience is so totally bizarre."

"It must have been a shock. How did he act at the party?"

"Well, as I said, I didn't know him very well. I had hung out with him and his friends at another party. Surprisingly he asked me to dance and then he wouldn't leave me alone. It was awkward, because he was older. My girlfriends kidded me about him, but he was funny and a real good dancer. Until he drank too much."

"Was he a gentleman?"

"At first he was. But he got drunk and, like fell down while we were dancing. He hurt himself, I think, and he blamed me. That pissed me off. Then later he suggested we go inside for a drink and sit on the couch. At that point, I was worried things could get out of hand and I told him I was leaving. He followed me and grabbed at my waist. I pushed him away, than ran to get my purse. As I was leaving, I told my brother what had happened and not to wait for me."

"That was Will?"

"Yes. Will was furious and headed towards Scottie."

Then Taylor described the scene between the two men and the fight.

"Afterwards, Will took me home. I felt safe with him. He wanted to call the police. I told him no and asked him not to tell our parents. I just wanted to get past everything."

"Those events must have been upsetting. Scottie's behavior was inexcusable. Did he talk about anything that stood out I your mind?"

"No. He mainly talked about my school, his job, friends at the club, the band, who was trying to hook up with who at the party—that sort of thing. Just talk."

"Did Scottie talk to anyone else?"

"His buddies—Zack Steward, Sam something, Art Carlson, his older brother, the Kings, Lou Upton—I'm sure there were others."

"Did he talk to anyone in the band?"

"Just before I left, Scottie nodded at someone he said was the manager."

"What did he look like?" Charlie asked.

"I don't remember. It was dark. But he was some big guy like maybe in his forties. He wore a coat and tie. White guy—although most of the band was black."

Charlie wrote down her description on a legal pad.

"Thank you, Taylor. You have been very helpful. I'm sorry you had to go through this ordeal."

"Yeah, me too. It was creepy. Will feels bad about it too."

They arranged a time to meet the next week to talk about her career, and ambitions, and then said goodbye. Charlie had learned nothing new from the conversation.

The band manager was still a wild card; so he became Charlie's next person of interest. He found the club's party invitation in his old emails. The band's name, *Motown Chicago*, led him to a website that listed a single contact, Lamar Goodens, and his email address and a phone number. Lamar was also identified as the band's drummer and booking agent.

Charlie reached Lamar on his first try.

"I am Charlie Bailey. I heard that you put on a great show at the Potawatomi Club. I might be interested in booking your group. Who's your band's manager?"

"We don't have no manager. I do all the bookings." Loud music in the background forced Charlie to concentrate on Lamar's words.

"Someone at the party said he talked to your manager."

"Like I said, we don't have no manager. You talk to me."

"A big, white man in a coat and tie standing near your band said that he's the manager."

"Yeah, I remember that dude. He's saying he's our manager? No way. Next time I see him, I'm gonna shut that dude down."

"I must have misunderstood," Charlie said quickly. "Anyway, are you free on the Saturday of Labor Day weekend?"

"Let me look," Lamar said. After a moment of silence, he said, "No man. We be booked."

Charlie smiled. He had guessed that would be the case.

"Oh, too bad. But I'll remember you and call again."

"Sure, man."

So who was the man? Why had he pretended to be someone else? Charlie did not have a name or more than a vague description, but he had confirmed a possible suspect. He was sure that Paul wouldn't believe him, so he didn't bother to call the investigator. It was up to him to find this man before the man found him or Kate.

*＊*＊

Kate was already in their room at The Colony when Charlie returned. She wore a plush white cotton hotel robe. She looked
healthy with wet hair, and glowing pink skin.

"Refreshed?" Charlie asked.

"After my afternoon of power shopping, I needed a shower,"
Kate laughed. "I learned how impressive Worth Avenue is."

She pointed and he saw glossy shopping bags lined up on
the floor, on the bed, and on a chair.

"You've been busy," Charlie said eyeing the bags.

Charlie knew what she meant. Worth Avenue was a retail
powerhouse of iconic proportions. It ranked with New York's
Madison Avenue, Chicago's North Michigan, Beverly Hill's
Rodeo Drive, London's Bond Street, and Paris' Rue de St.
Honoré, with the most expensive clothing, antiques, art, and jewelry stores in the world. Worth Avenue was at once international
and local, fashionable and traditional, serious and touristy. He
guessed that one-quarter of the shoppers came to buy; one-
quarter came to browse; and one-half came to look at the other
shoppers.

"Which was your favorite?"

"Ferragamo's. I wanted another pair of dressy black shoes—
in case you ever take me to a fancy restaurant. Hint, hint. I noticed
that the selection here hasn't turned up in Chicago yet. My friends
will love them."

"Can I help you with these purchases?"

"No, I put money away for just such a time."

"Great. How about Café Boulud tonight?"

"Terrific. That reminds me. You'll never guess who I ran into today coming out of Kassatly's."

"Who?" Charlie asked.

"Dottie Bradshaw. She wore a smart black dress despite the heat."

"In mourning?" Charlie said.

"I assume so. She looked terrible—dark circles under her eyes, and her face was drawn."

Kate shook her head sadly.

"I expressed my sympathy to her and her family."

"That was nice of you, Kate."

"She asked what I was doing in Palm Beach in the middle of the summer. When I said you and I decided to enjoy Palm Beach without the crowds, she agreed and asked if your mother had accompanied us.'

'Then she said, "I hope that rascal Charlie is courting you properly."'

"And you said?" Charlie asked as he wrapped his arms around her and nuzzled her neck.

"Everything is fine. Then she invited us to join her for dinner on Friday at their house. Henry and Jamie are flying down for the weekend."

"Did you accept?" Charlie asked.

"I did. I'm sorry I didn't check with you first, but when she said she needed to get her mind off Scottie, I could hardly refuse."

"You did the right thing. What a coincidence. We can pay our respects, and I can ask Jamie about the man who tried to pass himself off as the band manager at the party."

"What are you talking about," Kate said.

"I'll bring you up-to-date, but first I have another idea."

He reached down and tugged at the belt of her robe. She responded by laughing, putting her arms around him, kissing him, and letting the robe slip off her shoulders.

# CHAPTER FOURTEEN

Charlie and Kate kept busy until Friday evening—on the phone to the office, walking the beach, reading at the pool, lunching at Taboo, and dining at Café Boulud and Chez Jean-Pierre. Kate was unwinding from the stress of the snake incident. If she continued to relax Charlie planned to propose Saturday night. It was time. While she indulged in a facial and massage at the spa, he slipped away after Friday lunch and picked out an engagement ring at Tiffany's on Worth Avenue.

Unlike his usual confident self, Charlie felt on shaky ground discussing diamond solitaires with the elegantly dressed saleswoman. He was unfit to assess color, clarity, carets, and *cut*. *What if he made a mistake? Maybe Kate had a specific cut in mind? Did she want something showy or discreet? He wished he would have asked his mother for her opinion. Of course, he wouldn't have done that. She would have tried to talk him out of marrying Kate. The ring choice with Solange was easy. His mother gave him a family ring.*

The saleswoman who looked to be only in her twenties was both knowledgeable and sensitive to his concerns.

"Your girlfriend will be thrilled with any of the rings you are looking at. The key is that the ring is from you. She will have to bring it in to be sized. That's usual."

"Okay," Charlie was starting to relax. "I'll tell her that she can have another one if she wants."

"She'll want the one you choose."

Charlie picked out a multi-carat emerald-cut diamond on a platinum band, and he was happy when he left the store with the box in his pocket. He hid it in his dresser before she returned form the spa.

They took a taxi to the Bradshaw house. Charlie felt relieved the driver wasn't Stan Slutsky. The house was situated on four acres on the ocean on North County Road. Because of the high ficus hedge, only the massive ornamental wrought-iron gate safeguarding the driveway could be seen from the street.

The house was vintage Palm Beach- a large two-story Spanish-style stucco house with a staircase tower that Charlie recognized was designed in the 1920's by Maurice Fatio. He pointed to the entrance pillars that carried the house name, *Beaulieu sur Mer*. Kate nodded awareness and their taxi was buzzed in at the gate.

Charlie was surprised that he and Kate were the only guests that night. The Bradshaws must have thought that it was too soon after Scottie's death to be entertaining a crowd. Dottie greeted them in the foyer and told the butler to inform Henry and Jamie to meet the guests in the family room.

"Jamie's here," Charlie said cheerfully, "Wonderful. I've

been meaning to call him."

"Yes, I asked him. His plane arrived an hour ago. He needed a break from work."

The Bradshaws greeted Charlie and Kate warmly and they all walked with their drinks out to the pool deck overlooking the still glistening ocean. The sound of the breaking surf competed with the background music of Sinatra singing classic love songs.

Charlie noted Kate staring at the marvelous ocean views and a container ship plying the Gulf Stream far out. At this time of year daylight would ensure that the views would last for at least two more hours.

Charlie approached a haggard-looking Henry and offered his condolences.

"Thanks, Charlie. You and your mother have been terrific. I don't know what Dottie would do without Claire."

Jamie approached the two and stated, "I am so grateful to you, Charlie. We go back a long time. You are a true friend."

They hugged, and Charlie turned his head to hide a tear.

Henry deftly changed the subject to the favorite topic among Palm Beachers—the breathtaking price of real estate on the island. Except for brief periods of national recession or significant stock market declines when real estate prices flattened out, values in Palm Beach only climbed.

The extraordinary influx of investment bankers, traders, and corporate CEO's to this small island fueled the rise in prices. Only so many properties were available, and like Saudi princes, buyers had more money than they could spend. Those on the island who had bought their places decades before were astonished at the sales prices. Most long time residents admitted they could not afford to buy their home at current prices. Still they delighted at the legacies they would leave their children and their own wealth—on paper.

"I heard the Defresnes estate sold that old house in the Estates District for $21 million," Henry claimed. "It'll probably end up as a tear down. And that little Reynolds cottage on Banyan is listed at $12 million. Can you imagine? They probably paid $250 thousand in the fifties."

"Well, I'm glad I'm not in the market," Charlie said. "Mom and Dad—and you and Dottie—were clever to buy when you did."

"It was more luck than inspiration," Henry admitted. "We just wanted some place warm in the winter. Of course both our parents were already here and helped us with the finances. Mind you, a hurricane could come through and blow this all away. In fact I heard that this year a bad hurricane season is predicted—like 2004. I'm glad we weren't here for the Frances and Jeanne storms. Our poor neighbors up in Vero Beach really were hit that year."

"Dinner is served," the butler interrupted, and Dottie coaxed everyone toward the dining room. "Enough real estate. Kate, you must tell us about your work. You are so intelligent and successful. I wish I were artistic, too. And Charlie, how is your mother? I haven't had a chance to talk to Claire in the last day or two what with the arrangements and all. I've been so overwhelmed. Claire was so helpful with the singers in church."

"The soprano from the Lyric Opera was superb," Jamie added. "Inspirational. Thank your mother from all of us."

They walked through an enormous living room to the formal dining room with its tropical-themed wallpaper, Georgian side table, painted white Chippendale-style, chairs, glass candlesticks, and sisal rug. Charlie noted silently that Dottie's taste in decoration resembled his mother's in Lake Forest—old world reset in the tropics.

Once everyone was seated, the dinner conversation ranged from the prospects for Northwestern's football team (Henry's alma mater), Yale's building program, the stock market, and the President's latest speech.

As the butler removed the dessert plates, Jamie asked Charlie, "By the way, did you ever talk to Steve Keller?"

"Oh yes, he was very helpful. Thank you for the suggestion."

"Jamie, do you mean Scottie's boss?" Henry asked.

"Yes, Dad. Charlie wanted to talk to him for some estate purposes."

"Oh, right," Henry said. "I never thought Keller appreciated Scottie. All that business he brought in. Scottie was a handful at times, but his firm should have backed him up when he had his problems. I suppose they did in a way, but they could have done more."

"Charlie, are the police still talking to you about the accident?" Jamie asked.

"Gentlemen," Dottie interrupted. "This topic is painful to me. I need to excuse myself."

"I'm sorry, my dear," Henry said. "May I help?"

"No. I'll be okay in a bit." Dottie answered tearfully and left the room.

Henry appeared confused for a moment but then suggested they take their coffee into the library. "There's also cognac and port if you'd like it."

Kate looked a Charlie and shrugged her shoulders as if to ask if she should come. Charlie stood and helped her up. He said to Henry, "We're happy to join you and Jamie."

Henry led them into a library that could have been shipped in total from a Chicago townhouse—a walnut wood-paneled room filled with shelves of hard covered books. A massive mahogany desk dominated the room, facing a fireplace topped by a Haitian painting. Only the green and white needlepoint carpet might have been a Florida product.

Kate and Charlie passed on the offer of a drink after the wine at dinner and nursed their coffees. The two Bradshaws settled on a vintage, single malt scotch.

"Have you heard from the police lately?" Jamie asked again. "Is the investigation over?"

"I don't know," Charlie said. "A reporter from the *Trib* told me that the police concluded Scottie's death was an accident. Maybe they are finished. Do you think it was?"

"Of course," Jamie responded. "What else? I saw his condition at the party. He drank too much and even got into a fight. He fell and had to be picked up. I guess he went up to the locker room to pee and lost his balance near the pool. Makes sense."

"True," Charlie paused and glanced over at Henry, who was staring at his drink. "One of the staff mentioned a man who talked with Scottie. He tried to pass himself off as the band manager. Do you have any idea who he was or why he was there?"

Jamie frowned, thinking. "No, I was there until ten and didn't notice anyone unusual. Maybe he was a guest and knew Scottie? Who knows? I don't see the connection with the accident?"

"Me neither," Henry said, suddenly looking up. "Charlie, why are you talking to the club staff about the party? What interest is that to you?"

"The police grilled me as if I had something to do with Scottie's death, because I found him. That, and the bad publicity could impact my firm. So I asked around to see if I could clear my name by pointing the investigation in another direction."

"Preposterous!" Henry barked. "You only found the body. The police are nuts. You don't need to protect yourself. Anyways it sounds as if the police agree that Scottie fell and drowned."

Jamie stood up to refill his glass. "Dad's right. You don't have to do anything. The thing is over."

"I have closure. We buried Scottie," Henry said. "Dottie is very upset with the continuing notoriety in the press and even among our friends. I told Governor Bross that unless there was clear evidence that Scottie's death was foul play, he should shut down the police investigation. So you should stop as well. Let sleeping dogs lie."

"I understand," Charlie responded.

He shifted in his leather chair uncomfortable that the family was moving on. But he was certain the death was no accident.

# CHAPTER FIFTEEN

The next day Charlie felt nervous when he woke up. He planned to propose but he worried that Kate was still angry about his detective work. The conversation with the Bradshaws hadn't helped. He pretended to be his usual confident self at breakfast, then excused himself for his customary-on-holiday three-mile run. Later he hid in their room until lunch citing paperwork.

Around two o'clock Charlie received a call on his cell from Jamie Bradshaw. "I was going to call you and thank you for the marvelous dinner last night. Your mother went all out. I hope she is feeling better."

"Yes, she is," Jamie said. "But I am calling to apologize for being such a poor host. Dad was rather harsh at the end of the night regarding your efforts to help us with the Scottie situation. He and Mother are understandably on edge. However, I am grateful for whatever you have done to learn more about what happened. I admit that at one point I thought that Scottie might have been murdered, but now, after the police have concluded it was an accident, I agree with them. I just wanted you to know we appreciate your efforts."

"Don't worry. I wasn't offended," Charlie said. "But thanks for calling. I just wanted to help a family I have admired and respected for a long time."

After discussing schedules and planning a lunch in a few weeks, Charlie hung up. Jamie had acted as a good friend does. But Charlie was not finished with his investigation. More important at this moment though was what to say to Kate this evening.

At lunch on the patio by the pool Kate carried the conversation while he played with his salad.

"Leaving work, I did not expect to be as relaxed as I am."

"I am happy to hear that," Charlie mumbled.

"The dinner last night was delicious. It's too bad that Dottie had to leave."

"Yes."

"What did you think about the conversation with Henry and Jamie? You said nothing after we left."

Charlie paused. He expected her to ask his opinion and didn't want to upset her. He told her about Jamie's apologetic call but returned to last night's dialogue. "Henry was quite clear," Charlie began. "He thinks a dragged out investigation is harmful to Dottie's peace of mind. He's willing to chalk up Scottie's death to a tragic accident. I don't know if he really believes that, but, as a lawyer, he senses that if a killer wasn't found immediately the case would be newsworthy and a bother for a long time. He's satisfied as it is."

"Are you satisfied?"

"No, but the incident doesn't seem to be damaging our business. So maybe I should stop thinking about it. Then there's that snake and that phone call to you. Someone wants to quiet me by attacking you. You who I hold most dear. I can't ignore the threat."

"I understand. Thank you. I had been in Henry's camp until that phone call. Now we know there is a crazy man watching us. Complying with his demand may make him go away, but we know he probably killed Scottie. It's hard to turn away. I understand why you feel so strongly about your investigation. I'll stop criticizing you. But be careful."

"Thank you. Let's leave this argument behind."

Charlie felt instant relief. Now he could focus on the proposal. He was excited and excused himself to go for a walk.

By late afternoon he felt calm enough to return to their room. He tried to act nonchalant as he recited for Kate a description of the restaurant where he had made a reservation.

"Café L'Europe. Great food. Attentive service. Romantic. Booked solid in season"

"I like the 'romantic' aspect," she responded.

The restaurant was only a few blocks from their hotel, so they walked hand in hand. The owner greeted them as if he were a regular. Since Charlie was not there often, he merely dismissed this effusive behavior as off-season behavior.

During the excellent meal of local specialties, crabmeat cocktail and grilled yellowtail snapper, complimented by a light California sauvignon blanc, Kate began to ask about Charlie's history in Palm Beach. As many conversations as they had had about each other's personal life, for some reason Palm Beach had been only a footnote.

"Why did your grandparents settle in Palm Beach?"

"As you may have guessed, they wanted to escape the Chicago winters. They came here rather than to the Gulf Coast of Florida because their friends were coming here from Chicago, New York, and Boston. Remember, Henry Flagler, a partner of Rockefeller's in Standard Oil, was a great promoter of this sandbar—to the rich, naturally—with its superb fishing, golf, tennis, and polo. The glamorous crowd was attracted by being among other rich people."

"I understand. So the restaurants, hotels, high-end shops, galleries, and large homes simply followed catering to the fancy tastes."

"Precisely." Charlie said. "And the Florida politicians were smart in keeping taxes on estates and personal wealth low. Of course, a couple of real estate busts happened along the way, but it is amazing how the rich survive those setbacks. At any rate, my father's parents built their house here in the late 1920's."

"Let's go see it."

"Tomorrow. It's all shuttered up now. I should have taken you there today. My fault. Anyways, when my father married Mom, they stayed at his parents' house. She liked everything about Palm Beach but her mother-in-law."

"Oh no," Kate reacted.

"My grandmother liked to run the show, and even though

she admired my mother's intelligence, energy, and good looks—beauty, I suppose—she felt that her son's allegiance should be to her first. In her mind, a daughter-in-law was to be seen, not heard."

"I don't see your mother liking that."

"You're right. She chafed under that notion, but acted the obedient daughter-in-law—if you can believe it—but fumed underneath. My father kept waiting for something to trigger a confrontation, but it never came. At least I never heard of any fisticuffs. Of course, poor Dad bore the brunt of this difficult relationship, but he was a natural diplomat and loved my mother very much.'

'At any rate, my grandmother died young, sixty-one, and my grandfather followed a few years later. Then the big decision was whether to tear down the big house and rebuild or leave it and let my mother redecorate away most traces of my grandmother. Fortunately for the architectural heritage of Palm Beach, my parents decided to let the house stand—so we preserved an original Marion Sims Wyeth house. They added the John Volk guesthouse in the fifties."

"I've read about them," Kate said. "Great architects. But what about you? When did you first remember being here?"

"When I was really young. I remember the ocean and the beach at what must have been the Bath and Tennis Club. Once I started going to school, we would come down right after Christmas for two weeks and for a week or so in March during Easter break. My dad golfed at the Everglades Club, and my mother shopped and played tennis. Our nanny or James took us to various activities and kept us out of trouble. My parents went out almost every night to dances at the club, cultural events, and charity balls at the hotels. I should add that the Bradshaws were wonderful in introducing my family to Palm Beach society.'

'I spent time with my contemporaries whose parents are friends of my parents. As I grew up and noticed girls, my friends and I would go to the beach—ostensibly to play catch with a Frisbee and swim—but really to size up the precious young ladies.'

'When I reached prep school and college age I would invite down a couple of classmates, and we would do essentially the same thing—check out the girls. Only now we were really cool—with our sunglasses and convertibles, cruising South Ocean Boulevard and Worth Avenue."

"Did you have a girlfriend then?"

"No. Not really. Just the usual two-to-three month romances in college which broke up either with big tears or indifference. I don't think I was much of a catch. I was too intense and intellectual. Not much fun. Mother pressured me to go to dances. I would never have gone to those deb parties if my mother had not insisted."

"Did you know Jamie and Scottie Bradshaw?"

"Of course. Scottie was too young, but I played sports and went to the same parties as Jamie."

"What was he like as a boy?"

"He was competitive in everything. I thought he went out of his way to impress his father."

"I wish I knew you then," Kate said smiling and looking down.

"No, I was boring and a bit shy. How did we get on this subject?"

Charlie fidgeted on his chair. Kate looked gorgeous tonight, and he was impatient to get to the big moment. The waiter had just served coffee and the restaurant's famous key lime pie. He didn't like to be disrupted at this moment.

"You are never boring, Charlie."

"Tell me, Kate, are you enjoying your visit here? That is, do you like the people, the ambiance, the look of Palm Beach? Do you feel comfortable?"

"Well, I have been here only two days. I do like the weather, the beautiful landscaping, the cleanliness, the high-end stores, and restaurants. I don't know many people, but I love you, and because this place is a part of you, I like it—especially if we have a plane."

He motioned to the waiter to clean the dishes and searched in his coat pocket to make sure the box was there. When they were alone, Charlie reached over to take Kate's hand. He looked up into her eyes. She leaned forward and focused on him.

"Kate, I've been a fool for too long. I love you. You are everything I could want in a woman. You challenge me, put up with me, and keep me sane when I get too wound up. I should have asked you months ago, but will you marry me?"

Kate was smiling as he talked. He sensed she knew what he was going to ask. Now she did not hesitate. "Yes, darling Charlie. I will marry you."

"I promise you I'll take care of you and love you for all our lives."

She laughed, "You don't have to convince me. I've already said yes."

"Right. You did. I'm nervous. I do have something."

Charlie fumbled around in his pocket and pulled out the pale blue box wrapped by a white ribbon. As he opened the box, he was struck how the diamond sparkled in the table's candlelight. Looking at the excitement in her face he knew the ring was a good choice.

"It's perfect," she said softly. "I never expected such a lovely ring. But all I ever wanted was you. I love you, too."

He leaned over and kissed her.

"Champagne?" Charlie suggested, his confidence returning.

Charlie put the ring on her finger. It fit. He was smiling more than he thought he could. Why had he been so nervous? Kate had made the event so easy for him.

Suddenly he heard some applause from the couple at the next table. They must have seen what was happening. The applause spread to the other diners. A few raised their wine glasses in tribute. Kate blushed at the attention, and Charlie felt both embarrassed and happy. The scene was an unexpected triumph.

They acknowledged their new acquaintances with a nod and salute of their wine glasses. The waiter brought a bottle of champagne. "Courtesy of the owner."

Charlie felt all was good in the world. Kate sat back alternately glancing at her ring and drinking the champagne. She appeared as excited as he had every seen her. "I can't wait to call my parents."

After the formality of the check, Charlie walked her out to the sidewalk and draped his arm around her shoulder. He was delighted every time he caught her looking down at the ring. The streetlights made it sparkle in the darkness of the night.

They sauntered up to South Ocean Boulevard to enjoy the sight of the rising full moon reflecting over the waves. The street and the beach were deserted. They walked along the sidewalk, condominium buildings to their right, and the road and beach to their left. Every so often a car would pass, but other than the waves crashing on the beach, there was no noise.

As they crossed Chilean Avenue, Charlie heard a car engine roaring behind them. He turned to see the car swerving at them. Charlie grabbed Kate and flung himself violently right. They fell onto the grass next to the sidewalk. The car barely missed them. It barreled down the street and out of sight.

Charlie rolled off Kate, "Are you hurt?"

"Charlie! We could have been killed."

Charlie felt his own bloodied palm and knees and wondered if his body block had injured Kate. His tan pants were filthy, ripped at the knees. Pain shot through his wrist. Kate's elegant pink dress looked crumpled and soiled, black and green stains in back. He helped her up, held her, and felt a tremor in her shoulders.

Charlie was incensed. His right shoulder and knees hurt and his right hand was swelling up. It had happened so fast he had not seen the driver or license plates. A black SUV? He was not sure. It was dark out, but he could see a deep tire mark on the grass between the curb and the sidewalk.

"It was intentional," he seethed. "Otherwise, he probably would have stopped to see if we were all right."

"But who knows we were here?" Kate asked, "The snake man again?"

Charlie wondered if someone had been following him everywhere or if he had mentioned to someone at the office—other than Kathy- where they were going. Of course, his mother knew. Had Kate said something to her friends?

"I don't know," Charlie answered. "It does seem intentional though."

"This is all weird, spooky," Kate said. "Let's get back to the hotel quickly."

She tried to step away from Charlie but, stumbled and cried out in pain. Charlie moved quickly to catch her so she would not fall.

"My left knee and ankle," she sobbed. "I can't walk."

"I'm taking you to the emergency room at Good Sam's. Damn it. This is serious. That bastard."

Charlie took his cellphone from his sport coat pocket and speed-dialed the local ambulance company. He then lowered Kate to the curb to take all weight off her foot. He also called the police in the hope that they could identify the black SUV.

The ambulance and the squad car arrived almost together. The policeman helped Charlie maneuver Kate into the ambulance and took some notes from Charlie's description of the incident.

He said he would put out an APB on the SUV.

"Maybe we'll get lucky," he said. "Call us later tonight after you take care of your lady friend. I'll need more information."

The doctor on duty at the hospital took an x-ray and gave Kate a painkiller. No bones were broken but that the ankle was severely contused. She should stay off it and continue pain medication as needed. He asked Charlie if he was injured also, but Charlie lied and said "no" - because he wanted to get Kate quickly back to the hotel bed where she could sleep. Besides he would rather see his own internist when he returned to Chicago.

In what seemed forever to Charlie but was actually an hour, they were back in their room at the hotel — Kate with crutches.

"If I had minded my own business regarding Scottie, this would not have happened," Charlie admitted.

"True, but clearly there is a killer out there."

"Still, as you have told me several times, that's the job of the police. Killer or not, why am I putting you at risk? Palm Beach isn't the safe haven I promised. We might as well be in Chicago."

"I agree, Charlie. Let's go back."

"You need sleep, but I can call the plane and it will be ready in ninety minutes. We could be home in four hours."

"Great. I'll sleep on the plane."

Kate winced as she adjusted her position on the bed. Charlie was at a loss at what he could do.

"What a day, sweetheart," she mused. "I get engaged and end up in a hospital. Thing's aren't as I imagined. I'm so tired."

As she drifted off in sleep, Charlie wondered how she was feeling, about his proposal and the attack.

At three-thirty in the morning they reached Chicago. His mind hadn't stopped running at top speed trying to figure out who was targeting them.

He had slept fitfully on the plane. He ached from the fall and his wrist was still swollen. Kate had slept the whole time and had asked to go back to her apartment, when they landed. Charlie sensed she was traumatized by the incident and wanted to withdraw from him and interactions with others, but Charlie convinced her to stay at his place for the night. He worried about her left alone. The assailant could still be following them.

When they reached his place, he tucked her in bed and she turned over and immediately fell asleep. For his part, Charlie could not sleep. He kept thinking about how he could protect Kate from further assaults—and himself.

When she finally woke up before noon, Charlie suggested that they move up to his mother's home for the next few days—at least until he could have a security guard to watch over Kate day and night.

"You don't think what happened was due to a drunk driver?" Kate asked.

"No. Too many coincidences."

Because of the snake episode, Charlie had called Bob Underwood from his office in Palm Beach the day before regarding potentially protecting Kate. Bob had recommended a body guard named Roman Spartek, who had done work for his law firm.

Charlie suggested that Bob set up an interview as soon as possible at Charlie's office in Chicago.

"I'll have to pack some fresh clothes and catch up on my mail," Kate said agreeing to stay in Lake Forest. "Please pick me up at my apartment at three."

"I hope you know that I did not intend to spend the first few days of our engagement at Mother's. It just can't be avoided. I think it's safer there."

"You're such a romantic. Should I wear my ring?"

"Never take it off. I'll call Mom about it after I get you home."

"Promise me you'll talk to the police again."

"I'll call Paul Victor tomorrow. Maybe he'll be more helpful after learning what happened last night."

Charlie called his mother and explained how they escaped serious injury from the car assault. Without being asked, she offered to take them in until adequate security could be hired. Although he fidgeted in his chair, he also broke the news about the engagement. He expected her reaction.

"Why didn't you tell me in advance?" she asked, miffed. "Were you afraid that I'd try to stop you? I knew this was coming. You're a grown man. I'm sure you know what you're doing. I'll tell the staff to get ready for you and Kate."

*Not exactly a ringing endorsement*, he thought. *But hopefully she'll love Kate as she gets to know her better. She obsessed with social position matters. She needs to know the person. The world has changed.*

Claire met them in the foyer when they arrived in late afternoon. Kate was still on crutches. Claire seemed to glance down at Kate's left hand, but said, "Kate, dear. Charlie didn't say you were hurt this badly. How do you maneuver on those crutches? May I get you something?"

"No. Thank you. These crutches aren't so bad once you get the hang of it. I'll be off them in a day or two. I just won't be running the Chicago Marathon this year," she joked.

Claire grimaced at Kate's joke.

"Charlie, you have to take better care of Kate. A fine fiancé you are."

"Oh, you know," Kate said excitedly.

"Charlie told me a couple of hours ago. Best wishes, dear! You must tell me all about Charlie's proposal. I hope he was well-mannered and considerate."

"He was indeed," Kate said casting a smile and a wink at Charlie.

"Let me see your ring."

Claire hugged them both and started talking wedding matters. Her focus on that event was so complete that Charlie had the impression that she had already forgotten about the danger they were facing.

All through dinner Claire persisted in discussing wedding plans, even though Charlie and Kate had only discussed the matter in general terms.

"Mother, about the wedding: We have been so busy we haven't given it much thought. We want to hold off on an announcement until we think through the arrangements. Sorry to spoil your fun."

"I'll try to keep quiet," she responded with a frown.

Eventually Claire asked about Palm Beach and even then seemed more interested in news about the Bradshaws than the attempt on their lives.

At last she said, "So you went to Palm Beach to be safe and you were nearly killed. I am terribly concerned for you. It's just a topic I don't like to discuss. Your father would have known what to do. I'm at a loss. You must get the police to help. And, son, your fiancé needs protection. Hire some people."

"I'm working on it," Charlie promised. "You see why it's important that Kate be here. She can't be on her own."

"Of course. James can be helpful and he knows all the policemen in Lake Forest. But you need more than that. You need your own personal security. After young Scottie Bradshaw, this town cannot endure any more excitement. Sally Kitridge said that the last murder in this town was forty years ago—a crime of passion when an elderly husband happened upon his young wife in *flagrante delicto* with a tennis pro. The husband went back downstairs and found a shotgun and finished off both his wife and her lover. In the end, the town pressured the judge to go easy on the old guy."

"Wow!" Charlie laughed. "That story probably nipped in the bud several other such liaisons for fear of a similar reprisal."

"Afterwards the city fathers were especially concerned that our town would garner an unsavory reputation because of the shooting, but nothing came of it. Of course, a few unflattering jokes form our neighbors in Winnetka and Kenilworth surfaced."

"They were probably jealous of the notoriety," Charlie joked. "Maybe things aren't' as dull in Lake Forest as is thought."

Kate did not look as amused as the others. She struck a more serious tone, "What are people saying about Scottie's death?"

"They want to know the truth," Claire told her. "Personally, I think most people are pulling for a murder. It's juicier than an accident and gives them something to talk about, even at the risk of Lake Forest's reputation. Please don't tell Dottie I said that. She would not like to think that anyone is having fun over her son's demise."

Claire folded her napkin and set it beside her plate. She glanced over at James, who was standing by the door to the kitchen. Dinner was over.

"Well, if you don't mind, I am leaving you two lovebirds as I have to go to bed. It's no fun getting old."

After Claire left the room, Kate winked at Charlie and said, "Your mother is a pistol. I never know where she is going on a topic."

"She says what's on her mind. She may not be politically correct but her heart's in the right place."

After Claire had left and James had cleared the table, Kate asked, "Now that we are engaged, do you think your mother would be offended if we slept in the same room?"

Charlie started to laugh.

"We might not get the Pope's blessing or Mother's blessing overtly, but she'll be fine."

## CHAPTER SIXTEEN

Charlie looked across his desk at Roman Spartek and was impressed with the man's imposing size, obvious strength, and his decorum in wearing a suit to the interview. His bulk nearly filled the chair on which he sat erect and alert. Charlie thought mischievously that the Chicago Bears could use him on their offensive line or that the U.S. Olympic team had a sure winner in Roman on it's Greco-Roman wrestling squad. Apt name, Roman.

"What's your nationality?" Charlie had asked.

"Bulgarian."

"I see. What's your experience in security? Bob Underwood recommended you but didn't describe your background."

"I serve in the Bulgarian army, then emigrate to Cleveland—a patrolman there, then come to Chicago and start my own company."

"Very enterprising. What kind of work do you usually do?"

"Surveillance and protection. Follow someone and report back. Sometimes young person, sometimes old person. Stay in the shadows."

"Do the people know you are following them?"

"No. Never. I am very careful. I keep a distance but never lose a person."

"I want you to protect my fiancé."

Charlie explained what had happened to Kate so far and said he feared another attack. Roman appeared interested and leaned forward. "Twenty-four seven?"

"Most nights she'll be safe in my apartment or at my mother's house in Lake Forest. We might not need you then, depending on other factors. Do you have time limitations?"

"I make it work."

"This assignment may be dangerous," Charlie warned, checking for any body language suggesting fear or, alternatively, nonchalance.

"I am licensed," Roman declared, opening his suit jacket to display a Glock in a shoulder holster.

"All right. I see you are prepared. Can you start tonight?"

Charlie felt that Roman could do the job and that his demeanor and manners would make him acceptable to Kate and Claire.

"Right, boss."

After Roman left, Charlie felt relieved to have settled that matter. Hoping to allay Kate's fears, he called her at his mother's house to tell her about the imposing Roman Spartek.

"I'll be moving in today and remaining here day and night for the next week. I arranged for James to drive down to my apartment to pick up some clothes."

"How's your ankle?"

"I'm limping, but it can take some weight."

"I'll be up there after work."

That night Charlie and Kate sat down with Roman to explain their schedules and their needs. Roman nodded understanding. "Now is too risky to go to the city. You need to keep low profile."

Charlie was surprised. He was only thinking about Kate's safety while Roman was also thinking about his.

"I agree in principle," Charlie said. "But I need to be in the office. My clients are nervous with these volatile securities markets. Anyways, I'm more concerned with Kate than myself."

"And I need to be back at work as soon as I can walk," Kate added.

"No good," Roman stressed. "Usual routine. I need to protect. You make it easy for the bad guy."

"Look. You drive Kate to work when she feels better. Watch over her and drive her back home at nights. I'll go to work but be careful leaving the office. I'll be back here at night. However, knowing both of us, we'll get tired of being here in a few days. Then we'll have to strategize what we do downtown."

"Not the best plan," Roman warned. "But you the boss."

Charlie drove very early each morning to his office, and after three days, Roman drove a partially healed Kate in an old Toyota that Claire had kept in the big garage. She stayed in the office doing design work at her desk easel, ordering in deli food, and lying to her fellow workers about how she hurt her ankle.

This arrangement worked fine as they passed a peaceful

week. Charlie, however, knew hiding out the way they were was no long-term solution. He was more determined than ever to find out more about Scottie's murder and the thug trying to kill him and Kate.

At the end of the week Bob Underwood called to inquire how Roman was working out. "Are you going to keep him?"

"Yes. His blunt personality is hard to take. But I'd rather he be like that than be retiring or unassertive. Where did you find him?"

"A couple of my clients have used him. In fact, Jamie Bradshaw said Roman helped him in one of his cases."

"That's good enough for me. Jamie expects perfection."

One call that Charlie wanted was from Paul Victor. Charlie had called him from his plane and then after he and Kate had moved into Claire's house, but the investigator had not been in. Charlie hoped that the news about the attempted hit and run in Palm Beach would convince Paul to believe that a real threat existed and that Scottie Bradshaw's death could not have been an accident. Paul finally returned the call four days later,

"Mr. Bailey, I appreciate your concern. These incidents may or may not be connected to Mr. Bradshaw's death. They are curious but don't prove anything. No eyewitness to Mr. Bradshaw's death has come forward and there is no evidence of a struggle. In short, at this point we cannot characterize his death a homicide. There will be a public announcement momentarily. If you feel that your life or Miss Milano's life is in danger, you should notify your local police department.

Charlie frowned at the phone and felt blood rushing to his face. "But what about the bruises?"

"Right. Inconclusive." Paul said dismissively. "The deceased may have fallen and there are reports he was in a fight at the party. The bruises may be explained several ways. Anyhow, these issues are our concern—not yours. Now the case is closed. I have a meeting to go to now. Good day."

Charlie seethed at Paul's lack of interest. How could they be so stupid? Incredible! He could only conclude that he was on his own.

Once he had calmed down he considered what should be his next step. He reached for his phone. Charlie felt that he had not been direct enough with Keller before and that Keller might have an idea of who had reason to dislike Scottie.

"Mr. Keller, I need to follow up on a few questions regarding Scottie Bradshaw—for estate purposes," Charlie began.

"Go ahead, shoot."

"We want to make sure that we provide the lawyers with a complete list of Scottie's assets. Did he have a personal brokerage account at Collins, Lang?"

"Of course. But you have to talk to our lawyers if you want to look at it."

"Naturally. We'll do that. Now did he directly invest or co-invest with any of his clients in limited partnerships, non-liquid investments like real estate or private companies, or other types of non-regulated securities?"

"Not that I know of."

"Fine. When we talked last week, you said that he recommended a few investments that soured significantly. Were any of those clients sufficiently angered that they threatened to sue Scottie or this firm or even do bodily harm?"

"What does that have to do with his assets?" Keller raised a doubt.

Charlie had anticipated Keller's pushback. He did not hesitate to make a case: "Well, we need to know if there are potential claims or liens on the estate."

"There have been some angry clients, but I can't release their names. It would be unethical. Maybe you can talk to our lawyers on that as well."

Charlie leaned back in his chair. He knew he was on thin ice asking about clients but he had to try to get names. From Keller's unwelcoming response he surmised that this line of questioning was futile. Keller was familiar with the corporate script. There would be no lifting of the veil of privacy at Collins, Lang.

Charlie sighed inwardly and tapped a pen as he asked a few perfunctory questions while he considered whether there was another angle of approach to learn who might have had a motive to harm Scottie. At a minimum he wanted to match the names of Scottie's clients with the attendees at the party. After a few minutes he gave up with Keller. He had struck out.

Even if he failed to identify the clients at the party, Charlie understood that the list was his best source of information leading up to the murder. Someone may have noticed something unusual at the party or could identify the mysterious band manager poseur. Of course, Charlie assumed that the police had questioned the attendees earlier and, from Paul Victor's comments, had not gleaned sufficient information to think there had been a murder. Still Charlie recognized several individuals who had been there and decided to call four or five of them to see if could elicit anything useful.

Unfortunately most of his conversations went the wrong way. Everyone expressed sympathy for the Bradshaws. A couple of them said that they wish that they had accompanied Scottie to the men's locker room to prevent him from slipping and drowning. Two confirmed that Scottie looked like he had too much to drink. No one remembered a band manager.

Charlie felt that most of the individuals he talked to were guarded in their responses and signaled that they did not want to be pulled into any inquiry about the incident—with one exception: Eric Mancine. He was Charlie's best hope—especially after getting nothing from Keller. Charlie knew that Eric like to talk. He wanted to be considered an expert on everything—more curious and intelligent than anyone in the room. He challenged all points of view and offered his opinions with absolute self-assurance. He was a cocky braggart. Still in spite of his arrogance, Charlie thought Eric was observant so he called him at his office, "Eric, I heard you were at the eventful party on that Saturday. What happened?"

"Too bad you weren't there. Scottie was in rare form. Soused as usual. Slobbering over the cute girls. Falling on the dance floor.

Trying to clobber Billy Tansey. Very amusing if you ask me. I laughed a lot watching him."

"Was there anyone in particular egging him on?"

"No. He was a fool by himself."

"Did anyone get angry at him for his performance?"

"No. I would have noticed. Of course, Billie Tansey was pissed off that Scottie was messing with his sister. Stupid fight. Scottie was a joke when he was drunk. When wasn't he drunk?"

"Were you a client of Scottie's?"

"Are you kidding? I wouldn't let Scottie near my dough. I know ten times as much about markets as he does—or did."

"What happened to him? I assume he fell into the Roman bath."

"Sure. You found him. He was drunk enough to fall. But if you ask me someone pushed him and held him under. He has lots of enemies."

"Really, who?" Charlie asked picking up his pen.

"You name it. People say he lost a lot of client money at work and his father had to bail him out. He cheated on his wife— led to his divorce. He was always trying to get into the pants of anybody wearing a skirt."

"But who?"

"I best not say. Don't want to compromise anyone. But I'm never wrong. Ask around. Gotta run. Bad luck you found the body. Someone might think you did it."

Eric laughed and then added, "Just kidding, sport."

Charlie endured the conversation because he expected as

much from Eric. He was an insufferable bag of wind. Still he confirmed the earlier account of Scottie's actions. What he did not do was give Charlie any new names to consider. Charlie was disappointed and ground his teeth.

"Damn it. This business is serious and I've got nothing," he said to no one. "Kate is terrified—as well as she should be—and I can't make progress. This is hard. Get moving, Bailey."

| § |

# CHAPTER SEVENTEEN

Kate watched Claire fold her napkin and put it beside her dessert plate. She understood that Claire was signaling that the meal was over and that it was time to leave the dining room. This ritual was new to Kate. She was not familiar with Charlie's mother's unspoken commands. She and Charlie had spent the work week, and now Saturday, in Lake Forest. Living in Claire's world amounted to being pampered and safe—but also feeling like an outsider. Tonight's dinner was a good example. Although she and Charlie were dressed informally, the dinner itself was formal—four courses, three different wines, candles, starched linen, Baccarat goblets, antique silver flatware, and Chinese export china—all orchestrated by James. Onion soup, Caesar salad, veal medallions, and crème brûlée constituted a meal more in common to a fancy restaurant than home. As always Claire wore lovely and tasteful jewelry—a pearl necklace, gold bracelet, and Cartier watch.

She mentioned to Kate as they sat down, "I don't expect my children and their friends to dress like me at dinner but I love dressing up and presenting a gracious table. Dinner gives me a chance to show off and use my favorite table settings. Why have them otherwise? I also think conversation is better over excellent food and wine. This is who I am."

Kate agreed that tonight's discussion had been enjoyable — about the economy, politics, and travel. No one had mentioned the recent frightening incidents. Nevertheless, these dinners made Kate feel insecure. The dining room table was big enough for twelve. She didn't know where to sit until Claire told her. James acted like a footman, always standing near the wall and serving from the sideboard. She hoped that Charlie would not expect this grandeur and spectacle from her after they were married. At least he had not shown any interest in such a display with her so far. But these evenings threw her off. She felt she needed to keep up with Claire and Charlie — but that would be impossible. She found herself watching her words, being a little tongue-tied, and feeling ignorant about some of the topics. She worried that she would never be comfortable in their world.

They retired into the large drawing room with its French and English antique furniture, amply stuffed sofas and huge Aubusson rug. The grandfather clock in the hallway chimed nine times and Claire immediately declared that she was tired.

"I'm excusing James for the evening. Please set the alarm when you and Kate go up. What about the Bulgarian person?"

"I told him to go into the town to have dinner, introduce himself and his mission to the Lake Forest police — including his carrying a gun — and return at eleven."

Claire nodded, kissed them, wished them both goodnight, and left to go upstairs.

Then with the house settled down, Charlie spread out some papers and his laptop on a writing table in the drawing room to catch up on some work that has been forwarded to him. Kate decided to leave him alone and moved on into the adjourning library. She needed to escape and put down her guard. She picked a book from the shelves and sank into one of the oversized chairs by the fireplace. She had read George Eliot's *Middlemarch* before, but never from a book clad in leather like this edition. It had a wonderful feel of heft and permanence with its old-fashioned binding and a slight smell of saddle soap. *Maybe I could grow to like this world.*

A half-hour into her reading she heard the crackling of tires on the long gravel driveway outside the house. She shuddered at the noise. The car sounded as if it was driving slowly. Then it stopped. It must be Roman returning early. Yet she imagined a cold hand on her shoulder. Kate said to herself, *"Everything's alright. Settle down."*

She read on, struggling to concentrate. Nerves. In her anxious state she had lost her sense of time. Nevertheless she could hear fine, and she recognized Charlie's voice talking to someone in the next room. He sounded agitated, although she could not understand his words. Her curiosity compelled her to leave her comfortable chair and walk toward the voices. What Kate saw quickly awaken her from her sluggishness and she stood frozen on the spot. A large, bulky, dark-haired man twenty feet from Charlie held a gun pointed at her fiancé. He was saying something she could not understand and motioning the gun at Charlie and then toward the French doors leading out to the terrace. One of the doors was ajar. She saw no one else in the room. She took a slow step back, her head pounding.

Kate scanned the library, bewildered, scared, and frantic to do something. Where had the man come from? She had not heard the doorbell. Maybe he came from the terrace through that door. Where was something - some tool or heavy object—to help Charlie? Then she remembered the breakfront on the wall in the study off the library. Of course. This was a display case housing four master-crafted shotguns. A week ago Charlie had pointed out with pride his dad's two Purdey side-by-sides, a Winchester over-and-under, and a Mossberg pump. Before dinner he had taken Kate and Roman to the case. "Roman, you appreciate shotguns no doubt."

Growing up on a farm Kate fired shotguns before—not these elite, specimen types but basic models. She hoped that the distinctions were minor. She rushed to the case, hoping that it was not locked. Miraculously, it was not, and she quietly took down one of the Purdeys. She opened the breech and saw empty chambers, as she expected. Hurriedly she opened the drawers underneath the glass case, and in the bottom drawer in the back she found a box of shells. With her heart pumping hard and her hands shaking, Kate loaded the gun. It locked easily as if it had been oiled yesterday.

Gripping it close, she peered around the door into the

drawing room and onto the lit terrace. Then on the dimly lit patio beyond the room she saw Charlie and the gunman. To avoid being noticed in the bright room, she edged along the left wall, past the fireplace, to the wall with the French doors. Her ankle still hurt her but she gritted her teeth.

"... a meddler," the gunman was saying. "Everyone thought it was a drowning accident. I was home free—until you started asking questions. We figured you would find nothing, but then we thought what if he gets lucky? First, we tried to scare you off. But you left us no choice. I just missed you in Florida, but I won't now."

"Wait!" Charlie said. "If you shoot me, matters will be much worse. You have choices. You could walk away. I don't know who you are and won't say anything to anyone. And the police won't listen to me anyway. They think I am crazy."

Terrified, in pain and furious Kate inched closer to the door behind the gunman.

"Turn around, Bailey, and kneel. It'll be easier on you if you don't watch. Now."

"This is crazy," said Charlie. "My mother's employees live on the property. When they hear a gunshot, they won't let you get away."

"Shut up."

"Who put you up to this?"

Kate thought that Charlie had noticed her over the gunman's shoulder. She raised the shotgun. He slowly turned to kneel and moved to the left. She understood that he was positioning himself out of her line of fire. Encouraged, she stepped out onto the threshold. As the gunman raised his gun, she checked the safety. From about fifteen feet she emptied both chambers in the direction of the gunman. Charlie leapt away and hurled himself towards the patio furniture.

The force of the blasts blew the gunman off his feet. Since he had turned around towards her at the last second, he caught numerous pellets in his chest and face and flew back and down. His gun flew away, discharged once in the air, and skidded across the bluestone terrace. Kate went over to Charlie, dropped the shotgun, and picked up the handgun.

"Oh, God. Are you alright?" She burst into tears as he pulled her to him, hugging her legs.

Kate saw that Charlie was looking past her at the ground. Was the gunman alive? She turned and saw the dark mass inert, blood splattered all over the terrace. The intruder was not moving.

"It's over," he said. "You saved my life."

Charlie was slowly getting to his feet. He was bleeding from a nasty scrape on his face.

"I think you killed him."

"I didn't mean to. I had to shoot."

She started to sob and shake. The horror was overwhelming. She had killed a man. Blown away. Oh, God. Suddenly she broke away, "Maybe he isn't dead. What if he gets up?"

"Calm down, Kate. It's over. Let's go sit down."

He took the handgun from her.

"You were brave and resolute when you had to be. I'm so proud. Saved my life." He led her inside to a chair and put the gun on the rug.

All the extra outside spotlights suddenly came on and James ran out dressed in a robe. He saw the man and the blood and winced. "I'll call the police. I don't recognize that man. Let me get something for you. You are bleeding, Charlie. Can I bring you something, Miss Milano?"

"Please check on Mother. Tell her that there was an intruder and Kate and I are fine."

"Yes, sir."

"Kate watched James leave and noticed that she felt cold despite the summer's night warm temperature. She continued crying.

"Charlie, hold me again."

The next few hours were a blur to Kate. The local police came including the deputy chief and Paul Victor. They took statements. They roped off the terrace and the drawing room, took pictures, tagged the guns and pellets, and collected blood samples.

Roman came back at eleven and apologized for not being there when he was needed. He stood in the background quiet and embarrassed. At midnight just when Kate felt that she had to go to bed more police arrived. The endless stream of officials questioning her added to her near hysteria. They were doing their jobs, but Kate wanted to be alone with Charlie.

She was astonished by Charlie's calm, answering the same questions multiple times. After another round of questions, she became frustrated, "Stop. Let him attend to his lacerated face. Charlie do you need to go to the hospital?"

"I'm okay."

He came over to her to commiserate, console, and compliment her on her brave actions, but he was called away by yet another police officer.

James had recommended that Claire stay in her room until the police arrived in case there was further danger. When he gave her the all-clear, she rushed down to the drawing room wearing a silk robe, and her hair was uncharacteristically a mess.

"I'm shocked. Appalled. How are you both? Kate, you are as white as a sheet and soaking wet. Charlie, you are cut and bloody. James is coming with first aid."

"Mother, the police said they want to ask you some questions. Are you up to it? Or should I tell them to come back tomorrow?"

"Heavens, no. We must get this over with. They are ruining my house. They have no manners. Where is this awful person?"

"On the terrace. Don't go there. It's a gruesome site."

"We'll see." She marched outside and in five seconds returned. "Hideous man. Got what he deserved."

Calmly she turned to James, "Please tell these policemen to remove the body. And clean up the mess. That is their job after all."

For the first time since dinner Kate saw Charlie smiling. He must have been enjoying his mother's take-charge personality.

"What will my friends say? They probably heard the sirens. Charlie, did you shoot the man with your daddy's Purdey?"

"No. Kate did. The man was going to shoot me."

"Kate?" Claire paused, then smiled.

"Hooray for you. Who needs men anyway? The ladies can take care of things. Charlie, you are a lucky man."

"You are dead right, mother."

"Bad pun, son. Now be a gentleman and get Kate something powerful to drink. She looks like she needs it. Scotch? Kate, did I tell you that I like strong women?"

"Strong?" Kate thought. "I killed a person. I'm falling apart."

As she continued to wait, images appeared to her: the man with the gun, her lover on one knee about to be executed, and blood everywhere. She also thought about the Baileys. Her soon-to-be husband dealt with events coolly, efficiently, rationally, and occasionally with compassion. Her perspective mother-in-law was opinionated, and worried about what her friends would say. How could these distinct individuals be related? How would Kate fit in? Would Claire's friends accept Kate into their world? She shot someone. She was a killer.

After everyone but one police guard and apologetic Roman left, Charlie came over to Kate to take her up to bed.

"You are a bit unsteady, aren't you? Well, there is a bright side to all of this—no more snakes and wild cars," Charlie offered lamely.

"I feel sick. I don't know if I'll ever forget this day. Is it over?" Kate muttered weakly. "I heard part of the conversation before I shot. He said 'we'."

# CHAPTER EIGHTEEN

The report of a homicide at the Bailey house had compelled Paul Victor to reevaluate his view of Charlie's claims. As someone who was trained to accept as evidence only cold facts and sworn statements, wild stories about snakes and a car out of control late at night meant little. However, a dead body and a loaded handgun on Claire Bailey's bluestone terrace gave credence to Bailey's and Milano's accounts. At the crime scene Paul spent an hour with the crime team reconstructing the arrival of the gunman, the confrontation with Charlie, and the shooting by Kate. During the questioning, they were believable and lucid.

Only once did he break into the questioning by the deputy chief.

"Why do you think this man is tied to Bradshaw?"

"As I told the chief earlier, he mentioned the drowning specifically," Charlie said. "He called me a meddler and said he tried to scare us off—including recently in Florida. It all ties together."

Paul didn't comment but agreed inwardly. Still he wanted more confirmation. The Bradshaw case was very important to him. Four months before he had been accepted into the Major

Crimes Task Force as an investigator. Bradshaw was his first high-profile case. He desperately wanted to be right about it.

Although solving a homicide would be more satisfying for his ego and career, Paul believed the weight of evidence in Bradshaw had pointed to an accident. Now with this new death seemingly connected to the Bradshaw case, he was happy that he had kept some doubts despite being told otherwise by his colleagues.

He recalled his recent conversation with Commander Mayo, his senior officer, "I can't prove anything, but the neck bruises are severe enough for a crime to have been committed. Let's keep open the possibility of a murder for the time being and let me keep working on."

"No. The case is closed," Mayo insisted. "The murder evidence is weak and, besides, higher-ups want us to stop looking. Do as I order."

"Huh?"

"The Bradshaws know the Governor. They are probably irritated that the death is still news."

But this shooting was new evidence which Paul could not deny. The next morning he received a lot of information on the gunman. Based on his fingerprints the crime team identified the dead man as Joseph Vecchia.

Vecchia had served twelve years in a federal prison for various counts of armed robbery, assault, and conspiracy. His parole officer verified his address in Queens, New York City. The handgun was unregistered. This type of information was sufficient to resolve any possible culpability of Kate and Charlie in the shooting. Vecchia had come to shoot Charlie.

In his eight years as a cop Paul had never dealt with anyone like this gunman. He had been assigned to the Lake Forest Public Safety Department as a patrolman after graduation from the Police Academy. In this quiet wealthy town there were no gangs, no drug dealers, no prostitution, and no violent crimes to speak of. Lake Forest had a homogeneous, well-educated, predominately white population. Its crime profile consisted principally of speeding, drunk driving, and burglary. The police were respected and supported strongly by the residents.

Paul found the work often dull and routine. His fellow officers, the town's administrators, and the citizens were friendly and cooperative. Fortunately the police department offered many opportunities to take additional training and acquire new skills, adding to his credentials for a higher rank. His new job in Major Crimes was the culmination of years of preparation and dreams.

Sitting in his cubicle in his Waukegan office, he was excited about the turn of events. He was now the chief investigator of a murder case involving the son of a celebrated Chicago family and a hired gunman. He was convinced that Vecchia must have been hired by someone to stop Charlie Bailey from probing into Bradshaw's murder. A person like Vecchia does not just show up at an elderly widow's house in Lake Forest to try to kill her houseguests. There is a second conspirator in this case. Charlie's investigation had spooked someone. Plus Kate Milano's comment that she heard Vecchia say "we" in reference to his planning of Bailey's death. That partner may have killed Scottie himself or may have hired Vecchia to do the hit job. On that point Charlie had said that Vecchia had suggested that he had drowned Bradshaw.

As he thought, Paul doodled a diagram where Mr. X points to Vecchia, who then points to Scottie Bradshaw. Then he added another line from Vecchia to Charlie and a loop running from Charlie to Scottie. Then he wrote down Mayo and Henry Bradshaw to the side. He added a question mark next to Henry. Vecchia is the connection. The trouble is Vecchia is dead. Finding Mr. X will be hard.

When Commander Mayo arrived at the office that afternoon, Paul was waiting for him.

"We can't drop this case. There are leads and Bailey is the key. The person behind the killing had to be aware of Bailey questioning acquaintances of Bradshaw to know that. He must be in Bailey's circle of social or business contacts. As much as I hate to admit it, Bailey has done us a favor."

"Are you suggesting we use him?" Mayo asked.

"Yes. Look, after what happened Saturday night, Bailey's not going to stop. He knows that if Mr. X hired Vecchia to silence him, he could hire another hit man. Bailey might make himself as bait."

"Paul, you know I hate amateurs. Besides, our duty is to protect to the public—not put them in harm's way. Bailey could get hurt."

"He almost did already. We could offer him protection—although he obviously doesn't trust us. I learned he hired a security guard. He is named Roman Spartek. I talked to him at the house Saturday night. He was out getting dinner when incident took place."

"A lot of good he was."

"Yeah, poor timing," Paul agreed.

Paul looked across the commander's meticulously ordered desk at a small, lean man wearing a uniform with pressed creases showing in a shirt. The commander had stopped talking and was thinking. Paul admired this boss who had succeeded in a difficult job and guessed he was weighing the potential risk of employing a civilian in a dangerous case. Despite Paul's limited experience with him, he felt that Mayo was decisive and fearless.

"Okay. I'll make an exception here. Use who you like and keep investigating. The crime is murder involving white-collar types. You're new to this type of case, Paul. You came highly recommended so I'm going to take a chance with you. If anything— I mean anything—doesn't make sense to you, come back to me immediately. Understood?"

"Yes, sir," Paul answered, trying to hide his nervousness from his supervisor.

"Sometimes an informed person like Bailey can be an asset," Mayo added. "He is in the same industry and traveled in the same circles as Bradshaw. Whatever he learned from his personal questioning may be useful to us. Offer some sort of collaboration. However, it's your ass if Bailey gets hurt. Make sure he understands the risks."

Later that day Paul Victor felt more confident. He learned

that his contact at the FBI had discovered that $25,000 has been wired into Joseph Vecchia's checking account in New York from a shell corporation in the Cayman Islands a day after Scottie Bradshaw's death. This payment augmented a $5000 dollar transfer from the same source three weeks earlier. While the FBI could not pierce the corporate shell to its real owner due to Cayman bank secrecy laws, the deposit supported the evidence that Joseph Vecchia had something to do with the Bradshaw murder and that the person behind the money probably possessed a sophisticated knowledge of offshore banking arrangements. He was quick to report this news to Commander Mayo.

"Good going, Paul. Keep following the money. Don't take no for an answer. Bailey may be able to help you. He's a seasoned money guy. When do you see him next?"

"At five in his office."

"I think I'll join you."

*Fantastic. The commander is buying in. I'm on a roll.*

\* \* \* \*

The receptionist escorted Paul and the commander to Charlie's office where they found a hostile Charlie.

"Sit there, if you like," Charlie said pointing to the sofa but not getting up from his desk to shake hands. "If you had paid any attention to what I told you since the murder, my fiancée and I might not have been almost killed. And Kate would not have had to shoot a man—an act that may traumatize her for the rest of her life. Are you still going to diddle around or are you going to get serious?"

"Calm down, Mr. Bailey," Paul said gesturing with both palms pointed towards the floor. "Until recently we had little to go on, but now we are on the same page with you. I think you can be very helpful to the investigation. I hope you will work with us."

"Frankly, I have little confidence in you. What are your credentials anyways? Is this your first murder case?"

"Yes, but I have the whole Major Crimes Task Force behind me."

"As I feared, a rookie." He snorted.

"Our unit deals with scores of high profile crimes in Lake County each year and can call on all the local public safety departments in the county as well."

"One has to be highly recognized to be tapped for my unit," Mayo added. "Believe me, we'll solve this case."

"Well, you've got me," Paul said. "We can work together or not. Either way, I'm going to find Mr. Bradshaw's murderer. Do you want me to tell you about Joseph Vecchia or should I leave?"

Charlie frowned and tapped a green fountain pen on his desk saying nothing. Paul decided to wait him out.

After a short time Charlie leaned forward looking straight at both men and said,

"I'll probably regret this, but I'll try to trust you despite our history. What about Vecchia?"

"He's the killer."

Paul described Vecchia's background and the payments the killer had received. Charlie was pleased to learn this. He had asked Roman to gather similar information, but Roman had not come back yet.

"Obviously, Mr. Bailey, Vecchia did not act alone. We need to find out who financed him."

"Considering the money transfer through the Caymans," Charlie offered. "I think it will be impossible to identify the accomplice."

"Do you have any knowledge of Vecchia?" Mayo asked.

"No. But I suspect he was at the club's party that night. I talked to staff, members, and guests. He may have been the heavy set, mysterious man who passed himself off as the band manager. A staff member told me that he had talked to Scottie during the evening. Later a band member confirmed that they had no manager."

"I wish you had told me about this man earlier."

"With all due respect, you weren't listening."

"Well, I am now," Paul said sincerely. "I would like to hear everything you have unearthed since the murder—whom you talked too, what they said, and any evidence you have gathered."

"Only if you promise to provide some protection for Kate and are truthful in working with me," Charlie said describing his terms.

He paused and waited for answers. Paul looked at his boss, who nodded.

"I'll make sure you know what I know," Paul agreed. "The protection will involve some budget juggling, but we'll try our best."

Charlie reasoned that that was about all he could expect from the police. He thought he could go ahead and test out his theory and course of action.

"In my opinion, the person who hired Vecchia wanted Scottie dead because of bad investments and terrible advice. Revenge. Get even. You need to get his client list from his firm. Their names, activity, and asset sizes will reveal a lot. I tried but was turned down."

Paul took out a notebook and wrote something down.

"I welcome your assistance in those financial matters. Money often provides a motive, but we can't rule out other reasons."

Paul and Commander Mayo stood, and Charlie shook their hands. He wasn't sure if he trusted them but there was no turning back. The police had ready access to all sorts of information that he could not access. He would have to test their assurances soon.

He wished that Vecchia had survived. Kate might have felt better wounding rather than killing him and we would have had a chance to find out what Vecchia and Scottie had talked about at the party. Vecchia might even have confessed who had hired him. Why were he and Kate targeted? Charlie thought that he had uncovered very little in his investigation. How was he a threat? He was missing something. If he continued, would there be another thug in his life?

# CHAPTER NINETEEN

After Paul Victor and the commander left, Charlie remained at his desk to review what had happened and where to go next. He shut his door to signal to his staff to stay away. In his mind the death of Joseph Vecchia had opened another avenue. Vecchia had not acted alone. The money transfer was an interesting angle. He probably should not have been so negative with the police about tracing the money trail back through the Caymans. Offshore bank havens thrive precisely because they obfuscate the flow of money. Individuals seeking obscurity or privacy establish corporate shells or trusts in these jurisdictions, with local lawyers paid to serve as officers and trustees to ask no questions, and not respond to inquiries. An individual lawyer could be an officer of hundreds of corporations in name only. He performed no duties except to file legal documents and maintain the barest of banking records. Public officials in these havens wrote laws to support this structure so no one had any risk or liability.

If Paul isn't familiar with this situation, the FBI certainly is. They will have to be part of the effort to trace the money. They probably already are. Despite the well-known effectiveness of these offshore structures even those paid to be careful can make mistakes. There was a chance—albeit small- that an FBI investigation might uncover some useful information.

The personal security of Kate and himself was a real concern. Someone hired Joseph Vecchia and that same person could hire another killer. Charlie understood there was no turning back. All the more urgency to continue to dig for clues.

On the other hand, he knew that Kate and his mother would be livid that he agreed to work with the police. What could he do? There was no turning back. He needed to communicate the current situation delicately.

Initially he had focused on exposing Scottie's murderer at the party, but now he needed to identify an individual with a motive, the financial means, the savvy and experience to use foreign bank accounts, and the unsavory contacts to hire Vecchia. The obvious place to look was Scottie's business relationships. Many of those certainly had good reason to see him harmed.

The phone rang and Charlie picked it up when he saw that Bob Underwood was calling. "Are you, Kate, and your mother okay? The news of the shooting is all over the media."

"I'm fine, but Kate and Mom are still shell-shocked."

"This incident ties back to the Bradshaw incident. Right?"

"Yes. Same guy," Charlie acknowledged.

"Charlie, I told you not to pursue the matter."

"I know. I should have left well enough alone. I let my emotions and ego get the best of me. But then the Bradshaws did learn who killed their son. That's the one positive here."

"So it's done?" Bob asked quizzically.

"No. The man was a hired gun."

"Charlie, listen to me this time. Remove yourself from this situation. Next time you might not be so lucky."

"I hear you. But the man behind the murder may not let me. At least, the police are actively looking for him now."

Charlie hung up feeling admonished but understanding he could not rewrite history. He looked at his watch and guessed that Kate was finished with work and back at her apartment. His mother had offered that Kate should continue to stay at her house. Kate had clearly become much more acceptable to her after she had saved Charlie's life. She even praised her to Charlie the morning after the shooting. "Kate's quite handy and fearless." Claire had never said the like before.

Kate declined Claire's offer. She confessed to Charlie, "I need to be away from what happened there and I need to be alone. I love you, but I need to process what happened. Please understand."

Charlie did not want to invade her space now but needed to assure her that he would do anything to help her. But before calling her he had dialed up Roman.

"Where are you and how is Kate doing?"

"She's depressed. I'm in her lobby now, Boss. I was near her all day. She wanted to go work. Said it would take her mind off what happened. I saw nobody who looked suspicious."

"Okay. Stay alert tonight. Sleep tomorrow when she is safe at work."

Then he called Kate's number, but she did not pick up. So he left a message wishing her well.

Charlie pulled out a yellow legal pad from his desk to make a list of theories he should consider. He began with the several failures in Scottie's business dealings brought up by Steve Keller. He started with the gold fraud and the technology stock bubble episodes because so many other brokers had lost money for their clients in those mishaps. So what was unique about Scottie's involvement? Yes, he should have been smarter, but the same could be said about hundreds of other brokers and portfolio managers in these cases. Scottie's clients would be angry, but they would have blamed the fraud perpetrators and the financial markets at least as much as they would have blamed him. It did not seem likely that someone would so single out Scottie for fault enough to plot to murder him.

On the other hand, the instances involving the incompetent use of derivatives and the implied mutual-fund trading scandal appeared to be more a result of unique actions by Scottie. These actions resulted in losses for clients. In these cases Scottie would bear all the blame.

To Charlie derivatives are complex enough to scare ordinary investors. Derivatives are financial instruments based on an existing security, real estate or composites—like indices. A derivative may be designed to capture all or part of the financial characteristics of the underlying security, or it may work to negate these characteristics. In other words, it may serve to leverage an investment or hedge it. In the hands of a sophisticated, skilled investor, derivatives are elegant tools to achieve a desired outcome. In less skillful hands, they can produce disastrous results.

Based on Charlie's conversations with Keller and with his own staff he surmised that Scottie Bradshaw had more hubris than skill as a broker. Scottie was vocally envious of the successes of clever traders but apparently too lazy or dull to learn the nuances of sophisticated financial investments. Of course his clients would have had little understanding of the risk of these types of investments. To Charlie's own clients investing was largely an arcane art form—too removed from ordinary affairs. Nevertheless, the allure of large profits offered by the likes of Scottie Bradshaw could overcome fears of the unknown and lead clients to entrust part of their fortunes to apparent financial professionals like Scottie. If they assume Scottie understood in great depth that of which he spoke, greed could cloud their judgment. Charlie guessed that likely happened.

He wrote the word *derivatives* and underlined it. He recognized certain special factors which make these investments ideal for abuse. For instance, because derivatives are mostly specialized vehicles, they are rarely quoted in the daily papers. A client of Scottie's would not be able to verify independently the value of his investment. He would have to rely on Scottie even though brokerage firms are strictly regulated regarding the accurate pricing of securities and reporting of the valuation of client holdings. They generally send out reports on a monthly basis. In fact, Charlie's firm did the same. In the interim, a client had to depend on his broker or portfolio manager for pricing of derivatives.

Scottie's reputation was that he loved to brag to his clients when prices were climbing, but he shrank into a shell when values declined. He was a fair-weather broker. Derivatives were sufficiently complex and the pricing of them frequently opaque enough that Scottie could obscure negative news at least during the time between required reporting periods if he wanted to.

Unfortunately, lots of bad things can happen during the course of a month. Moreover, even after a broker distributed client reports, an unscrupulous broker could tell a client that the pricing of his account did not accurately capture the true value of the derivatives. From Charlie's experience in the industry, many clients accepted that explanation, simply because the subject matter was so confusing or complex—or they just wanted to believe in lucrative outcomes.

Charlie wrote down the words *leverage* and *losses* in capitals. He was emphasizing the mechanism that could lead to a dismal result for a client. He knew that a bad broker's purpose in obscuring the value of the client's holdings usually was to buy time—time during which the security might eventually recover its value. But no law in nature says that all investments increase in value. Some drop in value and never recover. To make matters worse, some derivatives are designed to leverage or amplify the change in valuation of the underlying security or asset. So a client could lose a great deal more than he thought he had at risk.

Charlie was stuffing his briefcase with research reports to take home when his cellphone rang. He checked caller ID and saw that it was Peaches. Charlie guessed that he was calling about the shooting and didn't want to talk to him. But he knew he could not avoid Peaches for long.

"Hello, friend," Charlie said amicably. "What can I do for you?"

"A lot. I need a scoop about the events at Mrs. Claire Bailey's house. Gunfire in toney Lake Forest. Not heard of in decades. Kate Milano takes down the desperado. Headline stuff. Was this guy the one who pushed young Bradshaw in the drink?"

"Hold on Peaches. Where did you get all this?"

"The press contact from the Lake County Police. She appeared to enjoy talking about this juicy incident. But she didn't explain why the gunman was threatening you. She said that motives were under investigation. But I know—wink, wink - that boring old you are in the middle of the Bradshaw case. The police messed up or were silenced by the powers upstairs, maybe? So what's up? Help a friend—and a client."

"Well, we had quite a scare. I never met this thug before. Beats me why he was after me. You'll have to ask the police if they are going to reopen the Bradshaw case and whether there is any a connection with the gunman."

"I tried already."

Charlie thought it might be useful if Peaches pushed ahead on the goal of the investigation. So he said, "If this guy did kill Scottie, I wonder why? Was he an angry client? Did he have a personal grudge? Did someone else pay him to do it? I suppose a lot will be clearer when the police tell us who this guy was."

"Interesting. Maybe someone paid him to knock off Scottie—and you. Are you suggesting that?"

"Never."

"Sure," Peaches laughed. "This story could be great. Fabulous intrigue. We'll be talking again."

"Okay. Time for dinner."

"One last thing. Where did Kate learn to shoot a shotgun?"

"On a farm. Birds and those pesky rabbits. I'm thankful."

"I imagine you are."

Early the next morning Charlie called Bob Underwood from his apartment. As much as Bob frowned on Charlie's involvement in the Bradshaw case, Charlie considered him useful in accessing certain information.

"Bob, understanding your disapproval, I need a favor. Would you canvass your legal contacts and ask if Collins, Lang settled any client claims in excess of seven figures due to Scottie Bradshaw's actions? And who were the clients?"

Charlie figured that if Scottie's employer had had to pay out such claims, then Scottie should have been fired. Since he had not, Charlie concluded that either Scottie had generated substantial revenues—making him too valuable to fire—or the Bradshaw name meant too much.

"I'll make a few calls," Bob said sounding unenthusiastic. "You know, lawyers are discreet regarding client names in lawsuits or impending actions before a settlement. Sometimes, though, they can be talkative afterwards."

Bob called back that afternoon. "In a surprise to me, several people confided a lot. I have eleven names. One of the plaintiff lawyers had a funny anecdote. She said that one of the big losses was in a Bradshaw family account at a big bank. She remarked cattily, "Scottie could lose his own family's money as fast as someone else's. His incompetence showed no favorites.""

Charlie shook his head and noted that Henry Bradshaw must have been aware of Scottie's performance.

"This information is privileged, Charlie. Don't mention it to the police without talking to me first. I need to protect my source. I'll courier this list over."

Although Charlie assumed that more clients had been harmed, this list was a good start. Upon review, no name stood out to Charlie. He knew three individuals, had heard of five others, and did not recognize the last three. He needed to do some research. He wrote all eleven names on his pad.

While he was searching for some background information on these injured clients, Charlie reviewed the press reports on the internet of the mutual-fund trading scandal of a few years before. He remembered that issue broadly and certainly was intimate with the regulatory impact the resulting reforms had on investment managers. Because of the sins of a few, all money managers—but only mutual-fund managers—had to incur hefty new costs in compliance and reporting measures. Practices that had served the industry well for decades were now considered inappropriate or fraught with potential conflicts of interest.

Instead of recognizing that the vast majority of people are honest and diligent, Congress and SEC had decided to legislate and regulate candor and independence into the daily affairs of business. Charlie was very distrustful of this effort. Crooks will always find a way to mislead and commit fraud, no matter what the rules, and the costs of regulations and compliance hit everyone—thief and honest man.

After a half hour of reading about the scandal; Charlie called Tony D'Angelo, his head of sales, to come to his office.

"Tony, remember the mutual fund scandal a couple of years ago? You were working at a mutual-fund company then. I've been reading the press accounts but I am not clear who the players were, how widespread the illegal actions were, and who was hurt?"

"Got some time? This was a big deal. I know a few people who were fired. Most were sales managers like me. I have no idea why they risked their jobs, but they did."

Tony took off his suit coat and loosened his Ferragamo tie as he sat back on the sofa. Charlie liked Tony. He dressed like an Ivy Leaguer but talked plainly, putting the listener at ease. He followed the industry practice of entertaining clients and prospects at lunches, dinners, and sporting events. From these activities he carried twenty pounds more than ideal. But he was good-natured about his weight and worked his physique into his ample supply of jokes. Beneath this jocular façade was a man Charlie knew to be serious, committed, and honest. Plus, he produced excellent sales results.

"The deal was late trading," Tony began. "Allowed for special clients—usually hedge funds. The *quid pro quo* that hedge funds offered the mutual funds was the investment of large sums of money and other investment products of the mutual-fund company — sometimes called *parking*. These other products charge high fees, which increase the mutual-fund company's profits. However, the cost to the hedge funds of investing or parking their funds with the mutual-fund companies was minor compared to the profits they made in after hours trading. So some hedge funds were tempted by an after hours arrangement even if their managers thought it improper."

"Okay. I think I get it," Charlie said carefully. "This arrangement was late trading of mutual-fund shares rather than individual stocks. Correct?"

"Yes. As you know, mutual funds price their portfolios once a day at four p.m. New York time."

"When the New York Stock Exchange closes trading."

"Precisely. Any information that develops after the close shows up in the prices of securities the next day when the market reopens."

"So if an important announcement comes out that will move prices when the market opens, and if I could buy or sell my mutual-fund shares back at the four p.m. close prices, I can't lose."

"Like shooting fish in a barrel."

"This arrangement would be particularly effective with investments of mutual funds in foreign markets in time zones that don't coincide with New York's."

"Correctomundo, Charlie. Because of the different open and close times, this arrangement is like betting on the outcome of the sporting event after it's over."

"And the victims are the honest, long-term holders of the mutual fund."

"Right. Of course the prospectus and legal documents of each mutual fund expressly prohibit doing this."

"That didn't stop some people."

"Mainly hedge funds—not all, of course, but a few of the big ones."

"Did they do it because they were lightly regulated?" Charlie asked.

"Maybe. But remember, it's not clear that the hedge funds were breaking the law. Rather, the mutual fund companies were violating their own prospectuses. They allowed—or maybe invited—the hedge funds to trade after hours for their *quid pro quo*."

"Knowing how aggressive most hedge fund managers are, that's like throwing a bloody carcass in piranha-infested waters," Charlie said with relish. "Those groups will immediately consume every last morsel of profit. If they aren't breaking the law, then the laws have a loophole."

"This arrangement reminds me of a short story by John O'Hara," Tony said. "A dull, unsuccessful broker commuting to New York City buys a *Wall Street Journal* one morning and finds that somehow the paper is the next day's edition. This situation occurs each day for a week. The broker decides to take advantage of having the next day's stock prices and puts in his trades. He profits every time. His wife, friends, and broker start to think he's a genius. Then after several weeks he buys the paper and the edition is the current day."

Charlie interrupts, "I know how this ends. He panics, tries trading anyway, and loses each day. Soon he is the same uninspired failure he always was—no longer a genius. Maybe those hedge fund investors wouldn't be so smart if they have to play by the same rules as you and I?"

"Like the man in the story, Charlie, eventually the game stopped. A disgruntled hedge fund employee blew the whistle. The SEC and the New York Attorney General investigated and identified several cases when this illegal post-close trading took place. As you probably read, they imposed fines and jail terms on several mutual fund executives."

"What outrages me," Charlie said with emotion, "is that the legitimate investors—unsuspecting individuals, institutions, and pension funds—lost the profits that the hedge funds skimmed. None of the punishments levied by the authorities made up for those losses."

Tony got up to leave. Charlie smiled as he kidded him, "Tony, I didn't know you read books, too. A man of many interests."

"I surprise even myself."

After Tony left, Charlie put a question mark on his pad next to the term *mutual-fund timing service*. Steve Keller had mentioned that the SEC inquiry had closed down Scottie's timing service around the time of the mutual fund trading scandal. If Scottie were involved, Charlie would have guessed he was small potatoes. Maybe he did more and acted as a middleman between a hedge fund and a guilty mutual fund? Keller has indicated that Scottie had a few of those types of clients.

*The idea was worth pursuing. I'm looking for angry clients. Maybe his new collaborator, Paul Victor, would use his authority to obtain a complete list of Scottie's clients. I am throwing a widening net now. I should catch some fish.*

| § |

# CHAPTER TWENTY

No one likes to be wrong. But Paul Victor admitted to himself that he had been. To Paul and his colleagues, the Bradshaw drowning appeared to be an accident. Paul knew that drownings are always difficult to analyze since little forensic evidence is discernible. Rarely does one willingly drown. Usually drowning occurs when the individual is under the influence of alcohol or heavy drugs which affects motor skills and perceptions, or when he suffers a natural occurrence such as a heart attack in or near a pool of water.

The deceased often exhibits abrasions of the head, face, hands, or knees from a fall near water, scraping against a rock or the size of a pool. Most autopsies—as was the case in Scottie Bradshaw—reveal water in the lungs and stomach and often a hemorrhage in the eardrums. Those facts do not prove death by drowning. But unless there is conclusive evidence of another cause such as unusual trauma events, the medical examiner will cite drowning as the cause of death through a process of elimination. Paul remembered that the medical examiner did note bruises on the right shoulder, forehead, and the neck but he did not conclude that they were caused by another person or that they even occurred at the time of the drowning - despite the account of a fight at the party. With this report, without a witness to attest to a homicide, and under pressure from Commander Mayo, Paul had felt comfortable at the time with the conclusion of an accidental drowning.

However, everything changed for Paul with Charlie's account of Vecchia's admission of killing Scottie. Paul had to admit before the coroner's report that he had half-hoped that the case was a murder. Considering the celebrity of the deceased family and the seriousness of murder, success in resolving this case might have brought him recognition and advancement in his career. But Scottie's family, the press, his commander, and everyone except Charlie had agreed with the official findings; so the case had gone cold. In fact, Mayo had talked to him on two occasions about dropping all work on Bradshaw and focusing exclusively on two violent crimes which had occurred in Waukegan that month. Mayo had said, "As I told you before stop thinking you are Dick Tracy and get back to work on that gang murder downtown. Mr. Fancy Bradshaw just got drunk and took a dive in the pool. Unfortunately for him, Michael Phelps wasn't there to save him. End of story."

The only considerations that had prevented him from dropping Bradshaw completely were Charlie Bailey's colorful recitals of a stalker, a snake, and a potential murderer. Paul had regarded Charlie as a classic busybody—a bit hysterical and whimsical. But the bottom line was that until the shooting Paul supported the department's conclusion of an accidental death.

Fascinating to Paul was that the case had become complex, reaching to New York, Palm Beach, Chicago, and the Cayman Islands. Never before had he worked on anything with this scope, requiring all the resources available to the Lake County Sheriff's Office—some of which he had never used before. But with Commander Mayo's support, Paul could access the FBI, IRS, and INS as well as bank records and multiple other databases to gather evidence. Such sources are rarely required in the normal crimes they investigated.

As exciting as this case was becoming, Mayo's and Paul's superiors were suddenly on his back to solve it quickly. This case could create budgetary stress for the Major Crimes Task Force. The local municipalities that funded his group did not normally have excess reserves available. In an apparent move to save money for Mayo, Paul had turned down his offer to assign someone to work for him. Paul's motive was not altruistic. In fact, he wanted the credit for solving the case himself. If he could, he would stun the politicians who had put pressure on Mayo before to drop the case.

Adding to the strain of the situation and the urgency, the press had asked his office about the recent Bailey shooting and whether there was any connection to the Bradshaw death. That reporter from the *Trib* was particularly persistent in pushing that theory. At some point his group would have to agree.

The task force team had had some help already from the New York Police Department and the FBI regarding Vecchia's history and his bank account. The Cayman Islands bank was no help, having hid behind local secrecy laws. However, these sources would likely find useful information as they dug into Vecchia's relationships.

Another promising avenue of inquiry was Bradshaw's client list. Angry clients might be suspects. Paul thought that he could get a court order to obtain the list. But while he went through that process, he decided to visit Bradshaw's supervisor without one to gauge how cooperative Mr. Keller would be. He might get lucky.

Despite arriving unannounced, Paul and John Riordan from the Chicago PD were shown in immediately. They sat on Steve Keller's couch facing him.

"Well, a lot has happened since we talked earlier this summer," Keller began. "Our firm's general counsel has instructed me to be helpful with the police—which I have been and would be anyway. Our counsel would have been here, but he had to be in court on some matter. What can I do for you?"

"In our previous conversation," Paul said looking at his notes, "you said that Mr. Bradshaw was a good employee, well liked by his coworkers, and a good producer for the firm. Do you have anything to add?"

Paul listened as Keller repeated some of the information he had told Charlie and that Charlie had passed along to him. Then Keller added, "Scott was notoriously late with paperwork—account forms, entertainment expenses, personal holdings reports, that sort of thing. He wasn't the only broker who was lax, but the worst. I was always after him."

"Anything else?"

"He certainly had some irate clients. Scottie had some of the biggest clients in the shop, and it stands to reason that they were the maddest over losses—because we are talking a lot of money. Some derivatives trades blew up on him. These things could happen to anyone, but not to the same degree."

"Mr. Keller, I would like to take with me a list of all of Mr. Bradshaw's clients for the past five years. Include activity in the accounts and dollar size and the reason some of them left."

Steve stiffened, scowled, and put down the pen he was playing with.

"Officer, I don't know. Those lists technically belong to the firm. I would have to get clearance."

"If necessary, I'll get a court order requiring your firm to produce them," Paul pressed on.

Keller frowned, pretending to write something on a yellow, legal pad. Paul thought he was acting put upon.

"I'll see what I can do. I don't think a court order will be necessary," he conceded.

"I would like them today or tomorrow at the latest."

"You're asking for a lot in a very short time."

"I'm sure most of it is on your computers. Next item: Was Mr. Bradshaw questioned by the SEC or any other authority regarding the ongoing investigation into illegal practices in the mutual fund industry?"

Keller paused and seemed unable to formulate a satisfactory

answer but eventually responded. As Keller recounted the story that Paul already knew from talking to Charlie, Paul had wanted to see Keller's body language and to assess his truthfulness. After all, Keller had reason to loathe Scottie. In general Keller recited the facts accurately but spiced with clear criticism of his former employee.

"The hedge fund here in Chicago that seemed to have profited most from late trading was one of Scottie's closest clients. In addition, Scottie knew the guy from the mutual fund, Paradigm funds, who was nabbed by the SEC in the same case. The man was fined—along with his company—and barred from the industry. I was uneasy with the situation because I remembered that a few years earlier Scottie had bragged about introducing a hedge fund portfolio manager to his buddy over at Paradigm."

"Did the SEC talk to you?"

"Briefly and only about the hedge fund client."

"Who was the client?" Paul asked.

"Pierson Partners. The head partner and portfolio manager is Lowell Hersey. Scottie knew him from golf."

"Did Mr. Hersey face punishment for his part in the illegal trading?"

"No, and that didn't seem fair. But Scottie's buddy at Paradigm, John Sweeney, kept his mouth shut. He admitted he had the late trades processed, but he did not confess to any *quid pro quo*. Still he lost his job. I guess that Pierson got off. I wouldn't be surprised if something was in it for Sweeney, but that never came out. I assume that the mutual-fund company profited by Pierson investing in other products of the company. I don't know."

"Is Pierson Partners still a client of yours?"

"Yes, I guess so. But, since Scottie died, we haven't done any business."

"Did Mr. Bradshaw have other hedge fund clients?"

"Yes, a handful—including our biggest client, BDS Partners."

"Was BDS implicated in the late trading scandal?"

"No, not that I know of. They do a ton of trading with us—long, short, mainly equities but also converts and options."

"Has their trading diminished since Bradshaw died?"

"A bit, but they still are huge with us."

"Mr. Bradshaw must have done a good job for BDS," Paul concluded, nodding to Detective Riordan.

"He did. That is why we put up with his lack of attention to administrative matters."

"Perhaps that is why your firm did not pursue the Paradigm Funds matter further?"

"No. The SEC was doing an investigation. That was good enough for us."

"From what you said, Pierson may have been trading heavily with you as a reward for Scottie facilitating its relationship with Paradigm. Was that the case?"

Keller did not answer, looking nervous. He seemed to fail to come up with a response. So Paul said, "Let me make this clear.

You said Bradshaw introduced Hersey to Sweeney. Hersey's firm profited because Sweeney allowed them to trade when they shouldn't have. Presumably Hersey was delighted. He thinks Bradshaw and your firm by doing a lot of business. Makes sense to me. Right?"

"Right," Riordan spoke up.

Keller swallowed hard and stammered, "W..w..wait a second. I never said there was an arrangement like you have described. It may have all been a coincidence. Our brokers know a lot of people in the financial industry. Anyway, the SEC found nothing."

"To tell you something about me," Paul said, leaning forward and looking Keller in the eyes, "I don't believe in coincidences—especially when it involves someone who is dead. I'm going to ask a judge to give me a subpoena to have your firm produce every memo, letter, and email regarding Paradigm Funds and Pierson Partners."

Paul kept pushing. He knew he was on a fishing expedition. He had no proof of any wrongdoing. What he was doing was testing Keller—see if he would say something incriminating.

Keller used his hand to wipe his forehead. Paul asked, "Are you okay? Too hot in here?"

"I'm fine," Keller mumbled. "You won't find anything."

"For your sake, I hope not. Let's go back to BDS for a minute. Did BDS purchase any Paradigm Funds?"

"Not that I know of," Keller answered. "Scottie serviced them well, and they like our trading desk."

"How much business did they direct to Mr. Bradshaw?"

"I don't know exactly, but at least five million dollars of commissions per year."

"Sounds like a lot of money. What could Mr. Bradshaw be telling them that was worth that much?"

"As I said, Scott spent a lot of time with them, and they appreciated his advice."

"Who did Mr. Bradshaw talk to there?"

"Ira Berkman, the head of the firm."

"Does BDS have a good investment record?" Paul asked.

"I am told they do very well for their clients. They are very smart people. Particularly Ira Berkman."

Keller appeared to be less rattled as the questions shifted away from Pierson Partners.

"Do they trade in mutual funds?"

"Not that I know of. I think they specialize in merger arbitrage."

"Excuse my ignorance, Mr. Keller, but what is merger arbitrage?"

"It's investing in an expected or announced merger between two companies. You can use several strategies, depending on the capital structures of the companies, the liquidity of the stocks, the time involved before the merger, the perceived likelihood of the merger actually happening, and other factors. The investor profits from the gap between the bid and ask narrowing."

"John, did you get that?" Paul asked with a smile.

"This type of investing seems very sophisticated and

technical to me," Detective Riordan responded, talking toward Paul. "From what I have heard of Mr. Bradshaw's competence, I am surprised that he could have been so helpful to BDS."

"I agree. What do you think, Mr. Keller?"

"Well, obviously he was," Keller snapped back. Now Keller was glaring at Detective Riordan.

"That's okay. Calm down. We are naturally suspicious. You see, you told us that Mr. Bradshaw lost lots of money for his clients, got in the middle of an arrangement between Pierson and Paradigm that appears to be shady, and then had a client who showered him with business. Seems inconsistent. By the way how much did Mr. Bradshaw keep from all those commissions?"

"The past two years he earned about $200,000—up substantially from earlier years."

"Why up?"

"His recommendations to clients improved."

"You supervised him. Right?"

"Yes!" Keller nearly shouted. "You know that."

"Just checking. We'll go now. Thank you and call me when you have the client information—tomorrow."

Paul stepped up to Keller in the middle of his office and shook a wet hand. Suddenly Keller asked a question that sounded as if he had been urgently waiting to ask, "Why did you come here today? I thought Scottie died in an accident. Was he murdered, as some of the press are suggesting?"

"We ask the questions. Do you think he was murdered?"

"How could I know?" Keller asked sounding defensive.

Outside the building Detective Riordan turned to Paul,
"Suspect?"

"We need to see that client list, but he sure was nervous.
Frightened maybe."

"And interested."

## CHAPTER TWENTY-ONE

Charlie drove into the pristine grounds of the Potawatomi Club trying to concentrate on the day's client outing. But an image of Scottie's bloated body blocked all other thoughts. If I find the killer, maybe this memory will fade. I must get closer today.

For twelve years every July, Charlie had entertained the athletic-minded clients of Bailey, Richardson and O'Neil at a golf and tennis outing at the club. His staff and clients looked forward to the one respite from the daily routine and becoming better acquainted in an informal setting. In addition, the Potawatomi Club itself was a draw, as many clients might never otherwise set foot on its grounds.

Potawatomi's Membership Committee, so sensitive that their names were known only to the club's officers, was extremely selective. New members were added only by attrition. Wealth was a factor, but social position was paramount. For many clients this event was their opportunity to play golf or tennis and take a peek at a social set they seldom saw.

The club strictly limited its use by members for large outings.

Since it was regularly closed on Mondays that was the day given over to the occasional member-sponsored event. Charlie was one of the handful of people to take advantage of this exception. He felt confident each year that his outing would be approved because the club, despite its healthy finances, could always use extra revenues.

Charlie's message to his guests this year was to be reassurance. Because the markets had been unremittingly poor since the Federal Reserve had begun raising interest rates, he wanted to convince his clients that what was happening was not unusual and that modestly rising interest rates alone were not sufficient to change their long-term investment programs. To this end, he had scheduled a brief talk during lunch before the athletic events.

Charlie's other unspoken intention was to advance his investigation. Included on his guest list were people he and Paul considered the most suspicious. After Paul's visit to Steve Keller, Charlie and the investigator had met to discuss their ideas. All of Charlie's names—a list generated by Bob Underwood—were on Collins, Lang's file of clients obtained by Paul. The names from the broker were complete, including both current and closed individual institutional accounts over the past three years, and the file detailed changes in asset values over that period.

Charlie and Paul agreed to concentrate on clients who had lost more than a third of the value of their portfolios during these years, clients who lost significant sums through derivatives trading, and clients who managed hedge funds. Of the thirty-four such clients, Charlie eliminated the Sisters of the Precious Blood; a Peoria, Illinois hospital; a widow who had no heirs; several bank administrated trusts benefitting children; and Scottie's family. None appeared likely to murder Scottie Bradshaw.

Of the remaining twenty-one names on their list, twelve had accepted Charlie's invitation to the outing—even though a few had been asked only a couple days before. Troubled by the appearance of a conflict of interest in the way he obtained their names, Charlie instructed his head of sales not to follow up on these twelve after the event. As for those who had not accepted, he would have to follow up with them later.

Charlie intended to meet each on the list at least briefly and to try to determine if anyone was worth further investigation. He even hoped that because the outing was at the scene of the crime, someone with a guilty conscience might be drawn to attend and once there become unsettled enough to stand out. Charlie recognized that this strategy was wishful thinking, but who could predict the outcome of bringing so many suspects to one place for five or six hours? Paul had encouraged him to pursue this approach and coached him on what to look for in identifying a true suspect and in eliminating the innocent. Charlie felt he was prepared and was eager to get started.

The firm invited everyone for eleven a.m. so that they had time to attend to business early, drive out to Lake Forest, change clothes, hit golf balls to warm up, and meet everyone in the group at lunch in the club. The first person he met in the parking lot was Jamie Bradshaw, dressed in business attire.

"Just come from the office?" Charlie asked.

"I had to take care of a few things this morning."

He paused, then added, "I think that this is my first time back since Scottie's death. I love this club, but I had not felt up to it."

"It's nice of you to come to our function," Charlie told him, and meant it.

"Even now I feel depressed, out of kilter, but I need to get back to a normal routine. You're providing a perfect opportunity. I'll know a lot of the people, and I'm sure they'll be sensitive to how difficult this has been for me."

"You are right. I hope you'll be able to relax and have a good time."

As they walked toward the clubhouse, Jamie asked, "How are you? I heard about what happened a couple of weeks ago at your mother's house. You might have been killed. Your mom confided in my mother what had happened. Then the police told Dad that the intruder may have had something to do with my brother's death."

"Yes, he admitted it." Charlie confirmed.

Jamie stopped walking, and turned to Charlie, "The police wouldn't tell Dad why the man targeted you. They couldn't or wouldn't say. Dad guessed that the man thought you saw something incriminating when you found the body. Did you? Dad had the impression that the shooting reopened the case. Is the investigation still active? We're family. We need to know. Have to have closure. My mother is in a terrible physical mental state. You saw a snippet of her condition in Palm Beach. This news is making her worse."

"Understandable. She's been through hell. You should ask the police about the investigation."

"Didn't you tell me at lunch that you intended to help the police?"

"I don't know what the police are doing," Charlie said, feeling miffed that Jamie thought he talked with the police. "After what happened at my mother's house, I would rather stand on the sidelines. I promised Kate I would. I cannot compromise her or my mother's safety. But if I hear anything, I'll let you know."

"Please do. It sounds like you are not allowed to tell me everything. I understand."

Charlie did not like the direction this conversation had taken, so he was relieved to spot two clients walking towards him. He seized on their appearance to excuse himself to greet them. His experience with Vecchia taught him that he gained nothing by talking about his involvement. He did not know if Jamie had talked to anyone else about their luncheon chat, but someone was aware of his personal investigation.

Jamie was interested in what Charlie knew and, since the shooting, the press was interested, too. Not only had Peaches connected Scottie's drowning with Vecchia's death, but most of the other local media reporters had called and left messages. Charlie had returned none. Violent deaths in Lake Forest were rare, and Charlie had been at both of them. Despite the interest, Charlie had vowed to refuse any comment about either incident. Unfortunately the reporters went ahead and speculated that Vecchia had

killed Scottie and had tried to kill Charlie because he knew something—yet to be confirmed.

After welcoming several guests as they arrived outside
Charlie headed to his locker to change. He immediately felt more
comfortable in his powder blue and white striped golf shirt, light
tan shorts, white sandal shoe-style golf shoes, and a blue base-
ball-style golf hat embroidered in front with the Potawatomi Club
emblem—a red "*P*" overlaying white eagle feathers. Outside again
he met two of his administrative staffers who were managing the
outing. He learned that so far no one had cancelled and that the
weather report remained encouraging—mid-seventies and no rain.

"Who is handling the tennis players?" Charlie asked.

Sarah Rinaldi, one of his security analysts, laughed and said.
"I am. I'll change into my whites in a minute. We have only two
men and one woman. I'll play to set up mixed doubles."

Pleased with that information, Charlie walked over to the
putting green, hit a few practice putts, greeted several clients
there, and finally walked back toward the clubhouse. Because of
the spectacular weather the club had set up a buffet on the patio
with a view of the eighteenth green.

Around noon the guests had selected their food and were sitting at tables scattered around on the bluestone patio chatting
freely. Charlie walked up to the front as several clients shouted
hello. He smiled and raised his hand for quiet.

"Thank you all for leaving your busy day and joining us,"
Charlie began. "I have just a few words to say. Keep eating,
please.'

'Thank you for your confidence and support in our firm. We are working diligently and intelligently on your behalf. We have been dealing with the difficult markets of the past few weeks. Now is not the time to panic. The current market correction is sowing the seeds for an eventual recovery. We have been through these periods many times before. I promise that your portfolio managers will be in regular contact with you. If for some particular reason your long-term investment objectives change, please let our managers know immediately. We'll make the necessary alterations.'

'And for those of you who are not clients, I invite you to schedule a visit to meet some of our staff. I think you will be impressed."

After taking and answering several timely questions from the crowd about the duration of the declining markets, the effect on technology stocks, and how high interest rates might go, Charlie changed the mood with some deprecating jokes about his golf game and then wished them all good luck during the afternoon's events.

As Charlie was returning to his table to pick up his golf hat, a short, stocky man with dark, curly hair came up and introduced himself as Ira Berkman.

"I run BDS Partners in the city. I am not sure why I was invited, but thank you. I thought your speech was reassuring. I don't know if your clients invest in hedge funds, but if they do, BDS would be happy to talk to them and to your portfolio managers."

I'm pleased to meet you, Ira," Charlie said, shaking his hand. "I have heard wonderful things about BDS from my colleagues.

Thank you for your offer. Many of our clients invest in hedge funds, and a couple are already in one of your funds. I agree that we should learn more about how you generate such impressive returns each year. I'll have Sam Dixon, one of my senior portfolio managers, call you to set up a meeting." He looked around, spotted Sam, and pointed him out to Ira. "There he is, the tall fellow with glasses and a moustache."

Ira looked briefly across the room and then faced Charlie. "Great." He cleared his throat. "Isn't this the place where Scott Bradshaw was killed? I read about it in the newspapers and wondered what this club looked like."

"You're right. This is where Scottie died. It was a shock to everyone. He was well liked. How close were you to him?"

"Oh, not close," Berkman answered, looking away. "I did some business with Scottie a while back. HE was helpful on some trades we did, but I never knew him socially. I liked his insouciant manner."

Did Berkman's body language mean anything? People with something to hide avoid eye contact. Paul had mentioned that.

Charlie chuckled, "Yes that was Scottie. I am a bit surprised that a large, active trader like you would find value in a small brokerage house like Collins, Lang."

"We didn't do a lot of business with them, but occasionally he had a good idea that we used. Now that he is gone, we rarely use them."

Ira continued to look off to the left as he spoke. Charlie wondered if he always spoke with people that way or whether he was nervous or uncomfortable with Charlie. He would have to observe Ira later with others.

"Call me when I can meet your portfolio managers," Ira said as he excused himself to warm up for golf.

Why did he bring up Scottie? Of all things to talk about in a first conversation with Charlie, Scottie. Curious. In addition Charlie could not reconcile how Scottie Bradshaw could have possibly been useful to a shrewd investor like Berkman.

Tee-offs began at each hole at the same time. Charlie had chosen Lowell Hersey of Pierson Partners, Peaches Kenney, and Tony Fitzpatrick to make up his foursome. Lowell Hersey had conspired with Paradigm Fund in the late-trading scandal. Scottie Bradshaw may have been the original go-between. Charlie, wanting to ferret out the connection, had invited Hersey personally, saying he wanted to meet him since their firms had a couple of co-managed accounts.

Next, Peaches' value was his outrageous banter, which might shake out a telling comment or two from the others. Finally, Tony, a client of Scottie's, had lost a good deal of money over the past three years. Charlie knew that he was a successful executive with a large printing company and that they had several mutual friends. Charlie felt that Tony certainly had good reason to dislike Scottie.

Since Charlie could not talk with everyone at the outing, he had asked Sam Dixon and Julian Anderson, the chief administrative officer of the firm, to include three clients of Scottie's in each of their foursomes and try to learn their feelings toward Scottie. Someone implicating himself was a long shot, but it was worth a try.

Because Charlie was the host, his foursome had the privilege of teeing off from the first tee in a shotgun format. When it was time to begin, he joined his playing partners on the tee, shook hands with the trio, and invited Lowell to go first.

As Charlie surveyed his fellow golfers, he was struck by the variety of their garb. Peaches was resplendent in his orange shirt with dark blue speckles, royal blue shorts, matching blue socks, and red shoes. His straw hat had a dark-blue band. This outfit would have been equally conspicuous at a beach resort as on the golf course. Tony—a tall, hefty man who would have benefitted by more time at a fitness center—wore a plain white shirt with a tan collar, beige shorts, white shoes, and no hat. His shirt was not fully tucked in. Lowell—a pencil-thin, fifty-some-year-old with angular features highlighted by wire rim glasses—was dressed in a black and beige golf shirt, long cream-colored light wool pants, and black shoes. He wore a black Ben Hogan style hat. Seeing this outfit, Charlie thought that Hersey was going to struggle in the eighty-five degree July heat and humidity.

Lowell Hersey must have read Charlie's mind. He said defensively, "I thought this club would prohibit shorts worn by men. That's why I wore these clothes."

"The club does have a reputation for being stuffy," Charlie responded. "But collared shirts for men and whites on the tennis courts are the only rules I am aware of. I hope we'll have a lake breeze to cool us off."

They teed off. Three of the four drives hit the fairway. But Peaches found the right rough. He turned to his partners and apologized for his dreadful game and promised to pick up if he was out of a hole.

As they walked forward, Charlie remarked that the course was designed by the famous golf architect Scotsman Donald Ross and played fairly. He cautioned, "Among the challenges you will face will be the greens, which tend to have a domed shape, and the ever-present wind blowing in from Lake Michigan."

Tony marveled at the impeccable conditioning of the fairways and greens and wished the greens keepers at his club did as good a job. The group chatted about golf, politics, the economy, and mutual acquaintances as they walked to their balls, analyzed their shots, hit them, and eventually came to the green.

On the second tee, Peaches tried to entertain the group with politically incorrect joke about the pope, a rabbi, and a minister playing golf. As it was well received by the group, Tony Fitzpatrick followed with one about a Scottish caddie. These jokes broke whatever ice was left among the three of the four players. Only Hersey, apparently unamused, was quiet and intense in his play.

It was obvious to Charlie that this foursome would never be entirely comfortable with each other. In addition to the differences in personalities, the disparity in golfing ability—he and Lowell were expert players, and Tony and Peaches were duffers—playing for exercise. In particular, he anticipated a clash between Hersey and Peaches.

On the third hole, Charlie asked for the scores and noted that Hersey declared a better score than he had shot. While the error could have been inadvertent, Charlie was on alert. Golf can reveal a great deal about someone's character, and an incorrect score always raises a red flag. To Charlie, golf was a gentlemen's game, and lying and cheating were *verboten*. Nevertheless, he reserved judgment, keenly interested to see if Lowell would lie again about his score.

On the next hole Peaches brought up the subject of Scottie Bradshaw as if he were reading a script prepared by Charlie.

"Lowell, didn't I hear that your firm had something to do with Scottie Bradshaw and the mutual fund that got into trouble? You know, this club is where Bradshaw was murdered."

"I didn't realize that. I knew Scottie a little bit," Hersey began, seemingly caught off guard. I remember that he died a few weeks ago. Sad. Poor man. He was murdered? I thought I read that he drowned accidentally. How do you know about this?"

"Well, you should read my columns. I might strike you as a simpleton society scribe, but believe me, he was killed—although the police wasted time dithering over the obvious."

'That reminds me," Peaches added, "In my research a few weeks back, I came across the Paradigm Funds story. Some thought Scottie introduced your people to Paradigm."

Charlie wondered what Peaches was doing. He saw Hersey's features harden. Hersey lifted his club in an aggressive fashion, then caught himself and let it drop.

Peaches struck a protective pose. When nothing happened,

Peaches continued, "I met John Sweeney, who took the fall. Nice man. Naïve, it turned out. I was surprised that Scottie and your company were never charged. I guess Pierson Partners did nothing wrong. Now that affair is over, maybe you can enlighten me as to what happened and satisfy my intense curiosity,"

Peaches' comments were clearly hostile. Ordinarily Charlie would have stepped in before his guests got into a fight. But he wanted to know how Hersey would respond.

"You're right about one thing," Lowell said with some heat. "That unfortunate event is past, done. The SEC dropped the case. Sweeney thought he was doing us a favor, but he sullied our reputation. We'll never accept another favor—from a broker or a mutual-fund guy."

"Right," Peaches drawled. "You made a fortune with your trading, and you consider yourself a victim. Please. Where do you get off, blaming John Sweeney? He'll never get another job. You financial types never do anything wrong. Censure the other guy. Colossal arrogance."

Hersey took two steps towards Peaches and raised his club again. "You have an awfully big mouth when the person you are insulting is ten feet away with a club in his hand."

"Gentlemen. Wait a second," Charlie quickly walked between them. "Lowell, Peaches makes a living goading people into losing their cool. That's why his columns are so widely read. Don't take offense."

He turned to Peaches, "And you, be a good boy."

"Well, I am not amused that this faggot is accusing my firm

of misconduct." He pointed his club at Peaches, who took a step back. Lowell's face was dark with fury. "Stick to your self-important society clowns."

"Temper, temper," Peaches teased. "I may look delicate but my pen is full of testosterone. Keep it up, and you may find yourself in my Sunday column."

"Gentlemen, please. Let's play golf!" Charlie shouted, and the threats stopped. But Charlie feared that Hersey would explode at any moment.

On the next hole, Hersey again misstated his score, and this time Tony spoke up. "I know you are upset, but you had a six instead of a five. I am not as good a golfer as you, but at least I know my score on each hole."

"What? Are you calling me a liar? I've had enough of this, Charlie. I'm going in. I'm sorry I came. I thought your clients would have more class."

With that valedictory, he stormed off toward the clubhouse. Charlie let him go. He had heard enough. He was convinced that Lowell Hersey was deceitful and lucky that the SEC had not come down hard on him. He had threatened Peaches. If Hersey suspected Scottie of talking to the SEC, who knows what he was capable of? Murder?

"Where does that guy get off?" Tony said. "He made a ton of money with Scottie Bradshaw. Scottie was my broker, too, and I lost a bundle. I had more reason than he to be pissed off. I wanted to wring Scottie's neck."

Tony stopped, seeming to regret what he said. So he

corrected, "I misspoke. I was mad, but I never would have hurt anyone."

"I understand that you are angry," said Charlie. "I have heard from several other people that Scottie lost money for them."

"To tell the truth the losses were probably my fault," Tony admitted. "I should have known better. After a couple of months, I knew Scottie was not very sharp. I should have closed the account, but I hung around because of the Bradshaw name and mystique. I counted on his being able to turn things around."

"Every family has a black sheep," Peaches offered. He seemed giddy with relief at Lowell's departure. "I just hope Charlie isn't the Baileys' black sheep. You have my trust fund, and Lord knows, I need the money."

"What you really need are some manners and a slew of golf lessons," Charlie said, attempting humor. "Shall we try again?"

"After you tell me about the delicious Kate Milano."

Charlie felt a minor heart pang at the mention of Kate. Since the shooting, his fiancée seemed to have distanced herself from him. Certainly that event had frightened and shaken her. She had said nothing, but she had reason to question Charlie. She had experienced a string of scary, unsettling episodes because of him. He had to regain her confidence. That might take time.

Charlie's playing partners stared at him, waiting for a snappy reply. All he could come up with was, "No comment."

Tony and Peaches laughed. The rest of the round was uneventful, and on the basis of Tony's comments and demeanor, Charlie decided that he was not a suspect. This conclusion pleased

Charlie, since he had decided that he wanted to get to know Tony better. He had a sense of humor and did not blame others for his feelings.

After the golf and tennis events the clients gathered at a reception with cocktails and hors d'oeuvres on the patio. They mingled while Charlie led Sam Dixon and Julian Anderson to a quiet place out of earshot of the others.

"Did you learn anything suspicious about Scottie?"

"Nothing from the golfers," Sam reported. "But Sarah said that the woman playing mixed doubles with her had mentioned Scottie in negative terms."

"Did Sarah tell you who?"

"One of our clients — Farah Irani," Sam said. "She contrasted our good investment returns with those of her former broker, Scottie. She said, 'I should not speak ill of the dead, but Scottie Bradshaw was dishonest, lazy, and incompetent. If I had found him in the pool, instead of your boss, I would have pushed him back under water.'"

"Sounds pissed" Charlie said.

"I'd hate to be on her bad side," Julian said.

"At least she likes us. It's time to hand out the prizes."

Charlie walked over to the scoreboard and announced the winners of the golf and tennis competitions. He then thanked everyone for coming and said he hoped he would see them again next year.

As he was changing his shoes by his locker, Javier walked by bringing back shoes he had cleaned for the golfers.

"Javier, it was good to see Jamie Bradshaw back here again after his brother's death. You and I remember that day very well."

"I certainly do. I still get nightmares. But I am not sure what you mean. I have seen Mr. Jamie here many times since his brother died. He came in the next day and cleaned out Mr. Scottie's locker and had been back here other times"

"Does he play golf?" Charlie asked.

"No. He comes in and goes to the men's room."

*Charlie was confused. Had Jamie lied to him? Was he obsessed by the murder and embarrassed to admit it or had he just misspoke? Maybe he forgot. Maybe he came here to grieve, as people do at a gravesite. Odd. Lowell and Jamie had lied to me today. Maybe "lie" is too strong a term in Jamie's case. I might be a little "off" if I lost my brother and not want to admit a desire to visit the scene of his death.*

## CHAPTER TWENTY-TWO

Paul and Charlie arrived at about the same time at Sal's Coffee Shop in Waukegan the next morning. They ordered breakfast quickly and then began in earnest.

"How did it go yesterday?" Paul asked. "Did anyone seem suspicious?"

"I met five of Scottie's former clients and my colleagues Sam Dixon, Julian Anderson, and Sarah Rinaldi chatted with the other seven guests of the twelve who agreed to come. Of this group Lowell Hersey stood out to me. He had a very short temper and almost came to blows with the *Tribune* reporter, Peaches Kenny, on the golf course. Peaches was questioning him about Scottie—actually goading him, and Hersey got riled up. He walked off the course in anger.

'Then another, Farah Irani, spoke very disparagingly about Scottie. She said she wanted him dead for his inept management. Of course, the fact that the others seemed normal doesn't mean they were not involved, but they gave us nothing to work with."

Paul was taking notes but looked up and asked, "Did Hersey have a motive for murder?"

"Possibly. He claims that he had done nothing wrong in the late trading episode with John Sweeney, but Scottie had introduced Hersey to Sweeney, Hersey may have been worried about what Scottie had to say to the SEC—or held back. Not knowing, Hersey might have been happy to see Scottie dead and he is the type to hire someone to do his dirty work. There may have been more to this that we don't know. What I don't understand is why Sweeney took the fall without implicating anyone else?"

"I think I can clarify that," Paul said. "Courtesy of the FBI we traced a series of small transfers totaling two hundred thousand dollars into a Sweeney bank account in Hinsdale."

"Why didn't the transfer trigger a Suspicious Activity Report from the bank?" Charlie asked.

"Every transfer varied between six and eight thousand dollars. Too small to trigger. We called him in yesterday and questioned him. He had a lawyer with him, and Sweeney agreed to provide us with a signed statement today linking the deposits to Pierson Partners and naming Scottie Bradshaw as the person who introduced Sweeney to Lowell Hersey."

"Bingo!" Charlie practically shouted. "So Hersey was complicit. How could the SEC have missed the payments?"

"They may have seen them but decided not to charge Hersey. Maybe Scottie wasn't talking then. This affidavit will be an important step but not sufficient evidence to tie Hersey to Mr. Bradshaw's murder. However, the Cook County District Attorney and the SEC should be very interested now in those payments."

Charlie was impressed. Maybe he has underestimated Paul. The police had ways to obtain information that he could never do himself.

"You're right," Charlie said. "That gives Hersey a motive to stop further investigations—especially if Scottie knew about the payments. But if Hersey were capable of murdering Scottie, why not kill Sweeney—another accident?"

"Let's not fix on Mr. Hersey yet. We need to question Sweeney further."

"I guess Sweeney is a suspect. Also he may have blamed Scottie for his problems."

"We'll add him to the list," Paul agreed.

"Maybe this is the breakthrough we have been searching for."

"Perhaps, but it is all circumstantial," Paul said looking down at his notepad. "Finish the names at your golf outing."

"Of course," Charlie paused. "Farah Irani. She ranted about Scottie's poor performance. I may sound too conspiratorial, but we understand that Mrs. Irani is an agent for some tribal families in the Middle East. They may settle their grievances more directly—and violently—than we do. Anyway, we should keep her on the suspect list."

Paul appeared to jot down her name. "Interesting supposition. I have her on the list."

"Two other conversations are worth noting," Charlie continued. "Ira Berkman from BDS partners had some significant business dealings with Scottie. Although he did not try to hide anything, I have trouble reconciling a big hitter like Berkman using a little broker like Scottie. He said something about 'good ideas from Scottie.' We have learned that the term 'good ideas' did not fit Scottie."

"No, he seemed to have more than his share of bad ones," Paul said, smiling.

"At any rate, Berkman wants to come over to Bailey, Richardson to pitch us on directing some of our wealthy clients' money his way. I am going to invite him over—but only to learn more about him."

"And the second conversation?"

"This may be nothing, but it was bizarre. I ran into Jamie Bradshaw in the club's parking lot, and he mentioned that he had not been there since Scottie's death. Later that day, the locker-room attendant recalled that Jamie had been there once or twice. I'm suspicious of someone who lies to me—especially about some matter that does not seem important."

Paul added Jaime to the list saying "I never eliminate a family member. Their motivations to kill may go back decades. How did they get along?"

"Not well, I think. Scottie was an embarrassment to the family, both how he did business and acted socially. Yet Jamie seemed stricken by his death—the whole family was. But last night I remembered something curious. He knew about my initial attempts to investigate the death. He happened to be in Palm Beach at the same time Kate and I were there and we had dinner with his parents."

"And the next night someone tried to run you down," Paul sat back and crossed his arms.

"Furthermore, one might speculate that he did not want me to know he had been at the club several times, because murderers can be obsessed by the scene of the crime and return to it again and again. Am I trying to hard to create something from these scenarios when nothing exists?"

"Possibly, but we should keep an eye on Jamie Bradshaw. Do you really think he could have drowned his brother himself?"

"No. He would have had to hire someone. Crazy idea, or ... forget I mentioned Jamie. Remember he is a very good friend, since we were boys," Charlie said feeling guilty. Then he changed the subject to the bigger picture. "So that was the golf outing — three, maybe four people worth watching."

"We'll take a closer look at each of them," Paul promised. "What about the rest of the client list? There are several who didn't attend the outing?"

"We'll have to follow up on the rest of the list over the next several weeks," Charlie concluded.

"I have news for you," Paul said. "The NYPD and the FBI are keeping alive their look at the wire transfers to Joseph Vecchia from the Cayman Islands. Recently they turned up a series of transfers amounting to $25,000 to Raymond Carome from the same shell corporation. Mr. Carome is a mid-level member of a New York crime family. The NYPD says that another transfer, for a lesser amount, went to a Carome shell company earlier this summer. Their theory is that Carome arranged for the Vecchia attack on Mr. Bradshaw and the murder attempt on you and Miss Milano."

"Why wouldn't the money go straight to Vecchia?" Charlie asked.

"Because Vecchia was—how I'll say it—so dumb. Incredibly dangerous but slow upstairs. He needed someone to tell him what to do. I mean, what murderer would drive up to his victim's front door and park his car there? Who would tell you that he killed Scottie before shooting you? Not slick."

I must admit I have wondered about those things," Charlie said.

"NYPD also thinks that Carome was freelancing—that he was working outside his family."

"So now what happens, with Vecchia being killed?"

"Carome doesn't seem to be giving up. He withdrew more of the Caymans' money immediately. He may be hiring a new hit man."

"And the target is me?"

"And possibly Miss Milano. I am flying to New York at noon to sit in on the NYPD interview of Mr. Carome. They are bringing him in. I might be able to help them with what questions to ask. Meanwhile you and Miss Milano must be very careful. I hope Carome has not hired anyone, but we have to assume that the person behind the money still views you as a threat."

"Talk about good news and bad news," Charlie said. "I always hoped something would come from the money trail. Now something really useful turns up. And Kate and I may be in the crosshairs. This situation gets worse and worse. How do I protect her—let alone myself? Now we are talking about Mafia types. Shit, how did this happen? I'm glad we hired a Roman Spartek."

"But he wasn't any good at your mother's," Paul added. "You need a second bodyguard."

"Do you think we could get some protection from the police now?"

Charlie knew the answer. His stomach felt queasy and his mind depressed. Of course, the targets remain the same.

"I requested it again today, but I can't promise anything."

Charlie wondered if he needed a third or fourth bodyguard. He could easily afford it. Still after Roman was absent the one time they needed him, he favored adding policemen-trained people who are authorized to shoot bad guys. Maybe Paul's boss would allow Charlie to hire one of his policemen off duty.

Charlie's car phone rang when he was halfway back to Chicago. Considering his conversation with Paul, Charlie shuttered when he saw on the dashboard display that the caller was Roman.

"Bad news boss. Miss Milano has been shot."

Charlie slammed his palm on the steering wheel and the car swerved suddenly half into the right lane cutting off an SUV.

"Shut up," Charlie yelled at the honking drivers.

"What, boss?"

"Not you. How is she?" Charlie stammered trying to gain control.

"Not sure. Ambulance is on the way. She was hit in the legs. Bleeding some. The doorman ran out with towels. I wrapped her legs and some neighbors are talking to her and trying to help. I called as soon as I could."

"Where the hell were you, Roman? You're supposed to be protecting her."

On the sidewalk in front of her apartment building."

How did it happen? Couldn't you stop it?"

"Too fast. We came out of her building. The doorman wasn't there; so I went to the curb and hailed a cab. As one was pulling up, I heard the shots. *'bam', 'bam'.*"

He paused, then added, "Had to be a shotgun. Twenty gauge. I saw a black car speeding away."

"Did you get the license number?"

"No. A car going the other way blocked it."

"What about Kate?"

"On the ground. Confused. In pain. I think just the legs." Charlie heard sirens in the background. "Better go," Roman said.

"Wait for God's sake," Charlie shouted. "Make sure they take her to the Northwestern Memorial emergency room. I'll be there as fast as I can. Keep me informed."

As frantic as he felt, Charlie had enough control to make a few phone calls while he pushed through the snail-like traffic. He thought that there must have been an accident ahead. His only alternative to quicken the pace was the shoulder—and hope that no cop saw him. He tried Samantha Milano, Kate's mother—a pretty, trim, intelligent older version of Kate. Both her home phone and cell asked for a message which Charlie gave in as calm and factual a manner as he could muster. He did not want to upset her more than she would be with the news.

"Samantha, Kate has been injured. Meet me at the Northwestern ER downtown as soon as you can. Please let Bill know as well."

Considering that the farm was west of DeKalb, Charlie knew that they would not arrive at the hospital for two hours. He winced at what he imagined Bill Milano's reaction would be. Kate's father was a large, voluble, and passionate man. He would be concerned about Kate but also irate at Charlie for exposing her to harm. Charlie had only met him a handful of times, but Kate had told Charlie about his reaction to the Palm Beach and Lake Forest incidents. He was a powder keg and this shooting would be the match. He would go at Charlie full bore and Charlie admitted that he would be justified.

Next, Charlie left a message for Dr. Bob McConnell, the family internist, to come as fast as he could. Finally, he managed to reach Gordon McAllister, head of the hospital, alerting him to Kate's presence in the ER.

"I am sorry to hear about Kate. I'll make sure she gets the best care," Gordon promised.

By then Charlie had given up on the Edens Expressway and was taking the cross streets to the hospital. He decided to tell his mother when he knew more. He would implore her to visit Kate in the hospital. He thought she might hesitate considering her lack of enthusiasm for Kate. Still, Kate was his fiancée had saved his life. Claire needed to accept reality and show good manners.

When he reached the emergency waiting room, he was happy to see Bob McConnell. Roman was there also.

"Bob, how is she?"

"I don't know, Charlie. She's in surgery. The good news is she had a great surgeon—Dr. Mehta. She came in in shock with several pellet wounds. I admitted her so I'll get a report—possibly in an hour. Go up to the surgery waiting room on five and sit down. I'll be back when they page me."

"Thanks, Bob."

Charlie took the elevator up followed by Roman. Angry that Roman had not prevented the shooting, Charlie sat far from him in the waiting room. Five minutes later Gordon McAllister arrived.

"We have the A team in there. Try to be patient."

"I feel powerless—and responsible."

"I'm not sure what you mean but your feelings are common by all loved ones. I have to go now but will stay on top of Kate's situation."

Charlie sat alone for about three minutes in the waiting room. Anger was swelling in him. He could no longer hold it in. He stood up and walked directly to a seated Roman.

"Oh boss, how is she? What's you want me to do?"

"You shit. I hired you to protect Kate. You failed. Twice - at my mothers and now this. Fucking incompetent. After the shooting, how could you leave her alone on the sidewalk outside the building? She could wait for her cab inside. You didn't even get the license plate."

When Charlie was talking, Roman was looking down, still sitting.

"Sorry boss. I'll do better next time."

"Next time?" Charlie shouted. "There's no next time. Kate might die. You're fired. Get your sorry ass out of here. You're finished."

Romans stood up suddenly, his face contorted.

"Shut up," Roman screamed venting emotion Charlie had not seen. "Or you'll be sorry. I'm a good bodyguard. Get yourself someone else."

He walked straight at Charlie and brushed his shoulder with his. He was gone by the time Charlie turned around.

"*Good riddance*," Charlie thought. He sat down and waited.

After an hour Bob McConnell came by. "Sorry. She is still in there. Her vitals are satisfactory but they are still digging out pellets. Hang in there. I'll be back."

Time dragged on slowly. After the second hour Charlie asked the nurse at the central station on five how Kate was doing. She said only that they were still in the OR.

Thirty minutes later Kate's parents arrived. Bill Milano headed straight for a standing Charlie. He was a muscular six-footer with slightly graying hair and the tan of a man who spent most of his days outdoors. He was still in his blue jeans and a short sleeve sport shirt. As he neared Charlie, Charlie thought he was preparing to throw a punch.

"Asshole!" he shouted, stopping two feet from Charlie's face. "We'll take care of our daughter. How could you put her in danger like this? Bastard! Maybe she shouldn't have saved your life!"

While Bill was bellowing at him Charlie backed away to create some distance. Samantha Milano was crying and begging Bill to stop.

"I'm so sorry," Charlie offered meekly. "You are right. I'll leave you alone."

Charlie walked outside of the waiting room and stopped in the hallway. He waited to let the Milano's comfort each other privately. However, he could not leave without hearing that Kate would be all right.

After another fifteen minutes Charlie noticed the nurse he had questioned before go into the waiting room and talk to them Milanos. They followed her toward the mechanical doors leading to the post-op area. Charlie started to follow them, but Bill turned back and pointed maliciously at him. "Stay away," he said.

So Charlie waited and worried. Roman had said that Kate had been hit by shotgun pellets in the legs and perhaps the lower body. *Would she survive? If so, would she walk again? Have her liver or kidneys been hit? Would she be able to have children? What would she think of me?*

*What about the shooter? That hood, Raymond Carome, may have hired him like Joseph Vecchia. And the guy who hired Carome? That guy was behind Scottie's murder in the first place. I hope that Paul Victor is successful in New York. I need to call him.*

Charlie was jolted from his thinking by the arrival of Dr.

Bob McConnell again.

"I talked to Dr. Mehta. Kate should be fine after she takes seven or eight weeks of rehab. The pellets missed any vital organs; the damage was localized in her legs. The reason the surgery took so long is that one pellet lodged in her knee and another was wedged under a major nerve. The team had to be precise in those removals. She is in post-op now and will be moved to a regular room soon.'

'Kate's parents are with her and left a strongly worded instruction that you are not to visit her. I'm sorry but the hospital must comply with their wishes."

"I understand, Bob. I am relieved by the outcome. Dr. Mehta and his team did a wonderful job. And thank you for your help."

Bob left and Charlie returned to a seat in the waiting room. He had started to think of security for Kate when Detective John Riordan came into the room.

"I heard about the shooting and asked to be assigned to this case as it clearly relates to the Bradshaw murder. I was just brought up to speed by the patrolman out in the hall. Eliminating Vecchia did not deter our killer/mastermind."

"Could you provide security for Kate?" Charlie pleaded.

"While she is here, we'll have uniforms twenty-four/seven. The hospital also has its security force. She should be safe. I would like to question your private guard. The man on the scene did not get a full description of the event. Is he here?"

"No. I fired him. He left. I can give you his cell phone and address. His name is Roman Spartek."

"Where did you find him?"

"My lawyer and a friend have used him and recommended him."

"If I can't reach Spartek, I'll need to talk to your referrals. What are their names?"

"Bob Underwood—here is his card - and Jamie Bradshaw."

"The same Bradshaw family?" the detective asked, raising his eyebrows.

"Yes."

"Okay. I heard she pulled through. That's one good thing."

Just in case the Milanos changed their minds, Charlie stayed in the waiting room. He called his mother and gave her the bad news.

"She's here at Northwestern for a couple of days, I imagine. The doctors think she'll recover fully. Physically that is; mentally and emotionally, I don't know."

"I'm shaking," Claire Bailey confessed. "Poor Kate. I'll come see her tomorrow morning. Let her rest tonight."

"That's nice of you to offer, but I'm afraid that's impossible. Her parents blame me and want nothing to do with the Baileys."

"They must be stressed to the limit. Don't they appreciate that you were nearly killed also? They should treat you better. Well, I offered.'

'I suppose this will be on the news tonight. I better call Dottie to warn her. She has been so depressed."

"Mother, I've been thinking I should hire some security for you. Don't be alarmed, but just in case. This evil guy seems to be getting after me by targeting those I love."

"I'm quite harmless. But if you think . . . but not that Roman guy. He gives me the creeps."

"I fired him today."

"Good. He failed Kate. Glad to see him go."

Charlie finally gave up twenty minutes later. As he was leaving the hospital he recognized a co-worker of Kate's, Marc D'Amboise, at the information desk. Marc was an artist in her department—average height with model-like looks and build.

"Marc, why are you here?"

"I came to see Kate. I heard the news. Her mother called the office. They said I might raise her spirits. Have you seen her?"

"No. But if you see her, tell her I was waiting for her. Okay?"

"Of course. You're engaged. Right? I saw the ring."

"Right."

Charlie left, feeling worse knowing that she would see Marc—not him. Somehow, he had to see her.

# CHAPTER TWENTY-THREE

Charlie was in no mood to go to the office; so he went home. His voicemail was blinking eight messages, all from friends and the press expressing concern and wanting comment on Kate's condition. Peaches' second call caught his attention.

"Charlie, good friend, give me the inside scoop on Kate. I feel so sorry for her. I hope she is okay. The Bradshaw murder just goes on and on. Is someone trying to get even because she shot that low-life Vecchia? You must know who's behind this. The police aren't talking. I'll be discreet."

As sobering as the events of the day had been, Charlie had to laugh. *Discreet* and *Peaches*, the words didn't belong together. But the last part of Peaches' message was especially alarming.

"One last thing. A source of mine noticed something as Kate was lifted into the ambulance. She had a sparkler on her left hand. You're engaged and didn't tell me. At least tell me about that."

*Once a society reporter, always a society reporter*, Charlie thought. He and Kate had decided to put off an announcement until his investigation was finished and they could make plans for the wedding. The topic seemed inappropriate at this time. So

Charlie made a note to request that Peaches hold off, promising in exchange a full report soon. That was the one call he planned to return later in the day.

Charlie turned his attention to Paul Victor in New York. On his first try Charlie was able to reach Paul on his cell while he was cabbing in from LaGuardia. The news about Kate did not seem to surprise him.

"I was worried that something like this could happen," Paul said. "How is she doing?"

"I think she'll be fine with the proper care. I'm told that she is scared but not hysterical—considering that she has been targeted again.

"My guess is that they did not mean to kill her—using a shotgun and seemingly aiming low."

"Unless the guy was just a bad shot," Charlie added.

"I'll call my contacts with the Chicago PD and see if they found something at the crime scene. A doorman or a passerby might have seen the car or the driver. In the meantime, my chances of providing you and Miss Milano some protection have improved."

"Great. But why do you think the man behind the murder is still trying to kill us—or scare us? He had no compunction about killing Scottie, but we can't be a big threat."

I don't know. The facts aren't consistent. Maybe he only wanted to scare you at your mother's house, but Vecchia freelanced on him. Maybe he knows you and Miss Milano. That may be threatening to him. Also now that Vecchia is dead, the picture may have changed for him. The stakes are higher. I wouldn't count on him backing off."

"Yes. With that possibility in mind, didn't you mention something about protection?"

"I have been working on Commander Mayo. He says protection is very unusual and not covered under his normal arrangements with the towns in the county which pay our expenses. However, he said he will be having a meeting with the chiefs soon, and he hopes to sell them on the idea."

"Okay. I'll take that as a 'maybe'. Anyway, I don't want to hold you up. I know you have to get into town for the Carome interview. That still seems to me the most fruitful lead. Good luck."

Despite his experience with Roman, Charlie then put in a call to Bob Underwood to find one or two new bodyguards.

Paul Victor directed his cab to the lower Manhattan office of the assistant district attorney, where the questioning was scheduled to take place. Since both the FBI and the NYPD had an interest in this case, they were cooperating in supervising the interrogation. In some cases Paul might be asked to participate in the questioning, since he knew the most about the details, but this time they all agreed the NYPD probably knew best how to deal with Carome. Accordingly Paul expected that when he arrived he would be asked simply to brief NYPD Detective Brian Malone on the Illinois case so far.

When he entered the building a security pass was waiting for him. He took the elevator to the fifth floor. There he was greeted by an FBI agent who introduced him to a handful of other FBI and police officials. Paul had never seen such an impressive array of personnel and resources in his life. They walked into a large room with steel case desks pushed together to create a central corridor and make for easy communication. The room looked like the squad room in Waukegan—only about five times bigger. Paul pulled an empty chair over to a space by a wall and studied the group standing and sitting on desktops assembled around him.

Paul began by describing to the group what had occurred to Kate this morning but emphasized he had few details. A wiry detective named Brian Malone wrote down a few notes in his pad and introduced himself as the one assigned to interrogate Carome. He mentioned that he had been briefed initially by Commander Mayo during a phone call in the morning while Paul was on the plane.

"I always get to interrogate hoods like Ray Carome. My specialty, so to speak, is the mob—the Mafia in New York. You have your 'outfit' in Chicago; we have our 'mob'. Carome is a third or fourth level operative; he does little jobs here and there. Some enforcement. Some collection. He must be working on his own on this case. Anyway, it looks like Carome worked fast. He must have been paid for speed. I always thought he was lazy. Maybe he has become more diligent since he screwed up the hit on Mr. Bailey. Miss Milano was the one who shot Joe Vecchia?"

"Right," Paul answered. "A shotgun also."

"I think she's lucky she's not dead. A shotgun from a moving car. Not a classic arrangement. No telling where the victim will be hit. So Paul, what does your prime suspect look like?"

"He may be a financial professional or a well-heeled client of the deceased, Scottie Bradshaw. His motive may be linked to financial losses or fear of disclosure of regulatory misconduct. At any rate, we figure the financier of the murder is a first timer and wants to keep his hands clean—hence the contract killer, Vecchia."

"Oh, I see Mr. Carome has arrived," Detective Malone said. "Our protocol is that I'll have my partner, Joe Pacelli, with me in the room taking notes while you watch the proceedings from the adjoining room."

At that point Raymond Carome and his lawyer entered the interrogation room and everyone else but detectives Malone and Pacelli took his place in the next room. The room had a two-way mirror and a wall-mounted speaker. Ray Carome wore a black, open-necked knit shirt, dark slacks, and a navy sport coat. He was short, under 5'7" tall, pudgy, with black hair and tanned skin. His companion was a tall, thin man with a mustache, wearing a shiny gray suit, white shirt, white tie, and wire glasses and carrying a briefcase. When everyone was in place sitting around the table, Malone began, "Ray Carome, nice of you to visit us again. Counselor Schwartz, I hope you will not impede this investigation."

"I am here to protect my client's well-recognized rights," the lawyer explained.

"Fine, let's begin. Mr. Carome, what is Broome Street Foods?"

"I don't know. But I know where Broome Street is."

"Let me refresh your memory. These incorporation papers, which I am handing to you, list you as president of Broome Street Foods, and this bank-account application in the same name lists you as signator. Now do you remember?"

"Oh, yes. It slipped my mind."

"What is the nature of Broome Street's business?"

"Import, export, foodstuffs—that sort of thing."

"Why is its address the same as your home address?"

"It is? What a coincidence. Business has been slow lately. I can't afford a separate office."

"Isn't it true that the only activity in this company is some deposits and withdrawals in its bank accounts?"

"Could be. As I said, business is slow."

"Recently Broome Street Foods received several wire transfers from a bank account in the Cayman Islands. Who was sending you money?"

"I never asked. I thought I just got lucky. Banks make mistakes, you know."

"The transfers amounted to $27,000. There was no mistake."

Raymond Carome then leaned close to his lawyer and whispered to him. After a few moments Mr. Schwartz got up.

"Mr. Carome doesn't need me any longer, so I am leaving."

"What's going on?" Paul asked the detective next to him. "Where's his lawyer going?"

"You'll see," the detective said. "Remember, Carome works for the mob, and Schwartz is a mob lawyer."

Paul nodded in understanding.

After the lawyer left, the detective explained more to Paul.

"I wondered how long that would take. Once Carome realized that we were looking at some moonlighting he has been doing, the last person he needed hearing that was the family's lawyer. He might just tell the mob of his freelancing."

"Schwartz's daughter has a piano lesson and he had to go," Carome said.

"Cut the crap. Who sent you the money?"

"The tooth fairy."

"Who is Joe Vecchia?"

"Never heard of him."

"This same Cayman Islands bank account transferred to Broome Street Foods and Joseph Vecchia significant amounts of money during the summer. Mr. Vecchia then committed a murder of a Scottie Bradshaw and was himself killed when he tried to commit a second murder. We have a witness who saw you meeting with Vecchia soon after he was released from prison last May. We think you hired Vecchia in fulfillment of a scheme of a Cayman Islands bank customer to commit the murder of Scottie Bradshaw and an attempt to harm Katherine Milano and Charles Bailey. When Vecchia failed to kill Mr. Bailey and was himself killed, we think you hired a new hit man shortly after more money came from the Cayman Islands."

"Hold on, Malone!" Carome shouted. He looked around the

room and back at Detective Malone. "What's all this bullshit? Murder? I never heard of any of these people. You got the wrong guy."

"You are in a world of hurt, Ray. This one is a lot worse then the penny-ante stuff you do for the family. You either start talking or we are going to come down on you a lot harder and we might want to tell Mr. Schwartz how you cut out the family by starting your own business."

Ray Carome shook his head and paused. To Paul he looked very uncomfortable from Malone's threats.

"No, you don't want to do that. Maybe I do recall Vecchia. He was a scumbag out of the slammer looking for a job. He probably misunderstood his assignment. I never told him to whack anyone. He was a screw-up. He gave me the creeps. He liked snakes and spiders and stuff like that. I heard that he had containers that had pet lizards and tarantulas and snakes."

Carome shuddered. Paul thought he was acting.

"He fed a live frog to a snake in front of his girlfriend, and she screamed so loud someone in the building called the cops."

He laughed.

"They thought he was killing someone but it was only a frog."

"Ha, ha." Malone said flatly looking at Detective Pacelli. "A comedian. Vecchia murdered a man at your instructions."

"Wait a minute! He either did that on his own, or someone else told him to do it."

"From the Caymans?"

"I dunno. Maybe."

---

"Who?" Malone asked, raising his voice.

"I don't know. A guy just called and sent money."

"So how did he get your name?"

"Another job I did a couple of years ago. A Wall Street guy who wanted to scare his wife's boyfriend."

"What is his name?"

"Johnson. Robert Johnson. A firm named Boylston something on Broad Street, near Wall. The boyfriend was named James Weston. Johnson must have liked what we done. Say, don't you think I should get some deal here? I'm giving you a lot."

"Keep talking and maybe we can speak to the DA. Was the Johnson job a family setup, Were you freelancing? You know, if you talk about the family, too, maybe we can get a better deal."

"I ate no snitch. Keep the family out of this. I want to live. Okay? I did the Johnson job by myself—no one else."

The detective next to Paul asked him, "Did you ever hear of Johnson?"

"No, the guy is news to me. He should be a good lead."

"Let's go back to Chicago," Malone continued. "Who did you hire to attack Miss Milano this morning?"

"No one."

Malone groans in disbelief. "Get serious or forget the DA. Understand. Who did it?" Malone shouts.

"Big Ferrol. Ferrol Lopez. I don't know where he is or how to get in touch with him. He calls me."

"When did you talk to him most recently?"

"This morning."

"Before or after he shot miss Milano?"

"After."

"He tried to kill her—on your instructions."

"You're wrong. Just scare her. Shoot at the sidewalk."

"Bullshit. He hit her bad."

"Mistake. Big Ferrol fucked up. He said so."

"His mistake was not killing her. You wanted revenge because she shot Vecchia." Malone said pointing at him.

"Who gives a shit about Vecchia?" Carome answered.

"You need to stop Lopez—now." Malone demanded.

"Don't worry. He is supposed to lay low until he hears from me."

"How do you get in touch with this guy who pays you?"

"I don't. He calls me."

"If he only calls you, then you did order Vecchia to kill Mr. Bradshaw and Mr. Bailey."

"No, no, you got it all wrong. Vecchia went overboard—on his own. I was only talking a rough-up, not a murder."

"Sure, and your brother is the Pope. Tell me, what did the money man from the Caymans say after Vecchia was shot?"

"He said, 'Get another man. Bailey and his girlfriend are snooping around too much. Scare them off. Stop them.'"

"Did he mention the police investigation?"

"No, he didn't seem to be worried about the police—just Bailey."

"That's dumb," Paul murmured to no one in particular in the next room.

"Did this guy tell you why he wanted Scottie Bradshaw dead?" Malone asked.

"As I said, Bradshaw must have been an accident. I didn't tell Vecchia to kill no one."

"We'll let that lay for a while. So did this guy who sent you a lot of money tell you why Bradshaw should be roughed up?"

"No. And I don't ask questions when someone wants to send me money."

"Okay. We'll stop there. Detective Pacelli will have a statement for you to sign in a few minutes. We'll have more questions in a few days. In the meantime, the officer outside will read you your rights and you go to lock-up."

Brian Malone left Carome sitting at the table and went to the viewing room next door.

."What do you think?" Detective Malone asked Paul.

"He's lying about the murder. Vecchia was under orders to drown Scottie Bradshaw. Why did you stop the questioning now? Carome knows things he isn't admitting."

"True. But he will tell us more after he has some time to consider his future. Arrangements we need to know more about: Johnson and Lopez and the communications from the guy Carome calls the Caymans. Besides, Carome isn't going anywhere."

Brian Malone and Joe Pacelli led Paul out to the large, open office and told him he could use the desk next to Joe's. Detective Pacelli immediately went to his computer, saying he would find what was available about Robert Johnson. Meanwhile Paul contacted Mayo and the Chicago PD to alert them about Ferrol

Lopez, the probably perpetrator of the drive-by shooting of Katherine Milano.

Paul Victor marveled once again at the resources that New York had and the powers of persuasion Detective Malone showed. Paul had to admit that the detective had done a better job of questioning than he would have. What was new to him was that, clearly, Carome was more worried about the wrath of his regular employer than of any federal, state, or municipal agency. Carome's mistake was hiring a hit man outside his mob family. He would not compound it by ratting on his own.

In Paul's mind Carome had divulged some excellent information. First, the gunman today was big Ferrol Lopez. Soon the NYPD would have his picture and physical description. Second, the police should be able to find a wealth of public information about Robert Johnson. With pressure he might talk. Johnson had recommended Carome to the man behind Bradshaw's murder. Third, the FBI and NYPD had been correct in linking Carome with Vecchia and Carome should prove to be a useful witness once the mastermind was apprehended.

While Paul was waiting for information on Robert Johnson, he called Charlie on his cell phone to bring him up to date. He reached Charlie at home.

"Good work." Charlie said. "Johnson is key. Perhaps you are near to identifying the man behind all this."

"One step at a time," Victor cautioned. "Have you ever heard of Johnson?"

"No one in particular comes to mind. But I have heard of

Boylston & Co. It is a small Boston-based investment banking firm. I think I remember that it has a New York office. I can check my sources to see if anyone knows Robert Johnson. I'll get back to you as soon as I can."

"That would be helpful. But let me caution you, Charlie. Don't assume that Carome is telling the truth about Ferrol Lopez. You and Miss Milano should not let your guard down. We need to catch Lopez, if he is who shot Miss Milano. Carome may be lying about that. We don't want anything else to happen to you two."

"I agree. Good advice. The problem is Kate has an important job, and I have a company to run and an obligation to my clients."

"You will have no obligations if you are dead. Be careful."

The *Tribune* ran an article on its Internet site that evening that justified Charlie's worst fears:

### GOLD COAST SOCIALITE ATTACKED

*Gold Coast executive and socialite*
*Kate Milano was shot by an unknown*
*assailant this morning as she was*
*hailing a cab outside her tony Gold*
*Coast apartment house. She suffered*
*multiple wounds from shotgun pellets.*
*She is at Northwestern Memorial*
*Hospital, where her condition is*
*listed as stable.*

The article went on to mention Scottie's murder and speculated that there may be a connection between that, the shooting of Vecchia at Claire Bailey's house, and what had happened to Kate this morning. Charlie was livid that Peaches had put all the incidents together without any proof. Charlie commented angrily to an empty room that the article belonged on the gossip page instead of the news section.

Now he would return Peaches' call. He reached the perpetrator of unbridled speculation on the second ring.

"Is this Mr. Discreet?" Charlie began in an antagonistic tone. "How could you write that article about Kate and bring up the Bradshaw murder again? Give us some peace. Kate doesn't need the press hounding her about an incident she had nothing to do with. She's hurting enough from her wounds."

"Sorry, Charlie. But if I didn't show the connection between the shooting and that creep Vecchia and her getting shot today, every other reporter would. It's too obvious. Understand, I am your friend. You take care of my little nest egg - what I desperately need for my retirement. But Kate's predicament is news. I have to cover it."

"Not in the way you did! I could wring your neck."

"Calm down. I'm no match for you. Next time return my phone calls and I might write a different article: more dry facts and less juicy conjecture. *Mea culpa*."

Charlie paused waiting for his anger to abate to a slow burn.

"Peaches, normally I put up with your behavior and smile at your outrageous banter. But you crossed the line this time. This matter is far too serious. I'm pissed."

"I hear that. I'll do better in the future." Peaches promised, then tried a different subject. "I don't suppose this is a good time to talk about that diamond ring?"

"What?" Charlie shouted and slammed down the phone.

After twenty minutes Charlie had cooled down enough to focus on Robert Johnson. He called a few business acquaintances who might know Boylston & Co. and maybe even Johnson.

Perry Duda said, "Sure, Boylston is a modest-sized investment banking firm specializing in small and start-up companies. It has a good reputation. I never heard of Robert Johnson."

After three similar responses, Charlie reached Peter Osgood, an investment banker at UBS. "I've met him. Once, at the Racquet Club. In the large men's barroom. He was seated at the big communal table. Let's see. The usual cast of characters who hang out there were present: Doug Smith, Farley Dugan, Josh Nathanson, others. Drinking and telling stories."

"What was his story?"

"He was visiting from New York. Had banking work in Chicago. He was a chatty guy who said he played a lot of squash at the NYC Princeton Club. Yeah, he went to Princeton and Columbia B-school. He already was lubricated with Bloody Marys. Brought up his messy divorce a few years ago. Why? I don't know. He bragged about it."

"What did he say?" Charlie asked, quite interested.

"The divorce dragged on for a couple of years. He was pissed by the delay. Blamed her. So when he heard that his ex had hooked up with some guy, he arranged something that scared the heck out of them. He laughed and said she deserved it."

"Sour grapes." Charlie commented. "Did he say how he scared her?"

"Nothing I remember. He did say it worked."

*<sub>*</sub>*<sub>*</sub>

Paul was pleased that Joe Pacelli had no trouble pulling up Robert Johnson's address, driver's license picture, social security number, and the notice of his divorce settlement. Otherwise Johnson had done nothing in his life that was relevant to any police investigation.

"A lot of information," Joe concluded. "But no reason to know Carome. They come from different worlds. Someone must have brought them together for the one job Ray talked about."

"Lopez is a different story," Joe said showing Paul a pile of police records. "Six arrests, two convictions, and multiple accounts involving physical violence and gun usage. Lopez is in his early forties and has done nine years in prison. His ex-wife and their two kids left him long ago and moved back to Puerto Rico. Currently he is in violation of his parole, and the NYPD has a warrant out for his arrest."

Paul reasoned that Lopez might be difficult to find in Chicago. Nothing in his file tied him to Chicago. In addition, since he had completed the assignment that Carome had given him, he might be traveling to another part of the country.

Detective Malone joined them by Joe's desk. Joe briefed him

on Johnson. Then Malone smiled and said, "We just brought him in for questions. He's in room *C*."

Paul noted that Johnson was well-dressed, trim, and of average height. He was in his mid-thirties and polished. Malone took him to the same room where he had questioned Carome. Pacelli joined Malone as before. Paul went to the adjoining room to watch and listen. He took out a notepad and pen.

Johnson appeared nervous and confused.

"Mr. Johnson," Malone began. "You may have relevant information pertaining to an investigation we are conducting. I expect you to answer my questions honestly and fully. Do you understand?"

"Yes, but what is this all about? Do I need a lawyer?"

"We aren't charging you now. You can decide that as we proceed. Please state your name, address, marital status, social security number, and occupation."

After the preliminary information gathering, Detective Malone asked simply, "Do you know Raymond Carome?"

Robert sank in his chair and did not answer. Paul feared that Johnson might become ill. A minute passed, and Malone waited patiently.

"I don't think so," Johnson answered finally. "Can you give me the context where I would know this gentleman?"

"Mr. Carome told us that you had hired him to threaten harm to your ex-wife's boyfriend, James Weston, a few years ago. We need you to verify this statement and tell us if Mr. Carome carried out the threats."

"Oh, this is terrible." Johnson gushed, shaking. "I never meant Weston any harm. I don't think anything serious happened. I only wanted to get even with Laura. Carome looked like central casting for a Mafia-type, so I thought it would work. I guess Carome scared him enough, because I learned Weston stop seeing Laura. I paid Carome $2000. I'm sorry if I did something wrong."

"How did you meet Mr. Carome?"

"Because the divorce took so long and was so painful, I complained about it openly. My secretary, Donna, was sympathetic to my situation and offered to help in any way. I made a stupid joke. I wondered if there was a way to get Weston to stop seeing my ex-wife. Donna said she knew someone who might be able to do that."

"Helpful secretary, Joe." Malone commented. Paul snorted.

"I met Carome at a coffee shop downtown, Larry's on Houston Street. I told him about Weston and left the specifics to him, but I said 'no violence'. I had nothing against Weston."

"Did you ever mention this incident to anyone?"

"Well, I might have bragged to some friends from time-to-time that I put Laura in her place. I was hurt and wanted to sound in control."

"What about recommending Carome to someone with a similar need?"

Paul thought that Malone was finally getting to the big question.

"There was a person who called me at the office last spring. He said he was a friend of a friend of mine in Chicago and wanted

to scare his wife who was cheating on him. I told him about Carome and gave him Carome's phone number."

"Who was that individual?" Malone pressed.

"He said his name was Harrison, I think. It may have been
a phony name. I never heard of him again."

The interview lasted another twenty minutes before Malone
told Johnson he could leave.

Johnson look surprised, then sighed in relief. Paul looked
down at his notes and saw he had written one name on the
notepad in capital letters: 'HARRISON'."

Malone came in to wish Paul good luck. He added,
"Harrison said he was from Chicago. Could he be your man?"

# CHAPTER TWENTY-FOUR

Paul called Charlie on his cell the next morning after he landed at O'Hare. They both had additional information to share on Robert Johnson.

"It's possible," Paul said. "That the man we are seeking in the Bradshaw murder was the man who identified himself as Harrison. Last night the FBI passed along all the phone records to Johnson's office from March through June. One of those calls might have been from Harrison. We'll research them all."

"Great," Charlie said enthusiastically. "Meanwhile I'll talk to Doug Smith. He was at that dinner with Johnson at the Racquet Club. I know him socially. If I approach Doug in a low-key way, he might remember if he repeated Johnson's story about Jimmy Weston and his wife to anyone. The police could follow up afterwards, if necessary. It's a long shot."

"Go ahead," Paul responded, "Since you know Doug Smith. An approach without us is irregular. I'm going to have to trust you."

"Are you through with Carome?" Charlie asked.

"I doubt we'll learn much more from him," Paul said. "He

appeared to be telling the truth when he said he never met Harrison. As long as the money showed up in his bank account Carome did not care to meet Harrison. But Carome gave us Johnson and Ferrol Lopez—as well as admitting to hiring Vecchia. We are checking Carome's cell phone records now on the off-chance that Harrison used an identifiable phone. Maybe we'll get lucky."

"I have an APB out for Lopez now. But he seems to be a loose cannon who could strike again at any time. You know Vecchia would have killed you had Miss Milano not intervened. We have to assume that now Lopez is out to kill you and Miss Milano."

"Do you think Vecchia and Lopez were ordered by Harrison to kill us?"

"Carome says no, that Vecchia was freelancing. We don't know about Lopez. Carome may be lying to try to reduce his downside. If Harrison finds out we have Carome, he'll try to reach Lopez directly. You should assume the worst."

"I do."

"Miss Milano has CPD protection until she leaves the hospital. Are you providing a bodyguard after that? Who was that Roman guy I met?"

"I fired him. I am looking for someone better now."

"We are still looking at the list we have of Scottie's clients. Nothing yet. Anything else for me?" Paul asked.

"Yes. Would you fax me a picture of Ferrol Lopez?"

"Of course. Mug shot from two years ago. Ugly scar above the right eye. Big guy, dark hair."

*␣*␣*

Charlie spent the morning at the office trying to reach Kate. His calls went to the nurse station instead of her room.

"I'm sorry, Mr. Bailey. We've been told by the family not to disturb Miss Milano with phone calls. They want her to rest. Recovery may take a long time."

Charlie heard this response three times that morning before he gave up in frustration, left the office and took a taxi to the hospital. As the taxi drove crosstown Charlie stared half consciously at the collection of high-end stores on Chicago's most celebrated shopping street, Michigan Avenue. Normally, he would be interested in the merchandise in the windows, but today he had only Kate on his mind. The taxi turned off the avenue into the maze of buildings that was Northwestern Memorial Hospital. Its multiple facilities covered many city blocks and were connected underground, on street level, and with overpasses. Charlie stopped the taxi at the main patient building.

The hospital had moved her overnight to a private room on the fifth floor. As he walked down the corridor he saw Roman outside her room.

"What the hell are you doing here?" Charlie demanded.

Roman stood up from his chair and commanded, "Stop. You aren't allowed in. Mr. Milano's orders. In other words, get lost."

"I fired you. Why are you here?"

"Mr. Milano hired me. Specially, he said you can't go in."

"Bullshit."

Charlie moved toward the door, but Roman stood his ground. They bumped shoulder to chest. Furious, Charlie pushed Roman but couldn't move him. Roman grabbed Charlie's shoulders and twisted him around, encircling Charlie's body with his arms.

"You're going nowhere."

Charlie realized that Roman was stronger than he was. He looked left and saw the CPD policeman down the hall.

"Officer! Get this thug off me. I need to see my fiancé."

The policeman came over and parted the two. "No visitors in that room, sir."

"Why?"

"Her father said she was hurt badly. Couldn't risk any excitement. Maybe try again to visit in a day or two."

Charlie was befuddled. What to do? He went over to the nurse's station and called the President's office. Gordon McAllister was out. Out of options, incensed, Charlie resigned himself to a temporary defeat.

\* \* \*

When he arrived home, he leafed through the great number of voicemails—from the press, friends, and close clients. The first one he selected was from Jamie Bradshaw.

"Thanks for calling me back, Charlie. How's Kate? Is she still in the hospital?"

"I haven't been able to talk to her, but I get the feeling that she is in dreadful shape. But she will survive."

"Mom and Dad asked about her as well. We hope she

recovers fully and soon. I feel bad that somehow we are responsible. Scottie's death appears linked to her being shot."

"God, Jamie, you are the victims. You shouldn't apologize. No, it's my fault. If I had let the police do their job, nothing would have happened to her."

"I know you were just trying to help us. Certainly I understand that if after what's happened you step aside. That's okay with me."

"Thanks. I'm sure the police will find the killer."

Charlie paused and then changed the subject. "We hired a bodyguard we heard you had used, Roman Spartek. Sound familiar?"

"Yes. My firm used him a few months ago. We had a client, a Middle Eastern sheik, who was apprehensive about his safety while staying in Chicago. He wanted locals to augment his team. We have a list of a few security firms we have used in the past. This time we used Roman. I think he did a good job. The sheik was happy."

"I wasn't. He flubbed two dangerous situations for us. I tell you to watch out for him."

"Thanks for the heads up. Call me if I can help with Kate."

"Say, Jamie. Since your firm uses other security firms, could you recommend someone to look after my mother?"

"Of course. We used a guy last month. His name is Jimbo Pavko—was in Special Forces. His presence and demeanor scared everybody. I have his number on my cell. I'll text it to you."

"Thanks. I'll interview him."

Charlie hung up and considered where he was. He had no intention of stopping his investigation. He and Paul Victor were making progress. His efforts were now intensely personal. He didn't scare off. Kate was seriously hurt and he was undoubtedly in the crosshairs. There was urgency and seriousness in what he was doing.

He took out his list of suspects and reviewed the names again. Who was Harrison? Lowell Hersey? Maybe. He showed me that he has a short fuse on the golf course. Scottie had undoubtedly put Hersey together with Sweeney of Paradigm Funds. Hersey had avoided SEC sanctions but if Scottie had wanted to he could have told the SEC how Hersey's firm had enticed Sweeney into breaking the law. So Scottie was a continuing threat to Hersey.

*What was harder to understand was why a savvy hedge fund like BDS did so much business with Scottie? What was the quid pro quo?*

Ira Berkman had come over to Bailey, Richardson a few days before, as he had promised. Ira was a blunt, tough, and unscrupulous man.

"Although we are both in the same money management business, we could work together—nothing formal or in writing— but a friendly understanding. People tell me that your analysts are excellent. We'd love to hear their best ideas. Also you could introduce some of your clients who need a hedge fund to diversify their portfolio holdings."

"Why would I do that?"

"Our investment returns have been spectacular. Your clients would benefit and for you we could make Bailey, Richardson a subadvisor to our largest fund."

"That arrangement seems fraught with conflicts of interest. I worry that it might work against the interests of most of our clients."

Beckman frowned, "Well, think about it. You might benefit quite a bit."

Charlie would never put his interests ahead of his clients' Still he wanted to hear more about how Beckman did business.

"Ira, describe another arrangement or partnership that worked for both partners. For instance, Scottie Bradshaw at Collins, Lang. They couldn't offer you much in research or trading."

"Of course not. But Scottie had some great merger and acquisition ideas. Clearly they didn't come from Collins, Lang. They were the kinds of intelligence that would come out of a large investment bank or a law firm specializing in mergers."

"Scottie must have had a contact there?"

"Precisely," Berkman said with emphasis. "He wouldn't tell us who, but after the first two deals worked out we listened to him. See, we like to work with people. We make it worthwhile. Your client base of the top executives and old money would be a great source."

Wow. How unethical! Charlie was blown away. He couldn't believe Berkman would be so candid and so shady. Charlie remembered he had ended the conversation with "Not us. We can't be a party to the arrangements you describe." He then had ushered Berkman out.

That memory was ugly and informative. Ira Berkman would have wanted Scottie alive—not dead. But the idea that Scottie had a source in a bank or a law firm willing to give him illegal insider information on potential financial deals added a whole new dimension to the Scottie story. A mole. Scottie had to be paying him or had some leverage that forced the mole to go along.

Charlie had decided to withhold this speculative theory from Paul, who was busy with Carome and Johnson. Charlie wanted to use his contacts at the Chicago and New York investment banks and law firms to try to confirm this intriguing lead. There were fifteen or twenty such firms. Plus, if Berkman made up the story, Charlie did not want to be embarrassed by it. Still he had been thinking about where to start. He needed some hard evidence before his snooping spooked the mole.

Charlie looked up Doug Smith's telephone number but then realized that he had set up a squash lesson with Adam, an assistant pro at the Racquet Club. The club was only five blocks away from his apartment; so he didn't need to hail a cab. He checked his watch and saw that he would be on time.

Darkness was deepening when Charlie reached the street. He looked up at the black clouds and decided it was going to rain. He judged that he could beat the rain, but he was happy he had brought an umbrella. The air was warm and noticeably muggy— a carryover from the earlier rain. Because of the humidity, Charlie was tempted to remove his suit coat, but he decided to wait to see if he would start to perspire on the walk. If so, then the coat would come off.

As he walked, he noticed the street lights were not yet on. Combined with the darkening sky and the leafy trees lining the streets, he felt as if it was nighttime. He couldn't see more than a block ahead.

As the darkness surrounded him, he noticed only two other walkers on the sidewalks. He heard footsteps behind him as he walked west. Instinctively, Charlie shivered and then his shoulders and neck were yanked back. He dropped the umbrella and tried to break away but his assailant was too strong. He yelled for help, leaned forward, and raised his right leg. Then he back-kicked with all his might and his heel struck his attacker's shin. The man cried out and lost his grip.

Charlie spun around and drove his elbow into the man's face. Lopez? His attacker slipped on the wet pavement and hit the ground. Charlie landed two quick kicks to the man's head and ribs. Again Charlie yelled for help.

The man rose quickly, pulling something from his pants pocket. Charlie chopped hard on that arm, and the man gasped in pain as a metal object hit the sidewalk. Charlie expected the man to attack again, but instead the man turned and ran into the darkness. In the moment they had faced each other Charlie had seen enough to know that despite the black hoodie he wore the man was Ferrol Lopez by the ugly scar above the right eye. Charlie looked at his watch and understood that the whole en-counter had lasted only a minute or two.

Charlie stood catching his breath. Two bystanders rushed over to ask him if he was all right. A man came out of the townhouse near where Charlie was standing. He asked how Charlie was and said he had called the police. Charlie thanked them and said he would be okay. As these people walked away, he looked down and saw to the left on the curb the weapon, a six-inch knife with a serrated blade. Charlie picked it up delicately, examined it, and put it in his suit pocket.

Charlie took out his cell phone and canceled his lesson. He walked slowly back the few blocks to his apartment. He would call the police later to report what happened. Upstairs he cleaned up. His cheek was bruised and the back of his hand bled slightly. Surely Lopez would come back for him. Kate was not enough. Now he was the target.

He called Paul at home.

"Paul, Lopez jumped me on the street."

"When?"

"Minutes ago. I was attacked. I have his knife. Can you run the fingerprints? He mugged me from behind near the Cardinal's residence. The light was bad but I recognized him from your mug shot."

"Obviously you survived. How?"

"I don't know. Everything went by fast. But he ran away. Then I found the knife."

"Did you pick it up?

"Put it in my pocket. I haven't touched it since."

"Did you call the police?"

"I'm talking now."

"Were there witnesses?"

"A couple of guys on the street."

"The Chicago police can investigate the scene for evidence. I'll call them and they'll contact you. They will want you to show them the crime scene and give a statement. Tell me more about Lopez."

"He was well over six feet tall, strong, with dark hair, dark pants, and he wore a black hoodie. Ugly scar like the picture. Frankly, I can't think of anyone who would have done this other than Lopez."

"Give the knife to the police. But don't touch it again. They might be able to match prints or even DNA. Sorry, but are you okay?"

"A little beat-up but I'll get over it."

Paul didn't say anything so Charlie asked, "The NYPD kept Carome in custody didn't they?"

"Yes. He is being charged on several counts."

"Then he couldn't have talked to Lopez. Either Harrison must have called Lopez and told him to find me or Harrison intended to go after me all along and Carome failed to tell you. Also, if Harrison tried to reach Carome since the NYPD has him, Harrison might be worried that things are falling apart on him. Maybe he blames me. We need to catch Lopez and make him talk."

"You're right. Harrison may be getting desperate. Two attacks in one week."

| § |

# CHAPTER TWENTY-FIVE

Two policemen from the Chicago PD came to Charlie's apartment an hour later. They took his statement, asked if Charlie had any bruises or injuries as the result of the attack, confirmed the exact street location, and placed the knife in a plastic evidence bag.

"I'm fine," Charlie asserted. "My attacker may be in worse shape. I elbowed him hard in the ribs and face and kicked his leg. After he dropped the knife, he ran off."

"Do you think you could recognize the man?" one officer asked.

"Yes, I think the man was Ferrol Lopez. Talk to Detective Victor of the Lake County Major Crimes Task Force for background."

Obviously confused, the officers exchanged glances but they wrote down the names and left shortly thereafter.

Charlie had little hope that the local police would find Lopez now but, if there was a Lopez fingerprint or DNA on the knife, that evidence might be useful in a trial some day. His body was hurting more, so he took a painkiller and sat down in the library to consider what had happened today - all bad. He might have been killed by Lopez and he was barred from seeing Kate. He was losing control of events.

\*\*\*\*

The phone call he wished for came around dinnertime the next day. Kate telephoned him on his cell while he was still at his apartment.

"Charlie, I'm sorry for not calling. I'm finally alone."

"Kate, sweetheart, how are you? I hope you are past the worst."

"I get to leave the hospital tomorrow. I'm going to my parents' house until I can return to work. I need rehab. The office has been very kind about taking my time."

"Great news! I'll drive out tomorrow."

"That's what I've wanted to talk about. I think I need some space—and time. You didn't intend for what has happened to me—but I have been beaten up badly. My dad says you are careless and responsible for everything. He insists I never see you again. I'm just so confused. And unhappy. We can't be engaged until I feel better and can think this through. I'll send back the ring. Don't try to see me. And please don't hate me."

Charlie could not believe what he was hearing. She sounded broken. Of course he was responsible. He had dragged her into this mess. He had known she was in danger and had failed to protect her.

She had every right to be angry at him. But he didn't want to lose her. He had to find a way to win her back.

---

"Kate, I love you. I've done you so much harm. Please let me make things better."

Charlie could hear her sobbing. He paused to let her release her emotion.

"I'm sorry," she whispered. "Not now. I have to go." She hung up.

He sat shocked and bewildered. His body tensed and started to ache. He felt devastated, profoundly sad, and alone.

Eventually the fog that engulfed his brain started to lift. The pain remained but he started to think again. I have to catch Harrison and Lopez. Then life had a chance to return to what it had been before Scottie died. Kate might remember the good times then. At a minimum she would be safe.

\* \* \*

Charlie skipped work the next day. He was too depressed. Unexpectedly his mother showed up at his door about ten that morning and swept past him going to the living room.

"Charlie, I just stopped by to say hello. Your office told me you were here. I talked Dottie into coming to town finally. There's a good speaker at the Contemporary Club today. We'll have lunch and talk mindless gossip. It'll do Dottie good."

"I hate to spoil things, but you should know that Kate has decided to call off our engagement."

Claire's sense of merriment faded immediately. She sat down in the nearest chair. She thought for a minute then began,

"I feel heart-broken for you, son. Such a loss. You two were so much in love. I must confess I was skeptical at first, but my feelings changed and I got to know her. But no wonder, getting shot at. Is she okay now?"

"She goes to her parents tomorrow."

"Thank heavens! The most important thing is she gets healthy. Once she is over the trauma, she will feel different about the engagement. You'll see."

"Thanks for being optimistic, Mom. But she is completely depressed now."

I don't suppose it would be welcomed if I call her or drop her a note at this time? I could send flowers."

"That's nice of you, but let's give her some space."

"Of course." Claire responded and appeared to think about something.

"Charlie, if Kate is resolute about ending your relationship, I can think of a couple of special young women who could take her place. Just yesterday Helen Chandler mentioned her niece, Wendy. She grew up in Winnetka and went to Princeton. Smart and is excellent athlete. Pretty, too. Make loans or something at Northern Trust. Anyway her marriage is breaking up. Her husband has been seeing—not too secretly—some well-endowed sales woman at Nordstrom's. Apparently he is more interested in boobs than brains. Wendy would be perfect for you. Good family."

Charlie stared at her. He didn't know whether to laugh or cry. His mother was so off-base at times.

"Cool it Mom. I love Kate and plan to win her back."

"Of course. I was only trying to help. Cheer you up. She'll come around."

"Thanks."

"Oh, one more thing. On the elevator coming up here a neighbor—floor four—mentioned that the police paid you a visit yesterday. She's nosey. What did the police want?"

Charlie smiled, thinking 'Who's nosey, Mom?' Charlie proceeded to tell her about the assault on the sidewalk.

Claire turned serious again. She pressed him for details. As he discussed the incident her right hand started to shake. She put it on her chest and slumped to the side. When Charlie mentioned the knife she gasped and sweat burst out on her face.

"Are you all right, Mother?"

Claire murmured something about dizziness and pills and slid almost off the chair. Charlie jumped up, dashed to her chair, picked her up and placed her on the couch. He rushed to her purse on a side table and found a bottle of pills—nitroglycerin. He hurried into the kitchen and filled a glass of water and returned to his mother with the glass and pills. He propped his mom up and fed her the pill and water.

Charlie laid her down and put a throw blanket over her. He hit the speed dial for medical emergencies on his phone and asked for an ambulance immediately.

Later that day, again at the Northwestern Hospital, Charlie learned of his mother's serious heart condition. She had hid the severity of it from him for over a year.

"Too much stress can suddenly trigger an episode," Dr.

Hogan, Claire's cardiologist, said. "She should have explained her condition to you. You acted promptly and maybe saved her life. She should be back home in a day or two. Given her age we want to be conservative."

After the doctor left, Charlie sat next to his mother's bed and reviewed what had happened. The mention of the knife coincided with her reaction. She must have concluded that Charlie could have been killed. That thought had been too much for her. *I never should have told her about the assault—or about Kate.*

He then remembered the bodyguard. He would talk to Jimbo Pavko tomorrow and hire him for his mother.

# CHAPTER TWENTY-SIX

*What else can go wrong? Mother's heart, the breaking with Kate,
the assault on both of us.* Charlie had left his mother well attended
and asleep at the hospital. He was sitting in his library depressed
and angry. Angry at himself for losing control of events. He had
to get more focused.

Let Paul Victor and the New York police focus on Harrison.
He needed to find Lopez. Lopez had botched his assignment on
the street. He would be back. Charlie felt sure of that. He needed
to create a trap. Lure Lopez into a place where he could be captured. He might be able to convince Paul to provide police surveillance of his movements. However, Lopez would probably be
looking for a protective tail. No, Charlie needed to do something
unusual to trick Lopez.

After a while a crazy scheme struck him. It would involve
his brother, Mike. Mike, the high-tech security buff. His place
on Lake Geneva. Charlie would need some police backup, of
course. But they could be invisible.

He had a screwball idea, but it might work. He snapped out of his funk and called Paul. Before Charlie could explain his plan, Paul brought him up-to-date,

"I have been trying to reach you. You should keep your cell phone on. Chicago police found Lopez's prints on that knife."

Charlie blurted, "I knew it. Great. We'll nail him when we find him."

The investigator agreed, then added, "I also had a call from New York—Mike Malone. Carome received two calls on his cell phone today. Malone let him answer. Part of our deal with Carome is that we have a taping device and speakers. He can't call out, only receive. One was from Lopez, and one was from Harrison."

"A breakthrough!" Charlie said.

"Yes. Malone played the calls for me. Lopez wants more money. He said that Harrison had called him directly twice. Two days ago he demanded that Lopez rough you up also. Harrison said that that was phase two of the job. Today he called to ask if that had happened. Lopez told Harrison that he had found Bailey and had jumped him on the street. Lopez said that unfortunately he couldn't finish the job because he saw other people down the street. He told Harrison and Carome separately that the police are now all over him, and unless he is given more money, it wasn't worth it to complete the job.'

'Then Carome shouted, 'I shouldn't have given Harrison your phone number. Everything should come through me. Ask me about a phase two. Ask me about money. I'm running this show.'

"So Lopez asked what he should do next—assuming more money was coming. Carome calmed down and said, 'I'll take care of the money to take out Bailey. Where are you?' Lopez said he was at a public phone on the South Side of Chicago and would call back when he had finished the job."

Charlie did not like that threat, but he felt more confident that Lopez would turn up at Lake Geneva.

Paul continued, "Harrison called a few hours later to complain that Lopez had failed to hurt Bailey. He said that he was frustrated because he had tried to reach Carome on Tuesday for an update, but his cell phone had been off. Carome told him not to worry. He said Lopez was a professional and had never failed before. However, the job—especially with a phase two—would cost more than he had expected. He asked Harrison if there was a number where he could reach him. But Harrison said no and that he only used public phones. Harrison and then demanded that he wanted the job done by the end of the week. Then they would talk about money. He hung up."

"So Malone could hear this complete conversation?" Charlie said. "I congratulate you. Could Malone trace this call?"

"Harrison wasn't on long enough. All we know is it came from a public phone in the old First Chicago building. We also recognized that Harrison was covering the mouthpiece with something to disguise his voice."

So close, yet so far," Charlie mused. "Could you get me the tape? I might recognize the voice anyway."

"Of course. Still, we know Harrison is watching, and Lopez

still has an assignment. We'll catch him. Now what's that plan you have to catch Lopez?"

Charlie explained his idea in broad terms. He had not thought through the details yet.

"Sorry, Mr. Bailey. Bad idea. Won't work. Besides, Lake Geneva is in Wisconsin. Out of my jurisdiction. And what's the bait?"

"Mr. Lopez will think I went to the lake house to hide from him."

"To put yourself in danger is another reason not to do it. Just be patient. We'll catch Lopez with standard police work."

"I'm leaving town anyway. Kate is recovering at her parent's in western Illinois. I need to get away from it all."

"Just don't try to capture Lopez. He's a very dangerous criminal."

"I hear you. But if Lopez does follow me, would you call the Lake Geneva police and notify them of my situation? I probably won't need them, but just in case . . . I'll email you my brother's address and phone number."

"I'll call. Meanwhile will be trying to locate Harrison."

# CHAPTER TWENTY-SEVEN

Charlie did not have to spend much time to persuade his brother, Mike, to join in his plan. Michael Bailey was a renowned orthopedic surgeon with privileges at Rush University Medical Center. He and his wife, Julie, and two preteen children lived near Charlie on Chicago's north side. They spent most weekends at the massive, vintage, fourteen-bedroom, shingle and stone "cottage" that Mike bought on Snake Road in Lake Geneva three years before. The house sat on a hill that sloped gently down a green carpet lawn to the lake. A large, two-story boathouse was home to Hinckley and Chris Craft runabouts and an upstairs guest apartment. Oak, elm, and pine trees lined most of the three-acre perimeter with the lake view completely open from the wraparound porch of the main house. Because the entrance driveway ran through two stone pillars, Mike named his house Stonegate.

While Charlie liked the way the house was positioned for observing most of the property down to the lake and the boathouse, what really appealed to him now were the surveillance and security systems his brother had installed. Mike had always been enamored with state-of-the- art technology. *Stonegate* was a prime example of his passion for the best, most expensive electronic security available. In a basement room looking out on the lawn Mike had installed a central control panel where he could monitor the grounds and operate lights, cameras, and sound all through the property. He had surveillance of the driveway, the exterior and interior of the main house and the boathouse, the perimeter of the grounds, in and among the trees, the shoreline, and the Lake Geneva Shore path that bisected the lower portion of the lawn. Lights, night vision lens in cameras, and audio monitors enabled him to see and hear anything twenty-four seven. Electronic tripwires in multiple locations could signal the control panel of any movement on the property. While this equipment was designed to keep track of roaming children and invading burglars, it usually alerted Mike to the migrating deer and ducks. Nevertheless, Mike loved his elaborate toys. You never failed to lead unsuspecting guests to the house down to this room, where acting like a proud father he sang the praises of his first-class security system.

Until now Charlie chuckled that his brother had gone overboard with this installation. It was a harmless folly. After all, crimes were rare in Lake Geneva. An over active watchdog was likely all you needed for security. But this system was the *sine qua non* of Charlie's plan to catch Lopez. Paul Victor had thought his plan was stupid—even dangerous. But Charlie had an enthusiastic partner in his brother. Mike was eager to put his creation to the test.

"Charlie, we'll nail your bad guy. We have the edge. We can monitor his every step. He won't know we are watching and listening."

Mike was normally a very busy doctor with surgery or visitations booked each weekday eight to six. Weekends were spent with family. This weekend he was free to work with Charlie because his wife and kids were away in California seeing her parents.

While visiting his mother in the hospital on Friday morning Charlie heard from her cardiologist that she would be on a mildly sedated precautionary watch through Monday at the hospital. Charlie decided he could leave her there with little risk. He would execute his plan and call in each day.

After a few hours in the office, Charlie left early. He made a point to tell his secretary, Kathy, and several members of his team that he was spending the weekend at his brother's place on Lake Geneva. He mentioned that same destination to his apartment's doorman, a porter, and the superintendent. Later he pulled his car out of the building's garage and left it in front idling while he went back upstairs, pretending he had forgotten something. If Ferrol Lopez was watching, Charlie wanted him to think he was going out of town for the next few days.

Charlie reached the small town of Lake Geneva on the eastern shore of the large lake ninety minutes later. There he stopped for a few minutes at the grocery store to buy enough food and drink to stock the refrigerator for a few days. He also visited the boat-rental business on the shore to talk to the owner, whom

Charlie had known for a couple of years. He described Lopez and asked the owner to give him a call if Lopez rented a boat — but not to mention that they had talked. Charlie explained that Lopez had a grudge against him and he wanted to be ready if Lopez intruded on his brother's property. Lastly he visited the local police chief.

"Detective Victor called me this morning and asked if I would watch over you. He said it was a serious matter. We're always happy to help."

"Thank you," Charlie said. "My brother and I are worried that an intruder may try to break into his cottage."

"Your brother has quite a security system out there. It connects to our switchboard, you know. If there's trouble, we can be there in less than ten minutes."

"I hope nothing happens," Charlie concluded, but secretly hoped it did.

Happy that these elements in his plan were arranged, Charlie drove onto Snake Road and headed to Mike's home. As he drove he considered this extraordinary and familiar place. Because of its beauty, clarity of water, size, and proximity to Chicago and Milwaukee, Charlie's social circle had been coming to Lake Geneva each summer for generations. Of course, some friends preferred instead rustic Door County on Green Bay or the dunes of Indiana and Michigan on Lake Michigan. To each his own.

Lake Geneva, though, had an undeniable cachet among the moneyed and successful in Chicago and southern Wisconsin. They bought large lakefront properties and built comfortable homes with countless bedrooms, wraparound porches, stone fireplaces, and boathouses. Some built structures on their properties—compounds designed to accommodate large families with each branch having its own cottage. Under this arrangement the children of the extended family would play together each summer, become lifelong friends with their cousins, and form alliances useful for their careers.

Charlie was pleased that Mike had joined this community. Since they both worked such long hours on their careers, they rarely seemed to have time to see each other. Thanksgiving, Christmas, Easter at Mother's were the exceptions. Other than that, phone calls and lunch maybe once a month constituted their contact. Since Charlie was only two years older, they had some of the same friends growing up. For instance, they both considered Jamie Bradshaw a friend. Several others also. Charlie remembered that when Solange was alive, they visited more often. Solange and Julie had been pals.

If Charlie remarried and had children, he was certain his family would be invited up to Lake Geneva often. Mike and Julie had told him that they adored Kate. So did he. After he took care of Lopez, he hoped he could patch things up with her.

Mike had offered his help when Kate had been shot. If there had been time he would have arranged for the best general surgeon at his hospital to operate on her. But Kate had been taken to the Northwestern Emergency Room before Charlie had called to tell him what had happened. Even though they lived separate lives, the brothers were always there for each other.

Charlie pulled into Mike's gravel driveway and pushed the call button at the iron gate. The caretaker, David, came on and opened the electronic gate. David welcomed him at the front door and offered to park Charlie's car in the garage. Charlie took his bag and proceeded to the guest room he usually stayed in. He unpacked and went to the enormous living room to read investment reports while waiting for Mike to arrive.

At six o'clock Mike showed up. David reported what was available for dinner and Mike chose some frozen dinners that he knew his brother would enjoy.

"Charlie, I see you have made yourself comfortable. What's your plan for this weekend?"

"I am going to be as visible as possible, while I prefer if you lay low. I'd like Lopez to think I'm alone."

"Okay."

"I called Carl Olsen for golf tomorrow at the Lake Geneva country club. He was happy to host me. Then tomorrow night I'll drive into town and have dinner alone at the bar in Gilbert's. Since it is on the lake and has a big parking lot, Lopez can see me coming and going without exposing himself."

"If he is here in Lake Geneva," Mike added.

"I'm counting on that."

Mike had gone to his bar and opened a bottle of Oregon pinot noir for them both. He joined Charlie in the middle of the room and sat across the coffee table.

"On Sunday morning, I'll go to church," Charlie said. "Then change my clothes and take out your Hinckley touring the lake for at least an hour. During the afternoon I'll read a book on the porch in full view from the lake. Before dinner I'll jog along the lake path east past the Bradshaw's cottage and back. If Lopez is here, he won't be able to miss me."

"Fine, I will hang out downstairs and monitor all activity at the lakefront and the perimeter of the property. If Lopez shows up, I'll call Police Chief Warren. This should be fun."

On Saturday nothing happened. Charlie played golf and ate in the busy restaurant. Mike saw strollers and joggers, countless boats on the lake, a family of deer, two hawks in the pines, and a neighbor's dog.

More of the same on Sunday. Then at about five p.m. Mike called Charlie on the home's intercom.

"Come down. I see someone."

Charlie hurried down to find Mike pointing at the northeastern monitor.

"There's someone behind that viburnum."

Just then the figure stood up and looked around. The man appeared to be about six feet tall and husky.

"That could be Lopez," Charlie said. "About the right size."

After a minute of scanning the area, the man moved south along the line of pines defining the property boundary. He reached the lake path and turned back to look at the house, then over towards the boathouse. Suddenly he was gone.

"I have the alarm system on the perimeter turned off. I didn't want to scare him. He's left the property now. I snapped a couple of pictures of him when he first stood up. I'll enlarge the face and body. Maybe you can recognize him."

The face of Ferrol Lopez became clear as Mike played with the pictures. Charlie grew excited.

"That's him. He was casing the joint. He didn't seem spooked. He'll probably come back when it's darker."

"I followed him initially from the trees around the driveway. If he comes back, I guess he would use the lake path or the lake itself. That way he wouldn't draw attention to himself. Everybody uses those approaches. But anyway I'll see him."

At seven Charlie appeared on the back lawn in his robe and swimming trunks. He walked out to the dock and dived into the cold water. He swam quickly out fifty yards, stopped, then returned to the dock. He climbed out of the water, put on his plush, white cotton robe, and walked up to a cluster of Adirondack chairs facing the lake and sat down on the middle one. He pulled out his cell phone from the robe's pocket and appeared to concentrate on the screen.

Every five minutes Mike would call Charlie on his phone.

"Nothing yet. Dusk is setting in. If he is coming, he can still see you now."

Charlie grew impatient for action. He had complete confidence in his brother to execute the plan as agreed. But he needed Lopez to come back.

Charlie's phone rang again. "I see a small outboard off to the right about 150 yards out in line with the boathouse. He's idling, looking this way. Despite his baseball hat and dark sunglasses he looks like the guy who was here earlier."

"Great," Charlie said. "I'll come in as planned."

He stood up and returned to the house. Charlie wanted Lopez to land his boat thinking no one was aware of his presence. Charlie would come back out once Lopez was hiding on property.

Charlie joined his brother and watched Lopez drive his small craft slowly toward the boathouse. Once there he tied it up and crept into the boathouse.

Mike's camera could zero in on him accurately.

"That's him for sure," Charlie pronounced. "I go out again."

He picked up a metal baseball bat and secreted it under his ankle-length robe. Four minutes later he was back in his lawn chair.

About ten minutes later as the sun neared the horizon and a full moon was climbing in the east, Mike called Charlie's vibrating cell. "He is on the move. Sneaking up the west border behind the bushes. I'm going to call Chief Warren now. Keep Lopez busy for ten minutes."

Charlie had a hard time not looking at Lopez advancing toward him. He relied on Mike's commentary.

"He's parallel with you. Maybe forty yards away. I don't see a weapon. He's behind your position now and has left the trees. He's in the open, walking fast towards the chairs."

Charlie could hear Lopez's footsteps on the lawn behind him. He sensed him quite near now. He pivoted toward him saying, "Welcome to Stonegate, Mr. Lopez. Perhaps you will tell me who put you up to this."

Lopez stopped moving. Then he leapt as Charlie bent forward. The high, wooden back of the chair impeded Lopez's attempt to put a garrote over Charlie's head.

At that moment huge spotlights around them lit up in the yard. Even though Charlie knew what was happening, he was temporarily blinded. Squinting over his shoulder, he saw a confused Lopez. Then eighteen flood lights shot on illuminating trees and the house. Anticipating this burst of light Charlie had shut his eyes. He opened them to see Lopez disoriented and stumbling. Sirens suddenly blared in all directions. Lopez dropped the garrote and fumbled to pull out a handgun from his pocket. Charlie took the bat and ran around the chair, and smashed Lopez's hand and then his skull. Lopez collapsed on the ground. Charlie swung at him one more time, then he picked up the gun. To his right he saw Mike race from the house shotgun in hand.

Lopez was bleeding from his hand and reaching around for his gun. Charlie hit him again in the arm. Lopez cried out in pain and still appeared to be lost. Mike arrived and pointed the shotgun at the doomed man's head.

"Charlie, I can hear the police sirens now adding to the blare. I told David to direct them down here. This is so cool. Your plan worked out. Helped by my system. I thought it was amateurish. But I didn't say anything, because I thought it was unlikely that Lopez would show. But he did and we have him. Wow!"

Charlie did not feel as giddy. When Lopez was behind him in the chair he realized that his plan had been needlessly dangerous. If Mike had been slow with the lights. If Lopez had used his gun instead of the garrote. If Lopez hadn't fumbled grabbing his gun. If Lopez brought an accomplice. Lots of "if's". He could be dead, if . . . *Was the risk worth it? Only if Lopez talks and we find Harrison.*

Five policemen and Chief Warren ran down the lawns to the brothers and Lopez. Charlie liked their drawn weapons.

"Is this the guy you mentioned on Friday?"

"Yes. Ferrol Lopez. Wanted in Chicago, Waukegan, and by the FBI."

One of the officers squatted beside Lopez and said, "A felonious assault here. What happened to him? He is beat up something awful. We need an ambulance."

"You did this, Mr. Bailey?" the Chief asked.

"He tried to strangle me and shoot me. I had to protect myself."

"Understood. We'll take it from here."

# CHAPTER TWENTY-EIGHT

"Mike, I think I'll be leaving to go home." Charlie was standing in the foyer with his packed suitcase at the door early the next morning. He hugged his brother and said, "We make quite a team. The Bailey boys. Against all logic and advice we caught a thug like Lopez. But without you I'd still be thinking about him."

"It was fun," Mike laughed. Scary but fun. Call me next time you need help with a bad guy."

Mike chuckled, then asked, "Which police group will get Lopez? Here, Lake County, or Chicago?"

"Beats me. But whichever one will want to talk to you further. And, if there is a trial, you'll be asked to testify. But that's a long time from now. For me I can get back to work and not worry who might be following me. I hope Lopez talks so we find out who hired him.

"Did you talk to Kate? She should be relieved."

"I called her cell last night. She didn't pick up so I left a message. I'll try again today. I also called Paul Victor—same result.

Chief Warren probably reached him last night. I'm sure Paul will call back. I want to needle him about how our plan worked."

"Do you think the Chicago press will pick up this story?"

"Yes, but I hope not for a few days. I want some calm."

Charlie didn't explain to Mike that no publicity was a good thing. If Harrison lost track of Lopez he might panic and call Carome. Then the NYPD might be able to trace the call. Even when Harrison learned that Lopez had been caught he might worry that he had lost control and might be vulnerable. So the police would try to identify Harrison through Carome. Charlie would try to find Harrison through Doug Smith. He needed to talk to him right away.

About an hour into Charlie's drive to Chicago Paul called.

"Congratulations. I heard from Chief Warren that they have Lopez in custody. I admit I thought your plan would never work or, if Lopez showed, you would survive. I'm happy to have been wrong."

"Sometimes hare-brained schemes succeed", Charlie said trying not to gloat. "The key is that we have Lopez. Now you have to get him to talk."

"First we have to get him back to Illinois. Chief Warren has a strong case of attempted murder. But so do we—and more. A decision will take a few days, but I think we'll bring him down here and get a first shot at Lopez. Having the FBI with us and a handful of federal charges on the table will help us. Don't worry about it."

"Your business. Go to it," Charlie said. "I'll be at the office when you want my statement. This happening should help your guys in New York."

"I hope so," Paul agreed. "More important, you and Miss Milano should feel safe now."

"Unless Harrison hires another Lopez."

"Don't even think about it. Harrison should be feeling pressure having lost Vecchia and Lopez. We'll let him know what happened in a few days through the media. In the meantime he may try to reach Carome and Lopez. We'll be listening."

"I'm sure you will be." Charlie said.

Charlie stopped to change at his apartment and then took a taxi to his office. He had trouble concentrating on work as he was disappointed that Kate had not called. Later in the day he gave up trying to work and called Doug Smith. They agreed to meet for a drink at the Racquet Club at six.

Charlie arrived first and waited in the lobby for Doug. Charlie knew him socially for at least ten years. They had some of the same friends, but Charlie could not recall talking to him one-on-one. Entering the club the tall, fit Doug seemed relaxed and happy to see Charlie.

"Nice to have the opportunity to see you, Charlie. Is anyone joining us?"

"No, just the two of us. With all that has happened to me the last couple of months, I wanted to ask you a few questions," Charlie said pleased that Doug seemed in a good mood.

As they walked up the stairs to the bar, Doug said, "I've always admired you—even if you did go Yale. You have a great reputation as an investor and your firm is the gold standard in giving all kinds of advice to the wealthy—financial and otherwise."

"You're too kind. But I am a bit sensitive to critical comments about Yale. Where did you go to school?"

"Williams. A more intimate version of Yale."

"True. We have a couple of Williams graduates in my firm. Very talented."

Coming into the bar, Charlie pointed, "Let's sit over in the far corner. It's quiet there."

Doug waved to a friend across the room. Charlie observed that the friend looked a bit like Doug—short brown hair, wire-rimmed glasses, preppy sport coat and tie, in his thirties. *I guess their tastes run the same*, Charlie thought.

"I remember that you are an architect. Are you working on anything locally?"

"We're in the early stages of designing a practice facility for the Blackhawks near the United Center."

"Win a few Stanley Cups and the team finds a way to spend the riches," Charlie joked.

"It's a fun project. Now what can I do for you?"

They quickly ordered two glasses of wine and settled back in their chairs.

"Before I forget," Doug said, "I read that Kate Milano was injured last week. Chicago is becoming a shooting gallery. Gang violence. I suppose it was a case of mistaken identity. I hope she is okay."

"Thank you for asking. She is home recuperating. Very unfortunate incident—though not a mistake. The shooter tried to kill her."

"Wow! So sorry."

Charlie leaned forward and said, "Apropos to this topic, I am told that you're friends with someone from New York, Rob Johnson. A few months ago he had a few drinks with you and some other people."

"That's right. We had a few pops one night. In fact, right here in this room. Why do you ask?"

"I'm told he had a rough divorce a little while back and hired a Mafia-type to scare his wife. Did he talk about that?"

"Yes, he did. I remember that he thought he was rather cool in doing that. Personally, I think that type of thing stinks. But he was proud of it."

"He didn't mention the name of the thug he hired, did he?"

"No, not that I remember. I hope you are not thinking of hiring someone like that!"

"No, but the police think this same guy may have had something to do with Kate's shooting."

"No kidding! That's scary. Rob may have been dealing with the wrong crowd."

"By any chance, did you tell the story of Rob and the thug to anyone?"

"Sure. It's an entertaining tale. I brought it up here in fact. I remember once Farley Dugan and I talked about it. Farley had heard the story from Rob also. We weren't certain if it was the truth, but it made a good story. We weren't the only ones there that night. We were sitting at a long communal table over there," Doug said, pointing at it.

"Do you remember who else was there?"

"Let's see. Several weeks ago. Neil St. Onge was there, I think. Jamie Bradshaw. Tony Fitzpatrick—I don't know if you know him. Toby Baird. Maybe someone else. Yeah, Lowell Hersey, a money manager like you. Kind of a horse's ass, if you ask me. Everyone was joking about who they would want to scare. Ha, ha."

Charlie reacted internally to Lowell Hersey's name. He had not followed up on him. Paul was supposed to check on Hersey's whereabouts on the night of Scottie's murder but had not mentioned any findings. Charlie would have to ask Paul.

"Did anyone want to scare anyone I know?"

"I don't know. No one was being serious. Mostly ex-girl-friends, mother-in-law, brokers, and bosses—the usual suspects. Jamie didn't think the joke about brokers was funny. That, I remember. Of course his brother was a broker. Then Scottie was killed a few weeks later. Weird. Of course, most people want to kill their broker. Right?"

"Only those who have lost a lot in the market," Charlie answered. "Did Lowell seem interested in and Rob Johnson's story?"

"Lowell didn't say much. I don't recall his reaction."

Doug leaned forward and said, intrigued, "So the police think the same guy shot Kate. You didn't say. I'm guessing, but what a coincidence! I hope Rob wasn't involved. He's a friend."

"If any of your friends talk about this topic, please let me know," Charlie asked.

"Of course, but I can't imagine any of them would want to harm Kate. So Rob introduced the thug to someone here?"

"Yes, named Harrison. Know him?"

"I know a Bill Harrison, but he lives in Houston. That's a common name."

Charlie walked home from the Racquet Club. He would call Paul in the morning to see if Lopez is talking and ask what the police found out about Lowell Hersey.

*\*\**

"Any luck with Lopez?" Charlie asked Paul Victor. Charlie rang him first thing in the morning before going to work.

"He's still in Wisconsin, but Chief Warren invited me to yesterday's interrogation. Good thing. Lopez was talking."

"How so?"

"He said he never intended to kill either you or Miss Milano. He only meant to scare you. He admitted he knew Raymond Carome. Carome contacted him a few weeks ago and promised him fifteen grand if Lopez would rough you and your girlfriend up a bit to convince you to stop looking for some guy named Harrison."

"What a pile of crap," Charlie spat out.

"It gets worse. So he agreed to take care of you both. First, he said he intentionally aimed low at Miss Milano. He could have easily killed her. With you he admitted that he screwed up the mugging."

"Did you ask about the knife?"

"Yes, he said it fell out of his pocket. He did not expect you to be so aggressive. He kept watching you and saw you preparing to leave town. He decided to follow you."

"As I planned," Charlie added.

"You were lucky," Paul added.

"Maybe."

"Lopez said he had never been to Lake Geneva. So he was out of his comfort zone."

Charlie recognized that Lopez was trying to minimize his action while making excuses why a professional like himself had failed. Big ego. Small brain.

"He said that after a day or two he felt familiar enough with the locale to come after you."

"With a garrote?" Charlie continued.

"We told him his story stunk. He meant to kill you just as he meant to kill Miss Milano, if he were a better shot. At that point Lopez offered to turn on Carome, if he could get a deal."

"Sounds like he threw in a towel," Charlie observed.

"We told him we would have to get a lot considering what he did. He said he had Carome's cell number and would ID him in court."

"What about Harrison?" Charlie asked.

"Of course, we asked. Lopez said he didn't know who he was but assumed he was behind Carome. He said he always believed the less he knew, the better it was."

"That's it? No Harrison," Charlie declared in frustration.

"When we get Lopez back in Illinois, we'll try some more. He's lying about a lot of things. Meanwhile I talked to Detective Malone in New York last night. Harrison called Carome yesterday afternoon. He wanted to know when Lopez was going to do his job. Had he disappeared with the money paid to him? Where was he now? Carome said he would try to locate him, but Carome needed to know how he could get back to Harrison with the information. Harrison said he could not be reached and would call back in two days."

"So, what do you want Carome to tell Harrison the next time?"

"We don't want Harrison—or Carome for that matter—to know we have Lopez. Angry people make mistakes. Yet we'll just have Carome tell Harrison that he is still looking. The call was from a public phone in Union station. Different ones each time—the Loop, Old Town, Logan Square. Of course, we have it on tape. The telephone calls to Robert Johnson were also from public phones in Chicago.

"After Harrison gets tired of waiting to hear about Lopez, do you think he will hire yet another hitman?" Charlie asked.

"It's always possible. But I am thinking that Harrison probably does not know of someone else like Raymond Carome. So either he tries Carome again—and we'll know—or he gives up on this approach."

"Do you think Harrison will try something himself?"

"That's not his M.O.. He hires people to do the messy work. He just might stop trying to hurt you. He might figure that, if we haven't found him by now, we never will—so he is home free."

"I hope you are right on his giving up," Charlie said. "I am tired of dodging bullets. Kate and I want to get back to normal lives. On the other hand, I hope you are not going to stop looking."

"Don't worry. We are not going to stop looking for a murderer."

"Good. I have something for you. Remember Doug Smith?"

"The friend who Robert Johnson told the story involving Carome?"

"Yes. I saw him yesterday. He recalled the scene at the Racquet Club when Johnson bragged about using Carome. I have a list of people who were there. I'll send it to you. One name stood out—Lowell Hersey. Did you check out his activities about that time? Could he have contacted Carome and sent funds to him?"

"Nothing has come up so far, but we need to look closer," Paul admitted. "Email me the list."

"Finally, do you know when the press will run a story on the arrest of Lopez?"

"No. The Chicago press is unlikely to pick up an arrest in Wisconsin unless they connect it with you and the shooting of Miss Milano. Usually we prefer no story while we are still interrogating the criminal, but a story involving a major crime in the Chicago area might ease our efforts to move Lopez back to Illinois. So after Harrison calls Carome again."

Charlie smiled and thought he knew just the person to write that story. Harrison might feel uneasy with Lopez in the hands of the Chicago Police and the FBI. He could call Peaches the next day.

# CHAPTER TWENTY-NINE

"Charlie, I'm all ears," Peaches declared, returning Charlie's call. "Did I hear 'exclusive'? So your cutie, Miss Kate Milano, is going to be Mrs. Charlie Bailey?"

Peaches sounded intensely excited. But he's so wrong. Charlie laughed inwardly.

"No, no. I called you about your other assignment."

Charlie then recounted the story of Lopez' appearance after Vecchia's death, his shooting of Kate, his attack on Charlie, and his capture in Lake Geneva. He concluded, "The police did a marvelous job. Otherwise, I'd be dead. Credit both the police in Wisconsin and Illinois."

"So this Lopez character is an assassin like Vecchia?" Peaches understood. "Someone wants you dead all right. And these attempts connect back to Scottie Bradshaw's murder. Wow. Big story! Why you? Do you know something?"

"Your guess is as good as mine. Ask the police."

"I will. Do you think Kate was a target because she knows something about the murder or because she knows you?"

"I'm certain the attack on her must have been a mistake. She barely knew Scottie."

"And you haven't talked to any other journalists?"

"Exclusive, as I said. Of course, after you break the story I'll get many calls. I'll have to talk to them."

"Understood. Thanks, Charlie. You are such a good friend."

Charlie hung up and sat back in his office chair. The *Trib* article should appear tomorrow. Then Harrison will know where Lopez is. He'll have to worry that Lopez will lead the police to Carome. Harrison will have to review all his contacts with Carome and may fear that somehow his conversations and money wires might be traced back to him. Charlie wanted Harrison on edge. He might make a mistake.

Kate would also see the newspaper story. Hopefully she'll recognize that she is no longer in danger. I want her back. I miss her. I need to find Harrison and put this nightmare behind us. He has harmed my relationship with Kate as well as has devastated the lives of my friends, the Bradshaw family.

Charlie did not have to wait long. The next day's *Chicago Tribune* ran Peaches' scoop on the front page — bottom left. The headline read "Alleged Hit man Captured in Wisconsin". The subhead added "Socialite Helpful". The story, which continued onto page seven, faithfully recited Charlie's account. Quotes from Chief Warren and Paul Victor merely confirmed the details.

By the time Charlie reached his office he had seventeen messages from reporters, friends, and clients regarding the *Trib* article. He had returned a handful of the calls when his mother telephoned.

"Son, Dottie phoned me just now about the article in the paper. You know, she has been distant with me ever since you got involved in the aftermath of Scottie's death. I'm so happy that Dottie seems please now with what you and Michael did. I guess she finally agrees that Scottie was murdered. I am sympathetic to her not wanting more notoriety after what she took to be an accident. Now she appears to be reconciled and is talking to me."

"Wonderful, Mom."

"Oh, I almost forgot. Congratulations to you and your brother in helping the police. I guess you both are heroes. I'm so proud. And now that that evil creature is behind bars everything will settle down. Back to normal. No more dangerous situations for you."

"Partly true. We still need to find the person behind all this."

"Of course, but the police can do that. You don't need to be involved."

"I hope so. I must run now. I am happy you and Dottie are friends again."

Charlie put down the phone and considered what his mother had said. He seethed that Dottie had treated his mother so badly. What a way to have behaved toward a decades-long friend! Charlie had only acted in the Bradshaw's best interests. He was trying to find Scottie's murderer. They should have been grateful rather than having shown mother a cold shoulder. *Mom seems more forgiving than I am. Nevertheless, I am still determined to catch Harrison.*

Later in the day Kate finally called. Charlie took the call immediately feeling nervous about her state of mind.

"Kate, I'm so glad to hear your voice. I hope you are healing from the ordeal."

"I'm getting better. My doctor says I can return to work when I want to. I might have to use a walker for a while. A cane at least. One of the reasons I am coming back to Chicago is to be near the Shirley Ryan Ability Lab- the top rehab hospital!'

'I am so far behind at work. Everyone has been so nice, but they have had to pick up the slack. I fear that their expressions of sympathy are wearing thin. After all, how can my colleagues explain the bizarre situation of an employee being shot on a busy street in the city? You were concerned about the effect of bad publicity might have had on your business, so you should understand how I feel, Charlie."

He sensed her frustration. She didn't deserve this—and she blamed him. The more she said, the icier she sounded. He faced an uphill task to win her back. Their conversation was awkward.

"I wish I could change things," Charlie offered weakly. "Your friends and associates must like and respect you to say what you describe. I'm sure they want you back on your own schedule."

"I hope so. My pal, Marc, has been especially helpful—visiting me at the farm, finishing one of my projects and covering for me."

He had no substantive reason to be jealous but the mention of Marc bothered him. At the moment Marc was closer to Kate than he was.

Kate continued, "I'll go in tomorrow. I'll need a taxi, but Marc said he would pick me up at my apartment house and drive me to work. I've been staying with my parents and taking physical therapy. Dad will take me back to Chicago tonight. I'll be that much closer to the office. I should be safe as Dad has insisted on retaining Roman to look after me Chicago until he can find a re-placement. That's not easy from a farm seventy miles away."

Charlie choked up at the mention of Roman. Roman's failure to protect Kate had resulted in her nearly being killed. Charlie bit his tongue and commented on her return to work, "Returning to the office is good news."

"I didn't call to talk about myself. I read today that you and Michael were involved in the police arresting the thug who shot me. Someday you can tell me what happened, but it's great news that he is behind bars. Congratulations. This is what you wanted. I feel safer now. I imagine you feel excited about how this adventure ended. The affair is over? Right?"

The Kate he was hearing was not the sweet, supportive woman he had loved the past couple of years. She was distant, matter-of-fact, and wary. He had to be careful what he said.

"Lopez was hired by a man with the code-name Harrison. The police and the FBI are zeroing in on him. It shouldn't be long."

Kate was silent. Charlie waited for her response. Finally she said, "I see. It's not done. Are you still involved?"

"I'm trying not to be," Charlie said uncomfortably. "If they ask me a question, I have to respond."

Charlie did not want to lie to her but he was feeling desperate. If he told her the truth, he feared he would lose her completely.

"I guess so," she said without conviction. "Take care of yourself. I have to run. I think my dad is knocking at my door."

"Kate, remember I love you."

"I know you do."

She hung up. Charlie was stunned. Had he lost her? This situation was new to him. Solange had never gotten angry at him. She let me do as I wanted. Kate is so different. A real challenge. So independent. But smart, courageous, loving. He had to find a way to get her back. And Marc?

| § |

# CHAPTER THIRTY

The next two days passed slowly for Charlie. He felt depressed and adrift. Unlike his usual responsive self he neglected answering most of the calls and emails he received after the Lopez news. He had no idea as to how to win her back. All he could do was hope that as her body healed, so would her heart. But a prolonged period did not match well with his impatient temperament.

Finally he called Paul from his office, hopeful that Lopez or Carome had revealed something.

"No. I am convinced Lopez never met Harrison. All communication went through Carome. We'll keep trying. I expect the Lake Geneva police will transfer him to Chicago tomorrow.'

'We keep waiting for Harrison to call Carome. After the news reports on Lopez we expected Carome would keep asking what Lopez knew about him. Maybe Carome had told Lopez the details of the Harrison-Carome arrangement—an unlikely event but worrisome to Harrison. We also wonder if Harrison will order up another hitman. So far, no. Probably not. Bottom line, Harrison has gone silent. We don't know what that means."

"Maybe he has given up?" Charlie suggested.

"I doubt it. He has to be nervous. His plans to eliminate you and Miss Milano have failed. Vecchia is obviously not talking but Carome or Lopez might be. The police and the FBI are investigating. Harrison's not home free. Only the murder of Mr. Bradshaw worked."

"True, but unless he slips up, we seem a long way from identifying him."

"He doesn't know that. Now let me ask you about that list you sent me. From the Doug Smith-Robert Johnson dinner."

"Of course."

"We have information on all six. You can add context—relationships, social milieu, history. That sort of thing."

"I'll try to be helpful," Charlie promised.

"Anthony Fitzpatrick is forty-two and lives in Winnetka with his wife and three children, ages six, eleven, and thirteen. He grew up in Oak Park, went to college at Marquette, and joined his father's printing business after college. When his father died twelve years ago, he took over and built the business significantly. Two years ago be sold the business to a major printing company and stayed on managing what he had sold. I suspect this arrangement was part of the deal. At any rate, he was paid a substantial sum for his company, and he invested part of the proceeds with Scottie Bradshaw. He also invests with a couple of other financial firms.

'Mr. Fitzpatrick seems like an upstanding citizen. He attends mass regularly, coaches his son's Little League team, was a Boy

Scout troop leader, vacations at a lake in northern Wisconsin, drives a Lexus, and occasionally plays golf with friends. He does not belong to the Racquet Club—so he must have been there as a guest. The house he lives in predates the buy-out of his company. In other words he did not change his lifestyle much after he became rich.'

'Based on the records we obtained from Collins, Lang, he lost about $375,000 in the two years prior to Mr. Bradshaw's death. That is a lot of money to me - enough to give Fitzpatrick a motive, but nothing in my research indicates that he would kill someone."

"I am not even sure if that motive holds up," Charlie interjected. "What did he clear on the sale of his business?"

"The buyer—a corporation—paid $23 million."

"After accounting for any debt the company may have had," Charlie said, "I would not be surprised if Fitzpatrick cleared $8-10 million after taxes. You could find out from his tax returns. My point is that while a $375,000 loss is significant, it may not have put a dent in Tony Fitzpatrick's net worth—certainly not enough of a hit to warrant his putting his family and himself at risk from a crime. Moreover, the markets have been down since the sale; and Tony's friends probably have talked about their losses as well. Losing what he did should not have made him feel persecuted."

"Not that we have discovered. We could talk to some of his friends and neighbors or could bring him in for questioning, but he just doesn't have the profile of a murderer."

Charlie agreed with Paul's conclusion. Paul then brought up Toby Baird and Neil St. Onge. He had found nothing to implicate either of them. Neither had financial dealings with Scottie.

"I know both Toby and Neil socially," Charlie added. "They are close friends of Jamie. So they had to have known Scottie. But I have never heard any stories that would suggest that they have a grudge against Scottie. The same with Doug Smith."

"Why don't we move on to Jamie and Lowell Hersey," Paul suggested.

"Jamie Bradshaw is 43 years old, lives in Chicago on Lake Shore Drive, is divorced, and has two children. He attended private schools in Lake Forest and graduated from Princeton University. He has a graduate degree in business from Northwestern. He started his career with Continental Bank, where he made loans to large companies. When he was 28, he married Brooke Wells. The marriage fell apart seven years later. After Continental Bank, he joined Goodman, Bates as an associate in investment banking. He is still there and is titled Managing Director."

"Okay, I know all that." Charlie said. "This family is well-known in Chicago. His father is head of a large law firm with his name on it. His grandfather ran for governor of Illinois at one point. He lost, but the exposure helped make the Bradshaw name famous in Illinois."

"James Bradshaw appears to be successful," Paul continued. "But I am not certain what an investment banker does. Since his divorce he seems to have dropped out of the social scene in which his mother and father still appear. In fact, he seems to be private—even secretive—in his personal life. This behavior contrasts with his visibility in the social columns when he was married."

"I wonder who told you that?" Charlie asked.

"We talk to lots of people," Paul said. "Let me go on. He is listed as a board member of a Chicago hospital and a museum, but both boards have a lot of members, so I don't know how involved he is. He belongs to several clubs in the city including The Racquet Club and, of course, the Potawatomi Club."

"Stop. Jamie is a friend from childhood. You have told me nothing that I don't know. Your facts are correct. But they say little about the person. We went to grade school together, attended the same dances, and played on the same sport teams. And our families have enjoyed a deep bond across generations. I could go on, but Jamie can't be the one we are looking forward. Move on."

"In a minute," Paul said with conviction. "Based on my experience we always look at family members. Jamie has to be considered—friend of yours or not."

"You're wasting your time. Get to Lowell Hersey."

"He was born, grew up, and attended schools in New York City. He earned a B.A. and M.B.A. from Columbia. His first job was with Chemical Bank in Manhattan. After ten years he moved to Chicago to join the hedge fund, Pierson Partners, as an analyst. He is now head of the firm. Now, the interesting parts. The FBI found two transfers to a bank in Luxembourg from Pierson Partners to an account named S. Bradshaw. These payments postdated the Paradigm mutual fund scandal."

"So Hersey must have had another arrangement with Scottie," Charlie suggested, feeling hopeful and excited.

"We asked Hersey into our office to explain what was going on, he lawyered up and said nothing."

"Will you arrest him?" Charlie asked.

"The D.A. needs more evidence. Clearly Hersey's relationship with Scottie went beyond the standard broker/client arrangement. Since Scottie can't talk and Hersey won't talk, we need someone else to come forward."

"Do you have someone in mind?" Charlie asked.

"We're working on it."

"Do you think Hersey is our man?" Charlie said.

"You said it, not me," Paul replied with a chuckle. "And since you know these men we just discussed, consider seriously who could plot a murder. Someone can have a motive but not the personality to act on it."

| § |

# CHAPTER THIRTY-ONE

Charlie looked at his watch and excused himself. He was late for an important meeting. He rushed down the hall to a conference room where his senior investment staff was waiting for him. Rumors were abounding that the general obligation bonds of the state of Illinois might be downgraded by the rating agencies, meaning the state would have to pay more to borrow. The governor and the state legislature were at an impasse regarding the need to raise taxes. The state's budget was projected to produce a huge deficit. Revenues had to increase significantly, or services would have to be cut.

No one had an easy solution. The situation had deteriorated significantly since the budget had been approved in the spring. Now politicians were blaming each other rather than working together on a solution. The rating agencies were intently following the dialogue between the governor and the legislature and were about to determine if the current crisis would drag on.

These developments were important to the clients of Bailey, Richardson because many of its clients were Illinois residents and held Illinois securities. A ratings downgrade would most likely lead to lower prices for these debt instruments. The firm's portfolio managers needed to evaluate how serious the threat of a downgrade was to agree on what actions if any, they needed to take and to develop a general communication to the clients.

The analysts and traders began by presenting what information they had gleaned from dealers and from Wall Street firms. Almost all the portfolio managers agreed that a downgrade was coming and they needed to warn their clients immediately of the implications.

As the meeting broke up, Charlie motioned to Sam Dixon to follow him into his office. He shut his door and directed Sam to sit down and said, "I don't want to hold you up more than a few minutes from making your calls but it struck me that I never asked you about any unusual payments out of Scottie Bradshaw's portfolio. Now I know the bank is the trustee, and they would not pay anything to Scottie directly unless the trust allowed it, but were any sums that seemed strange paid out to individuals or firms? Those that might have first occurred only a year or two ago?"

Charlie noticed a frown on his colleague's bespectacled face. Sam ran his hand through his thinning short brown hair. "When Scottie died, I did meet with the administrator from the bank trustee to review the trust. She showed me what she had. Scottie has not made many withdrawals over the past three years. But I did notice nine payments to Bradshaw, Evans—Scottie's father's firm. Eight were less than $10,000—small enough so that the payments would not have been scrutinized under the anti-money-laundering provisions. The one remaining payment was for almost $300,000."

"Wow. That was a big one," Charlie noted and wrote down the amount. "Did the bank know what it was for?"

"When I asked, the administrator said that there had been bills for services rendered for each payment to the law firm, so the bank had approved them. This explanation sounded legitimate to me, so I did not pursue the matter. I did wonder later, however, why a trust in existence for over twenty years would suddenly occur about $400,000 in legal fees. So two weeks ago—out of curiosity—I asked the bank to send me copies of the bills."

"Have you received them?" Charlie asked.

"Friday. They are all the same—a vague mention of 'legal services rendered'. Disturbed, I called the administrator and asked her why she approved such uninformative bills. She said she had called Scottie to find out whom to call at Bradshaw, Evans to get details. Scottie had given her the number of an associate, but when she called, the lawyer said that Scottie had asked him to have his firm review his trusts in light of decades of Illinois code provisions. Scottie had said he wanted to see if his status as the income beneficiary had changed. That explanation was sufficient for the trust administrator, and she approved the payments."

"Did you check the language of the trusts to see if the law firms' work is covered?" Charlie asked. "I find the lawyer's explanation a bit fishy—especially when there is a potential conflict of interest in using Bradshaw, Evans. Four hundred thousand dollars is a lot of money for a routine update, which the bank already does for the trusts."

Leaning forward in his chair, Sam said, "I looked at the language this morning. The trustee bank can hire legal advice in the course of its work, and the trust will pay. But the documents make no mention of recompense if the income beneficiary hires counsel. I don't think the bank should have approved the payment after the fact and without receipt of the legal work."

"Do you think Scottie was taking advantage of sloppy work by the trustee bank?"

"Possibly. What would Scottie have gotten out of the arrangement? Maybe he was checking to see if trusts could be altered so he could receive some of the principle of the trusts—calling it income somehow."

"You mean, could he break the trust," Charlie added. "Many income beneficiaries have tried that in the past."

"Most have failed. At least legal work would be a quasi-legitimate expense. Although such an expense really should have been Scottie's personally—if that is what he had asked the lawyers. The other possibility is that the bills are bogus. The money goes to his father's law firm in either case. I don't see how that would have helped Scottie."

"Wait. I may see a connection here," Charlie said slowly as he wheeled his chair to look out the window. "Scottie had no substantial money of his own. Right? If he could have used assets of his trusts to pay someone for help or a different kind of advice, then why not? Now what would he have found useful from Bradshaw, Evans, and what would motivate and associate there to send bogus bills?"

"I don't know," Sam responded.

"Try this," Charlie said. "If an associate bills more, he looks better to the senior partners. Correct? In a law firm, he who bills the most has the most power and takes home the most compensation. If he can bill for little or no work, that frees up time for him to bill real clients for real work. It would be lucrative if he could bill the same hours for work twice—for instance to Scottie's trust and to a real client. This situation would be a good deal for the junior lawyer. Now again what would Scottie have gotten out of it? By the way, who is this associate?"

"I wrote down the name," said Sam, reaching into his pocket. "Phillips Elliott. I never heard of him."

"Me neither. I'll call Bob Underwood to check him out. I'm guessing, but I suspect Mr. Elliott had something to offer Scottie beyond trust advice and was getting paid. Maybe he did figure a way to undermine the trusts. Probably something instead. The trust bills may have been a payoff. Sam, if these payments turn out to be important, I am going to kick myself. This information was right under our noses from day one. Had we thought to look at these bills in June, we might have saved a lot of time and trouble.'

"Charlie, I apologize. I should have caught this situation. Inexcusable on my part."

"I agree, your mistake and my mistake."

Then he shrugged his shoulders, moving on. "By the way, nice bowtie, Sam," Charlie smiled. "I need to get one or two myself. Goes with your mustache."

Sam shook his head in disapproval, then said, "I'll check back with you later - after talking to our clients."

*₊*₊

Once alone Charlie thought over the new information he had learned that day. The police and FBI had been busy digging up information on the suspects mentioned by Doug Smith. Based on wire transfers, Paul had been most interested in Lowell Hersey. Hersey's money seemed to be a kickback for secret information. Scottie may have been passing along intelligence that did not originate from his firm.

Was Scottie bribing a source in his dad's law firm for intelligence to give to Hersey? Maybe a connection existed between Phillips Elliott, Scottie, and Lowell Hersey? Scottie may have had a lucrative middleman arrangement.

*This line of thought intrigued Charlie. He thought: I'll talk to Elliot and bring in the police if I don't like his explanation for the money. After all, money is often a motive for murder. What kind of information coming from Hersey's law firm would be worth that sort of money?*

Minutes later, Charlie telephoned Bob Underwood, the firm's outside counsel, but because of Bob's schedule he was not able to reach him until late afternoon.

"Bob, I need a favor. Have you ever heard of Phillips Elliott," he asked. "He is an attorney at Bradshaw, Evans."

"No, but I can look him up in the lawyer's directory. Hold on. Here he is. B.A., Ohio State' L.L.B, Michigan law. He would be twenty-nine. He joined Bradshaw, Evans four years ago. He's in Mergers and Acquisitions."

"Not trust? M. and A.. That's strange. Is $400,000 a lot of money for an associate, by himself, to bill for a review of twenty-year-old trust documents?"

"Associates don't bill that kind of money by themselves."

"I bet something untoward was going on under our noses," Charlie declared.

"What?"

"Scottie Bradshaw directed large sums of money to Bradshaw, Evans for advice from Phillips Elliott, probably having to do with M. and A.. Scottie could have benefited materially from knowing all about impending mergers and acquisitions. He could invest in those deals himself and he could pass along information to eager clients who would do more business with him."

"Charlie, I don't like the sound of this."

"You're right to be concerned. Bradshaw, Evans has quite a reputation in M. and A., does it not?"

"Yes, they do lots of work in the area. After a handful of firms in New York, they are probably the busiest and most widely respected firm in the country in M. and A.. You don't think they're leaking insider information on prospective deals?"

"I don't know about 'they', but Phillips Elliott might have."

"I would be flabbergasted if Bradshaw, Evans was involved in anything of the sort. A law firm has nothing if it can't be trusted. Reputation is everything."

"I take it from your reaction that you have never heard anything to link Bradshaw, Evans with insider information. But that may be the case. Elliot may have been selling insider M. and A. information to Scottie Bradshaw, who used it to his benefit. A tidy, if illegal, scheme. I have to run but, now that you know what I am looking for, if you hear whispers or rumors, please call me."

Charlie sat back in his chair, thinking. The pieces were fitting together. If Elliot—and perhaps others—had sent Scottie insider information, Scottie could have passed it along to his hedge-fund clients, who would position their trades to score big. As a *quid pro quo*, Scottie would earn huge commissions from the large trading volumes from these hedge funds. Presumably, their trading would have been in different stocks from these deal stocks, so was not to connect the deal to Scottie. Of course, this construct was only a theory so far—and a guess of why one-way payments were sent.

The enormity and repercussions of such a plot were breathtaking—a premier law firm involved in fraudulent activities with the alleged mastermind being the son of the head of the law firm. Compounding the matter, everyone would assume that Scottie was working with his father's knowledge. The damage to Bradshaw, Evans would be colossal, perhaps fatal. So Scottie may have put not only his own future at risk but that of the family firm.

Further complicating the issue for Charlie was that the Bradshaw were friends and clients. Being knowledgeable of information potentially harmful to the Bradshaws presented multiple conflicts - legal responsibilities, client privacy requirements, personal relationships. However, not for an instance would he not report to the authorities what he might learn. Whatever the price in friendship and business relationships, Charlie knew he was ethically bound to tell the police and regulators about the arrangement he had uncovered—if he had uncovered something.

This contrivance could also provide a motive for murder. If, for instance, something has gone wrong in the scheme to break down the trust between Scottie and Elliot, Elliot might have wanted to silent Scottie. Conspirators often turn on each other.

Charlie's imagination was running full speed. Of course, he knew this theory was nothing more than speculation on top of speculation. Still, the stakes were high in terms of money and career, and Scottie had been murdered. And maybe this situation created motives for people Charlie had not even considered. Scottie, being no genius, might not have foreseen the consequences and risks to his life.

If this hypothesis is correct, Charlie saw where he fit in. Because of his professional experience he understood the technicalities of the financial scheme. In addition he had an unique window with Scottie's cash flows. Harrison must know these connections. So Charlie finding the body was bad luck for Harrison. The murderer would not have expected that someone of Charlie's background would have found himself with an incentive to solve this crime. Charlie saw clearly why he was a threat and therefore a target. Kate was close to him so she was a target also. Harrison must feel an urgency to get rid of Charlie. And Charlie must know Harrison. Elliot is the linchpin.

Charlie asked Kathy, his secretary, to arrange a luncheon meeting with Elliott as soon as possible.

"Explain to Mr. Elliott that I want to discuss an opportunity to advise me on a private equity fund being offered in the marketplace."

Fifteen minutes later Cathy had set up the meeting at noon the next day at The Chicago Club.

# CHAPTER THIRTY-TWO

Charlie met Phillips Elliott in the second floor dining room at precisely twelve. He was a short, pale, thin young man with horned-rimmed glasses and short brown hair. His tan, checkered suit and loud geometric tie struck Charlie as out of place for stuffy Bradshaw, Evans. Maybe, he thought, young, sharp lawyers were in short supply today — or Elliot was simply making a statement.

"Are you related to Woody Elliott?" Charlie began, trying to make him comfortable.

"Yes, he's my uncle."

"You resemble him somewhat. He's quite a squash player. I know him from the Racquet Club. Do you play squash as well?"

"No," Elliott chuckled, sitting back in his chair looking relaxed. "I did not inherit the family genes for sports. I am embarrassingly uncoordinated. Fortunately my two children take after my wife."

Charlie sensed Elliott was confident — certainly unsuspecting why Charlie had invited him.

They both ordered club sandwiches and iced tea. When the waiter disappeared, Charlie got down to business.

"Phillips, I am told that you are expert in private equity-fund situations," he ventured. "My firm is considering using those alternative investments more extensively in our clients' portfolios. I'd like to consider you to help us."

"I'm flattered. Who recommended me?"

"I feel awkward saying that Scottie Bradshaw did several months ago. With the unfortunate events of this past summer I am just getting back to the issue. You were a friend of Scottie's?"

Elliott shifted in his chair and took a sip of water.

"Not friends. I did some legal work for him. Tragic what happened to him."

"A colleague of mine, Sam Dixon, said you did some legal work related to the trusts we managed for Scottie."

Charlie paused, then "That sounds strange: an M. and A. lawyer doing trust work. I'm curious—how did that come about?"

Redness colored Elliott's neck and worked its way up to his cheeks. The waiter returned with their teas, and Charlie cursed the interruption. Elliott busied himself squeezing the lemon wedge into the tea avoiding eye contact with Charlie.

"Are you all right, Phillips? Does talking about your relationship to Scottie upset you?"

"I. . . I'm okay," he stammered. "You know I'm bound by confidentiality."

"Since you are not a trust lawyer," Charlie pressed on, "could it be that Scottie was paying you for information pertaining to your M. and A. work and masking it with bills for trust advice?"

Elliott flushed and seemed unable to speak. Suddenly he

pushed back his chair and stood up, looking offended. "I don't like your implications, Mr. Bailey. I feel you invited me under false pretenses and I don't appreciate it. Goodbye."

Elliott strode out of the dining room. Charlie did not follow him. Charlie had seen all he needed. Elliott was guilty of something in connection with Scottie. An innocent man would have reacted differently. Charlie had hit a guilty nerve. Now it was time for the police to follow up. He would ask Paul Victor to pry out the conspiracy from Elliott.

Back at his office Charlie called Paul in Waukegan. Not reaching him he left a detailed message of all that had happened. He ended the call with the thought, "*I fear that this scheme may go deeper in Bradshaw, Evans. It's one thing for a bank administrator to fail to question bills, but would the law firm not know that Elliott was billing for non-work? Maybe someone inside the firm was working with Elliott?*"

Charlie felt depressed by this situation. Poor Henry Bradshaw. He had worked so hard to build a reputation of expertise and integrity for his firm. Now a junior person like Elliott had most likely undermined and damaged the name of Bradshaw, Evans, perhaps destroying it.

\* \* \*

Paul Victor watched Detective John Riordan escort Phillips Elliott and his lawyer across the open office bullpen of the Chicago Police Downtown Precinct to Interrogation Room Two. Since he received Charlie's call two days ago he had accomplished a lot. With help from Detective Riordan and FBI Agent Terry O'Malley he had obtained court orders for Scottie's personal and office computers and passwords as well as Elliott's cellphone. A search of emails discovered numerous communications between the two regarding prospective deals Bradshaw, Evans was working on. They used codenames to identify each transaction, but the public record of the law firm's work easily matched the deals described in the emails. In addition, Scottie's trade records matched the time and pertinent stocks referenced in the emails. This material plus the billing payments from the trust to Bradshaw, Evans chronicled a fraud based on illegal insider information.

Paul and Agent O'Malley joined the group while Elliott and his lawyer were sitting down. Elliott complained immediately.

"Why did you have to tell our secretary you were asking me in here? She might have told others at the firm. It's damn embarrassing."

"Calm down. That's the least of your problems," Riordan answered. "I see you brought counsel. Welcome Mr. Lucas. From your card I see that you are also with Bradshaw, Evans."

Then Detective Riordan quickly dispensed with the preliminaries and asked,

"Mr. Elliott, what was your relationship with the late Scottie Bradshaw?"

"He was a client who hired me to review two trusts in which he was the beneficiary."

"Trusts? You are not a trust lawyer. Why you?

"Mr. Bradshaw hired him," Attorney Lucas interrupted. "Perhaps you should ask him."

"Ha, ha," the detective laughed derisively. "You know he is dead. This interview will go much easier if you let your client answer. I repeat, 'Why you'?"

"I knew Scottie socially," Elliott responded. "I felt the matter was routine. Technically, the bank trustee hired me. The bank must have thought my assignment was proper."

"The bank trustee hired you because Scottie Bradshaw told them to. If the matters were routine as you claim, why did you charge his trust more than $400,000?"

"I do good work and charge accordingly," Elliott answered.

Riordan was not amused. "Mr. Elliott, even if you charged $1,000 per hour, you would have had to work four hundred hours to do a routine review. Your bills mention a total of ten hours of work. So you are bull-shitting me. Do I look like an idiot? Don't lie to me. What was this money for?"

"My client answered that," his lawyer objected.

"Actually, the issue was not routine," Elliott finally confessed. "Scottie wanted me to see if the trusts could be broken so he could get more money out of them. Since our firm wrote the trusts, I thought it would be a waste of time to consult the trust lawyer. I studied trusts in law school, so I did the work. Unfortunately I saw no way to break the trusts and told Scottie as much. Scottie thanked me and had the trusts pay my fee."

"I guess we're done," his lawyer concluded, beginning to gather his papers.

Detective Riordan ignored the attorney and cast a stern look at Elliott. "Crap. What a story. You work on mergers and acquisitions matters. The information you see could be of great value to investors if they knew of it before it was make public. Scottie Bradshaw was a broker. His clients were investors. Isn't it true that Bradshaw paid you for inside information through a bogus trust fund review?"

"Don't answer that," the lawyer jumped in.

The detective pressed on, his voice rising, "Something went wrong, and now Bradshaw is dead. Didn't he pay you enough? Did he threaten you that he would expose you to the firm, to his father? Did you kill Scottie Bradshaw to silence him?"

"No!" Elliott screamed. "I didn't murder him!"

Lucas leaned in, but Elliott pushed him away.

"Look," Elliott began desperately, "Scottie was an acquaintance. He asked a favor. My boss is always after me to bill more. I looked at the trust. I never game him insider information."

"Don't continue to lie to us," Riordan said. "We have evidence that you repeatedly shared confidential information on upcoming deals. We have the emails you sent to Scottie."

Elliott visibly blanched. He put his head in his hands.

"Oh no. That idiot."

"What idiot," Riordan asked.

"Scottie."

"My client has nothing more to say," his lawyer broke in, gathered his notes, and reached for his briefcase.

Elliott went on anyway, "Scottie described an arrangement

that seemed a godsend. So I gave him tips on small deals. I don't make much as an associate and I have a family to support."

"Then you got greedy," the detective said.

Paul watched Elliott shrink into his chair. He looked defeated but resigned to the situation.

"Yes. I passed along something I knew would be a homerun for Scottie's investors. Why shouldn't I benefit too? So I billed $400,000. Scottie paid up. He seemed happy and my boss was happy, too. He didn't ask how I billed so much."

"None of your superiors knew of your scheme?"

"Not that I know of," Elliot said.

Paul thought that Elliott was telling the truth.

"If by chance someone in the firm suspected something," Elliot continued, "he would probably have gone directly to Henry Bradshaw. I doubted that Mr. Bradshaw would turn on his son. He would be very angry but would not take any action. In fact, I discussed this possibility with Scottie. He assured me with a story about another associate who had done a similar thing, and Mr. Bradshaw had turned the other way, fearing a backlash from the companies involved in the secret deal. Any publicity could ruin the firm's reputation. So Mr. Bradshaw ignored the breach."

From what Paul had learned in the investigation, he was amazed to hear this story. Henry's integrity was beyond question. Understanding Scottie's problem with the truth, Paul was skeptical about what Elliott had said. He would give Henry the benefit of the doubt.

"So you felt safe," Detective Riordan summarized, "And the scheme worked until Scottie Bradshaw died."

"Somewhat. I did feel that if our arrangement became known in the firm, Mr. Bradshaw would cover it up and ship me out to some corporate client of the firm where a general counsel was close to Henry. Exile, if you will."

"Perfect," Riordan observed. "Everyone made lots of money and no clients would know what happened. You were safe."

"But when Scottie died, the arrangement died with him," Elliott said. "So I had no reason to want him dead."

"But you still had expenses at home and were privy to insider information. Did you try to find another broker?" Riordan asked.

"Someone did approach me, but I turned him down."

"Who?" the detective asked.

Elliott's lawyer broke in again. "My client has told you enough. If you want more, offer him a deal."

"Let us hear what he says, and we'll consider his helpfulness."

The lawyer whispered to Elliott, and Elliott nodded.

Paul perked up. A possible connection with the murder investigation. The dialogue was getting good.

"Lowell Hersey. Scottie mentioned him as one of his investors. Scottie liked to boast of his contacts. Hersey runs a large hedge fund. In my opinion the man is a snake. When I was dealing with Scottie, Hersey approached me on the sly to propose we cut out the middleman. Hersey said that Scottie could not be trusted. He offered to pay much more than Scottie for an exclusive arrangement. The payments would come through an offshore bank account. I was nervous about Hersey and turned him down. Besides, Scottie afforded me protection from my firm's senior management."

"And after Scottie Bradshaw's death?"

"He came back within that week. I said no again. I thought he was a slime ball. Anyway I had had my fill. I felt too exposed. I was relieved that the risk of discovery was gone. Or at least until now."

"Are you certain that Scottie did not tell anyone else about your scheme—his father, lawyers in your firm, friends, clients?"

"I think he sold the information to several clients, but I don't know who."

"After Scottie's death, did you notice any change in Henry Bradshaw's attitude toward you?"

"No. I have little contact with him. I'm a nobody in his firm."

"Mr. Elliott, I'll prepare a statement for you to sign. The FBI and the SEC may have further questions."

The detective rose and went to the door. He beckoned an officer to enter and arrest Elliott. He recited his Miranda rights and told attorney Lucas that he would recommend to the D.A. that Elliott be held without bail as a flight risk.

"Frankly, the evidence here is extremely strong," Riordan asserted. "But I'll tell the D.A. that your client has been helpful."

After Elliott and his attorney left, the trio sat at the table to review what had happened. O'Malley said, "An open-and-shut case. Securities fraud. We'll need to follow up on Lowell Hersey and any other investors who received the information. Elliott's testimony can take them all down."

"And he'll want to trade his cooperation," Riordan added.

"Don't forget, I still have a murder case," Paul said.

"With all the money involved, there is ample motive to kill someone," Agent O'Malley said.

"So what's next?" Paul asked.

"Talk to Henry Bradshaw," O'Malley recommended. "He will be irate at Elliott whether Henry knew anything or not. He'll probably want to carve out Elliott and blame everything on him. Save the firm from a bad apple."

"How do you think he'll react to Scottie's involvement?" Paul asked.

"Scottie was an embarrassment," Riordan said.

"That, Detective, is an understatement," Paul said.

| § |

# CHAPTER THIRTY-THREE

Charlie was worried that he had not heard from Paul since he told him about Phillips Elliott three days before. He was certain that Elliott conspired with Scottie to pass along insider information. The police could not bungle this situation. They should have been able to pressure Elliott to implicate others. Anyone involved would be a possible suspect in Scottie's murder.

Finally, Charlie could not wait no longer and called Paul. Paul sounded upbeat over the phone. He related all that occurred during the investigation.

"He had a lawyer with him and stopped talking when we asked him who else was involved. He wanted to trade his testimony for a lesser sentence. After we arrested him, we decided to visit Henry Bradshaw to see what he knew.'

'The next day we called on him in his office—and what an office! Large, comfortable, antiques, Persian rugs, multiple TV screens on the wall, fantastic view of the park and lake. He took us into a conference room adjacent to his office and was very polite. He told us he had learned of the allegations against Mr. Elliott yesterday. He went on to say, "So Phillips confessed to this awful scheme. What a betrayal of our faith in him. We shall of course cooperate in any way we can.'

Riordan responded, 'We would like to interview Mr. Elliot's superiors and co-workers.'

"Then Mr. Bradshaw shut us down. He pointed out that Mr. Elliott was represented at this moment by an attorney of Bradshaw, Evans. That arrangement created a conflict for him. 'Mr. Elliott is a client now, and we have standards of practice. So we can't help unless he hires representation from another firm.'"

"I spoke up then and asked him if he had an interest in Scottie's murder.'

'He said that of course he did, but he failed to see the connection between his son's death and this scheme. He said that he didn't know Scottie was providing illegal, insider information until yesterday."

Charlie felt satisfied that the police were pursuing the securities-violations case efficiently. However, they were not near solving Scottie's murder.

Charlie asked Paul, "Was that all? Henry seems to be hanging Elliott out to dry. Right now having him as a client is useful, but eventually Henry will want to create maximum separation from the firm. The current arrangement allows Henry time to determine if anyone else in the firm was a participant in the scheme and to decide the best strategy to protect Bradshaw, Evans. Eventually Elliott will be characterized as a single bad apple, who took advantage of his son."

"You hit the nail on the head," Paul agreed. "We'll see if we can get a court order to penetrate the veil of lawyer privilege to investigate the firm. In the meantime one name has come up again — Lowell Hersey. He seems to have benefited from this arrangement."

Charlie hung up and tried to put the pieces together. The financial magnitude of Scottie's schemes and the potential damages to Bradshaw, Evans could provide motives to a number of people for a murder. He was skeptical that Elliott's superiors would not have known what was going on. Certainly something similar would have been unearthed by the compliance officer in his own firm rather quickly. At least he hoped so. If Henry's people knew of the problem, they would have told him.

One person who might be helpful in understanding Scottie's risk to Bradshaw, Evans was his mother. Reaching her was easy. She was at home in Lake Forest.

"Mom, remind me of your conversations with Dottie before and after Scottie's death."

"What on earth for? You're not still doing what the police should do?"

"Humor me. I think the police may have something crucial to understanding Scottie's murder."

"Oh."

"Before his death did Dottie ever say anything about Scottie being an embarrassment or a disappointment?"

"Dottie loved her baby boy. He was the life of the party, always in a good mood, solicitous of his parents. She said that if he did anything wrong, he did not mean it. He was a bit too trusting and may not have always thought through the consequences of his actions."

"Was she worried about anything specifically?"

"No. Nothing specific, but she did worry about him."

"As I recall, she and Henry insisted that Scottie's death was an accident, and resented anyone thinking otherwise. In other words, no on should pursue the possibility of murder, since a continued spotlight on the death was unnecessary and painful to the grieving family."

"True. And she was annoyed that you would not let it go but instead asked a lot of questions and kept the press interested. Because of you she became mad at me and was so cold—and after our friendship of forty years! Only recently did she seem to forgive me."

"Did she ever admit that Scottie was murdered?"

"She never used those words. I think she knows that it wasn't an accident, but the subject is distasteful. She expressed no interest in learning who killed her son. She wants to move on."

"I'm sorry I was a problem for you, Mom, and happy you two have reconciled."

Charlie decided to change the subject and asked her about her new bodyguard.

"He's been here only a couple of days. Jimbo is his name. It should be 'Jumbo'. He's in the kitchen a lot. Otherwise he lurks around and follows me wherever I go: the club, my hairdresser, the market, the bank, whatever. He rarely says a word to me. He's more comfortable talking to James. I can't see why you're wasting your money on him."

"Just bear with him for a little while," Charlie said.

"All right, but you can make life so difficult at times. If you are done, I have an awkward thing to tell you. Caroline Abbott called this morning. She said she saw Kate out with a man last night at Bice. Carolyn said he was very good looking. Kate came wearing black pants and a silk top and used a cane. The man looked fit and trim with his dark facial hair - generally appeared stylish. She said they were animated and familiar over dinner. Caroline voiced her disapproval, but then she did not know about your breakup.'

'I know this situation pains you. Whatever my early reservations, I've grown to like and respect Kate and I hate to see you unhappy. If there is anything I can do, I will do it: talk to her, invite Kate to something, anything."

"Thanks, Mom. You are so kind. We'll work it out. She has a right to be mad at me. I'll win her back."

# CHAPTER THIRTY-FOUR

Sensing a significant break in the case, Paul and Detective Riordan called on Lowell Hersey immediately and unannounced. When the receptionist said that they needed an appointment, John Riordan produced his badge and told her "Tell Mr. Hersey that he could meet us here or down at the precinct."

Within minutes Hersey ushered them in a conference room out of view from staff and clients.

"What can I do for you, officers? I wish you had called ahead so I could be prepared."

"No preparation necessary, Mr. Hersey," Paul said. "We just have a few questions relating to an ongoing investigation. You were familiar with Mr. Scottie Bradshaw?"

"Yes." Lowell appeared to frown.

"You were his client, and he provided you with useful investment information. Correct?"

"Yes."

"You traded securities with his firm for which he received commissions. Correct?"

"I don't know his financial arrangements with his firm, but most brokers work for commissions."

"You also know a lawyer named Phillips Elliott, who works for Bradshaw, Evans, do you not?"

Hersey appeared startled hearing Elliott's name. The cool confidence that he exuded up to then seemed to dissolve.

"Where is this going? Perhaps I should call my lawyer."

"You are not a suspect in this investigation at this time, but if you are uncomfortable, you have the right to an attorney being present. We were hoping you would be helpful."

"Oh," he said slowly. "I'll try, but if the questions get too personal, I'll have to call my attorney. Yes, I know Phillips Elliot."

"According to Mr. Elliott, he passed along certain information to Scottie Bradshaw regarding pending merger and acquisition transactions on which his firm worked. Mr. Bradshaw in turn told you what Mr. Elliott had told him. At one point you tried to go around Mr. Bradshaw and approached Mr. Elliot to obtain his information directly. He said no. But when Mr. Bradshaw died, you approached Mr. Elliott again."

"Yes, but he demurred again. I don't know why. If he was comfortable talking to Scottie, he should have been with me."

"After Mr. Elliott turned you down, what did you do? Did you contact anyone else at Bradshaw, Evans?"

"Yes. I met with Henry Bradshaw."

Paul had to restrain his excitement when he heard this. They had hit a jackpot. Henry Bradshaw knew months ago what was going on.

"When and where did that meeting take place, and what was the purpose?"

"I met with Henry in his office on the top floor in late June. I assumed his son had worked out the original arrangement through his father, and I complained that Elliott was backing out. I thought Henry might assign a new source to me because Elliott was reneging."

"Did you think that there was anything illegal in passing along this type of information?"

"It crossed my mind, but I expected that Bradshaw, Evans knew the rules. A respected firm like that wouldn't risk breaking the law. I'm not a lawyer. I'm just an investor paying for information that might benefit my clients."

Paul shook his head. Lowell was being disingenuous. He was a bright, sophisticated businessman playing dumb—and not doing a good job at it. He noticed that John Riordan looked disgusted with this guy.

"So what did Mr. Bradshaw say when you told him you were unhappy?"

"He was very gracious. He apologized for failing to meet with me earlier to let me know that he could not continue the arrangement. When I asked why not, he explained that his staff reconsidered certain potential conflicts of interest."

"So his answer was a polite no," Riordan asked.

"That's correct," Hersey confirmed.

"So in your opinion, Henry Bradshaw was aware of the arrangement you had with Scottie Bradshaw?" Paul said.

"Absolutely. As I was leaving he asked that, in deference to Scottie, I keep the arrangement in confidence. He said that some people might misinterpret things and he did not want Scottie's memory sullied."

"What did you make of Mr. Bradshaw's comments?"

"I thought it was a crock. He was willing to permit our arrangement as long as his son was profiting. With Scottie gone he was concerned about damage to his firm."

"Do you think Scottie Bradshaw had a similar arrangement with other investors willing to pay?"

"I am sure of it. Other hedge funds in town arbed some of the same deals I did. That hurt my profits, so I told Scottie I wanted an exclusive."

"What did Scottie say?" Paul asked.

"He turned me down. But no matter, his information was always accurate and timely, so we made a lot of money for our clients."

"Arbed?"

"Do arbitrage. There is always a bid/ask spread on a deal that narrows over time or changes if new information—like different terms—arises. When we know the information before others, we can take a position on the spread."

"Very good. I understand. Did you talk with anyone else at Bradshaw, Evans besides Henry Bradshaw and Phillips Elliott?"

"No."

Paul turned to Riordan and motioned that they step out to confer. They excused themselves and found an empty conference room down the corridor.

"I noticed he blanched when we mentioned Elliott," Paul said. "He regained his cool when he discussed Henry Bradshaw. I guess he thinks he can argue that he received a pass for his actions from the head of a prestigious law firm."

"That would be stupid. He's just playing a role. A good prosecutor will tear him apart. The SEC will shutter his firm, and he'll do time."

"Are we going to arrest him? He admitted a lot."

"Not now. Let him think we bought his story. We have a bigger fish in the esteemed Henry Bradshaw. We'll need Henry's testimony to nail him for securities violations as well as a lot of corroborating evidence. Hersey will want a deal. He'd be a fool to run."

They went back into the room and Riordan said, "Okay. That's all we have for you at this time. Don't talk about this conversation with anyone. Thank you, Mr. Hersey."

When the detectives reached the street, Paul turned philosophical, "I am disgusted that one greedy, dumbbell son can take down a whole family. What a shame that the Bradshaw name will be remembered for this rather than all the good they do for the community."

Riordan said, "Henry Bradshaw must have been apoplectic when he learned what his son had done with Elliott. Because Scottie was involved, Henry tried to cover it up. But both Scottie and Elliott were loose cannons. Trying to protect his son—and the name and the law firm—Henry was in an uncomfortable bind.

So do you think he would have hired someone to kill his own son?"

Paul stopped walking and waited for Riordan to turn around and look at him. "I do," he said. "And a man like him thought he would get away with it. But we'll need proof."

# CHAPTER THIRTY-FIVE

After talking to his mother, Charlie called Jamie Bradshaw. They agreed to meet for lunch at the Chicago Club grill. Charlie arranged with the maître d' to get the farthest table in the back — away from the other diners.

"It's been quite a summer for you," Jamie began as he sat down. "How is Kate? Is she at home or back to work?"

"She's working. I haven't seen her lately, but I'm told she is using a cane. She needs more time to heal."

"Is that temporary?"

"I hope."

"How about you?" Jamie asked.

Before Charlie answered, the waiter requested their orders. That done, Charlie told Jamie what had happened at Lake Geneva, explaining that Ferrol Lopez was in police custody and had confessed to shooting Kate.

"What a story! I hadn't read about it in the newspapers. I missed it somehow — maybe because it was out of state. I wonder why this Lopez fellow was involved? How did you know he might follow you to Lake Geneva?"

Charlie eyed Jamie carefully to gauge his body language. He seemed quite interested in what happened. He was probably lying about not hearing. Did that mean anything?

"The police alerted me. They identified him in their investigation. He seemed to be a part of the same plot to kill me earlier at Mother's."

Jamie was surprised. He nervously tapped the end of his fork on the table, looked to the side, then asked suddenly,

"You mean those attacks on you and Kate were connected?"

"Undoubtedly."

"Why were they after you?"

"Your brother's murder."

Jamie looked down and set the fork down slowly. He appeared shocked.

"That makes no sense. Do the police know who was behind it?"

"Someone named Harrison," Charlie said looking straight at Jamie. "Do you know anyone by that name?"

Jamie appeared unnerved. He sat up and thought for a moment. Then he answered, "I know Chris Harrison and Walter Harrison. It is a common name. As far as I know neither of them had anything against Scottie. His death seemed like an accident to me at first, but I now guess I was wrong."

"You were at the party when he died. Did you notice anyone named Harrison?"

"No. I don't know. I left very early."

Charlie noted that Jamie was bending the truth—unlike what

he said a few weeks ago. Maybe Jamie had misunderstood Charlie before.

Jamie changed the subject, "I am upset that Kate was injured. Roman Spartek didn't do a good job, did he?"

"After what happened to Kate, I fired him. But Kate's father hired him back."

"Oh, too bad. That's crazy. Did you hire the other bodyguard we talked about for you mother?"

"Yes. Jimbo Pavko. I hope she doesn't need him."

"Of course, but after all that has happened you can't be too sure."

Their food arrived, and their conversation lagged. Jamie was eating much faster than usual. Charlie decided to up the pressure while he had the chance.

"Jamie, there are two more things. I learned from Sam Dixon that someone in your father's firm worked with Scottie to profit from information regarding secret plans of clients' corporate actions. Mergers, stock offerings, buybacks, and more."

Jamie looked startled and stammered as he asked, "Who! Can't be! Insider information?"

"An associate named Phillips Elliott. Scottie passed along the information to his clients. You better warn your father, if he doesn't know."

"That's terrible. I'll go over to him now."

"One last thing. Sam told me that you occasionally transfer money from your account with us to a bank in the Cayman Islands. Why do you?"

"True. Tax strategies. But none of your business. It's my money."

"Sorry. Don't be offended. Just curious."

Jamie stood up and excused himself. "Must talk to Dad."

Obviously angry, Jamie stopped and turned back. "A thought just struck me. Maybe that Harrison targeted you because you became involved in the police's investigation. I told you not to do that—asking for trouble." Jamie walked away.

Charlie returned to the office. Market news distracted him for a few hours. But he wanted to assess his conversation with Jamie. So he left early to go home. He poured himself a bourbon and water and sat down with a legal pad in his library. Charlie recognized that he had thrown several bombshells at Jamie. His significant unspoken reactions confirmed Charlie suspicion that Jamie knew a lot about his brother's death that he was hiding. While it was inconceivable that he would kill his brother, something was very wrong. His lie about his attendance at the fateful party, his experience with Cayman Island banking, his nervousness about the insider information scheme, his feigned indifference to the Lopez information, and his presence in Palm Beach when the car nearly ran over Kate and himself all bothered Charlie. So many coincidences. Jamie had to be involved. But where was the proof? Carome and Lopez wouldn't know him. The bank in the Caymans wouldn't talk. Vecchia was dead. And what was his motive? Not money. Sibling rivalry? Hersey seems like a more likely suspect.

The ringing phone interrupted his thoughts. Angry, he picked it up. "Who's this?" he asked sharply.

"It's Peaches. Sorry to bother you at home."

"I didn't mean to snap at you. I was in the middle of something."

"You'll excuse me when I tell you my news. My sources in the Chicago PD just informed me that they are close to arresting Lowell Hersey in the Scottie Bradshaw case." Wraps it up, I suppose. That wouldn't surprise me at all. He's a bad person."

Charlie shook his head, maybe they are right.

"That's news," Charlie said simply. "But you better get confirmation before you stop the presses to print a story connecting Hersey with the murder. He may have done business with Scottie, but that might have been all."

"Charlie, don't throw cold water on my hot story. If I scoop this, I could get out of the fairy tale world of society. People would take me seriously for once."

"Only if you are right. Be careful."

"Nice guy you are," Peaches sniffed. "Spoilsport."

Charlie smiled. Peaches was so easily aroused. Charlie was merely trying to save him embarrassment.

Peaches retreated and struck back on another topic.

"Since I have you, someone told me that your Kate was out with a smartly dressed man. It looked like a date. Is there trouble in the upper echelon of elite society?"

"No comment."

"You know, I have so wanted to write up the Bailey-Milano wedding—the cathedral, the presiding Cardinal, hired opera singers, world renowned organs blaring, colorful flowers every-where, and pews fully occupied by the *haut monde* of business, fashion, government, and polite society. Don't disappoint me."

"I can't begin to address your fantasy," Charlie replied merrily. "You live in another world. But thanks for calling and lightening my mood."

Charlie hung up and wondered why the police wanted Hersey. If they are correct, my suspicions about Jamie are off-base. Did Hersey admit to doing something?

| § |

# CHAPTER THIRTY-SIX

Jamie almost ran the seven blocks to his father's law firm. He was too wound up to hail a cab or even notice the other people on the sidewalks. He was angry and scared—desperate. Up to now he felt that he had hid his involvement successfully—from the police, the media, and Charlie Bailey. He was the puppeteer behind the curtain confidently pulling the strings. But obviously Charlie knew too much. His questions at lunch came too close for comfort. He and his dad needed to deal with Bailey immediately.

While Jamie was walking he called on his cell phone to his father's office requesting an urgent meeting. He was on his way over. Henry Bradshaw's secretary said she would clear his schedule. Breathlessly Jamie entered the office and his father looked up with a frown.

"This better be important. I need to prepare to be in court tomorrow morning."

"Nothing trumps this. Bailey knows about Scottie and Phillips Elliott and is sniffing around my offshore money transfers."

"The police were here," Henry said adding to the serious-ness.

"Shit," Jamie spit out. "Charlie even knows the fake name I used with Carome. We have to rid of him as soon as possible."

Henry gestured for Jamie to stop. He then pointed to a chair near his desk for Jamie to sit.

"Calm down. We need clear heads to figure this out. We did the right thing. First, Elliott. Somebody—probably Charlie Bailey—figured out Scottie's scheme. I still kick myself for not shutting it down when I first heard about it last year. I should have called in the regulatory authorities immediately and exposed the arrangement. But I didn't want to end Scottie's career and stain this firm for not supervising its associates. It's insidious how a cover-up comes back to bite you—no matter how clever you are."

Seated, Jamie was no less agitated. He fidgeted while his father spoke.

"We can handle the Elliott situation minimizing the danger to the firm. I've assigned one of our litigators to Elliott's defense. He'll tell me what Elliott is thinking. We need to control him. We'll claim privilege to the authorities and start our own inves-tigation. Eventually we'll drop Elliott and let him get run over by authorities. We'll use the bad apple defense. Elliott was the bad apple in a massive law firm. We'll agree to a slap on the wrist and vow increased diligence in the future. We'll contend that Phil Elliott took advantage of my naïve son, that I was ignorant of the scheme and, we won't talk poorly of the dead. I am confident we'll survive this situation. The Bradshaw name and our law firm must and will prevail and prosper."

"No doubt—as regards the insider trading fraud," Jamie said trying to control his emotions. "It's the murder I'm worried about. You know we tried to talk some sense into Scottie's head. He was such an embarrassment and a loose cannon. This Elliott scheme was just the latest foolish act. He shamed us repeatedly: sexual abuse of young women, that illegal late-trading strategy, the insurance fraud. Many others, you bailed him out of all of them."

Henry gestured with open palms and said, "What else could I do? I'll protect our legacy at all costs."

"True. And we did the right thing. Even Mom was so disgusted that she agreed. We were all finished with Scottie. He had to go."

"He did," Henry agreed solemnly. "My feckless and reckless son. He would have brought down all we have built over decades. I had to stop him. We talked to him many times—showed patience, finally warned him. But he went on, disrespecting our name and our legacy. If there had been any other way."

"There wasn't," Jamie stated firmly.

"I know. No looking back. Our anger and our actions were justified. And you make the arrangements. It worked. The police thought it was an accident at least for a while. I convinced the governor to tell the police to call it off and stop bothering a grieving family."

"Until Charlie Bailey," Jamie added.

"Charlie is the whole reason we're in this situation. Unfortunate. Our families have been so close for so long. Too bad you couldn't scare him off. His father was like that. Persistent. Bulldog tenacity. So you think he suspects us?"

"Yes. We talked about this before. We need to eliminate him. The half-measures with his girlfriend only made him more determined."

"Don't forget you gave Joseph Vecchia the option of shooting him at Claire's house."

"That backfired," Jamie admitted. "I think Carome gave us a couple of inept hit men. And just now I learned that Lopez has been arrested. This revelation is new. I called Carome this morning and he knew nothing about Lopez's whereabouts. Bailey was involved in his capture. We're fortunate Lopez doesn't know us, but clearly he can't help us further."

Henry sank into his chair and rubbed his temples. Jamie thought he looked older.

"Now what are you going to do Jamie? Will you have "Harrison" request a new assassin?"

"No. I have some ideas. I could use the bodyguards. Remember I recommended them to watch over Kate Milano and recently Claire also. I pay Roman and Jimbo for information and secrecy. They are definitely for hire to kill."

"So do you have a plan?"

"Sort of. I'll need your help and Mom's. I would like to utilize a location where I could control the action. Could I use your Lake Geneva house?"

"Why?"

"I need a place agreeable to Charlie, Kate, and Claire. Familiar. Not suspicious."

"Then what?"

"I don't know specifically, but you won't be implicated. I'll be careful."

"Do you have a plan B, if your scheme doesn't work?"

"I'm working on it."

"Why Claire and Kate?"

"Charlie may have told them what he has discovered."

"I don't know if I like using our house," Henry said. "Dottie would have to invite the ladies. She might balk. Claire has been a dear friend. Of course, Dottie knows about what happened to Scottie. She had wished there had been another way—but agreed in the end. She'll need convincing."

"And how do you get Charlie to come?"

Jamie sat back. He was starting to relax after explaining his idea. The alternative of doing nothing and hoping Charlie would fail in his investigation had become untenable.

"So you think these two bodyguards, Spartek and Pavko, will agree to your plan?"

"Yes. Spartek in particular hates Bailey. Charlie fired him publicly. Roman wants to get even. Despite that this arrangement will be costly."

"Never mind the cost. Pay in laundered cash. Not traceable."

Henry paused thinking. Jamie sensed he was buying in.

"I wish you had more specifics in your plan. But we don't

have much time. This situation is deteriorating. Go ahead," Henry sighed.

"Fine."

"I am angry how this has turned out," Henry complained. "I had hoped that our friend, the governor, would have successfully quashed the police investigation. Kept the death as an accident. No, it's true; the cover-up is always more problematic then the crime."

As Jamie reached the door, his father turned his shoulder from behind and hugged him for five seconds. Jamie felt his eyes welling up but he held back the tears. He backed away and did not stop until he reached the street. His mind was in a daze.

# CHAPTER THIRTY-SEVEN

"I think I know who is behind Scottie's murder, but I don't know why," Charlie began his call to Paul the next morning. He was still in his pajamas—his night had been so restless.

Charlie described his conversation with Jamie and his body language. Charlie was surprised when Paul agreed with him.

Paul summarized his meetings with Phillips Elliott, Henry Bradshaw and Lowell Hersey. "Henry knew what was going on and did nothing to stop it. He miscalculated that no one would talk."

"But Hersey did talk." Charlie noted.

"Yes. But we can't see any reason for Hersey to have Scottie killed. The Bradshaws had much more to lose from Scottie's scheme if it were discovered!"

"Of course they did. But did they act?"

"We can't prove anything, but a new clue came yesterday. Harrison finally called Carome. He sounded agitated on the phone and did not try to muffle his voice. He demanded to know where Lopez was. Of course Carome had no news. But we heard Harrison's voice. It sounded familiar to me, but you might recognize it. When I get to the office, I'll call you with the recording."

Charlie hung up and felt excited. A breakthrough. As he was making breakfast he noticed a flashing light on his answering machine. Last night he was so preoccupied he had not noticed it. He punched the button and heard his mother's voice.

"Charlie dear, I wanted to tell you I'll be away this weekend. Dottie called and invited me up to her house on Lake Geneva— to go on a lake cruise. Stay overnight. I'm leaving early morning. She also suggested she invite Kate. I had told Dottie that I thought that was a great idea. I confessed that I had felt guilty not visiting Kate in the hospital and wanted to improve our relations—especially since she has turned cool to you lately. Dottie thought a day or two together at the lake would do the trick. Dottie called back to say Kate is coming. She said that she didn't mention that I would be there. Probably best. Dottie asked Jamie to drive her as Kate's legs are still injured. I'll try to mend some fences."

A chill crept through Charlie's body. This invitation sounded suspicious. Given what he was learning about Jamie and the Bradshaws, he feared for Kate's and his mother's health. But since Dottie was doing the organizing, he was possibly overreacting.

He heard a bell signaling his English muffin was done. As he was taking it out of the toaster the phone rang. He wanted to call his mother to prevent her going, but first he had to get rid of this call.

Charlie was surprised to hear Jimbo Pavko's voice.

"Mr. Bradshaw, I need to tell you that your mother decided to drive herself to Lake Geneva this morning and gave me the weekend off. You must talk to her for two reasons. First, she doesn't look too good. She has to take her meds. Sometimes she forgets. I remind her a lot.'

'Second, last night I was talking to Roman Spartek. We used to have a business together. Anyway, he has it in for you. You did a thing that really pissed him off—fired him in front of people. I'm afraid he might do something to get back at you—like hurt your mother. He is following Miss Milano up to the Bradshaws this morning. That's his job. I don't like it that your mother will be there alone. Should I go up there also?"

Charlie was frightened by this news. A perfect storm was forming. He did not hesitate. "Of course, go up there. And I'll join you. Meet me at the car park in front of the house. Do you know the address?"

"Yes, I can find it."

"The drive from here takes two hours. I'll meet you at 11:30."

His first thought was to call his mother, but he couldn't because she had not installed a car phone—on purpose. "Too distracting, unsafe!" Instead he called her cellphone. No response.

Scared, Charlie called to have his car brought up. He then went to the safe hidden in a wall cabinet in the library. He took out the handgun that he had secreted and rarely used—having fired it only twice at a local range. Fortunately the gun was clean and loaded.

He took the gun and his cellphone downstairs to find his BMW waiting for him. The drive north was difficult as he had to balance the traffic, his desire to speed to Lake Geneva as fast as possible, and his knowledge that the tollway to Wisconsin was heavily patrolled by traffic cops. He did not want to be stopped with a gun in the glove compartment.

Despite his anxiety he had the good sense to call Paul again. The situation had changed in only an hour. It did not help his fretful state that Paul did not answer. Instead Charlie left a message describing his intent and asked Paul to alert Chief Warren of the potential trouble at the Bradshaw cottage.

Was he overreacting? Perhaps. Lunch with Dottie Bradshaw at the Lake Geneva house sounded innocent enough. But Jamie and Roman were going to be there. So what? Why did he need a gun? Was he being foolish?

Still he became more frustrated and nervous as the time crept slowly by. At last he pulled into the long driveway of the Bradshaws cottage on the lake. Jimbo was waiting for him.

"Their butler said they are out back in the glass building—sort of a greenhouse called the Orangerie. They're having coffee and tea."

Just then Charlie's cellphone rang. He stepped away from Jimbo and took the call from Paul.

"I have the recording of Harrison. See if you recognize the voice."

Charlie smiled as he heard the voice. He knew it from forty years of friendship.

"Paul, that's Jamie Bradshaw. There can be no mistake."

"Yes, but I wanted you to confirm."

"Is there enough to arrest Jaime?"

'We'll see. I'd feel better if we had more evidence and a clear motive."

"Follow the money."

"The FBI will try again to get access to Jamie's offshore bank accounts. We need to match the cash flows with Carome's records."

"So we're on the same page. The Bradshaws."

"Yes, I admit you got there first."

"Forget that, Paul. I am at the Bradshaw's. Jamie should be here also. What should I do?"

"Be careful. Remember desperate men do desperate things. I'll have Chief Warren come by."

"The sooner the better." Charlie said hanging up.

"Follow me," Charlie ordered Jimbo. "I'll go in the Orangerie and you stay outside and wait for my signal. The structure is almost all glass; so you'll be able to see us from any direction."

Charlie saw the group immediately as he came around the corner of the mansion. He walked in without knocking. Dottie, Jamie, Kate, and his mother were sitting in comfortable chairs around a large glass table—each with a drink. This sitting area comprised about half the Orangerie while the remainder was filled with rows of wooden tables supporting scores of assorted terra cotta flowerpots.

Dottie was first to see Charlie. "What a surprise. Welcome Charlie. Sit down for a minute. You're just in time for the boat ride."

Next to Dottie was Claire, then Kate and then Jamie. There was about five feet between each person. Charlie saw an empty chair across the table and headed for it. He noticed that his mother looked flustered and Kate was frowning.

"Excuse me all, but I had to come," Charlie explained. "I'm afraid but there will be no boat ride."

"Charlie, don't be rude," Claire chastised him. "Why are you here?"

"To protect you."

"It's a beautiful day. The lake is calm, so we can have lunch across the lake at the club," Dottie said. "This is a peaceful place; no one needs protection. Now excuse me. I have to go up to the house and get a hat. I'll call the club to save a slip for our boat. Don't wait for me. Jamie can drive me over in our other boat. Charlie, please join us."

Dottie stood up and left quickly.

Charlie watched his mother start to gather her belongings as he thought what to do next.

A moment later Roman Spartek came in the same door that Charlie had just entered and announced, "The boats are ready. Follow me to the dock."

"Not today, Roman," Charlie answered.

Roman glanced at him and pointed, "Where did you come from?"

Roman half turned and pulled out a gun from his right pocket. "I said let's go people."

"No guns now," Jamie murmured.

"Shut up, Bradshaw. I'm in charge," Roman yelled. "I know what to do."

Claire moaned and slid down in her chair fighting for breath. Kate looked stunned at what was happening.

Charlie glanced outside behind Roman and spotted Jimbo. Charlie motioned him in with his hand.

Meanwhile Kate limped over to Claire to help her.

"Pills. In purse," Claire whispered with difficulty, pointing to her bag next to her chair.

"Sit down," Roman shouted at Kate.

She ignored him, searching in Claire's purse.

At that moment Jimbo entered with a drawn gun. He walked behind Roman and stood to his left. Charlie saw that the gun was pointed in his direction, not Roman's. Suddenly he understood. Jimbo and Roman were a team. They had tricked Charlie and the Bradshaws had planned to dupe him and the ladies, bringing them all together.

He cursed his forgetfulness in having left his gun in the car. He had been too excited and distracted when he arrived.

"Get up now," Jimbo ordered this time.

Jamie started to stand. Charlie used the slight diversion to act. He dove right at Jimbo's legs. He bumped and tackled the big man so that Jimbo fell down and over the supine Charlie. Jimbo's gun went off and struck the glass ceiling.

Instinctively Roman turned and shot rapidly at the figure on the floor. Terra cotta pots, dirt, flowers, and wood flew in multiple directions. Bullets also hit Jimbo in the back and neck on top of Charlie.

"Stop. You're screwing up," Jaime shouted at Roman and moved towards him.

"Fuck you, I'm running this show," Roman said and shot Jamie four times, killing him.

Charlie pushed the bleeding gunman off him and rolled under a wooden table. Jimbo's gun was within reach. Because of the table he could only see Roman's legs. So he shot three quick volleys at them connecting with two.

Roman shouted in pain and lost his balance. He dropped his gun but saw it near him as he hit the floor. As he grabbed at it, Charlie did not hesitate to empty his last two bullets into Roman's head.

Then the only noises Charlie heard were Claire screaming and Kate sobbing. As he pushed himself up he saw blood, dust, bits of flowers, and shards of clay. The smell of gunfire permeated the air. He rushed over to his mother. Kate was holding her as Claire breathed heavily. Kate cried out of control, but his mother was alive. Kate had found her pills and saved her life.

On the floor to the right was a lifeless Jamie. Four feet from him was Roman in a pool of blood. Jimbo was on the ground, bleeding out and beyond saving.

A shaken looking housekeeper had arrived at the door of the Orangerie, looking uncertain as to what to do.

Charlie told her gently, "Get a doctor. Call the police."

She turned and ran away. Charlie went back to Kate and his mother. And what seemed a moment but must have been five minutes, Charlie started to hear the approaching sirens of the local police and ambulances.

He leaned over the two most important women in his life and whispered, "It's over. It's over. It's over."

| § |

## CHAPTER THIRTY-EIGHT

Charlie looked at the back windows of his mother's drawing room watching the wind blowing dead leaves off the trees. Those that remained were bright red and yellow. He was certain that a hard rain and windstorm would finish off those that were left. Nature was preparing itself for winter.

The weather had convinced him that he should drop by the club on his way back to Chicago and get his golf clubs from the storage bins. He wouldn't need them until he flew down to Palm Beach at Thanksgiving.

"There you are," Claire said as James wheeled Claire into the large, elegant room. "Did Kate call you? I haven't heard from her since I invited her up last week."

James left them to answer the front door.

"I'm sure she's coming," Charlie said confidently. "She promised me two days ago. That bell might be her. I know what it is on your mind. We're not back where we were. She blames me for most of getting her hurt—as she should. I was too bull-headed. I've been walking on eggshells with her, but lately I am feeling reciprocal feelings. One thing I am happy about. She is not dating anyone else. At her low point, she was spending time with her coworker, Marc D'Amboise. He helped her through a tough time. But she's strong enough now not to need him. I am still giving her space and time. It's promising."

"Don't forget love, Charlie. My view of her has changed, you know. Don't forget, she saved my life at Dottie's. I had misjudged her. She wasn't like the young women in my social circle. Now I realize that she was better. Whatever happens between her and you, I think she and I will be close forever."

"Terrific. And how are you feeling health-wise? Your color looks better to me. Has the rehab program improved your strength?"

"Yes. But I only do it so I can throw away this damn wheelchair. It makes me look old. My heart doctor said last week that I was lucky to have avoided a full heart attack. I might have died or had a stroke. Kate found up my angina pills in the nick of time. Those thugs, Roman and Jimbo, would have scared anyone to death. I have you to thank. You found them."

"I relied on Jamie. My poor judgment."

"To think they were always there—next to me and Kate. I guess I should be happy that I'm not dead."

"Miss Milano has arrived and is powdering her nose," James said returning to the room. "Long drive from the city."

Just then Kate entered and went over to Claire and kissed her.

"You are looking good," she said. "Better than last time."

Charlie wondered if she had been in the corridor and had heard his conversation with his mother. He hoped she had.

Then Kate went over to Charlie and gave him a prolonged hug. He responded by kissing her on the lips and holding her tight. At last she sat down near Claire and turned down James' offer of tea or coffee.

"I'm sorry I'm late. The traffic was monstrous."

"Don't worry, dear. Lunch won't be ready for a while. Detective Victor is here, out on the stone patio. Charlie invited him over to bring us up to date on what the police are doing. I hope the topics won't be upsetting to you."

"No. I am curious. I like to see justice served."

Paul came into the room through the French doors. He asked politely about Claire's and Kate's health, sat down with them all, and then switched to the news about the players in the Bradshaw murder.

"First, Jamie Bradshaw arranged the murder of his brother. He hired Ray Carome to hire Joseph Vecchia who assaulted and drowned Scottie Bradshaw in the roman bath at The Potawatomi Club.'

'After you, Miss Milano, shot Vecchia at this house where he meant to kill all of you, Jamie instructed Carome to hire a replacement. Enter Ferrol Lopez. Mr. Lopez shot at you, attacked Mr. Bailey on the street, and tried to finish the job at Michael Bailey's house in Lake Geneva.'

'Lopez is incarcerated. He's a repeat offender in because he attempted to kill both of you. He'll be in an Illinois penitentiary for life. He offered to trade his confession for a lighter sentence, but he had no leverage as we already had Carome.'

'Carome, on the other hand, will receive less time. He will testify against Lopez. He also tried to give up Harrison. While he didn't know Jamie was Harrison, he did provide us with a matching Cayman Bank account that wired him the money. In my mind, his biggest concern is that his Mafioso boss might be so angry at him for moonlighting that mob loyalists may take care of him in prison."

"Why is the Cayman account so important?" Kate asked.

"Because the FBI was able to break through the Island's confidentiality laws to confirm that the owner of the account was Jamie. I knew we would have identified Jamie eventually."

"What you say jibes with what Charlie told me," Kate said. "But how did Roman and Jimbo fit in? They were killers."

"Jamie paid them," Paul began. "He probably was paranoid that Charlie would discover his involvement. He tried to convince Charlie to drop your efforts, but you would not stop. So Jamie thought he needed to know Charlie's every move. If he could plant someone near you, Miss Milano, and Mrs. Bailey later, he could keep tabs on Charlie's moves."

"So when I was shot at on the street," Kate surmised, "Roman intentionally did not move to protect me."

"Yes, at that point Jamie didn't know if Charlie was telling you what he was finding. But if you did know from Charlie, Jamie needed you dead as well. So while the attacks on you at first were to scare Charlie off from his investigation that changed when Lopez tried to kill you. Eventually he became so desperate, he included both you and Mrs. Bailey in that plan at the Bradshaw house on Lake Geneva. You were originally a pawn, then later at target."

"Wow. Was I lucky." Kate said looking puzzled.

Charlie broke in adding, "Jamie's plan backfired when Roman turned on him. Roman wanted to be in control. He didn't respect Jamie any more than me. And he hated me after I fired him publicly at the hospital. Jamie had hired Roman and Jimbo to kill us, but I suspect they didn't trust Jamie not to point the finger at them afterwards. They didn't want to be the fall guys for some rich person. So Jamie had to go, too."

"True," Paul agreed.

"Jamie was in over his head," Charlie added. "In hiring types like Carome and Roman he was naïve to think he could control them."

"Men like Jamie often think they command more than they do."

"So now that Jamie, Roman, and Jimbo are dead," Charlie said. "What about the others? Henry? Phillips Elliott? Lowell Hersey? What will become of them?"

"Let's start with Mr. Elliott," Paul said. "He'll go to jail for several years, pay a fine, and be disbarred. The Bradshaw, Evans firm dropped his defense. Hung him out to dry. They contend that Elliott concocted the scheme on his own and they were a victim of his actions as well."

"But they should have known what he was doing," Charlie argued.

"You're right, and the DA doesn't buy their story either. I suspect Bradshaw, Evans will cave and settle for a sizable fine. The DA will insist on a damning PR statement, but bottom line, I think they will survive. Collins, Lang will also be fined and sanctioned for securities violations and failure to supervise."

"Okay," Charlie said. "Lowell Hersey and the others using the insider information?"

"The law is vague on what they did. I doubt the DA and the SEC will spend their time going after those people."

"A shame," Kate declared shaking her head. "I think they are guilty because they had to know the information was fraudulently passed along."

"That leaves Henry Bradshaw," Charlie reminded Paul.

"Henry did nothing," Claire asserted with emotion. "He lost two sons. He wouldn't have approved of any of this."

"I don't know what was in his head, Mrs. Bailey," Paul began. "Regarding the insider information case, we have Lowell Hersey saying he went to Henry after Scottie Bradshaw died to try to continue the arrangement. And Henry turned him down. Henry should have gone to the authorities immediately to turn over Elliot but he will argue he lacked enough time to investigate Hersey's story. The DA says he's lying. We think he knew what his son was doing and failed to act in order to protect Scottie. He should go to jail at least, pay a fine, and be disbarred."

"That's not fair," Claire protested. "That would kill Dottie."

"He was complicit," Paul explained. "But he may get off lightly."

"And the murder?" Charlie asked.

"Jamie's dead. Who else would know if he talked to his father? Did Jamie act alone? Clearly the Bradshaws were looking at a potential calamity because of Scottie's illegal actions. Embarrassment, severe damage to their firm, blow to their lifestyle, time in jail—a disaster to a family held in esteem by most people. Maybe that was motive enough to want Scottie dead and silenced."

"A Greek tragedy." Charlie said sadly.

"I don't believe it," Claire repeated. "Poor Dottie and Henry. We should commiserate with them, not accuse them."

Charlie said nothing. He felt certain that Jamie would not have acted without Henry's blessing. Even Dottie may have been complicit. But there was no proof—and why quarrel with his mother? Henry would be getting off easy.

Paul stood up and excused himself. Charlie walked him to the door.

As he returned, he overheard his mother say to Kate, "Can you ever forgive him? You know he loves you. He's so headstrong."

"I know Mother Bailey. We're working it out. I've always loved him."

Encouraged, Charlie started into the room but stopped to take a cell phone call. It was Peaches.

"Charlie, my friend. Your case this summer has a silver lining for me. I have been promoted to a full time crime reporter. I still have to do the society news, but I get to write up provocative murders, robberies, gang wars, terrorist plots—the like. You'll take me much more seriously."

"Well, let's not go overboard. But congrats. Sounds titillating."

"Sure is. But you still owe me the scoop on your wedding date. So when?"

*Charlie smiled. Same old Peaches. I hope I'll be able to tell him someday.*

"You'll be the first to know."

Smiling, Charlie pocketed his phone and entered the room. He walked up to Kate and hugged her. He said softly, "This all is history. I want you always with me."

Kate said nothing at first, but kissed him long and hard. She put her head on his shoulder and whispered in his ear, "I hear that spring time here is ideal for special events."

| § |

# ACKNOWLEDGEMENTS

Any author will tell you that he doesn't create alone. He needs collaborators – partners in the process. I relied on many people for technical knowledge, advice, coaching, and old-fashion encouragement. Three professional editors had a significant impact on this novel. David Bischoff was an early influence on structure and use of POV. Marlene Adelstein revised carefully several drafts with particular emphasis on plot and character development. Finally and most noteworthy, Laurie Rosin worked tirelessly on every aspect of the book from line and copy editing, pacing, coaching, and storytelling. I thank them all.

As this book reached its final stages, a handful of individuals brought their skill and expertise to ready it for publishing: Heidi Vestrem, The Lake County Major Crimes Task Force, Jane Friedman, Lou Heffernan, and Mitch Engel. In the end, my marvelous and wise Elaine guided this project to conclusion. I am lucky to have her in my life.

Besides these collaborators I have been inspired by numerous others. I am grateful to Christopher, Brendan, and Alexander, my sons, for their tenacity, passion, and pure spirit. Also, I acknowledge that certain writers have energized me through

their work to tell my own stories: P.D. James, Ruth Rendell, Do-
rothy Sayers, Louis Auchincloss, Dick Francis, Robert Penn
Warren, John Mortimer, E.M. Forster, Wallace Stevens, Jo Nesbo,
John D. MacDonald, Scott Turow, and William F. Buckley, Jr.
They all helped shape me.

"The novel is the one bright book of life." – D.H. Lawrence

CPSIA information can be obtained
at www.ICGtesting.com
Printed in the USA
LVHW010023240922
729134LV00004B/404